Praise for the previous volumes

"Reading all of *Nebula Awards Showcase 2002* is a way of reading a bunch of good stories. It is also a very good way to explore the writing of tomorrow."
—John Clute, scifi.com

"Conveys a sense of the vitality and excitement that have characterized the field's internal dialogues and debate over the last few years. One of the most entertaining Nebula volumes in years." —*Locus*

"Stellar. . . . This is not only a 'must read' for anyone with an interest in the field, but a pleasure to read. . . . That's more reassuring than surprising, of course, given that this collection has little if any agenda besides quality writing, but it is reassuring to see that so many fresh voices are so much fun. . . . Worth picking up." —SF Revu

"While the essays offer one answer to the question of where does SF go now, the stories show that science fiction writers continue to re-examine their vision of the future. It's a continuing dialogue, and by including critical essays along with the stories, the *Nebula Awards Showcase 2002* does more to present the SF field as an on-going conversation and discussion of ideas than any of the other best of the year anthologies. It's a worthy contribution and a good volume to have on your shelf." —SF Site

"Every fan will have their favorites; there's pretty much something for everyone. . . . Overall, *Nebula Awards Showcase 2006* gets it right. I judge it a keeper." —Scifi Dimensions

"An essential index of one year in SF and fantasy." —*Booklist*

"The variety of taste shown by the SFFWA continues to be striking and heartening." —*Publishers Weekly*

"Invaluable, not just for the splendid fiction and lively nonfiction, but as another annual snapshot, complete with grins and scowls." —*Kirkus Reviews*

Mike Resnick has written fifty novels and two hundred short stories, and edited forty anthologies. His works have been translated into twenty-two languages. The winner of five Hugo Awards, among other major awards in the United States, France, Japan, Spain, Croatia, and Poland, he ranks fourth on *Locus*'s list of science fiction award–winning authors and first in the short fiction category.

NEBULA AWARDS©
SHOWCASE
2007

THE YEAR'S BEST SF AND FANTASY

Selected by the Science Fiction and
Fantasy Writers of America®

EDITED BY

Mike Resnick

A ROC BOOK

ROC
Published by New American Library, a division of
Penguin Group (USA) Inc., 375 Hudson Street,
New York, New York 10014, USA
Penguin Group (Canada), 90 Eglinton Avenue East, Suite 700, Toronto,
Ontario M4P 2Y3, Canada (a division of Pearson Penguin Canada Inc.)
Penguin Books Ltd., 80 Strand, London WC2R 0RL, England
Penguin Ireland, 25 St. Stephen's Green, Dublin 2,
Ireland (a division of Penguin Books Ltd.)
Penguin Group (Australia), 250 Camberwell Road, Camberwell, Victoria 3124,
Australia (a division of Pearson Australia Group Pty. Ltd.)
Penguin Books India Pvt. Ltd., 11 Community Centre, Panchsheel Park,
New Delhi – 110 017, India
Penguin Group (NZ), 67 Apollo Drive, Mairangi Bay,
Auckland 1311, New Zealand (a division of Pearson New Zealand Ltd.)
Penguin Books (South Africa) (Pty.) Ltd., 24 Sturdee Avenue,
Rosebank, Johannesburg 2196, South Africa

Penguin Books Ltd., Registered Offices:
80 Strand, London WC2R 0RL, England

Published by Roc, an imprint of New American Library, a division of Penguin Group (USA) Inc.

First Printing, March 2007
1 3 5 7 9 10 8 6 4 2

Copyright © Science Fiction and Fantasy Writers of America, 2007
Additional copyright notices can be found on p. 389
All rights reserved

 REGISTERED TRADEMARK—MARCA REGISTRADA

Set in Bembo
Designed by Elke Sigal

Printed in the United States of America

CONTENTS

NEBULA
AWARDS©
SHOWCASE
2007

INTRODUCTION

MIKE RESNICK

t's now been a little more than four decades since SFWA—the Science Fiction Writers of America—was formed, and since we began giving out the Nebulas.

A lot has changed since then.

- A number of science fiction writers were starving, but a small handful were making more than ten thousand dollars a year. A number are still starving, but an even bigger handful regularly signs six- and seven-figure contracts.
- There were well over a dozen science fiction magazines, and as fast as one would die, a new one would come along to take its place. These days there are four magazines, and the two most recent ventures both died in less than a year.
- The World Science Fiction Convention, numbering well under a thousand members, was the largest gathering of imaginative literature enthusiasts in the world. Today the Worldcon regularly draws 6,000 to 7,500 attendees—but the San Diego Comic-Con draws over 100,000, and Dragon*Con, which specializes in comics, media, anime, and gaming, regularly draws 50,000.
- When SFWA was formed, Stanley Kubrick was still a few years away from releasing *2001: A Space Odyssey*, *Star Trek* hadn't hit the small screen yet, and the typical science fiction film or TV show had unbelievable monsters traveling a few zillion miles to menace equally unbelievable girls. Today almost all the top-grossing movies are science fiction films, and television has produced one science fiction/fantasy hit after another. Hell, we even have the SciFi Channel.

- There were only a couple of theme parks back when SFWA was formed. These days a science fiction writer's agent negotiates the rights to theme park rides derived from the work.
- There were no personal computers when SFWA began. Today not only are almost all stories created on computer (and probably half are submitted without ever being transferred to paper), but the electronic venue may turn out to be the savior of the short story.

Like I said, the world is changing, and for the supplementary material in this volume, I thought it was time to ask some of our preeminent practitioners to address that fact, and its effect on science fiction.

Some old-timers find the changes disconcerting. This began as a short fiction field. It isn't anymore—and indeed, it's been more than half a century since a science fiction writer could make a living writing only short stories. It began as a field where science fiction movies were long and boring and pretentious, or short and cheap and silly; today they win Oscars. It began as a field where the Idea was All, where practitioners actually argued (in essays that came back to haunt them) that characterization wasn't very important (and our founding father, Hugo Gernsback, who knew a little something about electronics but was pretty much ignorant of the English language, claimed that the purpose of science fiction was to interest young boys in science). Today our best writers are considered literary artists inside and outside the field, and the girls that Gernsback had no use for dominate the editorial offices and more than hold their own in the awards and on the bestseller lists.

So I asked Ben Bova, Ellen Datlow, Bill Fawcett, Martin H. Greenberg, Kevin J. Anderson, Catherine Asaro, Lou Anders, John Picacio, Josepha Sherman, and Robert J. Sawyer to explain to us exactly how the science fiction world is changing, where those changes are likely to lead it, and how we should react and adjust to it. (And just to be fair, I asked Jack McDevitt to point out one way in which the world is not changing.)

The bulk of the book, as usual, will consist of the Nebula winners (and some of the nominees that most impressed the editor), plus the Rhysling (poetry) winners, and a seldom reprinted novella by our 2006 Grand Master, Harlan Ellison, introduced by multiple Nebula nominee Barry N. Malzberg.

Is there an emerging theme in the fiction here, something that points the way to the next New Wave or Cyberpunk movement? On the surface, no; but I think if you look a little more carefully and consider that the members of the Science Fiction Writers of America were able to give Nebulas to work by Joe Haldeman, Kelly Link, and Carol Emshwiller in the same year, there is indeed a theme, and the theme is that Quality Counts, and Damn the Narrow Definitions of Category. Hard science, soft science, fantasy—it's all secondary to quality, which is exactly as it should be.

SFWA has been around a long time, closing in on half a century. It's going to be around a lot longer time. The best thing I can say about the stories you're about to read (and about the integrity of the voting) is that every one of them would have contended for the awards back in 1965, and I'm sure they could contend for awards in 2050. Nothing wrong with that.

ABOUT THE SCIENCE FICTION AND FANTASY WRITERS OF AMERICA

The Science Fiction and Fantasy Writers of America, Incorporated, includes among its members most of the active writers of science fiction and fantasy. According to the bylaws of the organization, its purpose "shall be to promote the furtherance of the writing of science fiction, fantasy, and related genres as a profession." SFFWA informs writers on professional matters, protects their interests, and helps them in dealings with agents, editors, anthologists, and producers of nonprint media. It also strives to encourage public interest in and appreciation of science fiction and fantasy.

Anyone may become an active member of SFFWA after the acceptance of and payment for one professionally published novel, one professionally produced dramatic script, or three professionally published pieces of short fiction. Only science fiction, fantasy, and other prose fiction of a related genre, in English, shall be considered as qualifying for active membership. Beginning writers who do not yet qualify for active membership may join as associate members; other classes of membership include illustrator members (artists), affiliate members (editors, agents, reviewers, and anthologists), estate members (representatives of the estates of active members who have died), and institutional members (high schools, colleges, universities, libraries, broadcasters, film producers, futurist groups, and individuals associated with such an institution).

Anyone who is not a member of SFFWA may subscribe to *The Bulletin of the Science Fiction and Fantasy Writers of America.* The magazine is published quarterly, and contains articles by well-known writers on all aspects of their profession. Subscriptions are eighteen dollars a year or thirty-one dollars for two years. For information on how to subscribe to the *Bulletin,* or for more information about SFFWA, write to:

SFFWA, Inc.
P.O. Box 877
Chestertown, MD 21620
USA

Readers are also invited to visit the SFFWA site on the World Wide Web at the following address: www.sfwa.org.

NOVEL

Jonathan Strange & Mr Norrell, by Susanna Clarke (Bloomsbury, September 2004)

Camouflage, by Joe Haldeman (*Analog Science Fiction and Fact*, March–May 2004; Ace, August 2004)

Polaris, by Jack McDevitt (Ace, November 2004)

Going Postal, by Terry Pratchett (HarperCollins, October 2004)

Air, by Geoff Ryman (St. Martin's Press, September 2004)

Orphans of Chaos, by John C. Wright (Tor, November 2005)

NOVELLA

"The Tribes of Bela," by Albert Cowdrey (*The Magazine of Fantasy & Science Fiction*, August 2004)

"Magic for Beginners," by Kelly Link (*Magic for Beginners*, July 2005)

"Identity Theft," by Robert J. Sawyer (*Down These Dark Spaceways*, May 2005)

"Clay's Pride," by Bud Sparhawk (*Analog Science Fiction and Fact*, July/August 2004)

"Left of the Dial," by Paul Witcover (*SCI FICTION*, September 2004)

NOVELETTE

"Flat Diane," by Daniel Abraham (*The Magazine of Fantasy & Science Fiction*, October/November 2004)

"The People of Sand and Slag," by Paolo Bacigalupi (*The Magazine of Fantasy & Science Fiction*, February 2004)

"Nirvana High," by Eileen Gunn and Leslie What (*Stable Strategies and Others*, September 2004)

"Men are Trouble," by James Patrick Kelly (*Asimov's Science Fiction*, June 2004)

"The Faery Handbag," by Kelly Link (*The Faery Reel: Tales From the Twilight Realm*, August 2004)

SHORT STORY

"The End of the World as We Know It," by Dale Bailey (*The Magazine of Fantasy & Science Fiction*, October/November 2004)

"There's a Hole in the City," by Richard Bowes (*SCI FICTION*, June 2005)

"I Live With You," by Carol Emshwiller (*The Magazine of Fantasy & Science Fiction*, March 2005)

"Still Life With Boobs," by Anne Harris (*Talebones*, Summer 2005)

"My Mother, Dancing," by Nancy Kress (*Asimov's Science Fiction*, June 2004)

"Singing My Sister Down," by Margo Lanagan (*Black Juice*, March 2005)

"Born-Again," by K. D. Wentworth (*The Magazine of Fantasy & Science Fiction*, May 2005)

SCRIPT

"Act of Contrition"/"You Can't Go Home Again," by Carla Robinson, Bradley Thompson, and David Weddle (*Battlestar Galactica*, January 2005–February 2005)

Serenity, **by Joss Whedon** (Universal Pictures, September 2005)

ANDRE NORTON AWARD

Valiant: A Modern Tale of Faerie, **by Holly Black** (Simon & Schuster, June 2005)

Siberia, by Ann Halam (Wendy Lamb Books, June 2005)

The Amethyst Road, by Louise Spiegler (Clarion Books, September 2005)

Stormwitch, by Susan Vaught (Bloomsbury, January 2005)

GRAND MASTER NEBULA AWARD
Harlan Ellison

AUTHOR EMERITUS
William F. Nolan

HONORING ANDRE: THE ANDRE NORTON AWARD

JOSEPHA SHERMAN

The Year 2006 marked the debut of a new award, the Andre Norton Award for the Best Young Adult Science Fiction. I've asked Josepha Sherman, short story writer, novelist, editor, anthologist, and a woman with unimpeachable young adult credentials, to tell you about it.

Andre Norton (1912–2005), well loved as an author and as a person, has often been called the grande dame of science fiction and fantasy, both by the members of SFWA and indeed by all who knew her or her books. Over her long career of over seventy years, Andre wrote over 130 novels and over 100 short stories of fantasy, science fiction, and adventure for young people, as well as numerous anthologies, and has influenced more than one generation of writers. In fact, many of us who read the genre can remember first discovering the wonders of science fiction or fantasy through such works as *Star Hunter* or *Witch World*.

Andre was actually born Alice Mary Norton, but she soon discovered that while libraries might welcome female librarians—it was considered "ladylike" work, and female librarians could also be paid lower salaries than male librarians—it was not as easy for a woman to get published in anything but genteel "girls' books." Science fiction readers of the time were believed to be exclusively male, and male readers, especially the young ones, would not pick up anything with a woman's name on the cover. In 1934, Andre legally changed her name to Andre Alice Norton, and Andre Norton became her working name.

Until the 1950s, there was only a relatively small market for science fiction, and so Andre's earliest titles were adventure novels such as her first novel, *The Prince Commands* (1934). But she knew that she really wanted to write science fiction and fantasy, and write primarily for teenage readers, and in the 1950s she set out to do just that. Her first science fiction novel, *Star Man's Son 2250 A.D.*, was published in 1952, and after that, her solo or collaborative novels appeared regularly throughout the sixties and more sporadically after that, particularly as her health began to fail. She moved to Murfreesboro, Tennessee, where she worked to establish a writer's retreat that was to be called High Hallack. Unfortunately, her health kept that project from being finished.

When her health began its last decline in 2004, Andre was forced to part with a few of her beloved cats, but when she died, it was in the company of her oldest cat, RT, who stayed by her side until the end. Her last complete novel, *Three Hands for Scorpio*, was published in 2005, and her last collaborative novel, *Return to Quag Keep*, was published in 2006.

Andre was not ignored by the science fiction and fantasy world during her lifetime. She was the first woman to be inducted in the Science Fiction and Fantasy Hall of Fame; received the Skylark, Balrog, and World Fantasy awards; and was the first woman to win the Gandalf Grand Master Award in Fantasy and SFWA's own Nebula Grand Master Awards—as well as receiving the First Fandom Hall of Fame Award in 1994.

But even with all her successes, Andre knew that it still wasn't easy for women writers—particularly those with "girl" names—to get published in science fiction. She decried both prejudice and the "politically correct" movement that was rewriting even history texts to make them nicer. She had always wanted there to be an award for outstanding young adult work in fantasy and science fiction. In fact, she had established the Gryphon Award as a yearly honor for the best new fantasy or science fiction manuscript by a woman. But the Gryphon Award never really took hold, and died away as Andre's ill health continued.

However, the idea of an award did take hold, especially one that would honor both the best science fiction or fantasy young adult novel and the memory of Andre Norton. There was a great deal of online debate and exchanging of e-mails about such an award, what it should mean, how it could be made, what it should look like, and who should make it, from those on SFWA's Young Adult Committee: Catherine Asaro, Holly Black, David Brin, Andrew Burt, Jeffrey A. Carver, Marianne J. Dyson, Sean P. Fodora, Mel Gilden, James E. Gunn, Christopher McKitterick, Josepha Sherman, Janni Lee Simner, Sherwood Smith, and Jane Yolen. Pressure was on the committee, since we knew that Andre's health was precarious at best, and we wanted to get an award established before her death. The Andre Norton Award was voted into existence on October 17, 2004, with official SFWA recognition coming on February 20, 2005. The Andre Norton Award would be a new literary award given annually at the SFWA Nebula Banquet to recognize outstanding science fiction and fantasy novels for the young adult market. Any book published as a young adult science fiction or fantasy novel, including graphic novels, would be eligible, with no limit on word length.

The first Norton Award, which is a clear Lucite pyramid with a black base and a central pillar of golden "stars," was awarded at the 2006 Nebula Awards in May to Holly Black for *Valiant: A Modern Tale of Faerie.*

"We are thrilled to honor Ms. Norton with this new award," said Catherine Asaro, president of SFWA. "Many adults today, myself included, were first introduced to science fiction and fantasy through her books and have gone on to become readers, fans, and authors themselves. Andre Norton has done more to promote reading among young adults than anyone can measure."

Toward the end of her life, with her health failing, her beloved cats having to be given away, and her books slipping out of print, Andre was depressed, sure that she'd been forgotten. But fortunately, the Andre Norton Award was established before her death. Learning that the award had been established let her know that no, she had not been at all forgotten, and yes, she was still well loved and respected by us all.

KELLY LINK

If there is an emerging superstar in the field, I don't know who it could be except the remarkable Kelly Link. A few years ago almost no one had heard of her. Then, in less than a year, she won a Hugo and two Nebulas. This is the longer of the two, the winner of the Best Novella Nebula.

Everybody knows that fantasy stories don't win Nebulas, that only true-blue science fiction does.

Everybody used to know that men couldn't fly, too—and that if they sailed far enough out to sea, they'd fall off the edge of the world.

What they know now is that a fine story is a fine story, and to hell with the definitions.

Euphoria: The Librarian's Tonic—When
Watchfulness Is Not Enough.

MAGIC FOR BEGINNERS

KELLY LINK

Fox is a television character, and she isn't dead yet. But she will be, soon. She's a character on a television show called *The Library*. You've never seen *The Library* on TV, but I bet you wish you had.

In one episode of *The Library,* a boy named Jeremy Mars, fifteen years old, sits on the roof of his house in Plantagenet, Vermont. It's eight o'clock at night, a school night, and he and his friend Elizabeth should be studying for the math quiz which their teacher, Mr. Cliff, has been hinting at all week long. Instead, they've sneaked out onto the roof. It's cold. They don't know everything they should know about X, when X is the square root of Y. They don't even know Y. They ought to go in.

But there's nothing good on TV and the sky is very beautiful. They have jackets on, and up in the corners where the sky begins are patches of white in the darkness, still, where there's snow, up on the mountains. Down in the trees around the house, some animal is making a small, anxious sound: "Why cry? Why cry?"

"What's that one?" Elizabeth says, pointing at a squarish configuration of stars.

"That's The Parking Structure," Jeremy says. "And right next to that is The Big Shopping Mall and The Lesser Shopping Mall."

"And that's Orion, right? Orion the Bargain Hunter?"

Jeremy squints up. "No, Orion is over there. That's The Austrian Bodybuilder. That thing that's sort of wrapped around his lower leg is The Amorous Cephalopod. The Hungry, Hungry Octopus. It can't make up its mind whether it should eat him or make crazy, eight-legged love to him. You know that myth, right?"

"Of course," Elizabeth says. "Is Karl going to be pissed off that we didn't invite him over to study?"

"Karl's always pissed off about something," Jeremy says. Jeremy is resolutely resisting a notion about Elizabeth. Why are they sitting up here? Was it his idea or was it hers? Are they friends, are they just two friends sitting on the roof and talking? Or is Jeremy supposed to try to kiss her? He thinks maybe he's supposed to kiss her. If he kisses her, will they still be friends? He can't ask Karl about this. Karl doesn't believe in being helpful. Karl believes in mocking.

Jeremy doesn't even know if he wants to kiss Elizabeth. He's never thought about it until right now.

"I should go home," Elizabeth says. "There could be a new episode on right now, and we wouldn't even know."

"Someone would call and tell us," Jeremy says. "My mom would come up and yell for us." His mother is something else Jeremy doesn't want to worry about, but he does, he does.

Jeremy Mars knows a lot about the planet Mars, although he's never been there. He knows some girls, and yet he doesn't know much about them. He wishes there were books about girls, the way there are books about Mars, that you could observe the orbits and brightness of girls through telescopes without appearing to be perverted. Once Jeremy read a book about Mars out loud to Karl, except he kept replacing the word Mars with the word "girls." ("It was in the seventeenth century that girls at last came under serious scrutiny." "Girls have virtually no surface liquid water: their temperatures are too cold and the air is too thin." And so on.) Karl cracked up every time.

Jeremy's mother is a librarian. His father writes books. Jeremy reads biographies. He plays trombone in a marching band. He jumps hurdles while wearing a school tracksuit. Jeremy is also passionately addicted to a television show in which a renegade librarian and magician named Fox is trying to save her world from thieves, murderers, cabalists, and pirates. Jeremy is a geek, although he's a telegenic geek. Somebody should make a TV show about him.

Jeremy's friends call him Germ, although he would rather be called Mars. His parents haven't spoken to each other in a week.

Jeremy doesn't kiss Elizabeth. The stars don't fall out of the sky, and Jeremy and Elizabeth don't fall off the roof either. They go inside and finish their homework.

———————

Someone that Jeremy has never met, never even heard of—a woman named Cleo Baldrick—has died. Lots of people, so far, have managed to live and die without making the acquaintance of Jeremy Mars, but Cleo Baldrick has left Jeremy Mars and his mother something strange in her will: a phone booth on a state highway, some forty miles outside of Las Vegas, and a Las Vegas wedding chapel. The wedding chapel is called Hell's Bells. Jeremy isn't sure what kind of people get married there. Bikers, maybe. Supervillains, freaks, and Satanists.

Jeremy's mother wants to tell him something. It's probably something about Las Vegas and about Cleo Baldrick, who—it turns out—was his mother's great-aunt. (Jeremy never knew his mother had a great-aunt. His mother is a mysterious person.) But it may be, on the other hand, something concerning Jeremy's father. For a week and a half now, Jeremy has managed to avoid finding out what his mother is worrying about. It's easy not to find out things, if you try hard enough. There's band practice. He has overslept on weekdays in order to rule out conversations at breakfast, and at night he climbs up on the roof with his telescope to look at stars, to look at Mars. His mother is afraid of heights. She grew up in L.A.

It's clear that whatever it is she has to tell Jeremy is not something she wants to tell him. As long as he avoids being alone with her, he's safe.

But it's hard to keep your guard up at all times. Jeremy comes home from school, feeling as if he has passed the math test, after all. Jeremy is an optimist. Maybe there's something good on TV. He settles down with the remote control on one of his father's pet couches: oversized and reupholstered in an orange-juice-colored corduroy that makes it appear as if the couch has just escaped from a maximum security prison for criminally insane furniture. This couch looks as if its hobby is devouring interior decorators. Jeremy's father is a horror writer, so no one should be surprised if some of the couches he reupholsters are hideous and eldritch.

Jeremy's mother comes into the room and stands above the couch, looking down at him. "Germ?" she says. She looks absolutely miserable, which is more or less how she has looked all week.

The phone rings and Jeremy jumps up.

As soon as he hears Elizabeth's voice, he knows. She says, "Germ, it's on. Channel forty-two. I'm taping it." She hangs up.

"It's on!" Jeremy says. "Channel forty-two! Now!"

His mother has the television on by the time he sits down. Being a librarian, she has a particular fondness for *The Library*. "I should go tell your dad," she says, but instead she sits down beside Jeremy. And of course it's now all the more clear something is wrong between Jeremy's parents. But *The Library* is on and Fox is about to rescue Prince Wing.

When the episode ends, he can tell without looking over that his mother is crying. "Don't mind me," she says and wipes her nose on her sleeve. "Do you think she's really dead?"

But Jeremy can't stay around and talk.

Jeremy has wondered about what kind of television shows the characters *in* television shows watch. Television characters almost always have better haircuts, funnier friends, simpler attitudes toward sex. They marry magicians, win lotteries, have affairs with women who carry guns in their purses. Curious things happen to them on an hourly basis. Jeremy and I can forgive their haircuts. We just want to ask them about their television shows. Just like always, it's Elizabeth who worked out in the nick of time that the new episode was on. Everyone will show up at Elizabeth's house afterwards, for the postmortem. This time, it really is a postmortem. Why did Prince Wing kill Fox? How could Fox let him do it? Fox is ten times stronger.

Jeremy runs all the way, slapping his old track shoes against the sidewalk for the pleasure of the jar, for the sweetness of the sting. He likes the rough, cottony ache in his lungs. His coach says you have to be part-masochist to enjoy something like running. It's nothing to be ashamed of. It's something to exploit.

Talis opens the door. She grins at him, although he can tell that she's been crying, too. She's wearing a T-shirt that says I'M SO GOTH I SHIT TINY VAMPIRES.

"Hey," Jeremy says. Talis nods. Talis isn't so Goth, at least not as far as Jeremy or anyone else knows. Talis just has a lot of T-shirts. She's an enigma wrapped in a mysterious T-shirt. A woman once said to Calvin Coolidge, "Mr. President, I bet my husband that I could get you to say more than two words." Coolidge said, "You lose." Jeremy can imagine Talis as Calvin Coolidge in a former life. Or maybe she was one of those dogs that don't bark. A basenji. Or a rock. A dolmen. There was an episode of *The Library,* once, with some sinister dancing dolmens in it.

Elizabeth comes up behind Talis. If Talis is unGoth, then Elizabeth is Ballerina Goth. She likes hearts and skulls and black pen-ink tattoos, pink tulle and Hello Kitty. When the woman who invented Hello Kitty was asked why Hello Kitty was so popular, she said, "Because she has no mouth." Elizabeth's mouth is small. Her lips are chapped.

"That was the most horrible episode ever! I cried and cried," she says. "Hey, Germ, so I was telling Talis about how you inherited a gas station."

"A phone booth," Jeremy says. "In Las Vegas. This great-great aunt died. And there's a wedding chapel, too."

"Hey! Germ!" Karl says, yelling from the living room. "Shut up and get in here! The commercial with the talking cats is on—"

"Shut it, Karl," Jeremy says. He goes in and sits on Karl's head. You have to show Karl who's boss once in a while.

Amy turns up last. She was in the next town over, buying comics. She hasn't seen the new episode and so they all shut it (except for Talis, who has not been saying anything at all) and Elizabeth puts on the tape.

In the previous episode of *The Library,* masked pirate-magicians said they would sell Prince Wing a cure for the spell which infested Faithful Margaret's hair with miniature, wicked, fire-breathing golems. (Faithful Margaret's hair keeps catching fire, but she refuses to shave it off. Her hair is the source of all her magic.)

The pirate-magicians lured Prince Wing into a trap so obvious that it seemed impossible it could really be a trap, on the one-hundred-and-fortieth floor of The Free People's World-Tree Library. The pirate-magicians used finger magic to turn Prince Wing into a porcelain teapot, put two Earl Grey tea bags into the teapot, and poured in boiling water, toasted the Eternally Postponed and Overdue Reign of the Forbidden Books, drained their tea in one gulp, belched, hurled their souvenir pirate mugs to the ground, and then shattered the teapot which had been Prince Wing into hundreds of pieces. Then the wicked pirate-magicians swept the pieces of both Prince Wing and collectable mugs carelessly into a wooden cigar box, buried the box in the Angela Carter Memorial Park on the seventeenth floor of The World-Tree Library, and erected a statue of George Washington above it.

So then Fox had to go looking for Prince Wing. When she finally discovered the park on the seventeenth floor of The Library, the George Washington statue stepped down off his plinth and fought her tooth and nail. Literally tooth and nail, and they'd all agreed that there was something especially nightmarish about a biting, scratching, life-sized statue of George Washington with long, pointed metal fangs that threw off sparks when he gnashed them. The statue of George Washington bit Fox's pinky finger right off, just like Gollum biting Frodo's finger off on the top of Mount Doom. But of course, once the statue tasted Fox's magical blood, it fell in love with Fox. It would be her ally from now on.

In the new episode, the actor playing Fox is a young Latina actress whom Jeremy Mars thinks he recognizes. She has been a snotty but well-intentioned fourth-floor librarian in an episode about an epidemic of food-poisoning that triggered bouts of invisibility and/or levitation, and she was also a lovelorn, suicidal Bear Cult priestess in the episode where Prince Wing discovered his mother was one of the Forbidden Books.

This is one of the best things about *The Library,* the way the cast swaps parts, all except for Faithful Margaret and Prince Wing, who are only ever themselves. Faithful Margaret and Prince Wing are the love interests and the main characters, and therefore, inevitably, the most boring characters, although Amy has a crush on Prince Wing.

Fox and the dashing-but-treacherous pirate-magician Two Devils are never played by the same actor twice, although in the twenty-third episode of *The Library,* the same woman played them both. Jeremy supposes that the casting could be perpetually confusing, but instead it makes your brain catch on fire. It's magical.

You always know Fox by her costume (the too-small green T-shirt, the long, full skirts she wears to hide her tail), by her dramatic hand gestures and body language, by the soft, breathy-squeaky voice the actors use when they are Fox. Fox is funny, dangerous, bad-tempered, flirtatious, greedy, untidy, accident-prone, graceful, and has a mysterious past. In some episodes, Fox is played by male actors, but she always sounds like Fox. And she's always beautiful. Every episode you think that this Fox, surely, is the most beautiful Fox there could ever be, and yet the Fox of the next episode will be even more heartbreakingly beautiful.

On television, it's night in The Free People's World-Tree Library. All the librarians are asleep, tucked into their coffins, their scabbards, priest-holes, button holes, pockets, hidden cupboards, between the pages of their enchanted novels. Moonlight pours through the high, arched windows of the Library and between the aisles of shelves, into the park. Fox is on her knees, clawing at the muddy ground with her bare hands. The statue of George Washington kneels beside her, helping.

"So that's Fox, right?" Amy says. Nobody tells her to shut up. It would be pointless. Amy has a large heart and an even larger mouth. When it rains, Amy rescues worms off the sidewalk. When you get tired of having a secret, you tell Amy.

Understand: Amy isn't that much stupider than anyone else in this story. It's just that she thinks out loud.

Elizabeth's mother comes into the living room. "Hey guys," she says. "Hi, Jeremy. Did I hear something about your mother inheriting a wedding chapel?"

"Yes, ma'am," Jeremy says. "In Las Vegas."

"Las Vegas," Elizabeth's mom says. "I won three hundred bucks once in Las Vegas. Spent it on a helicopter ride over the Grand Canyon. So how many times can you guys watch the same episode in one day?" But she sits down to watch, too. "Do you think she's really dead?"

"Who's dead?" Amy says. Nobody says anything.

Jeremy isn't sure he's ready to see this episode again so soon, anyway, especially not with Amy. He goes upstairs and takes a shower. Elizabeth's family have a large and distracting selection of shampoos. They don't mind when Jeremy uses their bathroom.

Jeremy and Karl and Elizabeth have known each other since the first day of kindergarten. Amy and Talis are a year younger. The five have not always been friends, except for Jeremy and Karl, who have. Talis is, famously, a loner. She doesn't listen to music as far as anyone knows, she doesn't wear significant amounts of black, she isn't particularly good (or bad) at math or English, and she doesn't drink, debate, knit or refuse to eat meat. If she keeps a blog, she's never admitted it to anyone.

The Library made Jeremy and Karl and Talis and Elizabeth and Amy friends. No one else in school is as passionately devoted. Besides, they are all the children of former hippies, and the town is small. They all live within a few blocks of each other, in run-down Victorians with high ceilings and ranch houses with sunken living rooms. And although they have not always been friends, growing up, they've gone skinny-dipping in lakes on summer nights, and broken bones on each others' trampolines. Once, during an argument about dog names, Elizabeth, who is hot-tempered, tried to run Jeremy over with her ten-speed bicycle, and once, a year ago, Karl got drunk on green-apple schnapps at a party and tried to kiss Talis, and once, for five months in the seventh grade, Karl and Jeremy communicated only through angry emails written in all caps. I'm not allowed to tell you what they fought about.

Now the five are inseparable; invincible. They imagine that life will always be like this—like a television show in eternal syndication—that they will always have each other. They use the same vocabulary. They borrow each other's books and music. They share lunches, and they never say anything when Jeremy comes over and takes a shower. They all know Jeremy's father is eccentric. He's supposed to be eccentric. He's a novelist.

When Jeremy comes back downstairs, Amy is saying, "I've always thought there was something wicked about Prince Wing. He's a dork and he looks like he has bad breath. I never really liked him."

Karl says, "We don't know the whole story yet. Maybe he found out something about Fox while he was a teapot." Elizabeth's mom says, "He's under a spell. I bet you anything." They'll be talking about it all week.

Talis is in the kitchen, making a Velveeta-and-pickle sandwich.

"So what did you think?" Jeremy says. It's like having a hobby, only more pointless, trying to get Talis to talk. "Is Fox really dead?"

"Don't know," Talis says. Then she says, "I had a dream."

Jeremy waits. Talis seems to be waiting, too. She says, "About you." Then she's silent again. There is something dreamlike about the way that she makes a sandwich. As if she is really making something that isn't a sandwich at all; as if she's making something far more meaningful and mysterious. Or as if soon he will wake up and realize that there are no such thing as sandwiches.

"You and Fox," Talis says. "The dream was about the two of you. She told me. To tell you. To call her. She gave me a phone number. She was in trouble. She said you were in trouble. She said *to keep in touch*."

"Weird," Jeremy says, mulling this over. He's never had a dream about *The Library*. He wonders who was playing Fox in Talis's dream. He had a dream about Talis, once, but it isn't the kind of dream that you'd ever tell anybody about. They were just sitting together, not saying anything. Even Talis's T-shirt hadn't said anything. Talis was holding his hand.

"It didn't feel like a dream," Talis says.

"So what was the phone number?" Jeremy says.

"I forgot," Talis says. "When I woke up, I forgot."

Karl's mother works in a bank. Talis's father has a karaoke machine in his basement, and he knows all the lyrics to "Like a Virgin" and "Holiday" as well as the lyrics to all the songs from *Godspell* and *Cabaret*. Talis's mother is a licensed therapist who composes multiple-choice personality tests for women's magazines. "Discover Which Television

Character You Resemble Most." Etc. Amy's parents met in a commune in Ithaca: her name was Galadriel Moon Shuyler before her parents came to their senses and had it changed legally. Everyone is sworn to secrecy about this, which is ironic, considering that this is Amy.

But Jeremy's father is Gordon Strangle Mars. He writes novels about giant spiders, giant leeches, giant moths, and once, notably, a giant carnivorous rosebush who lives in a mansion in upstate New York, and falls in love with a plucky, teenaged girl with a heart murmur. Saint Bernard–sized spiders chase his character's cars down dark, bumpy country roads. They fight the spiders off with badminton rackets, lawn tools, and fireworks. The novels with spiders are all bestsellers.

Once a Gordon Strangle Mars fan broke into the Marses' house. The fan stole several German first editions of Gordon Strangle's novels, a hairbrush, and a used mug in which there were two ancient, dehydrated tea bags. The fan left behind a betrayed and abusive letter on a series of Post-It Notes, and the manuscript of his own novel, told from the point of view of the iceberg that sank the *Titanic*. Jeremy and his mother read the manuscript out loud to each other. It begins: "The iceberg knew it had a destiny." Jeremy's favorite bit happens when the iceberg sees the doomed ship drawing nearer, and remarks plaintively, "Oh my, does not the Captain know about my large and impenetrable bottom?"

Jeremy discovered, later, that the novel-writing fan had put Gordon Strangle Mars's used tea bags and hairbrush up for sale on eBay, where someone paid forty-two dollars and sixty-eight cents, which was not only deeply creepy, but, Jeremy still feels, somewhat cheap. But of course this is appropriate, as Jeremy's father is famously stingy and just plain weird about money.

Gordon Strangle Marses once spent eight thousand dollars on a Japanese singing toilet. Jeremy's friends love that toilet. Jeremy's mother has a painting of a woman wearing a red dress by some artist, Jeremy can never remember who. Jeremy's father gave her that painting. The woman is beautiful, and she looks right at you as if you're the painting, not her. As if *you're* beautiful. The woman has an apple in one hand and a knife in the other. When Jeremy was little, he used to dream about eating that apple. Apparently it's worth more than the whole house and everything else in the house, including the singing toilet. But art and toilets aside, the Marses buy most of their clothes at thrift stores.

Jeremy's father clips coupons.

On the other hand, when Jeremy was twelve and begged his parents to send him to baseball camp in Florida, his father ponied up. And on

Jeremy's last birthday, his father gave him a couch reupholstered in several dozen yards of heavy-duty *Star Wars*-themed fabric. That was a good birthday.

When his writing is going well, Gordon Strangle Mars likes to wake up at 6 A.M. and go out driving. He works out new plot lines about giant spiders and keeps an eye out for abandoned couches, which he wrestles into the back of his pickup truck. Then he writes for the rest of the day. On weekends he reupholsters the thrown-away couches in remaindered, discount fabrics. A few years ago, Jeremy went through his house, counting up fourteen couches, eight love seats, and one rickety chaise lounge. That was a few years ago. Once Jeremy had a dream that his father combined his two careers and began reupholstering giant spiders.

All lights in all rooms of the Mars house are on fifteen-minute timers, in case Jeremy or his mother leave a room and forget to turn off a lamp. This has caused confusion—and sometimes panic—on the rare occasions that the Marses throw dinner parties.

Everyone thinks that writers are rich, but it seems to Jeremy that his family is only rich some of the time. Some of the time they aren't.

Whenever Gordon Mars gets stuck in a Gordon Strangle Mars novel, he worries about money. He worries that he won't, in fact, manage to finish the current novel. He worries that it will be terrible. He worries that no one will buy it and no one will read it, and that the readers who do read it will demand to be refunded the cost of the book. He's told Jeremy that he imagines these angry readers marching on the Mars house, carrying torches and crowbars.

It would be easier on Jeremy and his mother if Gordon Mars did not work at home. It's difficult to shower when you know your father is timing you, and thinking dark thoughts about the water bill, instead of concentrating on the scene in the current Gordon Strangle Mars novel, in which the giant spiders have returned to their old haunts in the trees surrounding the ninth hole of the accursed golf course, where they sullenly feast on the pulped entrail-juices of a brace of unlucky poodles and their owner.

During these periods, Jeremy showers at school, after gym, or at his friends' houses, even though it makes his mother unhappy. She says that sometimes you just need to ignore Jeremy's father. She takes especially long showers, lots of baths. She claims that baths are even nicer when you know that Jeremy's father is worried about the water bill. Jeremy's mother has a cruel streak.

What Jeremy likes about showers is the way you can stand there, surrounded by water and yet in absolutely no danger of drowning, and not think about things like whether you fucked up on the Spanish assignment, or why your mother is looking so worried. Instead you can think about things like if there's water on Mars, and whether or not Karl is shaving, and if so, who is he trying to fool, and what the statue of George Washington meant when it said to Fox, during their desperate, bloody fight, "You have a long journey ahead of you," and, "Everything depends on this." And is Fox really dead?

After she dug up the cigar box, and after George Washington helped her carefully separate out the pieces of tea mug from the pieces of teapot, after they glued back together the hundreds of pieces of porcelain, when Fox turned the ramshackle teapot back into Prince Wing, Prince Wing looked about a hundred years old, and as if maybe there were still a few pieces missing. He looked pale. When he saw Fox, he turned even paler, as if he hadn't expected her to be standing there in front of him. He picked up his leviathan sword, which Fox had been keeping safe for him—the one which faithful viewers know was carved out of the tooth of a giant, ancient sea creature that lived happily and peacefully (before Prince Wing was tricked into killing it) in the enchanted underground sea on the third floor—and skewered the statue of George Washington like a kebab, pinning it to a tree. He kicked Fox in the head, knocked her down, and tied her to a card catalog. He stuffed a handful of moss and dirt into her mouth so she couldn't say anything, and then he accused her of plotting to murder Faithful Margaret by magic. He said Fox was more deceitful than a Forbidden Book. He cut off Fox's tail and her ears and he ran her through with the poison-edged, dog-headed knife that he and Fox had stolen from his mother's secret house. Then he left Fox there, tied to the card catalog, limp and bloody, her beautiful head hanging down. He sneezed (Prince Wing is allergic to swordplay) and walked off into the stacks. The librarians crept out of their hiding places. They untied Fox and cleaned off her face. They held a mirror to her mouth, but the mirror stayed clear and unclouded.

When the librarians pulled Prince Wing's leviathan sword out of the tree, the statue of George Washington staggered over and picked up Fox in his arms. He tucked her ears and tail into the capacious pockets of his bird-shit-stained, verdigris riding coat. He carried Fox down seventeen flights of stairs, past the enchanted-and-disagreeable Sphinx on the eighth floor, past the enchanted-and-stormy underground sea on the third floor, past the even-more-enchanted checkout desk on the first floor, and through the hammered-brass doors of the Free People's World-Tree Library. Nobody in *The Library,* not in one single episode, has ever gone outside. *The Library* is full of all the sorts of things that one usually has to go outside to enjoy: trees and lakes and grottoes and fields and mountains and precipices (and full of indoors things as well, like books, of course). Outside The Library, everything is dusty and red and alien, as if George Washington has carried Fox out of The Library and onto the surface of Mars.

"I could really go for a nice cold Euphoria right now," Jeremy says. He and Karl are walking home.

Euphoria is: *The Librarian's Tonic—When Watchfulness Is Not Enough.* There are frequently commercials for Euphoria on *The Library.* Although no one is exactly sure what Euphoria is for, whether it is alcoholic or caffeinated, what it tastes like, if it is poisonous or delightful, or even whether or not it's carbonated, everyone, including Jeremy, pines for a glass of Euphoria once in a while.

"Can I ask you a question?" Karl says.

"Why do you always say that?" Jeremy says. "What am I going to say? 'No, you can't ask me a question'?"

"What's up with you and Talis?" Karl says. "What were you talking about in the kitchen?" Jeremy sees that Karl has been Watchful.

"She had this dream about me," he says, uneasily.

"So do you like her?" Karl says. His chin looks raw. Jeremy is sure now that Karl has tried to shave. "Because, remember how I liked her first?"

"We were just talking," Jeremy says. "So did you shave? Because I didn't know you had facial hair. The idea of you shaving is pathetic, Karl. It's like voting Republican if we were old enough to vote. Or farting in Music Appreciation."

"Don't try to change the subject," Karl says. "When have you and Talis ever had a conversation before?"

"One time we talked about a Diana Wynne Jones book that she'd checked out from the library. She dropped it in the bath accidentally. She wanted to know if I could tell my mother," Jeremy says. "Once we talked about recycling."

"Shut up, Germ," Karl says. "Besides, what about Elizabeth? I thought you liked Elizabeth!"

"Who said that?" Jeremy says. Karl is glaring at him.

"Amy told me," Karl says.

"I never told Amy I liked Elizabeth," Jeremy says. So now Amy is a mind-reader as well as a blabbermouth? What a terrible, deadly combination!

"No," Karl says, grudgingly. "Elizabeth told Amy that she likes you. So I just figured you liked her back."

"Elizabeth likes me?" Jeremy says.

"Apparently everybody likes you," Karl says. He sounds sorry for himself. "What is it about you? It's not like you're all that special. Your nose is funny looking and you have stupid hair."

"Thanks, Karl." Jeremy changes the subject. "Do you think Fox is really dead?" he says. "For good?" He walks faster, so that Karl has to almost-jog to keep up. Presently Jeremy is much taller than Karl, and he intends to enjoy this as long as it lasts. Knowing Karl, he'll either get tall, too, or else chop Jeremy off at the knees.

"They'll use magic," Karl says. "Or maybe it was all a dream. They'll make her alive again. I'll never forgive them if they've killed Fox. And if you like Talis, I'll never forgive you, either. And I know what you're thinking. You're thinking that I think I mean what I say, but if push came to shove, eventually I'd forgive you, and we'd be friends again, like in seventh grade. But I wouldn't, and you're wrong, and we wouldn't be. We wouldn't ever be friends again."

Jeremy doesn't say anything. Of course he likes Talis. He just hasn't realized how much he likes her, until recently. Until today. Until Karl opened his mouth. Jeremy likes Elizabeth too, but how can you compare Elizabeth and Talis? You can't. Elizabeth is Elizabeth and Talis is Talis.

"When you tried to kiss Talis, she hit you with a boa constrictor," he says. It had been Amy's boa constrictor. It had probably been an accident. Karl shouldn't have tried to kiss someone while they were holding a boa constrictor.

"Just try to remember what I just said," Karl says. "You're free to like anyone you want to. Anyone except for Talis."

The Library has been on television for two years now. It isn't a regularly scheduled program. Sometimes it's on two times in the same week, and then not on again for another couple of weeks. Often new episodes debut in the middle of the night. There is a large online community who spend hours scanning channels; sending out alarms and false alarms; fans swap theories, tapes, files; write fanfic. Elizabeth has rigged up her computer to shout "Wake up, Elizabeth! The television is on fire!" when reliable *Library* watch-sites discover a new episode.

The Library is a pirate TV show. It's shown up once or twice on most network channels, but usually it's on the kind of channels that Jeremy thinks of as ghost channels. The ones that are just static, unless you're paying for several hundred channels of cable. There are commercial breaks, but the products being advertised are like Euphoria. They never seem to be real brands, or things that you can actually buy. Often the commercials aren't even in English, or in any other identifiable language, although the jingles are catchy, nonsense or not. They get stuck in your head.

Episodes of *The Library* have no regular schedule, no credits, and sometimes not even dialogue. One episode of *The Library* takes place inside the top drawer of a card catalog, in pitch dark, and it's all in Morse code with subtitles. Nothing else. No one has ever claimed responsibility for inventing *The Library*. No one has ever interviewed one of the actors, or stumbled across a set, film crew, or script, although in one documentary-style episode, the actors filmed the crew, who all wore paper bags on their heads.

When Jeremy gets home, his father is making upside-down pizza in a casserole dish for dinner.

Meeting writers is usually disappointing, at best. Writers who write sexy thrillers aren't necessarily sexy or thrilling in person. Children's book writers might look more like accountants, or ax murderers for that matter. Horror writers are very rarely scary looking, although they are frequently good cooks.

Though Gordon Strangle Mars *is* scary looking. He has long, thin fingers—currently slimy with pizza sauce—which is why he chose 'Strangle' for his fake middle name. He has white-blond hair that he tugs on while he writes until it stands straight up. He has a bad habit of suddenly appearing beside you, when you haven't even realized he was in the same part of the house. His eyes are deep-set and he doesn't blink very often. Karl says that when you meet Jeremy's father, he looks at you as if he were imagining you bundled up and stuck away in some giant spider's larder. Which is probably true.

People who read books probably never bother to wonder if their favorite writers are also good parents. Why would they?

Gordon Strangle Mars is a recreational shoplifter. He has a special, complicated, and unspoken arrangement with the local bookstore, where, in exchange for his autographing as many Gordon Strangle Mars novels as they can possibly sell, the store allows Jeremy's father to shoplift books without comment. Jeremy's mother shows up sooner or later and writes a check.

Jeremy's feelings about his father are complicated. His father is a cheapskate and a petty thief, and yet Jeremy likes his father. His father hardly ever loses his temper with Jeremy, he is always interested in Jeremy's life, and he gives interesting (if confusing) advice when Jeremy asks for it. For example, if Jeremy asked his father about kissing Elizabeth, his father might suggest that Jeremy not worry about giant spiders when he kisses Elizabeth. Jeremy's father's advice usually has something to do with giant spiders.

When Jeremy and Karl weren't speaking to each other, it was Jeremy's father who straightened them out. He lured Karl over, and then locked them both into his study. He didn't let them out again until they were on speaking terms.

"I thought of a great idea for your book," Jeremy says. "What if one of the spiders builds a web on a soccer field, across a goal? And what if the goalie doesn't notice until the middle of the game? Could somebody kill one of the spiders with a soccer ball, if they kicked it hard enough? Would it explode? Or even better, the spider could puncture the soccer ball with its massive fangs. That would be cool, too."

"Your mother's out in the garage," Gordon Strangle Mars says to Jeremy. "She wants to talk to you."

"Oh," Jeremy says. All of a sudden, he thinks of Fox in Talis's dream, trying to phone him. Trying to warn him. Unreasonably, he feels that it's his parents' fault that Fox is dead now, as if they have killed her. "Is it about you? Are you getting divorced?"

"I don't know," his father says. He hunches his shoulders. He makes a face. It's a face that Jeremy's father makes frequently, and yet this face is even more pitiful and guilty than usual.

"What did you do?" Jeremy says. "Did you get caught shoplifting at Wal-Mart?"

"No," his father says.

"Did you have an affair?"

"No!" his father says, again. Now he looks disgusted, either with himself or with Jeremy for asking such a horrible question. "I screwed up. Let's leave it at that."

"How's the book coming?" Jeremy says. There is something in his father's voice that makes him feel like kicking something, but there are never giant spiders around when you need them.

"I don't want to talk about that, either," his father says, looking, if possible, even more ashamed. "Go tell your mother dinner will be ready in five minutes. Maybe you and I can watch the new episode of *The Library* after dinner, if you haven't already seen it a thousand times."

"Do you know the end? Did Mom tell you that Fox is—"

"Oh shit," his father interrupts. "They killed Fox?"

That's the problem with being a writer, Jeremy knows. Even the biggest and most startling twists are rarely twists for you. You know how every story goes.

Jeremy's mother is an orphan. Jeremy's father claims that she was raised by feral silent-film stars, and it's true, she looks like a heroine out of a Harold Lloyd movie. She has an appealingly disheveled look to her, as if someone has either just tied or untied her from a set of train tracks. She met Gordon Mars (before he added the Strangle and sold his first novel) in the food court of a mall in New Jersey, and fell in love with him before realizing that he was a writer and a recreational shoplifter. She didn't read anything he'd written until after they were married, which was a typically cunning move on Jeremy's father's part.

Jeremy's mother doesn't read horror novels. She doesn't like ghost stories or unexplained phenomena or even the kind of phenomena that requires excessively technical explanations. For example: microwaves, airplanes. She doesn't like Halloween, not even Halloween candy. Jeremy's father gives her special editions of his novels, where the scary pages have been glued together.

Jeremy's mother is quiet more often than not. Her name is Alice and sometimes Jeremy thinks about how the two quietest people he knows are named Alice and Talis. But his mother and Talis are quiet in different ways. Jeremy's mother is the kind of person who seems to be keeping something hidden, something secret. Whereas Talis just *is* a secret. Jeremy's mother could easily turn out to be a secret agent. But Talis is the death ray or the key to immortality or whatever it is that secret agents have to keep secret. Hanging out with Talis is like hanging out with a teenaged black hole.

Jeremy's mother is sitting on the floor of the garage, beside a large cardboard box. She has a photo album in her hands. Jeremy sits down beside her.

There are photographs of a cat on a wall, and something blurry that looks like a whale or a zeppelin or a loaf of bread. There's a photograph of a small girl sitting beside a woman. The woman wears a fur collar with a sharp little muzzle, four legs, a tail, and Jeremy feels a sudden pang. Fox is the first dead person that he's ever cared about, but she's not real. The little girl in the photograph looks utterly blank, as if someone has just hit her with a hammer. Like the person behind the camera has just said, "Smile! Your parents are dead!"

"Cleo," Jeremy's mother says, pointing to the woman. "That's Cleo. She was my mother's aunt. She lived in Los Angeles. I went to live with her when my parents died. I was four. I know I've never talked about her. I've never really known what to say about her."

Jeremy says, "Was she nice?"

His mother says, "She tried to be nice. She didn't expect to be saddled with a little girl. What an odd word. Saddled. As if she were a horse. As if somebody put me on her back and I never got off again. She liked to buy clothes for me. She liked clothes. She hadn't had a happy life. She drank a lot. She liked to go to movies in the afternoon and to séances in the evenings. She had boyfriends. Some of them were jerks. The love of her life was a small-time gangster. He died and she never married. She always said marriage was a joke and that life was a bigger joke, and it was just her bad luck that she didn't have a sense of humor. So it's strange to think that all these years she was running a wedding chapel."

Jeremy looks at his mother. She's half-smiling, half-grimacing, as if her stomach hurts. "I ran away when I was sixteen. And I never saw her again. Once she sent me a letter, care of your father's publishers. She said she'd read all his books, and that was how she found me, I guess, because he kept dedicating them to me. She said she hoped I was happy and that she thought about me. I wrote back. I sent a photograph of you. But she never wrote again. Sounds like an episode of *The Library*, doesn't it?"

Jeremy says, "Is that what you wanted to tell me? Dad said you wanted to tell me something."

"That's part of it," his mother says. "I have to go out to Las Vegas, to check out some things about this wedding chapel. Hell's Bells. I want you to come with me."

"Is that what you wanted to ask me?" Jeremy says, although he knows there's something else. His mother still has that sad half-smile on her face.

"Germ," his mother says. "You know I love your father, right?"

"Why?" Jeremy says. "What did he do?"

His mother flips through the photo album. "Look," she says. "This was when you were born." In the picture, his father holds Jeremy as if someone has just handed him an enchanted porcelain teapot. Jeremy's father grins, but he looks terrified, too. He looks like a kid. A scary, scared kid.

"He wouldn't tell me either," Jeremy says. "So it has to be pretty bad. If you're getting divorced, I think you should go ahead and tell me."

"We're not getting divorced," his mother says, "but it might be a good thing if you and I went out to Las Vegas. We could stay there for a few months while I sort out this inheritance. Take care of Cleo's estate. I'm going to talk to your teachers. I've given notice at the library. Think of it as an adventure."

She sees the look on Jeremy's face. "No, I'm sorry. That was a stupid, stupid thing to say. I know this isn't an adventure."

"I don't want to go," Jeremy says. "All my friends are here! I can't just go away and leave them. That would be terrible!" All this time, he's been preparing himself for the most terrible thing he can imagine. He's imagined a conversation with his mother, in which his mother reveals her terrible secret, and in his imagination, he's been calm and reasonable. His imaginary parents have wept and asked for his understanding. The imaginary Jeremy has understood. He has imagined himself understanding everything. But now, as his mother talks, Jeremy's heartbeat speeds up, and his lungs fill with air, as if he is running. He starts to sweat, although the floor of the garage is cold. He wishes he were sitting up on top of the roof with his telescope. There could be meteors, invisible to the naked eye, careening through the sky, hurtling towards Earth. Fox is dead. Everyone he knows is doomed. Even as he thinks this, he knows he's overreacting. But it doesn't help to know this.

"I know it's terrible," his mother says. His mother knows something about terrible.

"So why can't I stay here?" Jeremy says. "You go sort things out in Las Vegas, and I'll stay here with Dad. Why can't I stay here?"

"Because he put you in a book!" his mother says. She spits the words out. He has never heard her sound so angry. His mother never gets angry. "He put you in one of his books! I was in his office, and the manuscript was on his desk. I saw your name, and so I picked it up and started reading."

"So what?" Jeremy says. "He's put me in his books before. Like, stuff

I've said. Like when I was eight and I was running a fever and told him the trees were full of dead people wearing party hats. Like when I accidentally set fire to his office."

"It isn't like that," his mother says. "It's you. It's *you*. He hasn't even changed your name. The boy in the book, he jumps hurdles and he wants to be a rocket scientist and go to Mars, and he's cute and funny and sweet and his best friend Elizabeth is in love with him and he talks like you and he looks like you and then he dies, Jeremy. He has a brain tumor and he dies. He dies. There aren't any giant spiders. There's just you, and you die."

Jeremy is silent. He imagines his father writing the scene in his book where the kid named Jeremy dies, and crying, just a little. He imagines this Jeremy kid, Jeremy the character who dies. Poor messed-up kid. Now Jeremy and Fox have something in common. They're both made-up people. They're both dead.

"Elizabeth is in love with me?" he says. Just on principle, he never believes anything that Karl says. But if it's in a book, maybe it's true.

"Oh shit," his mother says. "I really didn't want to say that. I'm just so angry at him. We've been married for seventeen years. I was just four years older than you when I met him, Jeremy. I was nineteen. He was only twenty. We were babies. Can you imagine that? I can put up with the singing toilet and the shoplifting and the couches and I can put up with him being so weird about money. But he killed you, Jeremy. He wrote you into a book and he killed you off. And he knows it was wrong, too. He's ashamed of himself. He didn't want me to tell you. I didn't mean to tell you."

Jeremy sits and thinks. "I still don't want to go to Las Vegas," he says to his mother. "Maybe we could send Dad there instead."

His mother says, "Not a bad idea." But he can tell she's already planning their itinerary.

In one episode of *The Library*, everyone was invisible. You couldn't see the actors: you could only see the books and the bookshelves and the study carrels on the fifth floor where the coin-operated wizards come to flirt and practice their spells. Invisible Forbidden Books were fighting invisible pirate-magicians and the pirate-magicians were fighting Fox and her friends, who were also invisible. The fight was clumsy and full of deadly accidents. You could hear them fighting. Shelves were overturned. Books were thrown. Invisible people tripped over invisible dead bodies, but you didn't find out who'd died until the next episode. Several of the characters—The Accidental Sword, Hairy Pete, and Ptolemy Krill, who (much like the Vogons in Douglas Adams's *The Hitchhiker's Guide to the Galaxy*) wrote poetry so bad it killed anyone who read it— disappeared for good, and nobody is sure whether they're dead or not.

In another episode, Fox stole a magical drug from The Norns, a prophetic girl band who headline at a cabaret on the mezzanine of The Free People's World-Tree Library. She accidentally injected it, became pregnant, and gave birth to a bunch of snakes who led her to the exact shelf where renegade librarians had misshelved an ancient and terrible book of magic which had never been translated, until Fox asked the snakes for help. The snakes writhed and curled on the ground, spelling out words, letter by letter, with their bodies. As they translated the book for Fox, they hissed and steamed. They became fiery lines on the ground, and then they burnt away entirely. Fox cried. That's the only time anyone has ever seen Fox cry, ever. She isn't like Prince Wing. Prince Wing is a crybaby.

The thing about *The Library* is that characters don't come back when they die. It's as if death is for real. So maybe Fox really is dead and she really isn't coming back. There are a couple of ghosts who hang around The Library looking for blood libations, but they've always been ghosts, all the way back to the beginning of the show. There aren't any evil twins or vampires, either. Although someday, hopefully, there will be evil twins. Who doesn't love evil twins?

"Mom told me about how you wrote about me," Jeremy says. His mother is still in the garage. He feels like a tennis ball in a game where the tennis players love him very, very much, even while they lob and smash and send him back and forth, back and forth.

His father says, "She said she wasn't going to tell you, but I guess I'm glad she did. I'm sorry, Germ. Are you hungry?"

"She's going out to Las Vegas next week. She wants me to go with her," Jeremy says.

"I know," his father says, still holding out a bowl of upside-down pizza. "Try not to worry about all of this, if you can. Think of it as an adventure."

"Mom says that's a stupid thing to say. Are you going to let me read the book with me in it?" Jeremy says.

"No," his father says, looking straight at Jeremy. "I burned it."

"Really?" Jeremy says. "Did you set fire to your computer too?"

"Well, no," his father says. "But you can't read it. It wasn't any good, anyway. Want to watch *The Library* with me? And will you eat some damn pizza, please? I may be a lousy father, but I'm a good cook. And if you love me, you'll eat the damn pizza and be grateful."

So they go sit on the orange couch and Jeremy eats pizza and watches *The Library* for the second-and-a-half time with his father. The lights on the timer in the living room go off, and Prince Wing kills Fox again. And then Jeremy goes to bed. His father goes away to write or to burn stuff. Whatever. His mother is still out in the garage.

On Jeremy's desk is a scrap of paper with a phone number on it. If he wanted to, he could call his phone booth. When he dials the number, it rings for a long time. Jeremy sits on his bed in the dark and listens to it ringing and ringing. When someone picks it up, he almost hangs up. Someone doesn't say anything, so Jeremy says, "Hello? Hello?"

Someone breathes into the phone on the other end of the line. Someone says in a soft, musical, squeaky voice, "Can't talk now, kid. Call back later." Then someone hangs up.

Jeremy dreams that he's sitting beside Fox on a sofa that his father has re-upholstered in spider silk. His father has been stealing spider webs from the giant-spider superstores. From his own books. Is that shoplifting or is it self-plagiarism? The sofa is soft and gray and a little bit sticky. Fox sits on either side of him. The right-hand-side Fox is being played by Talis. Elizabeth plays the Fox on his left. Both Foxes look at him with enormous compassion.

"Are you dead?" Jeremy says.

"Are you?" the Fox who is being played by Elizabeth says, in that unmistakable Fox voice which, Jeremy's father once said, sounds like a sexy and demented helium balloon. It makes Jeremy's brain hurt, to hear Fox's voice coming out of Elizabeth's mouth.

The Fox who looks like Talis doesn't say anything at all. The writing on her T-shirt is so small and so foreign that Jeremy can't read it without feeling as if he's staring at Fox-Talis's breasts. It's probably something he needs to know, but he'll never be able to read it. He's too polite, and besides he's terrible at foreign languages.

"Hey look," Jeremy says. "We're on TV!" There he is on television, sitting between two Foxes on a sticky gray couch in a field of red poppies. "Are we in Las Vegas?"

"We're not in Kansas," Fox-Elizabeth says. "There's something I need you to do for me."

"What's that?" Jeremy says.

"If I tell you in the dream," Fox-Elizabeth says, "you won't remember. You have to remember to call me when you're awake. Keep on calling until you get me."

"How will I remember to call you," Jeremy says, "if I don't remember what you tell me in this dream? Why do you need me to help you? Why is Talis here? What does her T-shirt say? Why are you both Fox? Is this Mars?"

Fox-Talis goes on watching TV. Fox-Elizabeth opens her kind and beautiful un-Hello-Kitty-like mouth again. She tells Jeremy the whole story. She explains everything. She translates Fox-Talis's T-shirt, which turns out to explain everything about Talis that Jeremy has ever wondered about. It answers every single question that Jeremy has ever had about girls. And then Jeremy wakes up—

It's dark. Jeremy flips on the light. The dream is moving away from him. There was something about Mars. Elizabeth was asking who he thought was prettier, Talis or Elizabeth. They were laughing. They both had pointy fox ears. They wanted him to do something. There was a telephone number he was supposed to call. There was something he was supposed to do.

In two weeks, on the fifteenth of April, Jeremy and his mother will get in her van and start driving out to Las Vegas. Every morning before school, Jeremy takes long showers and his father doesn't say anything at all. One day it's as if nothing is wrong between his parents. The next day they won't even look at each other. Jeremy's father won't come out of his study. And then the day after that, Jeremy comes home and finds his mother sitting on his father's lap. They're smiling as if they know something stupid and secret. They don't even notice Jeremy when he walks through the room. Even this is preferable, though, to the way they behave when they do notice him. They act guilty and strange and as if they are about to ruin his life. Gordon Mars makes pancakes every morning, and Jeremy's favorite dinner, macaroni and cheese, every night. Jeremy's mother plans out an itinerary for their trip. They will be stopping at libraries across the country, because his mother loves libraries. But she's also bought a new two-man tent and two sleeping bags and a portable stove, so that they can camp, if Jeremy wants to camp. Even though Jeremy's mother hates the outdoors.

Right after she does this, Gordon Mars spends all weekend in the garage. He won't let either of them see what he's doing, and when he does let them in, it turns out that he's removed the seating in the back of the van and bolted down two of his couches, one on each side, both upholstered in electric-blue fake fur.

They have to climb in through the cargo door at the back because one of the couches is blocking the sliding door. Jeremy's father says, looking very pleased with himself, "So now you don't have to camp outside, unless you want to. You can sleep inside. There's space underneath for suitcases. The sofas even have seat belts."

Over the sofas, Jeremy's father has rigged up small wooden shelves that fold down on chains from the walls of the van and become table tops. There's a travel-sized disco ball dangling from the ceiling, and a wooden panel—with Velcro straps and a black, quilted pad—behind the driver's seat, where Jeremy's father explains they can hang up the painting of the woman with the apple and the knife.

The van looks like something out of an episode of *The Library*. Jeremy's mother bursts into tears. She runs back inside the house. Jeremy's father says, helplessly, "I just wanted to make her laugh."

Jeremy wants to say, "I hate both of you." But he doesn't say it, and he doesn't. It would be easier if he did.

When Jeremy told Karl about Las Vegas, Karl punched him in the stomach. Then he said, "Have you told Talis?"

Jeremy said, "You're supposed to be nice to me! You're supposed to tell me not to go and that this sucks and you're not supposed to punch me. Why did you punch me? Is Talis all you ever think about?"

"Kind of," Karl said. "Most of the time. Sorry, Germ, of course I wish you weren't going and yeah, it also pisses me off. We're supposed to be best friends, but you do stuff all the time and I never get to. I've never driven across the country or been to Las Vegas, even though I'd really, really like to. I can't feel sorry for you when I bet you anything that while you're there, you'll sneak into some casino and play slot machines and win like a million bucks. You should feel sorry for me. I'm the one that has to stay here. Can I borrow your dirt bike while you're gone?"

"Sure," Jeremy said.

"How about your telescope?" Karl said.

"I'm taking it with me," Jeremy said.

"Fine. You have to call me every day," Karl said. "You have to email. You have to tell me about Las Vegas show girls. I want to know how tall they really are. Whose phone number is this?"

Karl was holding the scrap of paper with the number of Jeremy's phone booth.

"Mine," Jeremy said. "That's my phone booth. The one I inherited."

"Have you called it?" Karl said.

"No," Jeremy said. He'd called the phone booth a few times. But it wasn't a game. Karl would think it was a game.

"Cool," Karl said and he went ahead and dialed the number. "Hello?" Karl said, "I'd like to speak to the person in charge of Jeremy's life. This is Jeremy's best friend Karl."

"Not funny," Jeremy said.

"My life is boring," Karl said, into the phone. "I've never inherited anything. This girl I like won't talk to me. So is someone there? Does anybody want to talk to me? Does anyone want to talk to my friend, the Lord of the Phone Booth? Jeremy, they're demanding that you liberate the phone booth from yourself."

"Still not funny," Jeremy said and Karl hung up the phone.

Jeremy told Elizabeth. They were up on the roof of Jeremy's house and he told her the whole thing. Not just the part about Las Vegas, but also the part about his father and how he put Jeremy in a book with no giant spiders in it.

"Have you read it?" Elizabeth said.

"No," Jeremy said. "He won't let me. Don't tell Karl. All I told him is that my mom and I have to go out for a few months to check out the wedding chapel."

"I won't tell Karl," Elizabeth said. She leaned forward and kissed Jeremy and then she wasn't kissing him. It was all very fast and surprising, but they didn't fall off the roof. Nobody falls off the roof in this story. "Talis likes you," Elizabeth said. "That's what Amy says. Maybe you like her back. I don't know. But I thought I should go ahead and kiss you now. Just in case I don't get to kiss you again."

"You can kiss me again," Jeremy said. "Talis probably doesn't like me."

"No," Elizabeth said. "I mean, let's not. I want to stay friends and it's hard enough to be friends, Germ. Look at you and Karl."

"I would never kiss Karl," Jeremy said.

"Funny, Germ. We should have a surprise party for you before you go," Elizabeth said.

"It won't be a surprise party now," Jeremy said. Maybe kissing him once was enough.

"Well, once I tell Amy it can't really be a surprise party," Elizabeth said. "She would explode into a million pieces and all the little pieces would start yelling, 'Guess what? Guess what? We're having a surprise party for you, Jeremy!' But just because I'm letting you in on the surprise doesn't mean there won't be surprises."

"I don't actually like surprises," Jeremy said.

"Who does?" Elizabeth said. "Only the people who do the surprising. Can we have the party at your house? I think it should be like Halloween, and it always feels like Halloween here. We could all show up in costumes and watch lots of old episodes of *The Library* and eat ice cream."

"Sure," Jeremy said. And then: "This is terrible! What if there's a new episode of *The Library* while I'm gone? Who am I going to watch it with?"

And he'd said the perfect thing. Elizabeth felt so bad about Jeremy having to watch *The Library* all by himself that she kissed him again.

There has never been a giant spider in any episode of *The Library*, although once Fox got really small and Ptolemy Krill carried her around in his pocket. She had to rip up one of Krill's handkerchiefs and blindfold herself, just in case she accidentally read a draft of Krill's terrible poetry. And then it turned out that, as well as the poetry, Krill had also stashed a rare, horned Anubis earwig in his pocket which hadn't been properly preserved. Ptolemy Krill, it turned out, was careless with his kill jar. The earwig almost ate Fox, but instead it became her friend. It still sends her Christmas cards.

These are the two most important things that Jeremy and his friends have in common: a geographical location, and love of a television show about a library. Jeremy turns on the television as soon as he comes home from school. He flips through the channels, watching reruns of *Star Trek* and *Law & Order*. If there's a new episode of *The Library* before he and his mother leave for Las Vegas, then everything will be fine. Everything will work out. His mother says, "You watch too much television, Jeremy." But he goes on flipping through channels. Then he goes up to his room and makes phone calls.

"The new episode needs to be soon, because we're getting ready to leave. Tonight would be good. You'd tell me if there was going to be a new episode tonight, right?"

Silence.

"Can I take that as a yes? It would be easier if I had a brother," Jeremy tells his telephone booth. "Hello? Are you there? Or a sister. I'm tired of being good all the time. If I had a sibling, then we could take turns being good. If I had an older brother, I might be better at being bad, better at being angry. Karl is really good at being angry. He learned how from his brothers. I wouldn't want brothers like Karl's brothers, of course, but it sucks having to figure out everything all by myself. And the more normal I try to be, the more my parents think that I'm acting out. They think it's a phase that I'll grow out of. They think it isn't normal to be normal. Because there's no such thing as normal.

"And this whole book thing. The whole shoplifting thing, how my dad steals things, it figures that he went and stole my life. It isn't just me being melodramatic, to say that. That's exactly what he did! Did I tell you that once he stole a ferret from a pet store because he felt bad for it, and then he let it loose in our house and it turned out that it was pregnant? There was this woman who came to interview Dad and she sat down on one of the—"

Someone knocks on his bedroom door. "Jeremy," his mother says. "Is Karl here? Am I interrupting?"

"No," Jeremy says, and hangs up the phone. He's gotten into the habit of calling his phone booth every day. When he calls, it rings and rings and then it stops ringing, as if someone has picked up. There's just silence on the other end, no squeaky pretend-Fox voice, but it's a peaceful, interested silence. Jeremy complains about all the things there are to complain about, and the silent person on the other end listens and listens. Maybe it is Fox standing there in his phone booth and listening patiently. He wonders what incarnation of Fox is listening. One thing about Fox: she's never sorry for herself. She's always too busy. If it were really Fox, she'd hang up on him.

Jeremy opens his door. "I was on the phone," he says. His mother comes in and sits down on his bed. She's wearing one of his father's old flannel shirts. "So have you packed?"

Jeremy shrugs. "I guess," he says. "Why did you cry when you saw what Dad did to the van? Don't you like it?"

"It's that damn painting," his mother says. "It was the first nice thing he ever gave me. We should have spent the money on health insurance and a new roof and groceries and instead he bought a painting. So I got angry. I left him. I took the painting and I moved into a hotel and I stayed there for a few days. I was going to sell the painting, but instead I fell in love with it, so I came home and apologized for running away. I got pregnant with you and I used to get hungry and dream that someone was going to give me a beautiful apple, like the one she's holding. When I told your father, he said he didn't trust her, that she was holding out the apple like that as a trick and if you went to take it from her, she'd stab you with the peeling knife. He says that she's a tough old broad and she'll take care of us while we're on the road."

"Do we really have to go?" Jeremy says. "If we go to Las Vegas I might get into trouble. I might start using drugs or gambling or something."

"Oh, Germ. You try so hard to be a good kid," his mother says. "You try so hard to be normal. Sometimes I'd like to be normal, too. Maybe Vegas will be good for us. Are these the books that you're bringing?"

Jeremy shrugs. "Not all of them. I can't decide which ones I should take and which ones I can leave. It feels like whatever I leave behind, I'm leaving behind for good."

"That's silly," his mother says. "We're coming back. I promise. Your father and I will work things out. If you leave something behind that you need, he can mail it to you. Do you think there are slot machines in the libraries in Las Vegas? I talked to a woman at the Hell's Bells chapel and there's something called The Arts and Lovecraft Library where they keep Cleo's special collection of horror novels and gothic romances and fake copies of *The Necronomicon.* You go in and out through a secret, swinging-bookcase door. People get married in it. There's a Dr. Frankenstein's LoveLab, the Masque of the Red Death Ballroom and also something just called The Crypt. Oh yeah, and there's also The Vampire's Patio and The Black Lagoon Grotto, where you can get married by moonlight."

"You hate all this stuff," Jeremy says.

"It's not my cup of tea," his mother admits. Then she says, "When does everyone show up tonight?"

"Around eight," Jeremy says. "Are you going to get dressed up?"

"I don't have to dress up," his mother says. "I'm a librarian, remember?"

Jeremy's father's office is above the garage. In theory, no one is meant to interrupt him while he's working, but in practice Jeremy's father loves nothing better than to be interrupted, as long as the person who interrupts brings him something to eat. When Jeremy and his mother are gone, who will bring Jeremy's father food? Jeremy hardens his heart.

The floor is covered with books and bolts and samples of upholstering fabrics. Jeremy's father is lying facedown on the floor with his feet propped up on a bolt of fabric, which means that he is thinking and also that his back hurts. He claims to think best when he is on the verge of falling asleep.

"I brought you a bowl of Froot Loops," Jeremy says.

His father rolls over and looks up. "Thanks," he says. "What time is it? Is everyone here? Is that your costume? Is that my tuxedo jacket?"

"It's five-ish. Nobody's here yet. Do you like it?" Jeremy says. He's dressed as a Forbidden Book. His father's jacket is too big, but he still feels very elegant. Very sinister. His mother lent him the lipstick and the feathers and the platform heels.

"It's interesting," his father allows. "And a little frightening."

Jeremy feels obscurely pleased, even though he knows that his father is more amused than frightened. "Everyone else will probably come as Fox or Prince Wing. Except for Karl. He's coming as Ptolemy Krill. He even wrote some really bad poetry. I wanted to ask you something, before we leave tomorrow."

"Shoot," his father says.

"Did you really get rid of the novel with me in it?"

"No," his father says. "It felt unlucky. Unlucky to keep it, unlucky not to keep it. I don't know what to do with it."

Jeremy says, "I'm glad you didn't get rid of it."

"It's not any good, you know," his father says. "Which makes all this even worse. At first it was because I was bored with giant spiders. It was going to be something funny to show you. But then I wrote that you had a brain tumor and it wasn't funny any more. I figured I could save you—I'm the author, after all—but you got sicker and sicker. You were going through a rebellious phase. You were sneaking out of the house a lot and you hit your mother. You were a real jerk. But it turned out you had a brain tumor and that was making you behave strangely."

"Can I ask another question?" Jeremy says. "You know how you like to steal things? You know how you're really, really good at it?"

"Yeah," says his father.

"Could you not steal things for a while, if I asked you to?" Jeremy says. "Mom isn't going to be around to pay for the books and stuff that you steal. I don't want you to end up in jail because we went to Las Vegas."

His father closes his eyes as if he hopes Jeremy will forget that he asked a question, and go away.

Jeremy says nothing.

"All right," his father says finally. "I won't shoplift anything until you get home again."

Jeremy's mother runs around taking photos of everyone. Talis and Elizabeth have both showed up as Fox, although Talis is dead Fox. She carries her fake fur ears and tail around in a little see-through plastic purse and she also has a sword, which she leaves in the umbrella stand in the kitchen. Jeremy and Talis haven't talked much since she had a dream about him and since he told her that he's going to Las Vegas. She didn't say anything about that. Which is perfectly normal for Talis.

Karl makes an excellent Ptolemy Krill. Jeremy's Forbidden Book disguise is admired.

Amy's Faithful Margaret costume is almost as good as anything Faithful Margaret wears on TV. There are even special effects: Amy has rigged up her hair with red ribbons and wire and spray color and egg whites so that it looks as if it's on fire, and there are tiny papier-mâché golems in it, making horrible faces. She dances a polka with Jeremy's father. Faithful Margaret is mad for polka dancing.

No one has dressed up as Prince Wing.

They watch the episode with the possessed chicken and they watch the episode with the Salt Wife and they watch the episode where Prince Wing and Faithful Margaret fall under a spell and swap bodies and have sex for the first time. They watch the episode where Fox saves Prince Wing's life for the first time.

Jeremy's father makes chocolate/mango/espresso milk shakes for everyone. None of Jeremy's friends, except for Elizabeth, know about the novel. Everyone thinks Jeremy and his mother are just having an adventure. Everyone thinks Jeremy will be back at the end of the summer.

"I wonder how they find the actors," Elizabeth says. "They aren't real actors. They must be regular people. But you'd think that somewhere there would be someone who knows them. That somebody online would say, hey, that's my sister! Or that's the kid I went to school with who threw up in P.E. You know, sometimes someone says something like that or sometimes someone pretends that they know something about *The Library*, but it always turns out to be a hoax. Just somebody wanting to be somebody."

"What about the guy who's writing it?" Karl says.

Talis says, "Who says it's a guy?" and Amy says, "Yeah, Karl, why do you always assume it's a guy writing it?"

"Maybe nobody's writing it," Elizabeth says. "Maybe it's magic or it's broadcast from outer space. Maybe it's real. Wouldn't that be cool?"

"No," Jeremy says. "Because then Fox would really be dead. That would suck."

"I don't care," Elizabeth says. "I wish it were real, anyway. Maybe it all really happened somewhere, like King Arthur or Robin Hood, and this is just one version of how it happened. Like a magical After School Special."

"Even if it isn't real," Amy says, "parts of it could be real. Like maybe the World-Tree Library is real. Or maybe *The Library* is made up, but Fox is based on somebody that the writer knew. Writers do that all the time, right? Jeremy, I think your dad should write a book about me. I could be eaten by giant spiders. Or have sex with giant spiders and have spider babies. I think that would be so great."

So Amy does have psychic abilities, after all, although hopefully she will never know this. When Jeremy tests his own potential psychic abilities, he can almost sense his father, hovering somewhere just outside the living room, listening to this conversation and maybe even taking notes. Which is what writers do. But Jeremy isn't really psychic. It's just that lurking and hovering and appearing suddenly when you weren't expecting him are what his father does, just like shoplifting and cooking. Jeremy prays to all the dark gods that he never receives the gift of knowing what people are thinking. It's a dark road and it ends up with you trapped on late-night television in front of an invisible audience of depressed insomniacs wearing hats made out of tinfoil and they all want to pay you nine-ninety-nine per minute to hear you describe in minute, terrible detail what their deceased cat is thinking about, right now. What kind of future is that? He wants to go to Mars. And when will Elizabeth kiss him again? You can't just kiss someone twice and then never kiss them again. He tries not to think about Elizabeth and kissing, just in case Amy reads his mind. He realizes that he's been staring at Talis's breasts, glares instead at Elizabeth, who is watching TV. Meanwhile, Karl is glaring at him.

On television, Fox is dancing in the Invisible Nightclub with Faithful Margaret, whose hair is about to catch fire again. The Norns are playing their screechy cover of "Come On, Eileen." The Norns only know two songs: "Come On, Eileen," and "Everybody Wants to Rule the World." They don't play real instruments. They play squeaky dog toys and also a bathtub, which is enchanted, although nobody knows who by, or why, or what it was enchanted for.

"If you had to choose one," Jeremy says, "invisibility or the ability to fly, which would you choose?"

Everybody looks at him. "Only perverts would want to be invisible," Elizabeth says.

"You'd have to be naked if you were invisible," Karl says. "Because otherwise people would see your clothes."

"If you could fly, you'd have to wear thermal underwear because it's cold up there. So it just depends on whether you like to wear long underwear or no underwear at all," Amy says.

It's the kind of conversation that they have all the time. It makes Jeremy feel homesick even though he hasn't left yet.

"Maybe I'll go make brownies," Jeremy says. "Elizabeth, do you want to help me make brownies?"

"Shhh," Elizabeth says. "This is a good part."

On television, Fox and Faithful Margaret are making out. The Faithful part is kind of a joke.

Jeremy's parents go to bed at one. By three, Amy and Elizabeth are passed out on the couch and Karl has gone upstairs to check his email on Jeremy's iBook. On TV, wolves are roaming the tundra of The Free People's World-Tree Library's fortieth floor. Snow is falling heavily and librarians are burning books to keep warm, but only the most dull and improving works of literature.

Jeremy isn't sure where Talis has gone, so he goes to look for her. She hasn't gone far. She's on the landing, looking at the space on the wall where Alice Mars's painting should be hanging. Talis is carrying her sword with her, and her little plastic purse. In the bathroom off the landing, the singing toilet is still singing away in German. "We're taking the painting with us," Jeremy says. "My dad insisted, just in case he accidentally burns down the house while we're gone. Do you want to go see it? I was going to show everybody, but everybody's asleep right now."

"Sure," Talis says.

So Jeremy gets a flashlight and takes her out to the garage and shows her the van. She climbs right inside and sits down on one of the blue-fur couches. She looks around and he wonders what she's thinking. He wonders if the toilet song is stuck in her head.

"My dad did all of this," Jeremy says. He turns on the flashlight and shines it on the disco ball. Light spatters off in anxious, slippery orbits. Jeremy shows Talis how his father has hung up the painting. It looks truly wrong in the van, as if someone demented put it there. Especially with the light reflecting off the disco ball. The woman in the painting looks confused and embarrassed, as if Jeremy's father has accidentally canceled out her protective powers. Maybe the disco ball is her Kryptonite.

"So remember how you had a dream about me?" Jeremy says. Talis nods. "I think I had a dream about you, that you were Fox."

Talis opens up her arms, encompassing her costume, her sword, her plastic purse with poor Fox's ears and tail inside.

"There was something you wanted me to do," Jeremy says. "I was supposed to save you, somehow."

Talis just looks at him.

"How come you never talk?" Jeremy says. All of this is irritating. How he used to feel normal around Elizabeth, like friends, and now everything is peculiar and uncomfortable. How he used to enjoy feeling uncomfortable around Talis, and now, suddenly, he doesn't. This must be what sex is about. Stop thinking about sex, he thinks.

Talis opens her mouth and closes it again. Then she says, "I don't know. Amy talks so much. You all talk a lot. Somebody has to be the person who doesn't. The person who listens."

"Oh," Jeremy says. "I thought maybe you had a tragic secret. Like maybe you used to stutter." Except secrets can't have secrets, they just *are*.

"Nope," Talis says. "It's like being invisible, you know. Not talking. I like it."

"But you're not invisible," Jeremy says. "Not to me. Not to Karl. Karl really likes you. Did you hit him with a boa constrictor on purpose?"

But Talis says, "I wish you weren't leaving." The disco ball spins and spins. It makes Jeremy feel kind of carsick and also as if he has sparkly, disco leprosy. He doesn't say anything back to Talis, just to see how it feels. Except maybe that's rude. Or maybe it's rude the way everybody always talks and doesn't leave any space for Talis to say anything.

"At least you get to miss school," Talis says, at last.

"Yeah," he says. He leaves another space, but Talis doesn't say anything this time. "We're going to stop at all these museums and things on the way across the country. I'm supposed to keep a blog for school and describe stuff in it. I'm going to make a lot of stuff up. So it will be like Creative Writing and not so much like homework."

"You should make a list of all the towns with weird names you drive through," Talis says. "Town of Horseheads. That's a real place."

"Plantagenet," Jeremy says. "That's a real place too. I had something really weird to tell you."

Talis waits, like she always does.

Jeremy says, "I called my phone booth, the one that I inherited, and someone answered. She sounded just like Fox and she told me—she told me to call back later. So I've called a few more times, but I don't ever get her."

"Fox isn't a real person," Talis says. "*The Library* is just TV." But she sounds uncertain. That's the thing about *The Library*. Nobody knows for sure. Everyone who watches it wishes and hopes that it's not just acting. That it's magic, real magic.

"I know," Jeremy says.

"I wish Fox was real," Fox-Talis says.

They've been sitting in the van for a long time. If Karl looks for them and can't find them, he's going to think that they've been making out. He'll kill Jeremy. Once Karl tried to strangle another kid for accidentally peeing on his shoes. Jeremy might as well kiss Talis. So he does, even though she's still holding her sword. She doesn't hit him with it. It's dark and he has his eyes closed and he can almost imagine that he's kissing Elizabeth.

Karl has fallen asleep on Jeremy's bed. Talis is downstairs, fast-forwarding through the episode where some librarians drink too much Euphoria and decide to abolish Story Hour. Not just the practice of having a Story Hour, but the whole Hour. Amy and Elizabeth are still sacked out on the couch. It's weird to watch Amy sleep. She doesn't talk in her sleep.

Karl is snoring. Jeremy could go up on the roof and look at stars, except he's already packed up his telescope. He could try to wake up Elizabeth and they could go up on the roof, but Talis is down there. He and Talis could go sit on the roof, but he doesn't want to kiss Talis on the roof. He makes a solemn oath to only ever kiss Elizabeth on the roof.

He picks up his phone. Maybe he can call his phone booth and complain just a little and not wake Karl up. His dad is going to freak out about the phone bill. All these calls to Nevada. It's 4 A.M. Jeremy's plan is not to go to sleep at all. His friends are lame.

The phone rings and rings and rings and then someone picks up. Jeremy recognizes the silence on the other end. "Everybody came over and fell asleep," he whispers. "That's why I'm whispering. I don't even think they care that I'm leaving. And my feet hurt. Remember how I was going to dress up as a Forbidden Book? Platform shoes aren't comfortable. Karl thinks I did it on purpose, to be even taller than him than usual. And I forgot that I was wearing lipstick and I kissed Talis and got lipstick all over her face, so it's a good thing everyone was asleep because otherwise someone would have seen. And my dad says that he won't shoplift at all while Mom and I are gone, but you can't trust him. And that fake-fur upholstery sheds like—"

"Jeremy," that strangely familiar, sweet-and-rusty door-hinge voice says softly. "Shut up, Jeremy. I need your help."

"Wow!" Jeremy says, not in a whisper. "Wow, wow, wow! Is this Fox? Are you really Fox? Is this a joke? Are you real? Are you dead? What are you doing in my phone booth?"

"You know who I am," Fox says, and Jeremy knows with all his heart that it's really Fox. "I need you to do something for me."

"What?" Jeremy says. Karl, on the bed, laughs in his sleep as if the idea of Jeremy doing something is funny to him. "What could I do?"

"I need you to steal three books," Fox says. "From a library in a place called Iowa."

"I know Iowa," Jeremy says. "I mean, I've never been there, but it's a real place. I could go there."

"I'm going to tell you the books you need to steal," Fox says. "Author, title, and the jewelly festival number—"

"Dewey Decimal," Jeremy says. "It's actually called the Dewey Decimal number in real libraries."

"Real," Fox says, sounding amused. "You need to write this all down and also how to get to the library. You need to steal the three books and bring them to me. It's very important."

"Is it dangerous?" Jeremy says. "Are the Forbidden Books up to something? Are the Forbidden Books real, too? What if I get caught stealing?"

"It's not dangerous to you," Fox says. "Just don't get caught. Remember the episode of *The Library* when I was the little old lady with the beehive and I stole the Bishop of Tweedle's false teeth while he was reading the banns for the wedding of Faithful Margaret and Sir Petronella the Younger? Remember how he didn't even notice?"

"I've never seen that episode," Jeremy says, although as far as he knows he's never missed a single episode of *The Library*. He's never even heard of Sir Petronella.

"Oh," Fox says. "Maybe that's a flashback in a later episode or something. That's a great episode. We're depending on you, Jeremy. You have got to steal these books. They contain dreadful secrets. I can't say the titles out loud. I'm going to spell them instead."

So Jeremy gets a pad of paper and Fox spells out the titles of each book twice. (They aren't titles that can be written down here. It's safer not to even think about some books.) "Can I ask you something?" Jeremy says. "Can I tell anybody about this? Not Amy. But could I tell Karl or Elizabeth? Or Talis? Can I tell my mom? If I woke up Karl right now, would you talk to him for a minute?"

"I don't have a lot of time," Fox says. "I have to go now. Please don't tell anyone, Jeremy. I'm sorry."

"Is it the Forbidden Books?" Jeremy says again. What would Fox think if she saw the costume he's still wearing, all except for the platform heels? "Do you think I shouldn't trust my friends? But I've known them my whole life!"

Fox makes a noise, a kind of pained whuff.

"What is it?" Jeremy says. "Are you okay?"

"I have to go," Fox says. "Nobody can know about this. Don't give anybody this number. Don't tell anyone about your phone booth. Or me. Promise, Germ?"

"Only if you promise you won't call me Germ," Jeremy says, feeling really stupid. "I hate when people call me that. Call me Mars instead."

"Mars," Fox says, and it sounds exotic and strange and brave, as if Jeremy has just become a new person, a person named after a whole planet, a person who kisses girls and talks to Foxes.

"I've never stolen anything," Jeremy says.

But Fox has hung up.

Maybe out there, somewhere, is someone who enjoys having to say good-bye, but it isn't anyone that Jeremy knows. All of his friends are grumpy and red-eyed, although not from crying. From lack of sleep. From too much television. There are still faint red stains around Talis's mouth and if everyone wasn't so tired, they would realize it's Jeremy's lipstick. Karl gives Jeremy a handful of quarters, dimes, nickels, and pennies. "For the slot machines," Karl says. "If you win anything, you can keep a third of what you win."

"Half," Jeremy says, automatically.

"Fine," Karl says. "It's all from your dad's sofas, anyway. Just one more thing. Stop getting taller. Don't get taller while you're gone. Okay." He hugs Jeremy hard: so hard that it's almost like getting punched again. No wonder Talis threw the boa constrictor at Karl.

Talis and Elizabeth both hug Jeremy good-bye. Talis looks even more mysterious now that he's sat with her under a disco ball and made out. Later on, Jeremy will discover that Talis has left her sword under the blue fur couch and he'll wonder if she left it on purpose.

Talis doesn't say anything and Amy, of course, doesn't shut up, not even when she kisses him. It feels weird to be kissed by someone who goes right on talking while they kiss you and yet it shouldn't be a surprise that Amy kisses him. He imagines that later Amy and Talis and Elizabeth will all compare notes.

Elizabeth says, "I promise I'll tape every episode of *The Library* while you're gone so we can all watch them together when you get back. I promise I'll call you in Vegas, no matter what time it is there, when there's a new episode."

Her hair is a mess and her breath is faintly sour. Jeremy wishes he could tell her how beautiful she looks. "I'll write bad poetry and send it to you," he says.

Jeremy's mother is looking hideously cheerful as she goes in and out of the house, making sure that she hasn't left anything behind. She loves long car trips. It doesn't bother her one bit that she and her son are abandoning their entire lives. She passes Jeremy a folder full of maps. "You're in charge of not getting lost," she says. "Put these somewhere safe."

Jeremy says, "I found a library online that I want to go visit. Out in Iowa. They have a corn mosaic on the façade of the building, with a lot of naked goddesses and gods dancing around in a field of corn. Someone wants to take it down. Can we go see it first?"

"Sure," his mother says.

Jeremy's father has filled a whole grocery bag with sandwiches. His hair is drooping and he looks even more like an ax murderer than usual. If this were a movie, you'd think that Jeremy and his mother were escaping in the nick of time. "You take care of your mother," he says to Jeremy.

"Sure," Jeremy says. "You take care of yourself."

His dad sags. "You take care of yourself, too." So it's settled. They're all supposed to take care of themselves. Why can't they stay home and take care of each other, until Jeremy is good and ready to go off to college? "I've got another bag of sandwiches in the kitchen," his dad says. "I should go get them."

"Wait," Jeremy says. "I have to ask you something before we take off. Suppose I had to steal something. I mean, I don't have to steal anything, of course, and I know stealing is wrong, even when *you* do it, and I would never steal anything. But what if I did? How do you do it? How do you do it and not get caught?"

His father shrugs. He's probably wondering if Jeremy is really his son. Gordon Mars inherited his mutant, long-fingered, ambidextrous hands from a long line of shoplifters and money launderers and petty criminals. They're all deeply ashamed of Jeremy's father. Gordon Mars had a gift and he threw it away to become a writer. "I don't know," he says. He picks up Jeremy's hand and looks at it as if he's never noticed before that Jeremy had something hanging off the end of his wrist. "You just do it. You do it like you're not really doing anything at all. You do it while you're thinking about something else and you forget that you're doing it."

"Oh," Jeremy says, taking his hand back. "I'm not planning on stealing anything. I was just curious."

His father looks at him. "Take care of yourself," he says again, as if he really means it, and hugs Jeremy hard.

Then he goes and gets the sandwiches (so many sandwiches that Jeremy and his mother will eat sandwiches for the first three days, and still have to throw half of them away). Everyone waves. Jeremy and his mother climb in the van. Jeremy's mother turns on the CD player. Bob Dylan is singing about monkeys. His mother loves Bob Dylan. They drive away.

Do you know how, sometimes, during a commercial break in your favorite television shows, your best friend calls and wants to talk about one of her boyfriends, and when you try to hang up, she starts crying and you try to cheer her up and end up missing about half of the episode? And so when you go to work the next day, you have to get the guy who sits next to you to explain what happened? That's the good thing about a book. You can mark your place in a book. But this isn't really a book. It's a television show.

In one episode of *The Library,* an adolescent boy drives across the country with his mother. They have to change a tire. The boy practices taking things out of his mother's purse and putting them back again. He steals a sixteen-ounce bottle of Coke from one convenience market and leaves it at another convenience market. The boy and his mother stop at a lot of libraries, and the boy keeps a blog, but he skips the bit about the library in Iowa. He writes in his blog about what he's reading, but he doesn't read the books he stole in Iowa, because Fox told him not to, and because he has to hide them from his mother. Well, he reads just a few pages. Skims, really. He hides them under the blue-fur sofa. They go camping in Utah, and the boy sets up his telescope. He sees three shooting stars and a coyote. He never sees anyone who looks like a Forbidden Book, although he sees a transvestite go into the women's restroom at a rest stop in Indiana. He calls a phone booth just outside Las Vegas twice, but no one ever answers. He has short conversations with his father. He wonders what his father is up to. He wishes he could tell his father about Fox and the books. Once the boy's mother finds a giant spider the size of an Oreo in their tent. She starts laughing hysterically. She takes a picture of it with her digital camera, and the boy puts the picture on his blog. Sometimes the boy asks questions and his mother talks about her parents. Once she cries. The boy doesn't know what to say. They talk about their favorite episodes of *The Library* and the episodes that they really hated, and the mother asks if the boy thinks Fox is really dead. He says he doesn't think so.

Once a man tries to break into the van while they are sleeping in it. But then he goes away. Maybe the painting of the woman with the peeling knife is protecting them.

But you've seen this episode before.

It's Cinco de Mayo. It's almost seven o'clock at night, and the sun is beginning to go down. Jeremy and his mother are in the desert and Las Vegas is somewhere in front of them. Every time they pass a driver coming the other way, Jeremy tries to figure out if that person has just won or lost a lot of money. Everything is flat and sort of tilted here, except off in the distance, where the land goes up abruptly, as if someone has started to fold up a map. Somewhere around here is the Grand Canyon, which must have been a surprise when people first saw it.

Jeremy's mother says, "Are you sure we have to do this first? Couldn't we go find your phone booth later?"

"Can we do it now?" Jeremy says. "I said I was going to do it on my blog. It's like a quest that I have to complete."

"Okay," his mother says. "It should be around here somewhere. It's supposed to be 4.5 miles after the turn-off, and here's the turn-off."

It isn't hard to find the phone booth. There isn't much else around. Jeremy should feel excited when he sees it, but it's a disappointment, really. He's seen phone booths before. He was expecting something to be different. Mostly he just feels tired of road trips and tired of roads and just tired, tired, tired. He looks around to see if Fox is somewhere nearby, but there's just a hiker off in the distance. Some kid.

"Okay, Germ," his mother says. "Make this quick."

"I need to get my backpack out of the back," Jeremy says.

"Do you want me to come, too?" his mother says.

"No," Jeremy says. "This is kind of personal."

His mother looks like she's trying not to laugh. "Just hurry up. I have to pee."

When Jeremy gets to the phone booth, he turns around. His mother has the light on in the van. It looks like she's singing along to the radio. His mother has a terrible voice.

When he steps inside the phone booth, it isn't magical. The phone booth smells rank, as if an animal has been living in it. The windows are smudgy. He takes the stolen books out of his backpack and puts them in the little shelf where someone has stolen a phone book. Then he waits. Maybe Fox is going to call him. Maybe he's supposed to wait until she calls. But she doesn't call. He feels lonely. There's no one he can tell about this. He feels like an idiot and he also feels kind of proud. Because he did it. He drove cross-country with his mother and saved an imaginary person.

"So how's your phone booth?" his mother says.

"Great!" he says, and they're both silent again. Las Vegas is in front of them and then all around them and everything is lit up like they're inside a pinball game. All of the trees look fake. Like someone read too much Dr. Seuss and got ideas. People are walking up and down the sidewalks. Some of them look normal. Others look like they just escaped from a fancy-dress ball at a lunatic asylum. Jeremy hopes they've just won lots of money and that's why they look so startled, so strange. Or maybe they're all vampires.

"Left," he tells his mother. "Go left here. Look out for the vampires on the crosswalk. And then it's an immediate right." Four times his mother let him drive the van: once in Utah, twice in South Dakota, once in Pennsylvania. The van smells like old burger wrappers and fake fur, and it doesn't help that Jeremy's gotten used to the smell. The woman in the painting has had a pained expression on her face for the last few nights, and the disco ball has lost some of its pieces of mirror because Jeremy kept knocking his head on it in the morning. Jeremy and his mother haven't showered in three days.

Here is the wedding chapel, in front of them, at the end of a long driveway. Electric purple light shines on a sign that spells out HELL'S BELLS. There's a wrought-iron fence and a yard full of trees dripping Spanish moss. Under the trees, tombstones and miniature mausoleums.

"Do you think those are real?" his mother says. She sounds slightly worried.

" 'Harry East, Recently Deceased,' " Jeremy says. "No, I don't."

There's a hearse in the driveway with a little plaque on the back. RECENTLY ~~BURIED~~ MARRIED. The chapel is a Victorian house with a bell tower. Perhaps it's full of bats. Or giant spiders. Jeremy's father would love this place. His mother is going to hate it.

Someone stands at the threshold of the chapel, door open, looking out at them. But as Jeremy and his mother get out of the van, he turns and goes inside and shuts the door. "Look out," his mother says. "They've probably gone to put the boiling oil in the microwave."

She rings the doorbell determinedly. Instead of ringing, there's a recording of a crow. *Caw, caw, caw.* All the lights in the Victorian house go out. Then they turn on again. The door swings open and Jeremy tightens his grip on his backpack, just in case. "Good evening, Madam. Young man," a man says and Jeremy looks up and up and up. The man at the door has to lower his head to look out. His hands are large as toaster ovens. He looks like he's wearing Chihuahua coffins on his feet. Two realistic-looking bolts stick out on either side of his head. He wears green pancake makeup, glittery green eye shadow, and his lashes are as long and thick and green as Astro Turf. "We weren't expecting you so soon."

"We should have called ahead," Jeremy's mother says. "I'm real sorry."

"Great costume," Jeremy says.

The Frankenstein curls his lip in a somber way. "Thank you," he says. "Call me Miss Thing, please."

"I'm Jeremy," Jeremy says. "This is my mother."

"Oh please," Miss Thing says. Even his wink is somber. "You tease me. She isn't old enough to be your mother."

"Oh please, yourself," Jeremy's mother says.

"Quick, the two of you," someone yells from somewhere inside Hell's Bells. "While you zthtand there gabbing, the devil ithz prowling around like a lion, looking for a way to get in. Are you juthzt going to zthtand there and hold the door wide open for him?"

So they all step inside. "Iz that Jeremy Marthz at lathzt?" the voice says. "Earth to Marthz, Earth to Marthz. Marthzzz, Jeremy Marthzzz, there'thz zthomeone on the phone for Jeremy Marthz. She'thz called three timethz in the lathzt ten minutethz, Jeremy Marthzzz."

It's Fox, Jeremy knows. Of course, it's Fox! She's in the phone booth. She's got the books and she's going to tell me that I saved whatever it is that I was saving. He walks toward the buzzing voice while Miss Thing and his mother go back out to the van.

He walks past a room full of artfully draped spider webs and candelabras drooping with drippy candles. Someone is playing the organ behind a wooden screen. He goes down the hall and up a long staircase. The banisters are carved with little faces. Owls and foxes and ugly children. The voice goes on talking. "Yoohoo, Jeremy, up the stairthz, that'thz right. Now, come along, come right in! Not in there, in here, in here! Don't mind the dark, we *like* the dark, just watch your step." Jeremy puts his hand out. He touches something and there's a click and the bookcase in front of him slowly slides back. Now the room is three times as large and there are more bookshelves and there's a young woman wearing dark sunglasses, sitting on a couch. She has a megaphone in one hand and a phone in the other. "For you, Jeremy Marth," she says. She's the palest person Jeremy has ever seen and her two canine teeth are so pointed that she lisps a little when she talks. On the megaphone the lisp was sinister, but now it just makes her sound irritable.

She hands him the phone. "Hello?" he says. He keeps an eye on the vampire.

"Jeremy!" Elizabeth says. "It's on, it's on, it's on! It's just started! We're all just sitting here. Everybody's here. What happened to your cell phone? We kept calling."

"Mom left it in the visitor's center at Zion," Jeremy says.

"Well, you're there. We figured out from your blog that you must be near Vegas. Amy says she had a feeling that you were going to get there in time. She made us keep calling. Stay on the phone, Jeremy. We can all watch it together, okay? Hold on."

Karl grabs the phone. "Hey, Germ, I didn't get any postcards," he says. "You forget how to write or something? Wait a minute. Somebody wants to say something to you." Then he laughs and laughs and passes the phone on to someone else who doesn't say anything at all.

"Talis?" Jeremy says.

Maybe it isn't Talis. Maybe it's Elizabeth again. He thinks about how his mouth is right next to Elizabeth's ear. Or maybe it's Talis's ear.

The vampire on the couch is already flipping through the channels. Jeremy would like to grab the remote away from her, but it's not a good idea to try to take things away from a vampire. His mother and Miss Thing come up the stairs and into the room and suddenly the room seems absolutely full of people, as if Karl and Amy and Elizabeth and Talis have come into the room, too. His hand is getting sweaty around the phone. Miss Thing has a firm hold on Jeremy's mother's painting, as if it might try to escape. Jeremy's mother looks tired. For the past three days her hair has been braided into pigtails. She looks younger to Jeremy, as if they've been traveling backwards in time instead of just across the country. She smiles at Jeremy, a giddy, exhausted smile. Jeremy smiles back.

"Is it *The Library*?" Miss Thing says. "Is a new episode on?"

Jeremy sits down on the couch beside the vampire, still holding the phone to his ear. His arm is getting tired.

"I'm here," he says to Talis or Elizabeth or whoever it is on the other end of the phone. "I'm here." And then he sits and doesn't say anything and waits with everyone else for the vampire to find the right channel so they can all find out if he's saved Fox, if Fox is alive, if Fox is still alive.

BEN BOVA, ELLEN DATLOW,
BILL FAWCETT, AND MARTIN H. GREENBERG

You'll notice that, as usual, three of the four Nebula awards for prose fiction went to short fiction—a short story, a novelette, and a novella. The standard venue for short fiction has traditionally been the magazines.

That may not be the case for much longer. When I was a kid, back in the early 1950s, there were fifty-two science fiction and fantasy magazines being published. Today there are four professional print magazines, paying professional rates, being regularly published in the United States, and two more in England. So what is the future of the short story? Is it moribund? If not, where are you going to find short fiction in the future?

To answer that, I put the question, via round-robin e-mail, to four of the most knowledgable people in the field of short fiction:

Ben Bova—former editor of *Analog* and *Omni*, six-time winner of the Best Editor Hugo
Ellen Datlow—former editor of *Omni* and SciFi.com, two-time winner of the Best Editor Hugo
Bill Fawcett—writer, editor, packager, anthologist, a jack of every literary trade
Martin H. Greenberg—editor/producer of more than 1,700 anthologies. (Yes, 1,700.)

QUESTION: Ellen, you've edited print magazines, electronic magazines, and anthologies. Clearly the four remaining magazines could be in better health. Just as clearly, your own online magazine and most of your competitors were in even poorer health. And publishers are convinced that anthologies don't sell well, and hence they don't put as much money into them as into novels, thereby guaranteeing they don't sell well. So what is the future of the short story? Where are writers going to go five, ten, and twenty years from now to get paid for their short fiction—or won't they?

ELLEN DATLOW: Well, first of all, *SCI FICTION* was not in poor health. It was decided (probably by marketing) that fiction was no longer a part of the mix the company wanted to offer on the site. That's a bit different.

I'm still selling anthologies and earning royalties from some of them, so I don't see that anthologies are doing any worse than they ever were—particularly in the young adult market. I think the short story will muddle on as it always has done. New markets are consistently arising: in the past year two new online magazines have launched: Orson Scott Card's and Jim Baen's. In the past five years several other new online magazines have started to publish SF: Nature Online publishes short shorts on a weekly basis (although I feel that 950 words is a very limited form), and Salon has occasionally published SF and fantasy, as have *The New Yorker, Esquire,* etc. *McSweeney's* has published SF/F writers in its anthologies. *Conjunctions* has published fantasy material. I see our genres propagating into mainstream markets. Subterranean is now publishing a magazine by the same name that's paying professional rates, as is PS Publishing (*Postscripts*).

Also, the boutique magazines have been springing up like mushrooms. Most pay a pittance, but that doesn't mean they won't start paying writers better if they thrive.

So I see the same thing happening now that has happened all through science fiction and fantasy's history: Magazines start up. Some thrive; some die quickly. Some last a few issues. Others last several years.

QUESTION: Ben, you also had the experience of a highly praised electronic magazine—GalaxyOnline.com—that went under. Was your experience similar to Ellen's, or do you feel other factors were involved? And what kind of future, immediate and long-term, do you see for e-magazines as well as print magazines?

BEN BOVA: GalaxyOnline was doomed before it started, I think, because the management was more interested in selling shares of its IPO than anything else. The science fiction stories were more or less a front to attract investors, and not the company's primary interest. I agree with Ellen in that I think electronic publishing will become a stronger part of the market for short fiction, although payment rates will be (as usual) pretty damned low.

QUESTION: Bill, you've edited a lot of anthologies over the years, along with being a writer yourself. So what's the outlook? Is the decreasing number of magazines good for anthologists (either because there's a demand for short fiction that the magazines can't fill, or because you've got a lot of hungry short fiction writers out there)? Or is it bad, because there isn't the demand for short fiction there once was?

BILL FAWCETT: Electronic publishing, if there's a way to make it financially feasible, may play a major role in the future of short stories, assuming there *is* a future for them. Having packaged books mostly in the print medium, about forty anthologies myself, I'll comment here mostly on how that market has changed.

In print the publishers are getting much more selective. It used to be that some major publishers had a slot where they alternated reprints and anthologies. The list of paperback titles each month for Ace SF in the mid-eighties had five slots, and the fourth slot was always used to publish either a classic reprint or a new anthology. But since then, even with smaller publishers, there has to be more than just a good idea there. Today paper publishers look at any anthology and ask why, rather than what. There has to be a reason to print the anthology, one that shows it can sell up there with a novel. This can vary from just as simple a thing as the fact that the idea is popular or relates to an upcoming movie. More often you have collections: stories all by one author or set all in a popular shared universe, rather than anthologies. That's another format that has also basically dried up: There are very few new "shared universes" today. Back in the later 1980s there was a plethora of shared worlds, varying from my own (and Dave Drake's) *The Fleet* and *Thieves' World* to less prominent series such as *Heroes in Hell*. While new volumes of *Thieves' World* are again appearing, virtually no new shared-world anthologies are being created. They have, to some degree, been replaced by collections of stories set in worlds that first appeared in novels. Baen Books has successfully marketed a number of these, including *1632* and *Man-Kzin War* collections. But these too are less common. But even within those books, what we see today is perhaps less than half as many anthologies as we did twenty years ago—and it's an even smaller percentage from major publishers. There are some great anthologies there, but perhaps this is all the result of the new "businesslike" attitude of the major publishers. The painful truth is that few, if any, anthologies have the potential to become national best sellers.

Publishers want and need the occasional book that sells in very big numbers. It provides the money to cover ever-increasing costs. With publishing being so much about profits today, the limited top end alone may explain why we see fewer anthologies. Now, is there fiction to buy? As someone who is approached several times every convention by authors who have written or would like to write a short story, I have to say there are or could be plenty of short stories. When I do get the chance to ask an author to create a short story, I invariably get an enthusiastic yes—perhaps, sadly, because such invitations are so rare today.

QUESTION: Marty, you're "Mr. Anthology." Is it getting harder to sell them, or just harder for everyone else? Are there certain types of anthologies that are more in demand today, certain types that are more difficult to sell today? I know you don't limit yourself to science fiction; how do anthologies sell in other markets these days? And do you see an upturn or downturn to the current trends?

MARTIN H. GREENBERG: I think the short story will be fine—between the Internet and small publishers, everyone who has a publishable story should be able to find a home for it. However, these markets don't pay very well, and compared to the situation we all grew up with—magazines galore, lots of anthologies, etc., most paying decently—it is really another world (at least to an old dead-tree guy like me).

As to anthologies, there is still a market out there, but it seems to get smaller and smaller, at least in terms of the number of publishers who will (a) give you a contract for one, and (b) give you enough money not to insult your writers (either reprinted or original work). As of today, and counting some handshake deals, we have 296 forthcoming books: 43 anthologies (nine reprint and 34 original), but well over half of these are with one publisher, and a number of them are mystery/suspense and one Western. Almost all the reprint anthologies are with small (and small-paying) publishers, and only two in our genres, both with best-selling authors, have advances over $10,000. The others consist of 244 novels and nine nonfiction books. The 14.5 percent that are anthologies are probably an all-time low in terms of percentages of our books. I expect that even this figure will decline over time.

QUESTION: Okay, the Nebulas are over, and two of the three short fiction awards went to stories that did not appear in print or electronic magazines, but in small press collections. Is this the future of the awards? Are voters going to have to start buying every collection that comes down the pike, rather than relying on the pay scale of the magazines to at least give some indication of where the best stories are likely to be found? And is this ultimately where writers are going to have to sell their short fiction?

BEN BOVA: I think the future market for short fiction will be more electronic than print. The pay scales will be low, but pay scales for short fiction have always been low. The key "invention" that needs to be made is to convince potential readers that they should pay for receiving the fiction they want to read. Internet users are accustomed to getting everything for free.

ELLEN DATLOW: My first reaction is that I'm not sure that's such a horrible thing (of course, I'm biased, as I published the anthology from which one of the winners came).

But other points are that one of the two winners was published in a collection first, yes, but appeared in a magazine within the same year. So really, only one winner was from an original anthology. In addition, obviously people out there are already reading some SF/F collections, and anthologies or the novelette I published (and which was subsequently reprinted in the author's collection) would not have made the ballot.

So again I ask, Why is that such a horrible thing? My original anthologies pay as well as or better than the magazines. My anthologies are not "open," so writers I don't already work with or whose work I'm not familiar with have a harder time breaking into them. But as far as readers go, they're getting a good deal: over a hundred thousand words of good fiction in a lasting book rather than over several issues of a magazine.

Slightly on a tangent, I've been reading short horror fiction for *The Year's Best Fantasy and Horror* for going on twenty years, and from the very start most of the best horror fiction has been coming from the anthologies and collections rather than the magazines. The situation is admittedly different for horror than science fiction, the latter of which has traditionally been published regularly in magazines. Most of the horror magazines that *do* exist don't pay at a professional level, and many don't publish at a professional level, so I wouldn't wish that situation on the SF/F field.

BILL FAWCETT: Being a typical American, I have faith that technology will come along and save the day. At one point I would have said that anything that has a chance in electronic books has to have major advantages over the paperback, including price per book. But with the resurgence of hardcover books, it can be argued that price is a bit less of an issue. So it all comes down to a matter of convenience. There are platforms coming that can be read as easily as a book, screen brightness and weight being the major factors, and both are advancing rapidly. The questions are whether or not there is any advantage to the reader to have these devices rather than individual books, and what disadvantages there are. The obvious answer to the first is that a book contains, well, one book. If I am going on a long trip this means a suitcase with possibly several pounds of books. Any electronic equivalent would likely contain hundreds of books and stories with no added mass. The two big issues are cost and being easy on the eyes. Cost-wise we are watching as people who had twenty-dollar DVD music players replace them with $150-plus iPods. So that ground is broken. Why do they do this? Because they can be customized. The same pattern could easily follow for books. The iPod has already evolved to show video (if poorly), so when a book-Pod appears the public will be ready to accept it. The real tech breakthrough will be the screen, and maybe a device sturdy enough to let you drop it and take it to the beach without worrying. Are these likely? Yes.

How will the new technology, some of which we are seeing a good start on today, affect short stories? Length will cease to be a real measure, except maybe of cost. The reason novels are so much more popular today is not only the story format, but also the perceived value. Certainly to the publisher, where they have to offer something that is worth eight dollars to the reader. Why does every "Wheel of Time" story have to be a full book? Obviously it does not, and already we see short stories set in major series. With electronic publishing hitting mass proportions, that will cease to be a consideration. The next advance in the *Honor Harrington* series might be a novella that contains a crucial event. In electronic publishing that length is just fine, and David Weber could get paid proportionally to the time spent writing it; for the publisher, you can sell eight one-dollar items as efficiently on a Web site (almost) as one eight-dollar item. And the advantages of being a complete story on one subway ride or even one trip to the bathroom will be accentuated.

This change may be inevitable with the rapid increase in pricing of paperbacks. It will literally demand the market for an electronic reader. Mass-market books are already visibly at the point where their high cost encourages those to whom price is not a factor to buy hardcovers. How long before that increasing price point, driven by paper and production costs, forces the paperback cost even higher? This is the exact pattern that, in the fifties, as hardcover books increased rapidly in price, led to the popularity of the paperback format (then costing around thirty-five cents). So the cost of paperbacks, as eighteen-dollar record albums did with downloaded music, may soon drive the public to something electronic. And once there the short story, even single stories, may follow the same pattern as albums and singles have today. Where the album once ruled in music, now online the single-song download is dominant. If the pattern transfers to literature, once there is a viable, portable electronic device, then we might not only see resurgence in the popularity of short stories, but someday see even the snooty *New York Times* begin listing the best-selling short story downloads just as has happened in music. Someday only us lonely bibliophiles will be in the stores buying actual books, everyone else reading Mike Resnick's next Hugo-winning short story the day he finishes it.

MARTIN H. GREENBERG: I agree with all of the above, but with a considerable degree of sadness. For a dinosaur like myself, I will miss (I probably won't be around to see it) the smell and especially the feel of a printed book. Not that it matters in the cosmic flow of things, and even though the stories may be exactly the same, reading them on a screen just doesn't cut it for me.

So there will always be short stories, there will always be single-author collections, and there will always be anthologies. In fact, I can see a future in which selling a "regular" printed anthology will constitute a subrights sale, with the electronic edition being both the originator and main edition of the book—the phrase "I'm going to wait for the paperback" will have a different meaning—and one that I will personally embrace.

Carol Emshwiller is the widow of one of science fiction's finest artists, the late, great Ed Emshwiller. I think if he were around today, he'd be proud to be known as the husband of one of science fiction's finest writers. Carol has been turning out critically acclaimed fiction for quite some time now, and "I Live With You," the Nebula-winning short story, is clearly one of her very best.

I LIVE WITH YOU

CAROL EMSHWILLER

I live in your house and you don't know it. I nibble at your food. You wonder where it went . . . where your pencils and pens go. . . . What happened to your best blouse. (You're just my size. That's why I'm here.) How did your keys get way over on the bedside table instead of by the front door where you always put them? You *do* always put them there. You're careful.

I leave dirty dishes in the sink. I nap in your bed when you're at work and leave it rumpled. You thought you had made it first thing in the morning and you had.

I saw you first when I was hiding out at the book store. By then I was tired of living where there wasn't any food except the muffins in the coffee bar. In some ways it was a good place to be . . . the reading, the music. I never stole. Where would I have taken what I liked? I didn't even steal back when I lived in a department store. I left there forever in my same old clothes though I'd often worn their things at night. When I left, I could see on their faces that they were glad to see such a raggedy person leave. I could see they wondered how I'd gotten in in the first place. To tell the truth, only one person noticed me. I'm hardly ever noticed.

But then, at the book store, I saw you: Just my size. Just my look. And you're as invisible as I am. I saw that nobody noticed you just as hardly anybody notices me.

I followed you home—a nice house on the outskirts of town. If I wore your clothes, I could go in and out and everybody would think I was you. But I wondered how to get in in the first place? I thought it would have to be in the middle of the night and I'd have to climb in a window.

———————

But I don't need a window. I hunch down and walk in right behind you. You'd think somebody that nobody ever notices would notice other people, but you don't.

Once I'm in, right away I duck into the hall closet.

You have a cat. Isn't that just like you? And just like me also. I would have had one were I you.

The first few days are wonderful. Your clothes are to my taste. Your cat likes me (right away better than he likes you). Right away I find a nice place in your attic. More a crawl space but I'm used to hunching over. In fact that's how I walk around most of the time. The space is narrow and long, but it has little windows at each end. Out one, I can look right into a tree top. I think an apple tree. If it was the right season I could reach out and pick an apple. I brought up your quilt. I saw you looking puzzled after I took the hall rug. I laughed to myself when you changed the locks on your doors. Right after that I took a photo from the mantel. Your mother, I presume. I wanted you to notice it was gone, but you didn't.

I bring up a footstool. I bring up cushions, one by one until I have four. I bring up magazines, straight from the mail box, before you have a chance to read them.

What I do all day? Anything I want to. I dance and sing and play the radio and TV.

When you're home, I come down in the evening, stand in the hall and watch you watch TV.

I wash my hair with your shampoo. Once, when you came home early, I almost got caught in the shower. I hid in the hall closet, huddled in with the sheets, and watched you find the wet towel—the spilled shampoo.

You get upset. You think: I've heard odd thumps for weeks. You think you're in danger, though you try hard to talk yourself out of it. You tell yourself it's the cat, but you know it's not.

You get a lock for your bedroom door—a deadbolt. You have to be inside to push it closed.

I have left a book open on the couch, the print of my head on the couch cushion. I've pulled out a few gray hairs to leave there. I have left a half full wine glass on the counter. I have left your underwear (which I wore) on the bathroom floor, dirty socks under the bed, a bra hanging on the towel rack. I left a half-eaten pizza on the kitchen counter. (I ordered out and paid with your stash of quarters, though I know where you keep your secret twenties.)

I set all your clocks back fifteen minutes but I set your alarm clock to four in the morning. I hid your reading glasses. I pull buttons off your sweaters and put them where your quarters used to be. Your quarters I put in your button box.

Normally I try not to bump and thump in the night, but I'm tired of your little life. At the bookstore and grocery store at least things happened all day long. You keep watching the same TV programs. You go off to work. You make enough money (I see the bank statements), but what do you do with it? I want to change your life into something worth watching.

I begin to thump, bump, and groan and moan. (I've been feeling like groaning and moaning for a long time, anyway.)

Maybe I'll bring you a man.

I'll buy you new clothes and take away the old ones, so you'll *have* to wear the new ones. The new clothes will be red and orange and with stripes and polka dots. When I get through with you, you'll be real . . . or at least realer. People will notice you.

Now you groan and sigh as much as I do. You think: This can't be happening. You think: What about the funny sounds coming from the crawl space? You think: I don't dare go up there by myself, but who could I get to go with me? (You don't have any friends that I know of. You're like me in that.)

Monday you go off to work wearing a fuzzy blue top and red leather pants. You had a hard time finding a combination without stripes or big flowers or dots on it.

I watch you from your kitchen window. I'm heating up your leftover coffee. I'm making toast. (I use up all the butter. You thought there was plenty for the next few days.)

You almost caught me the time I came home late with packages. I had to hide behind the curtains. I could tell that my feet showed out the bottom, but you didn't notice.

Another time you saw me duck into the hall closet but you didn't dare open the door. You hurried upstairs to your bedroom and pushed the deadbolt. That evening you didn't come down at all. You skipped supper. I watched TV . . . any show I wanted.

I put another deadbolt on the *outside* of your bedroom door. Just in case. It's way up high. I don't think you'll notice. It might come in handy.

(Lacy underwear with holes in lewd places. Nudist magazines. Snails and sardines—smoked oysters. Neither one of us like them. All the things I get with your money are for *you*. I don't steal.)

How do you get through Christmas all by yourself? You're lonely enough for both of us. You wrap empty boxes in Christmas paper just to be festive. You buy a tree, a small one. It's artificial and comes with lights that glimmer on and off. The cat and I come down to sleep near its glow.

But the man. The one I want to bring to you. I look over the personals. I write letters to possibilities but, as I'm taking them to the post office, I see somebody. He limps and wobbles. (The way he lurches sideways looks like sciatica to me. Or maybe arthritis.) He needs a haircut and a shave. He's wearing an old plaid jacket and he's all knees and elbows. There's a countrified look about him. Nobody wears plaid around here.

I limp behind him. Watch him go into one of those little apartments behind a main house and over a garage. It's not far from our house.

It can't be more than one room. I could never creep around in that place and not be noticed.

A country cousin. Country uncle more likely, he's older than we are. Is he capable of what I want him for?

Next day I watch him in the grocery store. Like us, he buys living-alone kind of food, two apples, a tomato, crackers, oatmeal. Poor people's kind of food. I get in line with him at the check-out. I bump into him on purpose as he pays and peek into his wallet. That's all he has—just enough for what he buys. He counts out the change a penny at a time and he hardly has a nickel left over. I get ready to give him a bit extra if he needs it.

He's such an ugly, rickety man. . . . Perfect.

There's no reason to go into his over-the-garage room, but I want to. This is important. I need to see who he is.

I use our credit card to open his lock.

What a mess. He needs somebody like us to look after him. His bed is piled with blankets. The room isn't very well heated. The bathroom has a curtain instead of a door. There's no tub or even shower. I check the hot water in the sink. It says HOT, but both sides come out cold. All he has is a hot plate. No refrigerator. There's two windows, but no curtains. Isn't that just like a man. I could climb up on the back fence and see right in.

There's nothing of the holidays here. Nothing of any holidays and not a single picture of a relative. And, like our house, nothing of friends. You and he are made for each other.

What to do to show I've been here? But this time I don't feel much like playing tricks. And it's so messy he wouldn't notice, anyway.

It's cold. I haven't taken my coat off all through this. I make myself a cup of tea. (There's no lemons and no milk. Of course.) I sit in his one chair. It's painted ugly green. All his furniture is as if picked up on the curb and his bedside table is one of those fruit boxes. As I sit and sip, I check his magazines. They look as though stolen from somebody's garbage. I'm shivering. (No wonder he's out. I suppose it's not easy to shave. He'd have to heat the water on the hot plate.)

He needs a cat. Something to sleep on his chest to keep him warm like your cat does with me.

I have our groceries in my backpack. I leave two oranges and a doughnut in plain sight beside the hot plate. I leave several of our quarters.

I leave a note: I put in our address. I sign your name. I write: Come for Christmas. Two o'clock. I'll be wearing red leather pants! Your neighbor, Nora.

(I wonder which of us should wear those pants.)

I clean up a little bit but not so much that he'd notice if he's not a noticing person. Besides, people only notice when things are dirty. They never notice when things are cleaned up.

As I walk home, I see you on your way out. We pass each other. You look right at me. I'm wearing your green sweater and your black slacks. We look at each other, my brown eyes to your brown eyes. Only difference is, your hair is pushed back and mine hangs down over my forehead. You go right on by. I turn and look back. You don't. I laugh behind my hand that you had to wear those red leather pants and a black and white striped top.

————

He's too timid and too self-deprecating to come. He doesn't like to limp in front of people and he's ashamed not to have enough money hardly even for his food, and not to have a chance to shave and take a bath. Though if he's scared by me coming into his room, he might come. He might want to see who Nora is and if the address is real. His pretext will be that he wants to thank you for the food and quarters. He might even want to give them back. He might be one of those rich people who live as if they were poor. I should have looked for money or bank books. I will next time.

When the doorbell rings, who else could it be?

You open the door.

"Are you Nora?"

"Yes?"

"I want to thank you."

I knew it. I suppose he wants more money.

"But I want to bring your quarters back. That was kind of you but I don't need them."

You don't know what to say. You suspect it's all because of me. That I've, yet again, made your life difficult. You wonder what to do. He doesn't look dangerous but you never can tell. You want to get even with me some way. You suppose, if he *is* dangerous, it would be bad for both of us so it must be all right. You ask him in.

He hobbles into your living room. You say sit down, that you'll get tea. You're stalling for time.

He still holds the handful of quarters. He puts them on the coffee table.

You don't know how those quarters got to him or even if they really are your quarters. "No, no," you say, and "Where did these come from?"

"They were in my room with a note from you and this address. You said, Come for Christmas."

You wonder what I'll like least. Do I want you to invite him to stay for supper? Unlikely, though, since you only have one TV dinner and you know I know that.

"Somebody is playing a joke on me. But the tea. . . ."

You need help getting started so I trip you in the hall as you come back into the room. Everything goes down. Too bad, too, because you'd used your good china in spite of how this man looks.

Of course he pushes himself up and hobbles to you and helps pick up the things and you. You say you could make more but he says, It doesn't matter. Then you both go out to the kitchen. I go, too. Sidling. Slithering. The cat slides in with us. Both your and his glasses are thick. I'm counting on your blindness. I squat down. He puts the broken cups on a corner of the counter. You get out two more. He says, these are too nice. You say, they're Mother's. He says, "You shouldn't use the Rosenthal, not for me."

There now, are you both rich yet never use your money?

The cat jumps on the table and you swipe him off. No wonder he likes me better than you. I always let him go where he wants and I like him on the table.

You're looking at our man—studying his crooked nose. You see what neither of us has noticed until now. The hand that reaches to help you wears a ring with a large stone. Some sort of school ring. You're thinking: Well, well, and changing your mind. As am I.

He's too good for you. Maybe might be good enough for me.

We are all, all three, the same kind of person. When you leave in the morning, I've seen you look out the door to make sure there's nobody out there you might have to say hello to.

But now you talk. You think. You ask. You wonder out loud if this and that. You look down at your striped shirt and wish you were wearing your usual clothes. I'm under the table wearing your brown blouse with the faint pattern of fall leaves. I look like a wrinkled up paper bag kicked under here and forgotten. The cat is down here with me purring.

It never takes long for two lonely people living in their fantasies to connect—to see all sorts of things in each other that don't exist.

You've waited for each other all your lives. You almost say so. Besides, he'd have a nice place to live if . . . if anything comes of this.

I think about that black lacy underwear. That pink silk nightie. As soon as I have a chance, I'll go get them. I might need them for myself.

But how to get you moving? You're both all talk. Or *you* are, he's not talking much. Perhaps one look at the nightie might get things rolling. That'll have to be for later. Or on the other hand. . . .

I reach back to the shelf behind me and, when neither he nor you are looking, I bring out the sherry. They'll both think the other one got the bottle out.

(They do.)

You get wineglasses. You even get out your TV dinner and say you'll split it. It's turkey with stuffing. You got it special for Christmas.

Of course he says for you to eat it all, but you say you never do, anyway, so you split it.

I'm getting hungry myself. If it was just you, I would sneak a few bites, but there's little enough for the two of you. I'll have to find another way.

You both get tipsy. It doesn't take much. You hardly ever drink and it looks like he doesn't either. And I think you want to get drunk. You want something to happen as much as I do.

Every now and then I take a sip of your drinks. And on an empty stomach it takes even less. With the drone of your talk, talk, talking, I almost go to sleep.

But you're heading upstairs already.

I crawl out from under the table and climb the stairs behind you. I'm as wobbly as you are. Actually I'm wobblier. We, all three, go into your bedroom. And the cat. You push the deadbolt. He wonders why. "Aren't you alone here?"

You say, "Not exactly." And then, "I'll tell you later."

(You're right, this certainly isn't the time for a discussion about me.)

First thing I grab our sexy nightie from the drawer. I get under the bed and put it on. That's not easy, cramped up under there. For a few minutes I lose track of what's happening above me. I comb my hair as you always have it, back away from your face. I have to use my fingers and I don't have a mirror so I'm not sure how it comes out. I pinch my cheeks and bite my lips to make them redder.

The cat purrs.

I lean up to see what's going on.

Nothing much so far. Even though tipsy, he seems shy. Inexperienced. I don't think he's ever been anybody's grandfather.

(We're, all of us, all of a piece. None of us has ever been anybody's relative.)

You look pretty much passed out. Or you're pretending. Either way, it's a good time for me to make an appearance.

I crawl out from under the bed and check myself in the mirror behind them. My hair is a mess but I look good in the silky nightgown. Better than you do in your stripes and red pants. By far.

I do a little sexy dance. I say, "She's not Nora, I'm Nora. I'm the one who wrote you that note."

You sit up. You were faking being drunk. You think: Now I see who you are. Now I'll get you. But you won't.

I stroke the cat. Suggestively. He purrs. (The cat, I mean.) I purr. Suggestively.

I see his eyes light up. (The man's, I mean.) Now there'll be some action.

I say, "I don't even know your name."

He says, "Willard."

I'm on his good side because I asked, and you're not because you didn't. All this talk, talk, talk, talk and you didn't. You slither away, down under the bed. You feel ashamed of yourself and yet curious. You wonder: How did you ever get yourself in this position, and what to do now? But I do know what to do. I give you a kick and hand you the cat. Willard. Willard is a little confused. But eager. More than before. He likes the nightgown and says so.

I take a good long look at him. Those bushy eyebrows. Lots of white hairs in them. I help him take off his shirt. His is not my favorite kind of chest. He does have a nice flat stomach though. (I liked that about him from the start—back when I first saw him wobbling down the street.) I look into his green/gray/tan eyes.

But what about, I love you?

I say it. "What about I love you?"

That stops him. I didn't mean to do that. I wanted to give Nora a good show. Of course it's much too soon for any sort of thing that might resemble love.

"I take that back," I say.

But it's too late. He's putting on his shirt. (It's a dressy white one. He's even wearing cufflinks engraved with WT.)

Is it really over already?

I pick up the cat, hurry out, slam the door, and push the deadbolt on the outside, then turn back and look through the keyhole. I can see almost the whole bed.

Now look, his hands are . . . all of a sudden . . . on her and on all the right places. He knows. Maybe he actually *is* somebody's grandfather after all. And you . . . you are feeling things that make your back arch.

He tells you he loves you. *Now* he says it. He can't tell us apart. He'll love anything that comes his way.

I have what I thought I wanted . . . a good view of something interesting for a change, except. . . .

Actually I can't see much, just his back and then your back and then his back and then yours. (How do they do that, still attached?)

Until we're all, all of us, exhausted.

———

I go downstairs. . . . (I like how this nightgown feels. I'm so slinky and slippery. I bump and grind just for myself.) I make myself a peanut butter sandwich. I feel better after eating. Things are fine.

I might leave you milk and cookies. Bring it now while you sleep so I can lock you both in again. But I don't suppose that lock will hold against two people who *really* want to get out.

I think about maybe both of you up in my crawl space. He's taller than we are. He'd not like it. I think about your job at the ice cream factory unfolding boxes to put the ice cream in. I wouldn't mind that kind of job. You sit and daydream. I saw you. You hardly talk to anybody.

I think about how you can't prove you're you. You'll go to the police. You'll say you're you, but they'll laugh. Your clothes are all wrong for the you you used to be. They'll say, the person who's lived here all this time dresses in mouse colors. You've lived a claustrophobic life. If you'd had any friends it would be different. Besides, I can do as well as you do, unfolding boxes. I've done the same when I had jobs before I quit for this easier life. I won't be cruel. I'd never be cruel. I'll let you live in the crawl space as long as you want.

Your daydream is Willard. Or most of him, though not all. For sure his eyes. For sure his elegant slim hands and the big gold ring. You'll ask if it's a school ring.

Or one of us will.

Then I hear banging. And not long after that, the crash. They break open the door. It splinters where the deadbolt is. If I'd put it in the middle of the door instead of at the top, it might have held better.

By the time the door goes down I'm right outside it, watching. They run downstairs without seeing me.

I go and look out the window. He's leaving—hurries down the street with only one arm in his coat sleeve and it's the wrong sleeve. Other hand holds up his pants. What did you do to send him off so upset?

I open the window and call out, "Willard!" But he doesn't hear or doesn't want to. Is he trying to get away? From you or me?

What did you do to scare him so? Everything was fine when I came down to eat. But maybe getting locked in scared him. Or maybe you told him to go and never come back and you threw his coat at him as he left. Or he thinks you're me and is in love with me even though he told you he loved you. Or, like most men, he's unwilling to commit to anybody.

But here you go, out the door right behind him. You have your coat on properly and your clothes all straightened up. Now you're the one calling, "Willard."

You'd not have done that before. You've changed. You'll take back your life. Everybody will make way for you now. You'll have an evil look. You'll frown. People will step off the sidewalk to let you go by.

I want for us to live as we did but you'll set traps. I'll trip on trip wires. Fall down the stairs in the middle of the night. There won't be any more quarters lying around. You'll put a deadbolt on the crawl space door. Or better yet, you'll barricade it shut with a dresser. Nobody will even know there's a door there.

I made you what you are today, grand and real, but you'll lock me up up here with nothing but your mousey clothes. Your old trunks. Your dust and dark.

I dress in the wornout clothes I wore when I came. I pack the night-gown, the black underwear. I grab a handful of quarters. I don't touch your secret stash of twenties. I pet the cat. I leave your credit cards and keys on the hall table. I don't steal.

WHY NEBULAS MATTER

JACK McDEVITT

There are a lot of awards in the field of science fiction. There's the Hugo, the Campbell, the Campbell Memorial, the Sturgeon, the Tip-tree, the World Fantasy, a number of others—and, of course, there is the Nebula, voted on by the members of the Science Fiction Writers of America. With so many awards, I asked a man who's won his share of them, and a frequent Nebula nominee, Jack McDevitt, to explain why the Nebulas really do matter.

Occasionally we hear talk of abolishing the Nebulas. They don't really mean anything. The readers don't care. They've been around too long and it's time to find a different way to recognize outstanding work. The notion that if you won a Nebula you could retire to a beachside condo and spend your time doing interviews with Wolf Blitzer has proved questionable. And the evidence is in that a Nebula on the shelf doesn't guarantee a substantial boost in advances.

Do Nebulas matter other than as an ego boost for the individual writer? Are they simply chunks of plastic and glitz that come with handshakes from one's colleagues and maybe a few extra sales down the road? Or do they provide a substantive benefit that we tend to overlook?

I think a case can be made that their significance extends well beyond honoring a few writers.

I often have the opportunity to speak to groups composed of people who think science fiction is primarily about space battles and monsters. I rarely do one of these engagements without being asked whether I believe in UFOs. (The question usually comes with a smirk.) There is also, inevitably, the guy who approaches me afterward to remark that "I don't read the stuff myself, but my nephew does." The tone implies that the kid has other problems as well.

I sympathize with these people. They've never known what it is to catch the midnight express to Capella, to look back on our own era from the far future. To be first to set foot on another world. And usually it's too late for them. The train has left the station. They've developed a mind-set that has inoculated them against imagination. They've never really understood Tennyson's desire to sail beyond the sunset.

I can't remember when I started reading science fiction. In South Philadelphia, somewhere around 1940, I discovered Buck Rogers and those magnificent rocket ships with blinking lights on the panels. I was five years old, and I never recovered. By the time I was thirteen, I was devouring *Startling Stories* and Robert Heinlein and *The Legion of Space*. But when I got to high school, life became busy.

I drifted away from the field, and stayed away, with few exceptions, for fifteen years. Don't ask me why. I have no idea, unless it was the absurd films they were making. I can still remember fighter planes trying to take down something that looked like a giant buzzard. My closest connection with sf during that period was Raymond J. Healy's *Famous Science Fiction Stories*, which I read while stationed in the Far East. In 1962, I was driving a taxi and dropped off some fans at Penn Center who were headed for the Philadelphia Science Fiction Convention. I remember they were talking about Asimov.

A year later I'd become an English teacher and was confronting the realities of trying to persuade often reluctant students in Levittown, Pennsylvania, that reading could be a pleasure. We were using a textbook based on the admirable notion that high school kids should become acquainted with the great writers. Segments of Hemingway and Fitzgerald were included. And Lamb and Shelley. There was also a complete novel: George Eliot's *The Mill on the Floss*. It's a novel that packs a punch, but most of the kids couldn't get past the title. And unless you're a genius, the narrative requires a perspective that fifteen-year-old kids simply don't have. (Titles are important. My all-time favorite is Nancy Kress's "Out of All Them Bright Stars," which took the 1986 short story Nebula. I think Nancy had my vote from the moment I saw the title.)

The problem was that my students did not charge out afterward to read Lamb's comments on mortality. Or Browning's on human relations. They still measured the worth of a novel inversely by its length.

I wanted to demonstrate the sheer joy that could come from a good book. Get it up onstage where everyone could see it. If I could manage that, I thought they'd find Dostoevsky and Tolstoy and Dickens on their own. So I went looking for a turn-on.

I tried Mark Twain first. He might have worked, but a lot of my students associated him with the school board. If the school board liked him, he was suspect. Ring Lardner didn't go well with the girls. They all thought Damon Runyon was corny. Even Sherlock Holmes got nowhere.

In the spring of 1966, the Science Fiction Writers of America—I'm not sure I'd known the organization existed—showed up in the news with its first round of Nebula awards. Frank Herbert won for *Dune*. Brian Aldiss's *The Saliva Tree* and Roger Zelazny's *He Who Shapes* tied for the novella award. Zelazny became the first multiple winner, scoring again for his novelette, *The Doors of His Face, the Lamps of His Mouth,* and Harlan Ellison checked in with " 'Repent, Harlequin!' Said the Ticktock Man."

I picked up a copy of *Dune*, read it across two or three nights—my impression now is that I went through it in a single sitting, but that can't be right—and have never been the same. I couldn't find the short fiction winners at the time, but I wandered down to the local drug store and picked up all the SF magazines I could find. And several novels. I wish I could say everything was on a level with Herbert and the others. I quickly found out there was a lot of drivel out there. But there's always drivel. Before you can have work that stands out, you have to have drivel. It's a rule. Drivel even shows up sometimes in the same work as the brilliancies. If you want to go to sea with Ahab and Ishmael, you have to learn how to skin a whale.

I didn't think SF would work well with my students. They were, if anything, down-to-earth. By no means unimaginative, understand, but inclined toward practicality. I doubted they would have a taste for starships and machine intelligences. But I tried. The results were explosive. They not only gobbled down the prizewinners, but they began showing up with Jack Williamson and Ray Bradbury and Robert Heinlein. I've never forgotten one young man waiting for me to start class, sitting wiping his eyes while he read "The Green Hills of Earth."

I have no evidence to prove this, but I believe, in 1967, *Flowers for Algernon* became far and away the most popular novel in the history of the school.

Samuel R. Delany took home consecutive Nebulas in 1967 and 1968 for *Babel-17* (which was one of the more challenging books I'd seen) and *The Einstein Intersection*. Several students read Michael Moorcock's *Behold the Man,* which led to a spirited after-school discussion one day. I had by then moved to Rhode Island and was teaching at

Mount Saint Charles Academy, a Catholic school, so it was okay to talk about religion. Delany also won in 'sixty-eight for "Aye, and Gomorrah . . ." in the short story category, becoming the second person to win twice in the same year. Fritz Lieber also showed up, and some of us read not only "Gonna Roll the Bones"—there was something marvelously appealing about playing dice with Death—but we also discovered Fafhrd and the Gray Mouser.

Those were good years. The truth is I'd forgotten what sheer pleasure it could be to look at the lost Earth through the eyes of a young girl just coming to maturity, handled so powerfully in *Rite of Passage*; to ride one of Anne McCaffrey's telepathic dragons; to hang out with Richard Wilson and the last couple on Earth; and to watch Kate Wilhelm's scientists try to ignite monkey intelligence. A year later, I discovered Ursula K. Le Guin and *The Left Hand of Darkness*. That was 1970, a brilliant time even for the Nebulas. Harlan Ellison returned with *A Boy and His Dog*. Samuel Delany won with "Time Considered as a Helix of Semi-Precious Stones," and Robert Silverberg produced "Passengers."

We moved to New Hampshire the following year, and I tried the same tack there that had succeeded so well in Levittown and at Mount Saint Charles: using science fiction to promote enthusiasm for reading. I started with Nevil Shute's *On the Beach*. Word filtered back to me that someone on the school board didn't like seeing paperbacks used in the school. He was quoted as saying, "We all know what gets published in paperbacks."

But we charged ahead. To make everything more convenient we established a bookstore inside the main entrance. *The Martian Chronicles* became our number one seller. Larry Niven's *Ringworld* was a big mover. DC Comics contributed a truckload of titles, which we used with the freshmen and sophomores. (Yes. Really. And it wasn't that the kids were lagging. Batman and his friends knew how to deliver a solid sentence, and they were all reasonably literate.) Over a two-year period, the school's SAT scores soared. Was there a connection? Who knows? But there was a fair amount of voluntary reading going on.

That's all a long time ago. Before *Rendezvous with Rama* and "The Death of Dr. Island," before "If the Stars Are Gods" and *The Forever War*. Fred Pohl hadn't yet ventured into *Gateway*. Alice B. Sheldon hadn't yet written "Houston, Houston, Do You Read?" and "The Screwfly Solution."

In the mid-seventies, life changed. My wife, Maureen, began having children, and we needed money to pay the mortgage. So I broke away from teaching. I took a job as a customs officer. And, thinking it would be nice to live in a remote place, we moved to Pembina, North Dakota.

Pembina is cold. A place where temperatures in winter could easily reach forty below. Where smoke freezes to the chimneys. It seemed also to be dark, a town where it was always the middle of the night. Maybe it was because you could stand outside the border station, look west, and not see a single artificial light. There was nothing out there except the curve of the Earth. You could literally feel the planet turning beneath your feet. Pembina was a magic place. If dinosaurs were going to show up anywhere, that would have been the spot.

You might be aware that *The Thing from Another World*, that marvelous North Pole film with blizzards and giant snowbanks and howling winds, was made in Fargo, North Dakota. We were a hundred and fifty miles north of Fargo. So when I tell you that three a.m. at the border station could be quiet, you can grasp my meaning.

I can remember sitting up there in the middle of winter, with a fifty-mile-an-hour wind coming at us straight off Hudson's Bay, and the northern lights rippling through the night. It was a time that called for a good book. During my first year, I spent several evenings in Vonda McIntyre's apocalyptic world, *Dreamsnake*. And I discovered space elevators in Arthur Clarke's *The Fountains of Paradise*. I read Gregory Benford's *Timescape* during the summer, which means, in that part of the world, the weekend of the Fourth. I also discovered Howard Waldrop, Ed Bryant, and Barry Longyear. They are, in my mind, forever wedded to polar-cap weather.

But I discovered something: Science fiction just wasn't as much fun without my students. I began to realize that this is a literature that needs to be shared. Sitting up there in a frozen dawn, watching Poul Anderson or Connie Willis or Greg Bear manipulate reality, and do it in such startlingly diverse ways, and not be able to talk to someone about it, except maybe an occasional driver hauling lumber south, it just wasn't the same.

Pembina customs was also responsible for manning the airport at Grand Forks, eighty miles south, and when the inspector down there wanted time off, one of us got assigned to do a relief stint. Eventually my turn came, and I was mildly interested to discover it coincided with a science fiction convention. I wandered in on Saturday, expecting to have a Coke, buy a couple of books, maybe get something signed by one of the writers, and head back to my hotel room. But I got hooked. I enjoyed the panels. And I got into a debate about Clifford Simak's "Grotto of the Dancing Deer." And, to the extent the airport could spare me, I stayed the rest of the weekend. It was like coming home.

I still hear occasionally from some of my former students. Some have become fans of the genre. Some not. I like to think a substantial majority have discovered the sheer pleasure to be derived from a good book. I hope so.

When they get in touch with me, they want to credit my enthusiasm. I know that I was equally enthusiastic about Sherlock Holmes. But I'll take whatever they're willing to grant me. The truth, of course, is that they get most of the credit themselves. The rest of it goes to people like Michael Swanwick and Pat Murphy and Kim Stanley Robinson.

Mike Resnick asked me to comment on why Nebulas still matter. It's obvious that they matter to the reader of *this* book. The reader has made that decision by investing time and money in the volume. But they matter also because they call attention to a literary genre that is often misrepresented by the electronic media. Most people outside the genre think science fiction is more or less as portrayed on the movie and TV screens: It's all monsters and alien invasions and experiments gone horribly wrong. There's some of that, sure. It can be fun when handled, say, by a Greg Bear or a Michael Bishop. But there's a great deal more to it. It is not so much a literature of the future as of discovery. It is a way to look past narrow horizons. To see ourselves in a different perspective.

Do I believe in UFOs? Better to ask whether I believe in magic.

At a time when I was anchored in the present, and thoroughly earthbound, the Nebulas reminded me what could be done by a Theodore Sturgeon or a Connie Willis or a Robert Silverberg. And I in turn was able to pass it along. I suspect a lot of it gets passed along. And that, ultimately, is what the Nebulas are: Pass it along.

This is Dale Bailey's second Nebula nomination (to go along with three International Horror Guild Award nominations, including a winner in 2002). "The End of the World as We Know It," clearly inspired by the events of 9/11, is a deceptively difficult story to pull off, and yet Dale never misses a beat. No surprise that he teaches writing at Lenoir-Rhyne College.

THE END OF THE WORLD AS WE KNOW IT

DALE BAILEY

Between 1347 and 1450 AD, bubonic plague overran Europe, killing some 75 million people. The plague, dubbed the Black Death because of the black pustules that erupted on the skin of the afflicted, was caused by a bacterium now known as *Yersinia pestis*. The Europeans of the day, lacking access to microscopes or knowledge of disease vectors, attributed their misfortune to an angry God. Flagellants roamed the land, hoping to appease His wrath. "They died by the hundreds, both day and night," Agnolo di Tura tells us. "I buried my five children with my own hands . . . so many died that all believed it was the end of the world."

Today, the population of Europe is about 729 million.

Evenings, Wyndham likes to sit on the porch, drinking. He likes gin, but he'll drink anything. He's not particular. Lately, he's been watching it get dark—really *watching* it, I mean, not just sitting there—and so far he's concluded that the cliché is wrong. Night doesn't fall. It's more complex than that.

Not that he's entirely confident in the accuracy of his observations.

It's high summer just now, and Wyndham often begins drinking at two or three, so by the time the Sun sets, around nine, he's usually pretty drunk. Still, it seems to him that, if anything, night *rises*, gathering first in inky pools under the trees, as if it has leached up from underground reservoirs, and then spreading, out toward the borders of the yard and up toward the yet-lighted sky. It's only toward the end that anything falls—the blackness of deep space, he supposes, unscrolling from high above the Earth. The two planes of darkness meet somewhere in the middle, and that's night for you.

That's his current theory, anyway.

It isn't his porch, incidentally, but then it isn't his gin either—except in the sense that, in so far as Wyndham can tell anyway, *everything* now belongs to him.

End-of-the-world stories usually come in one of two varieties.

In the first, the world ends with a natural disaster, either unprecedented or on an unprecedented scale. Floods lead all other contenders—God himself, we're told, is fond of that one—though plagues have their advocates. A renewed ice age is also popular. Ditto drought.

In the second variety, irresponsible human beings bring it on themselves. Mad scientists and corrupt bureaucrats, usually. An exchange of ICBMs is the typical route, although the scenario has dated in the present geo-political environment.

Feel free to mix and match:

Genetically engineered flu virus, anyone? Melting polar ice caps?

On the day the world ended, Wyndham didn't even realize it *was* the end of the world—not right away, anyway. For him, at that point in his life, pretty much *every* day seemed like the end of the world. This was not a consequence of a chemical imbalance, either. It was a consequence of working for UPS, where, on the day the world ended, Wyndham had been employed for sixteen years, first as a loader, then in sorting, and finally in the coveted position of driver, the brown uniform and everything. By this time the company had gone public and he also owned some shares. The money was good—very good, in fact. Not only that, he liked his job.

Still, the beginning of every goddamn day started off feeling like a cataclysm. *You* try getting up at 4:00 A.M. every morning and see how you feel.

This was his routine:

At 4:00 AM, the alarm went off—an old-fashioned alarm, he wound it up every night. (He couldn't tolerate the radio before he drank his coffee.) He always turned it off right away, not wanting to wake his wife. He showered in the spare bathroom (again, not wanting to wake his wife; her name was Ann), poured coffee into his thermos, and ate something he probably shouldn't—a bagel, a Pop Tart—while he stood over the sink. By then, it would be 4:20, 4:25 if he was running late.

Then he would do something paradoxical: He would go back to his

bedroom and wake up the wife he'd spent the last twenty minutes trying not to disturb.

"Have a good day," Wyndham always said.

His wife always did the same thing, too. She would screw her face
into her pillow and smile. "Ummm," she would say, and it was usually
such a cozy, loving, early-morning cuddling kind of "ummm" that it almost made getting up at four in the goddamn morning worth it.

Wyndham heard about the World Trade Center—*not* the end of the
world, though to Wyndham it sure as hell felt that way—from one of his
customers.

The customer—her name was Monica—was one of Wyndham's reg-
ulars: a Home Shopping Network fiend, this woman. She was big, too.
The kind of woman of whom people say "She has a nice personality"
or "She has such a pretty face." She did have a nice personality, too—at
least Wyndham thought she did. So he was concerned when she opened
the door in tears.

"What's wrong?" he said.

Monica shook her head, at a loss for words. She waved him inside.
Wyndham, in violation of about fifty UPS regulations, stepped in after
her. The house smelled of sausage and floral air freshener. There was
Home Shopping Network shit everywhere. I mean, *everywhere*.

Wyndham hardly noticed.

His gaze was fixed on the television. It was showing an airliner flying
into the World Trade Center. He stood there and watched it from three
or four different angles before he noticed the Home Shopping Network
logo in the lower right-hand corner of the screen.

That was when he concluded that it must be the end of the world.
He couldn't imagine the Home Shopping Network preempting regularly scheduled programming for anything less.

The Muslim extremists who flew airplanes into the World Trade Center, into the Pentagon, and into the unyielding earth of an otherwise
unremarkable field in Pennsylvania, were secure, we are told, in the
knowledge of their imminent translation into paradise.

There were nineteen of them.

Every one of them had a name.

Wyndham's wife was something of a reader. She liked to read in bed. Before she went to sleep she always marked her spot using a bookmark Wyndham had given her for her birthday one year: It was a cardboard bookmark with a yarn ribbon at the top, and a picture of a rainbow arching high over white-capped mountains. *Smile*, the bookmark said. *God loves you.*

Wyndham wasn't much of a reader, but if he'd picked up his wife's book the day the world ended he would have found the first few pages interesting. In the opening chapter, God raptures all true Christians to Heaven. This includes true Christians who are driving cars and trains and airplanes, resulting in uncounted lost lives as well as significant damages to personal property. If Wyndham *had* read the book, he'd have thought of a bumper sticker he sometimes saw from high in his UPS truck. *Warning*, the bumper sticker read, *In case of Rapture, this car will be unmanned.* Whenever he saw that bumper sticker, Wyndham imagined cars crashing, planes falling from the sky, patients abandoned on the operating table—pretty much the scenario of his wife's book, in fact.

Wyndham went to church every Sunday, but he couldn't help wondering what would happen to the untold millions of people who *weren't* true Christians—whether by choice or by the geographical fluke of having been born in some place like Indonesia. What if they were crossing the street in front of one of those cars, he wondered, or watering lawns those planes would soon plow into?

But I was saying:

On the day the world ended Wyndham didn't understand right away what had happened. His alarm clock went off the way it always did and he went through his normal routine. Shower in the spare bath, coffee in the thermos, breakfast over the sink (a chocolate donut, this time, and gone a little stale). Then he went back to the bedroom to say good-bye to his wife.

"Have a good day," he said, as he always said, and, leaning over, he shook her a little: not enough to really wake her, just enough to get her stirring. In sixteen years of performing this ritual, minus federal holidays and two weeks of paid vacation in the summer, Wyndham had pretty much mastered it. He could cause her to stir without quite waking her up just about every time.

So to say he was surprised when his wife didn't screw her face into her pillow and smile is something of an understatement. He was shocked, actually. And there was an additional consideration: She hadn't said, "Ummm," either. Not the usual luxurious, warm-morning-bed kind of "ummm," and not the infrequent but still familiar stuffy, I-have-a-cold-and-my-head-aches kind of "ummm," either. No "ummm" at all.

The air-conditioning cycled off. For the first time Wyndham noticed a strange smell—a faint, organic funk, like spoiled milk, or unwashed feet.

Standing there in the dark, Wyndham began to have a very bad feeling. It was a different kind of bad feeling than the one he'd had in Monica's living room watching airliners plunge again and again into the World Trade Center. That had been a powerful but largely impersonal bad feeling—I say "largely impersonal" because Wyndham had a third cousin who worked at Cantor Fitzgerald. (The cousin's name was Chris; Wyndham had to look it up in his address book every year when he sent out cards celebrating the birth of his personal savior.) The bad feeling he began to have when his wife failed to say "ummm," on the other hand, was powerful and *personal*.

Concerned, Wyndham reached down and touched his wife's face. It was like touching a woman made of wax, lifeless and cool, and it was at that moment—that moment precisely—that Wyndham realized the world had come to an end. Everything after that was just details.

Beyond the mad scientists and corrupt bureaucrats, characters in end-of-the-world stories typically come in one of three varieties.

The first is the rugged individualist. You know the type: self-reliant, iconoclastic loners who know how to use firearms and deliver babies. By story's end, they're well on their way to Reestablishing Western Civilization—though they're usually smart enough not to return to the Bad Old Ways.

The second variety is the post-apocalyptic bandit. These characters often come in gangs, and they face off against the rugged survivor types. If you happen to prefer cinematic incarnations of the end-of-the-world tale, you can usually recognize them by their penchant for bondage gear, punked-out haircuts, and customized vehicles. Unlike the rugged survivors, the post-apocalyptic bandits embrace the Bad Old Ways—though they're not displeased by the expanded opportunities to rape and pillage.

The third type of character—also pretty common, though a good deal less so than the other two—is the world-weary sophisticate. Like Wyndham, such characters drink too much; unlike Wyndham, they suffer badly from *ennui*.

Wyndham suffers too, of course, but whatever he suffers from, you can bet it's not *ennui*.

We were discussing details, though:

Wyndham did the things people do when they discover a loved one dead. He picked up the phone and dialed 9-1-1. There seemed to be something wrong with the line, however; no one picked up on the other end. Wyndham took a deep breath, went into the kitchen, and tried the extension. Once again he had no success.

The reason, of course, was that, this being the end of the world, all the people who were supposed to answer the phones were dead. Imagine them being swept away by a tidal wave if that helps—which is exactly what happened to more than three thousand people during a storm in Pakistan in 1960. (Not that this is *literally* what happened to the operators who would have taken Wyndham's 9-1-1 call, you understand; but more about what *really* happened to them later—the important thing is that one moment they had been alive; the next they were dead. Like Wyndham's wife.)

Wyndham gave up on the phone.

He went back into the bedroom. He performed a fumbling version of mouth-to-mouth resuscitation on his wife for fifteen minutes or so, and then he gave that up, too. He walked into his daughter's bedroom (she was twelve and her name was Ellen). He found her lying on her back, her mouth slightly agape. He reached down to shake her—he was going to tell her that something terrible had happened; that her mother had died—but he found that something terrible had happened to her as well. The same terrible thing, in fact.

Wyndham panicked.

He raced outside, where the first hint of red had begun to bleed up over the horizon. His neighbor's automatic irrigation system was on, the heads whickering in the silence, and as he sprinted across the lawn, Wyndham felt the spray, like a cool hand against his face. Then, chilled, he was standing on his neighbor's stoop. Hammering the door with both fists. Screaming.

After a time—he didn't know how long—a dreadful calm settled over him. There was no sound but the sound of the sprinklers, throwing glittering arcs of spray into the halo of the street light on the corner.

He had a vision, then. It was as close as he had ever come to a moment of genuine prescience. In the vision, he saw the suburban houses stretching away in silence before him. He saw the silent bedrooms. In them, curled beneath the sheets, he saw a legion of sleepers, also silent, who would never again wake up.

Wyndham swallowed.

Then he did something he could not have imagined doing even twenty minutes ago. He bent over, fished the key from its hiding place between the bricks, and let himself inside his neighbor's house.

The neighbor's cat slipped past him, mewing querulously. Wyndham had already reached down to retrieve it when he noticed the smell—that unpleasant, faintly organic funk. Not spoiled milk, either. And not feet. Something worse: soiled diapers, or a clogged toilet.

Wyndham straightened, the cat forgotten.

"Herm?" he called. "Robin?"

No answer.

Inside, Wyndham picked up the phone, and dialed 9-1-1. He listened to it ring for a long time; then, without bothering to turn it off, Wyndham dropped the phone to the floor. He made his way through the silent house, snapping on lights. At the door to the master bedroom, he hesitated. The odor—it was unmistakable now, a mingled stench of urine and feces, of all the body's muscles relaxing at once—was stronger here. When he spoke again, whispering really—

"Herm? Robin?"

—he no longer expected an answer.

Wyndham turned on the light. Robin and Herm were shapes in the bed, unmoving. Stepping closer, Wyndham stared down at them. A fleeting series of images cascaded through his mind, images of Herm and Robin working the grill at the neighborhood block party or puttering in their vegetable garden. They'd had a knack for tomatoes, Robin and Herm. Wyndham's wife had always loved their tomatoes.

Something caught in Wyndham's throat.

He went away for a while then.

The world just grayed out on him.

When he came back, Wyndham found himself in the living room, standing in front of Robin and Herm's television. He turned it on and cycled through the channels, but there was nothing on. Literally nothing. Snow, that's all. Seventy-five channels of snow. The end of the world had always been televised in Wyndham's experience. The fact that it wasn't being televised now suggested that it really *was* the end of the world.

This is not to suggest that television validates human experience—of the end of the world or indeed of anything else, for that matter.

You could ask the people of Pompeii, if most of them hadn't died in a volcano eruption in 79 A.D., nearly two millennia before television. When Vesuvius erupted, sending lava thundering down the mountainside at four miles a minute, some sixteen thousand people perished. By some freakish geological quirk, some of them—their shells, anyway—were preserved, frozen inside casts of volcanic ash. Their arms are outstretched in pleas for mercy, their faces frozen in horror.

For a fee, you can visit them today.

Here's one of my favorite end-of-the-world scenarios, by the way:
    Carnivorous plants.

Wyndham got in his car and went looking for assistance—a functioning telephone or television, a helpful passer-by. He found instead more non-functioning telephones and televisions. And, of course, more non-functioning people: lots of those, though he had to look harder for them than you might have expected. They weren't scattered in the streets, or dead at the wheels of their cars in a massive traffic jam—though Wyndham supposed that might have been the case somewhere in Europe, where the catastrophe—whatever it was—had fallen square in the middle of the morning rush.

Here, however, it seemed to have caught most folks at home in bed; as a result, the roads were more than usually passable.

At a loss—numb, really—Wyndham drove to work. He might have been in shock by then. He'd gotten accustomed to the smell, anyway, and the corpses of the night shift—men and women he'd known for sixteen years, in some cases—didn't shake him as much. What *did* shake him was the sight of all the packages in the sorting area: He was struck suddenly by the fact that none of them would ever be delivered. So Wyndham loaded his truck and went out on his route. He wasn't sure why he did it—maybe because he'd rented a movie once in which a post-apocalyptic drifter scavenges a U.S. Postal uniform and manages to Reestablish Western Civilization (but not the Bad Old Ways) by assuming the postman's appointed rounds. The futility of Wyndham's own efforts quickly became evident, however. He gave it up when he found that even Monica—or, as he more often thought of her, the Home Shopping Network Lady—was no longer in the business of receiving packages. Wyndham found her face down on the kitchen floor, clutching a shattered coffee mug in one hand. In death she had neither a pretty face nor a nice personality. She did have that same ripe unpleasant odor, however. In spite of it, Wyndham stood looking down at her for the longest time. He couldn't seem to look away.

When he finally *did* look away, Wyndham went back to the living room where he had once watched nearly three thousand people die, and opened her package himself. When it came to UPS rules, the Home Shopping Network Lady's living room was turning out to be something of a post-apocalyptic zone in its own right.

Wyndham tore the mailing tape off and dropped it on the floor. He opened the box. Inside, wrapped safely in three layers of bubble wrap, he found a porcelain statue of Elvis Presley.

Elvis Presley, the King of Rock 'n' Roll, died August 16, 1977, while sitting on the toilet. An autopsy revealed that he had ingested an impressive cocktail of prescription drugs—including codeine, ethinimate, methaqualone, and various barbiturates. Doctors also found trace elements of Valium, Demerol, and other pharmaceuticals in his veins.

For a time, Wyndham comforted himself with the illusion that the end of the world had been a local phenomenon. He sat in his truck outside the Home Shopping Network Lady's house and awaited rescue—the sound of sirens or approaching choppers, whatever. He fell asleep cradling the porcelain statue of Elvis. He woke up at dawn, stiff from sleeping in the truck, to find a stray dog nosing around outside.

Clearly rescue would not be forthcoming.

Wyndham chased off the dog and placed Elvis gently on the sidewalk. Then he drove off, heading out of the city. Periodically, he stopped, each time confirming what he had already known the minute he touched his dead wife's face: The end of the world was upon him. He found nothing but non-functioning telephones, non-functioning televisions, and non-functioning people. Along the way he listened to a lot of non-functioning radio stations.

You, like Wyndham, may be curious about the catastrophe that has befallen everyone in the world around him. You may even be wondering why Wyndham has survived.

End-of-the-world tales typically make a big deal about such things, but Wyndham's curiosity will never be satisfied.

Unfortunately, neither will yours.

Shit happens.

It's the end of the world after all.

The dinosaurs never discovered what caused *their* extinction, either.

At this writing, however, most scientists agree that the dinosaurs met their fate when an asteroid nine miles wide plowed into the Earth just south of the Yucatan Peninsula, triggering gigantic tsunamis, hurricane-force winds, worldwide forest fires, and a flurry of volcanic activity. The crater is still there—it's 120 miles wide and more than a mile deep—but the dinosaurs, along with seventy-five percent of the other species then alive, are gone. Many of them died in the impact, vaporized in the explosion. Those that survived the initial cataclysm would have perished soon after as acid rain poisoned the world's water, and dust obscured the Sun, plunging the planet into a years-long winter.

For what it's worth, this impact was merely the most dramatic in a long series of mass extinctions; they occur in the fossil record at roughly thirty-million-year intervals. Some scientists have linked these intervals to the solar system's periodic journey through the galactic plane, which dislodges millions of comets from the Oort cloud beyond Pluto, raining them down on Earth. This theory, still contested, is called the Shiva Hypothesis in honor of the Hindu god of destruction.

The inhabitants of Lisbon would have appreciated the allusion on November 1, 1755, when the city was struck by an earthquake measuring 8.5 on the Richter Scale. The tremor leveled more than twelve thousand homes and ignited a fire that burned for six days.

More than sixty thousand people perished.

This event inspired Voltaire to write *Candide*, in which Dr. Pangloss advises us that this is the best of all possible worlds.

Wyndham could have filled the gas tank in his truck. There were gas stations at just about every exit along the highway, and *they* seemed to be functioning well enough. He didn't bother, though.

When the truck ran out of gas, he just pulled to the side of the road, hopped down, and struck off across the fields. When it started getting dark—this was before he had launched himself on the study of just how it is night falls—he took shelter in the nearest house.

It was a nice place, a two-story brick house set well back from the country road he was by then walking on. It had some big trees in the front yard. In the back, a shaded lawn sloped down to the kind of woods you see in movies, but not often in real life: enormous, old trees with generous, leaf-carpeted avenues. It was the kind of place his wife would have loved, and he regretted having to break a window to get inside. But there it was: It was the end of the world and he had to have a place to sleep. What else could he do?

Wyndham hadn't planned to stay there, but when he woke up the next morning he couldn't think of anywhere to go. He found two non-functional old people in one upstairs bedroom and he tried to do for them what he had not been able to do for his wife and daughter: Using a spade from the garage, he started digging a grave in the front yard. After an hour or so, his hands began to blister and crack. His muscles—soft from sitting behind the wheel of a UPS truck for all those years—rebelled.

He rested for a while, and then he loaded the old people into the car he found parked in the garage—a slate-blue Volvo station wagon with 37,312 miles on the odometer. He drove them a mile or two down the road, pulled over, and laid them out, side by side, in a grove of beech trees. He tried to say some words over them before he left—his wife would have wanted him to—but he couldn't think of anything appropriate so he finally gave it up and went back to the house.

It wouldn't have made much difference: Though Wyndham didn't know it, the old people were lapsed Jews. According to the faith Wyndham shared with his wife, they were doomed to burn in hell for all eternity anyway. Both of them were first-generation immigrants; most of their families had already been burned up in ovens at Dachau and Buchenwald.

Burning wouldn't have been anything new for them.

Speaking of fires, the Triangle Shirtwaist Factory in New York City burned on March 25, 1911. One hundred and forty-six people died. Many of them might have survived, but the factory's owners had locked the exits to prevent theft. Rome burned, too. It is said that Nero fiddled.

Back at the house, Wyndham washed up and made himself a drink from the liquor cabinet he found in the kitchen. He'd never been much of a drinker before the world ended, but he didn't see any reason not to give it a try now. His experiment proved such a success that he began sitting out on the porch nights, drinking gin and watching the sky. One night he thought he saw a plane, lights blinking as it arced high overhead. Later, sober, he concluded that it must have been a satellite, still whipping around the planet, beaming down telemetry to empty listening stations and abandoned command posts.

A day or two later the power went out. And a few days after that, Wyndham ran out of liquor. Using the Volvo, he set off in search of a town. Characters in end-of-the-world stories commonly drive vehicles of two types: The jaded sophisticates tend to drive souped-up sports cars, often racing them along the Australian coastline because what else do they have to live for; everyone else drives rugged SUVs. Since the 1991 Persian Gulf War—in which some twenty-three thousand people died, most of them Iraqi conscripts killed by American smart bombs—military-style Humvees have been especially coveted. Wyndham, however, found the Volvo entirely adequate to his needs.

No one shot at him.

He was not assaulted by a roving pack of feral dogs.

He found a town after only fifteen minutes on the road. He didn't see any evidence of looting. Everybody was too dead to loot; that's the way it is at the end of the world.

On the way, Wyndham passed a sporting goods store where he did not stop to stock up on weapons or survival equipment. He passed numerous abandoned vehicles, but he did not stop to siphon off some gas. He *did* stop at the liquor store, where he smashed a window with a rock and helped himself to several cases of gin, whiskey, and vodka. He also stopped at the grocery store, where he found the reeking bodies of the night crew sprawled out beside carts of supplies that would never make it onto the shelves. Holding a handkerchief over his nose, Wyndham loaded up on tonic water and a variety of other mixers. He also got some canned goods, though he didn't feel any imperative to stock up beyond his immediate needs. He ignored the bottled water.

In the book section, he *did* pick up a bartender's guide.

Some end-of-the-world stories present us with two post-apocalypse survivors, one male and one female. These two survivors take it upon themselves to Repopulate the Earth, part of their larger effort to Reestablish Western Civilization without the Bad Old Ways. Their names are always artfully withheld until the end of the story, at which point they are invariably revealed to be Adam and Eve.

The truth is, almost all end-of-the-world stories are at some level Adam-and-Eve stories. That may be why they enjoy such popularity. In the interests of total disclosure, I will admit that in fallow periods of my own sexual life—and, alas, these periods have been more frequent than I'd care to admit—I've often found Adam-and-Eve post-holocaust fantasies strangely comforting. Being the only man alive significantly reduces the potential for rejection in my view. And it cuts performance anxiety practically to nothing.

There's a woman in this story, too.
    Don't get your hopes up.

By this time, Wyndham has been living in the brick house for almost two weeks. He sleeps in the old couple's bedroom, and he sleeps pretty well, but maybe that's the gin. Some mornings he wakes up disoriented, wondering where his wife is and how he came to be in a strange place. Other mornings he wakes up feeling like he dreamed everything else and this has always been his bedroom.
    One day, though, he wakes up early, to gray pre-dawn light. Someone is moving around downstairs. Wyndham's curious, but he's not afraid. He doesn't wish he'd stopped at the sporting goods store and gotten a gun. Wyndham has never shot a gun in his life. If he did shoot someone—even a post-apocalyptic punk with cannibalism on his mind—he'd probably have a breakdown.
    Wyndham doesn't try to disguise his presence as he goes downstairs. There's a woman in the living room. She's not bad looking, this woman—blonde in a washed-out kind of way, trim, and young, twenty-five, thirty at the most. She doesn't look extremely clean, and she doesn't smell much better, but hygiene hasn't been uppermost on Wyndham's mind lately, either. Who is he to judge?
    "I was looking for a place to sleep," the woman says.
    "There's a spare bedroom upstairs," Wyndham tells her.

The next morning—it's really almost noon, but Wyndham has gotten into the habit of sleeping late—they eat breakfast together: a Pop Tart for the woman, a bowl of dry Cheerios for Wyndham.
    They compare notes, but we don't need to get into that. It's the end of the world and the woman doesn't know how it happened any more than Wyndham does or you do or anybody ever does. She does most of the talking, though.
    Wyndham's never been much of a talker, even at the best of times.

He doesn't ask her to stay. He doesn't ask her to leave.

He doesn't ask her much of anything.

That's how it goes all day.

Sometimes the whole sex thing *causes* the end of the world.

In fact, if you'll permit me to reference Adam and Eve just one more time, sex and death have been connected to the end of the world ever since—well, the beginning of the world. Eve, despite warnings to the contrary, eats of the fruit of the Tree of Knowledge of Good and Evil and realizes she's naked—that is, a sexual being. Then she introduces Adam to the idea by giving him a bite of the fruit.

God punishes Adam and Eve for their transgression by kicking them out of Paradise and introducing death into the world. And there you have it: the first apocalypse, *eros* and *thanatos* all tied up in one neat little bundle, and it's all Eve's fault.

No wonder feminists don't like that story. It's a pretty corrosive view of female sexuality when you think about it. Coincidentally, perhaps, one of my favorite end-of-the-world stories involves some astronauts who fall into a time warp; when they get out they learn that all the men are dead. The women have done pretty well for themselves in the meantime. They no longer need men to reproduce and they've set up a society that seems to work okay without men—better in fact than our messy two-sex societies ever have.

But do the men stay out of it?

They do not. They're men, after all, and they're driven by their need for sexual dominance. It's genetically encoded so to speak, and it's not long before they're trying to turn this Eden into another fallen world. It's sex that does it, violent male sex—rape, actually. In other words, sex that's more about the violence than the sex.

And certainly nothing to do with love.

Which, when you think about it, is a pretty corrosive view of male sexuality.

The more things change the more they stay the same, I guess.

Wyndham, though.

Wyndham heads out on the porch around three. He's got some tonic. He's got some gin. It's what he does now. He doesn't know where the woman is, doesn't have strong feelings on the issue either way.

He's been sitting there for hours when she joins him. Wyndham doesn't know what time it is, but the air has that hazy underwater quality that comes around twilight. Darkness is starting to pool under the trees, the crickets are tuning up, and it's so peaceful that for a moment Wyndham can almost forget that it's the end of the world.

Then the screen door claps shut behind the woman. Wyndham can tell right away that she's done something to herself, though he couldn't tell you for sure what it is: that magic women do, he guesses. His wife used to do it, too. She always looked good to him, but sometimes she looked just flat-out amazing. Some powder, a little blush. Lipstick. You know. And he appreciates the effort. He does. He's flattered even. She's an attractive woman. Intelligent, too.

The truth is, though, he's just not interested.

She sits beside him, and all the time she's talking. And though she doesn't say it in so many words, what she's talking about is Repopulating the World and Reestablishing Western Civilization. She's talking about Duty. She's talking about it because that's what you're supposed to talk about at times like this. But underneath that is sex. And underneath that, way down, is loneliness—and he has some sympathy for that, Wyndham does. After a while, she touches Wyndham, but he's got nothing. He might as well be dead down there.

"What's wrong with you?" she says.

Wyndham doesn't know how to answer her. He doesn't know how to tell her that the end of the world isn't about any of that stuff. The end of the world is about something else, he doesn't have a word for it.

So, anyway, Wyndham's wife.

She has another book on her nightstand, too. She doesn't read it every night, only on Sundays. But the week before the end of the world the story she was reading was the story of Job.

You know the story, right?

It goes like this: God and Satan—the Adversary, anyway; that's probably the better translation—make a wager. They want to see just how much shit God's most faithful servant will eat before he renounces his faith. The servant's name is Job. So they make the wager, and God starts feeding Job shit. Takes his riches, takes his cattle, takes his health. Deprives him of his friends. On and on. Finally—and this is the part that always got to Wyndham—God takes Job's children.

Let me clarify: In this context "takes" should be read as "kills."

You with me on this? Like Krakatoa, a volcanic island that used to exist between Java and Sumatra. On August 27, 1883, Krakatoa exploded, spewing ash fifty miles into the sky and vomiting up five cubic miles of rock. The concussion was heard three thousand miles away. It created tsunamis towering one hundred twenty feet in the air. Imagine all that water crashing down on the flimsy villages that lined the shores of Java and Sumatra.

Thirty thousand people died.

Every single one of them had a name.

Job's kids. Dead. Just like thirty thousand nameless Javanese.

As for Job? He keeps shoveling down the shit. He will not renounce God. He keeps the faith. And he's rewarded: God gives him back his riches, his cattle. God restores his health, and sends him friends. God replaces his kids. Pay attention: Word choice is important in an end-of-the-world story.

I said "replaces," not "restores."

The other kids? They stay dead, gone, non-functioning, erased forever from the Earth, just like the dinosaurs and the twelve million undesirables incinerated by the Nazis and the five hundred thousand slaughtered in Rwanda and the 1.7 million murdered in Cambodia and the sixty million immolated in the Middle Passage.

That merry prankster God.

That jokester.

That's what the end of the world is about, Wyndham wants to say. The rest is just details.

By this point the woman (You want her to have a name? She deserves one, don't you think?) has started to weep softly. Wyndham gets to his feet and goes into the dark kitchen for another glass. Then he comes back out to the porch and makes a gin and tonic. He sits beside her and presses the cool glass upon her. It's all he knows to do.

"Here," he says. "Drink this. It'll help."

DARING THE BOUNDARIES

CATHERINE ASARO

Catherine Asaro, Nebula winner and former president of SFWA, is known not only for her science fiction but for her romances. With the advent of a major new line of fantasy romances, Luna, and the willingness of some established publishers to blur the lines between fields, I asked her to give us her well-informed opinion on "crossover" fiction.

I never noticed the word *crossover* until my first books were published. They were called hard sf because of my use of science, but that isn't particularly unusual in our field. What I didn't expect was the controversy over the "romance." At the time, mixing of science fiction with romance was considered daring, even blasphemous. I'm certainly not the first to do it; Ursula K. Le Guin, Anne McCaffrey, Marion Zimmer Bradley, Lois McMaster Bujold, Vonda McIntyre, and Joan Vinge, just to name a few, have all mixed the genres. A danger exists in talking about the crossover aspects of your own work, though; it can set up preconceived ideas that turn off some readers who would otherwise enjoy the stories. Crossover work may be riskier than fiction that stays within the boundaries, but at its best it is also among the most exciting and versatile areas of fiction.

Does crossover work? It certainly has in anthologies such as *Down These Dark Spaceways*, which mixes science fiction and mystery; or *Irresistible Forces*, a compilation of science fiction and fantasy romances by writers from all three genres. Crossover succeeds when the authors enjoy, read, and understand the genres they are mixing. If a story isn't true to the genres it draws on, it will alienate its potential audiences. Readers can tell if an author doesn't understand the genre. A book full of clichéd plots, stereotypes, or characters who could have stepped off a bad movie set is more likely to hit the wall than hit the spot with readers. Unless the author writes really well, a story about, say, a giant plant that eats people will inspire groans rather than satisfaction. But if the work is done well, it can become a classic. How would we categorize *Little Shop of Horrors*? Well, horror, yes. Fantasy? Modern American musical? Satire? Mystery? Romance? Whatever labels we give it, the story isn't likely to vanish into obscurity. Because it *works*. It is true to all of the genres it incorporates.

My novella "The City of Cries" in *Down These Dark Spaceways* mixes science fiction and mystery. When I asked my editor for suggestions on how to approach the story, he pointed me toward Raymond Chandler. So I read *The Big Sleep*. At the risk of earning eternal glowers from my esteemed editor, I must confess I didn't much like the book—the first time through. I knew if I was going to write a science fiction mystery with a nod to that style, I needed to feel more connection with the writing.

My first decision was to set the story in a universe I created, the Skolian Empire. I asked myself, could any incident in those books involve a mystery? An answer immediately came to mind: a role-reversed situation where a young prince who has lived in seclusion since birth runs away because he can no longer abide his constrained life. The matriarch of his noble house calls in a hard-boiled detective to find him. Given the role reversal, of course the PI had to be a woman, a style I enjoy writing. Throw in a murder, smugglers, kidnappers, and the PI's shady ex-boyfriend, and I had my "writer's hook"—characters and a plot that drew me in. The writing flowed. By the time I was done, "The City of Cries" had become one of my favorite stories. Just as important, I had developed an appreciation of Chandler's work. It was why, ultimately, the story worked for me; I found satisfaction in *both* styles.

The novella pushes other boundaries. Whether or not role reversal can be called genre crossing is harder to answer. One might say it crosses into feminist fiction, but feminism and popular fiction have always maintained an uneasy relationship. Science fiction does have a history of role-reversed plots that explore what it means to be male or female (or something between), including Wen Spencer's *A Brother's Price*, Lois Bujold's *Ethan of Athos*, and my own *The Last Hawk*. To succeed, these works have to achieve the same goal as crossover fiction: They must reach potentially disparate groups of readers, in this case the audience for a genre traditionally considered male-oriented and an audience that accepts and enjoys the reversal of male and female roles in fiction. If the writer is uncomfortable reversing the roles, readers will know. In my experience, cross-genre works are more likely to succeed if authors write what comes naturally to them rather than trying to meet the expectations of any one audience.

Although "The City of Cries" has romantic elements, it isn't a romance. Other of my books include stronger romantic story lines. When I wrote *The Quantum Rose*, I questioned whether it would even be published. A retelling of "Beauty and the Beast" in a science fiction setting, it is also a classic marriage-of-convenience romance. I was pleasantly surprised when Tor made an offer and Stan Schmidt accepted the first half of the book as a serial for *Analog*. When it made the final Nebula ballot, I was flabbergasted. I'm told that at the awards ceremony, after they announced it as the winner, I sat in my chair for almost thirty seconds before I went to the stage. I only remember feeling shock. Delighted shock, yes, but it took a moment for the news to sink in.

Crossover work between romance and science fiction was less accepted at that time. Critics in each genre tended to disparage the other genre, and readers tended to assume that if they liked one, they wouldn't like the other. Yet *The Quantum Rose* also won several romance awards. As to why the book succeeded in crossing over, it's hard to say, but I think the most important point is that I enjoy both genres and I particularly liked writing them in that story.

Any book that pushes boundaries is likely to create controversy, no matter how successful the work. That includes crossover from genre to mainstream fiction, as in works by Mary Doria Russell, Margaret Atwood, and Kurt Vonnegut. Some critics would deny that works by those authors can even be called science fiction. If anything, the better written the story, the greater the controversy. It is easy to dismiss a book that is truly bad or speaks to few readers. It's not so easy when the book is well written and reaches a wide audience. The more people who read it, the more it shakes up genre assumptions. And those assumptions are intricately interwoven with our culture. Such works challenge the reader to think beyond cultural expectations.

Successful cross-genre work appeals to a large audience because it speaks to more readers. To find that audience, a writer needs to appreciate all the genres they write in—and also to turn off that internal editor whispering, "Don't do it. You know it will annoy people." The writer must be true to her or his sense of the story.

Once every few years a story begins with a sentence that is such a grabber, so fascinating that no matter what you're doing, you know you're not going to get back to it until you read the rest of the story. "Still Life With Boobs" is one of them. If Anne Harris had been Andy or Arnie Harris, an awful lot of editors would have been afraid to touch it for fear of charges of sexism . . . but thankfully Anne is Anne and the delightful "Still Life With Boobs" garnered her first Nebula nomination. (She has also been a Spectrum winner.)

STILL LIFE WITH BOOBS

ANNE HARRIS

She could no longer ignore the fact that her breasts were going out at night without her. Gwen stood in front of the bathroom mirror and gave George and Gracie a long hard stare. They bore marks she knew they had not acquired in her presence; scratches, smears of dirt and other, less identifiable substances.

"Shit," she swore under her breath. "What do you want from me?" But George and Gracie just stared back at her innocently with their cold-puckering nipples, like two children caught making mud pies in their Sunday clothes.

They hadn't looked so innocent when she'd caught up with them last night in the back room of Menzer's Art Supply.

She'd fallen asleep in front of the television again. That was her routine these days, plop on the couch with a carton of peppermint stick ice cream and let prime time rob her of the capacity for coherent thought.

When she and David were still together they'd have stimulating conversations about art and politics. She'd watch him paint or they'd go to art openings. She hadn't minded her job back then, because she was working to foster something she believed in; David's art.

It was David who named her breasts George and Gracie. He had a regular puppet show he'd do. "Say good night, Gracie," he'd say in a deep voice, jiggling the left one. In a high-pitched voice he'd answer, "Good night Gracie," as he jiggled the right one. And then he'd kiss them, his mouth soft and open, with a flicker of his tongue that still sent shivers down her spine, just thinking about it. Gwen sighed and stepped into the shower.

She'd nodded off last night sometime between *Law & Order* and *Conan O'Brien*, awakening again around two-thirty in the morning. An old black-and-white movie painted the room in flickering shades of noir and the ice cream had melted and leaked out the bottom of the carton, forming a pink lake in the middle of the coffee table.

When she got up to clean the mess she realized her breasts were gone. She ran her hands over the blank, flat place where George and Gracie should be, and felt a tremor of panic deep inside. She'd had this dream before, she thought, and pinched the featureless flesh hard. It hurt. The ice cream dripped off the edge of the table. She wasn't dreaming.

She threw on a sweater, sweatpants, and a pair of slippers and ventured out into the hallway of the apartment building just in time to see the elevator doors closing. Without stopping to consider if breasts even know how to use an elevator, Gwen plunged down the stairs.

But the lobby was deserted. She ran out onto the street and fancied she saw two small round objects rolling around the corner. She hurried after them and found herself in an alley behind a row of shops. The night was windy and damp. She shivered and wondered how her breasts could stand it. Up ahead, a door was just closing. Gwen ran to it, pulled on the handle and found it unlocked.

There was a small step up into a short hallway. Light leaked out from a doorway up ahead and she moved toward it. The muted thump of an insistent disco beat grew louder with every step she took. Gwen peeked around the edge of the doorway into a storeroom lit with Christmas lights. A disco ball made out of foil candy wrappers hung from the ceiling. Somewhere a stereo pounded out "Do You Wanna Touch Me?" by Rod Stewart.

Dozens of detached body parts cavorted about the room. There were penises, pussies, breasts, mouths, and even a couple of asses. She spotted George and Gracie off in one corner, wobbling lustily up and down the shaft of some rampant dick.

Shocked, Gwen started toward them, wading ankle-deep through bundles of bobbing flesh. George and Gracie froze in their cavorting, their nipples swiveling to face her like dark brown bull's eyes. They made a little squeal she didn't know breasts were capable of and darted for the doorway.

She ran after them. George and Gracie were remarkably swift for having no feet. They were out the back door before she could catch up with them. Gwen burst through the doorway and completely forgot about the step. She pitched forward, landing hard on the concrete. Groaning, she lifted her head and saw a pair of men's brown oxford shoes. She gasped, staggering to her feet. "Hey, careful now. You okay?" said the guy, and she got a vague impression of light brown hair and a white shirt. He put his hands out to steady her, but just grazed her sleeve as she fled down the alley.

She never did catch up with George and Gracie, but they came home sometime before dawn, and when she awoke, there they were, looking pretty much as she would have expected. Grimacing, Gwen got a good lather going on her body puff, closed her eyes, and scrubbed.

Late for work again, Gwen charged into her bedroom and grabbed panties and pantyhose from the clean pile by the bed. But she couldn't find a bra. She definitely needed a bra. She rummaged around in the bottom of the closet where she generally threw everything she didn't want to deal with. She really had to clean this mess up, she thought as she tossed aside a butterfly net she'd had since she was six.

Finally she found a black lace bra she'd bought back when she was still with David. It was far from ideal. Under the circumstances, she'd prefer full coverage and reinforced straps, but there was no time to worry about that. She sniffed the bra to determine if it was clean enough, decided it was, and put it on.

After work that day Gwen and her friend Tammi browsed through racks of bras at Target. They both worked at J. Thomas Design, Tammi in sales, Gwen in accounts receivable.

"I can't believe you put up with that crap from Charlie Axel, Gwen," said Tammi, tilting her curly brown head to one side and flashing her a glistening lip-gloss grimace. "I don't care how great a designer he is, he wouldn't call me a lower life form and walk away from it."

"I believe his exact words were, 'I won't put up with this constant badgering from some low-level bean counter,'" Gwen corrected her.

"Yeah, after he dumped a foot-high stack of memos and specs on your desk and told you to sort through them yourself. And you probably will. Why does that guy have you so whipped? Don't tell me it's the artist thing."

Gwen shrugged. "He *is* talented," she admitted. "His multi-media piece, 'Bart Simpson's Guernica,' won first prize in a juried show at the Pierce Gallery."

Tammi gave her a sour look and changed the subject. "So, what's the occasion for new lingerie? Could it be the ice age has ended at last? Do you have a date? Who is it?" Tammi grinned and elbowed Gwen in the ribs. "Is it the new guy in accounting? He's got a cute butt."

Gwen shook her head. "It's not for a date. It's for my breasts."

"Well, duh!" Tammi held up a leopard print underwire with black lace trim and eyed it critically.

"No," Gwen shoved aside a frothy lavender concoction and pulled out a white cotton sports bra. "I mean I need something more substantial, something . . . architectural, if possible."

Tammi cast a doubtful eye at Gwen's bust line. "I don't know if they make those kind in your size. You usually don't see those 'foundation garment' grandma bras in anything less than a 40 C. Besides, you don't need it. All you need is a little underwire, a little shaping." She took the sports bra from Gwen and hung it back up again. Twisting her bangle bracelets, she shrugged and said, "Maybe a little padding?"

Gwen rolled her eyes. "I need a lot more than that."

Tammi frowned. "Oh come on! What are you complaining about? You're beautiful." Her mouth quirked in irritation. "You wouldn't have any trouble finding guys if you'd just get out a little more. Which reminds me, Buzz wants to go to Moosejaw's next Friday for dinner and drinks. He's got this friend Tom, and I was thinking, he could bring Tom, and you could join us." She wiggled her eyebrows.

Gwen sighed and turned to the Playtex stand, rifling through the cardboard boxes, trying to find something in her size. "I don't think so, Tammi. I'm not much in the mood for dating right now."

Tammi rolled her eyes. Her chewing gum gleamed pink between her whitened teeth. "Gwenny, I love you, but you have got to get out of this rut."

She was in a rut, Gwen admitted to herself. She'd thought it was a comfortable rut, but now that had changed. You could hardly describe a rut in which your breasts were detaching from your body and getting into God knows what as being comfortable. "All right," she said. "I'll go."

That night Gwen sat cross-legged on the floor of her closet, rooting through old clothes and boxes still packed from when she'd moved here after her breakup with David.

In a far corner of the closet, beneath a red sequined dress Tammi had talked her into buying, she unearthed a carefully sealed cardboard box about the size of a bowling ball. For a split second she had no recollection of it, and then, like the sinking of an unsinkable ship, her mind capsized, plunging into remembrance and giving her a good long look at the rest of the iceberg.

She was seventeen, and she was going to be a famous sculptor.

Unbidden, Gwen's hands peeled back the tape on the box.

She loved the smooth, slippery feeling of wet clay, the act of molding it in her hands, the damp earth smell and the rich golden-red color.

The flaps of the box squeaked against each other as she pulled them open. The newspaper rustled and fell away like shed scales as she lifted the statue out.

Sitting in her room at night, naked in front of the mirror, seeing herself . . . touching herself . . . as a woman for the first time. In art class the next day molding the clay with her memory as a model. Forming her face, her body, with her hands, exploring herself as she sculpted the figure. And when she was finished, her art teacher, Mr. Teslop, standing over her, telling her that it was "exquisite" and "very advanced." Her body rushing with pleasure at his words. She quickly agreed to his suggestion to enter it in the district art competition.

And she won. Oh, how sweet it had felt, standing there in the Menamanee County Convention Center as the judge tied the blue ribbon around her statue and she smiled into popping flashbulbs and they ran her picture in the paper. Her statue went on display back at the high school, right in there with the football and wrestling trophies. She got a little jolt every time she passed it.

Gwen sat cross-legged on the floor of her closet and held herself in her lap, running her fingertips over her tiny clay face, her shoulders, her breasts. Trapped in their new, full coverage bra, George and Gracie tingled. What pleasure it had been to feel the clay taking form in her hands, to see a thing of beauty and to think, I made that.

And then came the next day. The last day of her sculpting career. Walking to civics class with her "friend" Charlene Ryans.

"Oh, is that your statue?" asked Charlene as the display case came into view. And Gwen's own prideful, foolish, "Yes."

They paused before the statue as Charlene peered at it, and Gwen's heart swelled with more pride, more idiotic self-satisfaction.

"Oh my God, Gwen," said Charlene and Gwen prepared to receive her admiration for this great work of art. Then Charlene turned to her and said, "Is that you?"

Gwen's big, swollen prideful heart was ripped right out of her. Her face went red. Charlene laughed, and very loudly in the crowded hallway cried, "Oh my God, Gwen, you sculpted yourself naked. It's a self-portrait!"

Soon after that her sculpture was removed from the case of honor and returned to her in a square cardboard box. But long after it was gone, the statue haunted her. She was "Boobs" Bramble after that, all the way through high school.

Gwen sighed and put the statue back in its box. She was about to close it when she hesitated, and then all at once, not giving herself time to consider it, she took it back out, ran into the living room and set it down on the coffee table. She stood back, waiting for what she didn't know, an explosion, or Charlene Ryans pounding on her door. But nothing happened.

Moosejaw's was a new wilderness-themed restaurant next to Costco. The menu was sprinkled indiscriminately with game in much the same manner as the walls were festooned with every kind of backwoods paraphernalia imaginable. There was even a stuffed bear standing just inside the door, a box of menus wedged between its paws. Gwen had to admire the logic. There *was* something about sitting beneath an owl rowing a birch bark canoe that made eating boar empanadas seem normal.

"So I said, the best way to maximize your potential is to proactively pursue advantageous opportunities and contacts," said Tom. He was in his mid-forties with wavy chestnut-brown hair and freckles. "Be an evangelist of your product. People can't resist a prophet, or a profit. Hey, I like that! Be a prophet of profit." He whipped a Palm Pilot out of his breast pocket and jotted his bon mot down. "I'm collecting all these inspirational sayings for my book, *101 Things To Do When There's Nothing You Can Do*. See, the first lesson is, there's always something you can do." Tom took a drink of his Rusty Nail and leaned closer to her. "Look at me. Two years ago I was at rock bottom. My second marriage had just fallen apart, I owed the IRS $75,000 in back taxes, and I hated my job. Now thanks to Maxway, I'm living proof that no dream is out of reach if you can identify it." He fixed her with a manic stare. "Do you have a dream, Gwen?"

George and Gracie stirred inside her bra, and Gwen crossed her arms to quell them. "I—I don't know," she stammered, but obviously her breasts were of a different opinion. They quivered and surged. She tightened her arms.

"It's okay," said Tom, "I was afraid at first too, but realizing what you really want is the hardest part. Once you do that, the rest is easy."

George and Gracie wiggled beneath her entrapping arms. "No, really, I'm very happy."

Tammi snorted. "Yeah, right."

Gwen's breasts gave up trying to pry free from her arms and started sliding down instead. George made a break for it and Gwen grabbed at her, elbowing her wine glass in the process. The glass twirled on its base and Gwen reached for it, her fingers glancing off the rim and knocking it off orbit. The glass tumbled to the table, spilling Chardonnay across the nachos with venison and sage sausage.

"Oh!" cried Gwen as George and Gracie squeezed through the bottom of her bra and rolled out from beneath the hem of her blouse. She thrust her hands into her lap, grasping for their warm, pliable flesh, but they tumbled free. Gwen ducked her head beneath the polyurethaned raw oak table, but it was dark down there, and the pale mound beside Buzz's shoe was only a crumpled paper napkin.

The rest of the evening was agony. Gwen kept spotting her breasts everywhere; in the bric-a-brac on the walls, on people's plates. She nearly had a heart attack when Buzz uncovered the rolls, and her quail and wild asparagus croquettes were a trial to her.

Finally they were down to coffee and Gwen thought she might get out of this with only minor humiliation. Buzz and Tammi were discussing their plans for Labor Day, and Tom was calculating the tip on his Palm.

"We're either going to Four Bears Water Park or Six Flags," said Tammi. "Six Flags has better roller coasters, but Four Bears has all the water slides and stuff—Oh!" Something over Gwen's left shoulder caught Tammi's eye. "Oh look! I hadn't noticed that before. That's really funny!"

"Geez," said Buzz. "I'm surprised they can get away with that. This is supposed to be a family place."

"Wow," said Tom. "I guess it's a girl bear."

Before she even turned around, Gwen knew what they were looking at. George and Gracie had been found. She craned her neck around to look, and there they were, each nestled in a crook of the bear's arms. By now other people were pointing and murmuring. Laughter ran through the restaurant as more and more people noticed that the bear was wearing Gwen's breasts.

Gwen's head felt light and the restaurant swayed around her. "Excuse me," she said, fumbling money out of her wallet and standing up. "I have to go now. I forgot I—I have to do something. It was nice meeting you, Tom."

Gwen fled the restaurant, glaring at George and Gracie as she passed them, but they didn't seem to notice. Caught up, no doubt, in being the center of attention. She managed to make it all the way to her car before losing her croquettes on the blacktop.

Gwen lay on the couch eating peppermint stick ice cream and brooding over her fate. George and Gracie were back again, but she knew it didn't mean anything. They could leave again at any moment and no bra could stop them. She wondered if she really needed them anyway. Maybe they were more trouble than they were worth.

She put down the ice cream and lifted up her shirt, looking down through the neck hole. They were pretty breasts, she had to admit. Gracie a little more so than George, who was larger and kind of droopy, but they both had a soft roundness to them which was very appealing. She snaked her arms beneath her shirt and ran her hands under them, hefting them in her palms, enjoying their watery weight and warmth. A thought occurred to her. If they could detach . . .

She cradled George in her hands, raised the jiggling lump of flesh to her mouth and rolled the nipple over her tongue. A jolt of pleasure shot down her body, making her toes tingle. Restless, Gracie rolled into her lap and burrowed at her crotch. Gwen relaxed her legs even as she continued sucking on George's nipple. It felt good. It felt so good it was almost certainly wrong, but so what? Her life was already ruined, why not wallow in whatever debased pleasures the situation offered? Stuffing as much of George into her mouth as she could, she unfastened her jeans and reached for the ice cream.

Gwen lay in a sticky stupor on the couch, the ice cream carton tucked into the crook of her arm. Inside George and Gracie lolled indolently in the melted pink froth. They really loved that stuff. Gwen sighed and gazed at the ceiling with blissful satisfaction, not caring, at least for the moment, why and how she felt that way.

Someone knocked on the door. "Gwenny?" came her mother's voice from the other side.

Gwen shot up off the couch, grabbing the lid to the ice cream and shoving it over George and Gracie. She refastened her jeans and wiped away the worst of the ice cream film with a paper napkin. "Just a second, Ma!" she yelled, racing into the bedroom to throw on a bulky sweater.

She answered the door and her mother swept in dressed in a powder blue micro-fiber jogging suit, her bleached curls sticking out from around a coordinating headband. "Sweetheart, I was just over at Kohl's, and they have the cutest little sweater sets that'd be just perfect for you." She leaned forward to give Gwen a kiss.

Gwen quickly pecked her mother's cheek and backed away before she could get a hug in.

"They're on sale," her mother continued. "I thought maybe we could go back together—maybe have a little lunch while we're out."

Gwen took a deep breath to steady herself. "Oh, no thanks, Mom. I'm uh, kind of busy right now."

"Hmm. I can see that." Her mother glanced around the disordered apartment and then turned to eye Gwen closely. "Are you okay?"

"Oh yeah! Yeah, I'm fine." Desperately Gwen searched for something to distract her mother. "H-hey, look what I found," she said, pointing at the statue on the coffee table.

"Oh, isn't that pretty!"

Gwen flushed. "Thanks, Mom."

"Where did you buy it? Was it on sale?"

Gwen stared at her. "Mom, I made it. In high school, remember?"

Her mother shook her head. "I don't remember you ever sculpting, Sweetie. You've always been such a good, practical girl." She looked around the apartment again in disapproval. "I just wish you weren't so messy. I mean look," she picked the ice cream carton up from where Gwen had left it on the floor, "how can you just leave this sitting out like this?"

"Mom, please . . ."

But her mother ignored her. "I bet it's all melted now," she said, opening the lid.

Her eyes widened briefly and then she froze, staring into the carton. It wobbled slightly as her hand shook. She shot a glance at Gwen, taking in her bulky sweater, and then looked back into the carton. She replaced the lid carefully and set it down on the coffee table next to Gwen's statue. She sat down on the couch. "They are yours?"

Open mouthed, Gwen nodded.

"Well, that's something, at least." Her mother sighed. "Dotty Green-field's boy wound up with somebody else's testicles and he got his girl-friend pregnant with them. It was a mess."

Gwen couldn't contain the laughter that burst inappropriately from her lips.

Her mother scowled, frown lines standing out around her mouth. "Oh, you think that's funny, do you?"

Helplessly, Gwen nodded her head and sank to the couch, weeping with laughter. She laid her head on her mother's shoulder and suddenly her giggles became sobs.

"Oh, now. There, there, Honey," said her mother, wrapping her arms around Gwen and rocking her, just like when she was a little girl. "Come on now, don't cry. It's not so bad."

Gwen sat back up, rubbing her eyes. "Not so bad? How can you say that? You're not the one whose breasts are gallivanting all over town!"

"No, but I was, once."

"What?" Shock made Gwen's hands and feet tingle.

Her mother sighed again. "Oh yes. I was a little older than you, but they say every generation matures earlier, so . . ."

Gwen shook her head. "So you're saying this happens to everyone? How come I've never heard about it before?"

"Well, it doesn't happen to everyone, dear. Just an unlucky few. And of course no one talks about it. I mean, it's just too embarrassing, isn't it?"

She nodded in agreement, and for a while they sat in silence, staring at the ice cream carton. At last Gwen said, "But it happened to you?"

"Mmm-hmm."

"B-but it doesn't anymore?"

"No. Thank God."

Gwen turned and looked at her mother. "So what happened?"

She shrugged. "One day, they just didn't come back."

"Oh my God! How horrible!"

"No." Her mother shook her head and took Gwen's hands in hers, gripping them tightly. "No. It was the best thing that ever happened to me. And the best thing for you to do is tape that ice cream carton shut, pop it in the freezer and never take it out again. Take it from me Gwenny, you'll be better off without them."

Gwen stared at her mother in horror. "How can you say that?"

"Because they'll destroy your life if you let them. Unless you give them exactly what they want, they will publicly humiliate you over and over again, until you lose your friends, your job, everything." She released Gwen's hands and folded her arms.

"What they want?"

"Mmm-hmm." Gwen's mother gave her a sinister look.

Running a hand over her sticky jeans, Gwen thought she had a pretty good idea what George and Gracie wanted.

Gwen's mother patted her knee and stood up. "Now you need to get your mind off all of this, Gwenny. Focus on something else." She smiled brightly and clasped her hands together. "I know, why don't you put the ice cream away and come shopping with me? Mervyns has some lovely oversized knits you might like."

Gwen shook her head. "No thanks, Mom. I think I'd like to be alone for a little while."

Her mother sighed and pursed her lips. "Suit yourself," she said as she headed for the door, "but believe me, you'll feel a lot better once you take matters into your own hands."

"I'm sure you're right, Mom," said Gwen, following her. "And thanks." She gave her a big hug. "Thanks for stopping by."

Armed with a cost-estimate form and the bulging Pottery Barn file, Gwen approached Charlie Axel. Charlie was on the phone, so Gwen stood in front of his desk waiting. Her arms ached from holding the huge file, but with the enormous graphics monitor, the scanner, and countless printouts and CDs, there wasn't a square inch of space open on his desk.

"Okay, I'll email you a thumbnail this afternoon, and as soon as you approve it, I'll go ahead with the final layout . . . Great. Bye." Charlie hung up and immediately dialed another number. "Hey, Baby, how you doing? . . . Ha! . . . Me? Not much . . . Hey, you want to go to the Icebox tonight? DJ Jah Love is spinning."

"Um. Excuse me," said Gwen.

Charlie glanced at her and put his hand over the receiver. "Just a sec," he said.

Gwen stood there for fifteen minutes while Charlie and his girlfriend made plans for the evening, discussed the local music scene and critiqued their friends' fashion sense.

"Dean should have stuck with black work. His new Elvis tattoo clashes with his hair . . . Oh, you gotta go? . . . Catch you later then baby, bye."

"Excuse me Charlie," said Gwen, edging closer to the desk as he hung up and returned his gaze to the monitor. "I need to talk to you about the Pottery Barn account."

"Sure, what do you need to know?" he asked, fingers briskly tapping at the keyboard. He never took his eyes off the monitor.

"Well—" Gwen shifted her weight and adjusted her grip on the file as a blush crept over her face. Suddenly she was furious with this smart, smarmy, hotshot young "artist," sitting there, not even looking at her, barely acknowledging her as a human being.

What gave him the right? What made him better than her? That he had talent? Well everybody has talent, just not everybody gets to use theirs. He was lucky. He was lucky and that meant he could treat her like a moderately bright stapler? "There's a few things," she said sweetly as she very gently shoved half the crap on his desk onto the floor and made room for the Pottery Barn file.

"What the hell are you doing?" She had Charlie's undivided attention at last. He gaped at her as she walked around his desk toward him.

"I have to file an invoice for this job tomorrow," she said, brandishing the cost-estimate form. "And I don't have one useful piece of information in this whole stack!" She smacked the Pottery Barn file with her other hand.

The noise made Charlie jump. "Geez, chill out! It's just an invoice. That's valuable work you just threw on the floor, dude!"

"Not if we can't bill for it," she said, resting one hand on his desk and leaning in toward him. "It may be 'just an invoice' to you, but it's my freaking job, *dude*. For weeks now, you haven't been letting me do my job."

Charlie blinked. "Okay, okay. Relax. Just leave the form with me and I'll fill it out and get it back to you tomorrow."

"Oh no," she said as she hauled a chair over beside his. "We're going to fill in the information on the form right now. And then I'll have what I need, and I can leave you alone, which is what we both want. And next time, you can avoid all this by filling out the form yourself." She looked Charlie in his bratty, talented, dumbstruck face, and she smiled.

When Gwen got to the elevator the new guy in accounting was just stepping inside. He held the door for her. He had sandy brown hair and an earnest, slightly perplexed expression. "Thanks," she said, and then wondered if he'd witnessed her little freak out with Charlie. She blushed and stood very still, staring at the brushed stainless steel of the elevator doors.

"I hate that guy," he said conversationally. "My first day here he kept me waiting at his desk for half an hour while he negotiated a new deal with his cellular provider. All I needed was his signoff on a Fed-Ex receipt. What a jerk."

Gwen smiled and glanced at him, and found him smiling back.

"That needed to be done," he said, and his smile became a grin. He swept one arm out in front of him. "Swoosh!"

Though her social life was in ruins and her job hung by a thread, Gwen's relationship with her breasts had improved considerably. They seemed to appreciate the attention she gave them. They didn't go out quite as much, and when they did they always came back in the manner of excited children eager to share their adventures. Gwen would wake up around four or five in the morning, her breasts bouncing on top of her chest. She'd fondle them for a little while, until they got sleepy and nudged away the covers so they could reattach themselves.

One night she awoke to find three blobs of flesh wiggling on her. She fumbled for the bedside lamp and beheld in the amber glow George and Gracie perching proudly on either side of a semi-flaccid penis. It was a testament to her reconciliation with her situation that she didn't scream and fling the thing across the room. Clearly, her breasts had meant well, but there was no telling where this little cock had been, and no way she was going to let it join their nocturnal games.

Groaning, Gwen sat up and stared at the penis, which regarded her with cycloptic innocence. She took a slip from the floor by the bed, draped it over the wayward penis and scooped it up, padding across the room to her dresser. She placed the penis gently in her underwear drawer, shut it, and went back to sleep.

The following afternoon was J. Thomas Design's annual office party. They'd taken over the lobby of the Hilton for the event. Towering posters of award-winning advertising images stood about, guests mingling among them. Gwen almost didn't mind being there. Since she'd been pleasuring her breasts there'd been no more public incidents and she felt more in control of her life than she had in weeks.

". . . so I figured, at least with accounting I could always find a job," said the new guy in accounting. "All in all, I think I did the right thing, switching majors."

Gwen, who'd been taking full advantage of the open bar, smiled pleasantly and allowed herself to focus on his nicely formed shoulders.

He smiled back at her, but at the same time his eyes darted nervously over her shoulder, like he was looking for someone. He seemed to catch himself and refocus on her. "So what about you, how do you like working here?" he asked her.

"Oh, it's great," she said, feeling her smile calcify into a rigid grin. "J. Thomas is a great company to be with and I love working around creative people." As she paused to drain her third whisky sour, she distinctly felt something warm and soft roll free from under her bra and drop down the front of her dress. She looked down in time to see George scampering beneath the hors d'oeuvres table.

No. Oh God no, not now. Swearing under her breath, Gwen ran after her left breast. She pulled up the tablecloth and stuck her head under the hors d'oeuvres table. George was nowhere in sight.

A pair of men's brown oxfords appeared beside the table. "Did you lose something?" asked the new guy in accounting.

She straightened, slamming the back of her head against the underside of the table, creating a minor shower of pigs in blankets. The new guy in accounting helped extricate her from the tablecloth. "Careful now. Are you okay?"

"Oh! Oh yeah." She folded her arms across her chest, as much to imprison Gracie as to hide George's absence. "I—I, um, lost my earring."

He wrinkled his brow. "But you have two now."

"Oh, oh yeah."

At the far end of the room stood an enormous poster of a model in a dress comprised entirely of pink balloons. The crowd before it parted momentarily, and she thought she saw George rolling behind it. "Excuse me," she said, and dashed off to investigate.

The poster stood in an alcove, one side pushed up against the wall, forming a little cul-de-sac behind it. And there in the shadows was her breast. Gwen got to her hands and knees and squeezed behind the poster. George rolled to the far corner, but could not escape. With a cry of exultation, Gwen grabbed her.

Awkwardly she managed to unbutton the top of her dress and push her bra down, but as she tried to put George back in her rightful place, the breast bucked, causing her to bump the poster with her elbow. The foam-board wobbled, and then, with a whooshing sound, toppled over. Gasps erupted and everyone turned to stare, and then silence fell as they saw Gwen, on her knees, naked from the waist up, clutching her left breast in her hands.

Still shaking with humiliation, Gwen rummaged in her bedroom closet until she found the box she'd kept her statue in. She got a roll of duct tape out of the junk drawer and put them both on the coffee table next to her high school masterpiece. Now maybe she'd be able to keep her job, she thought, steeling herself. Now maybe she'd meet someone and settle down to a nice, ordinary life. She stripped to the waist, and took George and Gracie lovingly in her hands. "I don't want to do this, but you've left me no other option," she told them.

As she grasped them more firmly, George and Gracie wiggled free from her hands. They rolled under the couch and she shoved it over onto its back. They fled to the bedroom and tried to hide in the bed covers. Gwen fished the butterfly net out of the closet and pulled the covers back in a whoosh. She swiped at them with the net, missed and dashed across the bed after them as they rolled into the bathroom.

Twenty minutes later she had them trapped behind the refrigerator. She rousted them out with the handle of the net and almost got them as they slipped out between the refrigerator and the stove. As they raced back into the living room, Gwen was right behind them. They sprinted across the carpet, heading for the television, but the overturned couch was in their way.

They thought they were being clever; George went one way around, Gracie the other, but Gwen leapt onto the couch and caught them on the other side. Unable to stop themselves, they rolled into her waiting net and she swung it up with a shout of triumph.

Her breasts hung heavy and limp in the swaying net, and Gwen reached forward to grab it and trap them inside. She overbalanced and the next thing she knew she was flying forward off the couch, right into her sculpture sitting on the coffee table. As she slid across the table, clutching the net in one hand, she reached for the sculpture, but it sailed free of her grasp and crashed to the floor, smashing into hundreds of pieces.

Gwen lay across the coffee table on her stomach, panting, her breasts struggling feebly in the net. She stared at her sculpture, her beautiful sculpture, destroyed, and then glanced at the box lying on its side nearby and suddenly great wracking sobs welled up inside her and shook her body. Hot tears streamed down her face and she couldn't stop crying.

The net slipped from her hand as she crawled off the coffee table and knelt beside the shattered remains of her sculpture. She sifted through the fragments, but much of the clay had turned to powder when it hit the floor. There was no repairing it. The one thing she'd ever done that she was really proud of was gone. It wasn't worth it, she thought. It just wasn't worth it. George and Gracie rolled into her lap and nuzzled against her as if to comfort her. She held them to her and cried until she was empty, and then she got the broom.

She struggled through the doorway with the block of clay and took it into the living room. With one foot she cleared the coffee table of dirty dishes and magazines and dropped the clay on top of it with a slam. She got a bowl of water from the kitchen, sat down on the couch and sank her fingers into the soft moist clay. It was smooth and cool, receptive to her every thought, every twitch of her fingers.

She didn't think about what she was doing, what form she wanted to wrest from the blank block, she just did it, molding and smoothing, feeling all her sadness, fear and self-doubt ebb away as she gave herself up to the task at hand. With wonder she watched the forms take shape as if of their own volition, emerging whole and perfect from between her fingers.

When she was finished, her arms, face, pants and blouse were streaked with red-brown clay. She sat back with satisfaction and looked at what she had created. An assemblage of fruit—apples, pears, bananas and peaches, and among them two round, disembodied breasts, almost indistinguishable from the fruit until you looked at it a while. And then you began to wonder about that banana. She decided instantly on a name, "Still Life with Boobs."

Gwen smiled, more pleased with herself than she'd been in years. She didn't care if the piece was good or not, she didn't care if anyone laughed at it, or her. She was through living for appearances. It wasn't worth it. It made you miss out on the really good stuff. It made you forget why you were alive in the first place.

Someone knocked on her door. Startled, Gwen wiped her hands on her jeans and opened it.

The new guy from accounting stood there, shifting restlessly from foot to foot. "Um. Hi. I—uh, I'm sorry to bother you but . . . Geez, this is embarrassing. I—uh, I lost my—I lost something and I was wondering if . . ." His blue eyes wandered past her to peer into the apartment, desperation and dread warring on his face.

Gwen suddenly remembered the penis in her dresser drawer. Good Lord. "Why don't you come in?" she said.

He looked relieved.

"Sit down," she said, gesturing to the couch. "I'll be right back."

She went to the bedroom and rummaged through her underwear drawer until she found the penis. But she couldn't just go out there with it in her hand. It seemed too . . . personal. She emptied the basket where she kept her scrunchies and placed the penis inside, then took a scarf and arranged it on top, as if it were a loaf of bread she wanted to keep warm.

She went back out. He was still sitting on the couch, hands clenched on his knees, his head tilted down, peering at his crotch. Bingo.

"Is this yours?" she asked.

He took the basket, tentatively lifting up one corner of the scarf. He heaved a sigh of relief. "Oh my God. Thank you . . . I—Could you excuse me a moment?"

She smiled. "Sure, bathroom's down that way, second door on the left."

When he came back he looked a lot more relaxed. She offered him a beer and they sat on the couch, drinking together in companionable silence for a few minutes. At last she said, "It was my breasts. They brought . . . him here. It wasn't me."

He laughed. "Oh, I know. Anyway, knowing him, he probably talked them into it."

She smiled. "How did you know he came here?"

"It's Frank, by the way." He stuck out a hand.

"How did you know Frank came here?"

"No, I'm Frank, he's Clyde. As in Bonnie and Clyde? It was a thing my old girlfriend would always say, back before we broke up."

"Oh, I'm sorry."

"Not your fault." He looked away. "Anyway, to answer your question, I followed him. I saw them all come in here, only at the time, I didn't have the guts to knock on the door. I was hoping he'd just come back, he usually does, but he's never been gone this long before and I was pretty desperate."

"I can imagine."

"So, has this been happening to you for long?" he asked.

She shrugged, caught up in the square line of his jaw, the compact sturdiness of his shoulders. She'd like to sculpt him. "About six weeks."

"Heh, me too. It's insane isn't it? I mean, I thought I was, until . . . until now." He leaned closer to her, his face intent, as if he were discovering something.

"Yes," she said, her voice a husky whisper. "Maybe we are crazy, but I don't care anymore, do you?"

He shook his head ever so slightly. "No."

"Me neither," she said, and she kissed him.

Their lips, soft and crushable, locked onto one another with sudden urgency. He ran his hands down her arms, across her back, holding her tight, and she brought her own arms around and up, to play with the hair at the back of his neck, to clutch his shoulders and crumple the starchy whiteness of his shirt between her fingers.

They parted, and his gaze focused on the sculpture. "Hey, that's beautiful. Did you do that?"

In her blouse George and Gracie tingled, and Gwen smiled broadly. "Yeah."

"Wow. That's great that you do something creative like that. I wish I could be creative. I used to love to draw, but I haven't done it for years."

"You should pick it back up again."

He looked pleased. "Really, you think?"

"Oh, definitely."

WHITHER CANADIAN SF&F?

ROBERT J. SAWYER

Robert J. Sawyer is a Nebula winner for Best Novel, a Hugo winner for the same, a multiple Seiun (Japanese Hugo) winner for the same, and has recently become a publisher as well. He lives in Canada, and has done more to promote Canadian science fiction than just about anyone. So when it came time to see how Canadian science fiction is doing, there was only one man to ask.

What's wrong with this picture?

The largest publisher of Canadian science fiction is Tor Books, based in Manhattan. Its Canadian roster includes Charles de Lint, Cory Doctorow, Candas Jane Dorsey, Dave Duncan, Phyllis Gotlieb, Terence M. Green, Ed Greenwood, Matthew Hughes, Donald Kingsbury, Spider Robinson, Robert J. Sawyer, Karl Schroeder, Peter Watts, Jack Whyte, and Robert Charles Wilson.

And the number two publisher of Canadian SF&F? That's doubtless DAW, also based in New York. It's home to Canadians Julie E. Czerneda, Tanya Huff, Fiona Patton, Sean Russell, Michelle West, and Edward Willett.

Why is this? It's not as though Canada doesn't have publishing companies of its own, including giants such as McClelland & Stewart, Penguin Canada, and Random House Canada. Nor is it that Canadian houses are averse to genre fiction. All the major players do lots of mystery fiction, and Harlequin—headquartered in Toronto—practically owns the worldwide romance market.

But these publishers shy away from fantasy, and they're even more reluctant to put out science fiction—possibly because Harlequin's brief foray into that, the cheapjack Laser Books line of 1976–77, was an abysmal failure. And so our major writers, with only a few exceptions, are edited and published by Americans.

Yes, there's a small-press publishing scene in Canada. *On Spec* magazine is good and hasn't missed a quarterly issue since debuting in 1989; the *Tesseracts* anthology series is reliable (*Tesseracts Nine*, edited by Nalo Hopkinson and Geoff Ryman, came out in 2005; *Tesseracts Ten*, edited by Edo van Belkom and Robert Charles Wilson, was released in 2006); and French-Canadian SF has always been a small-press operation, led by the venerable magazine *Solaris*, founded in 1974.

But if a Canadian SF or fantasy writer wants a readership measured in tens of thousands, rather than just hundreds, he or she has to look outside Canada for a publisher—and that means the writing must be a good match for the personal tastes and economic models of foreign editors. Not to look a gift horse in the mouth, but can this really be a good thing?

There's a parallel in the TV industry. Most of the leading SF programs of the last decade or so were filmed in Canada (and usually in Vancouver): the new *Battlestar Galactica*, *Stargate SG-1*, *Stargate Atlantis*, *Gene Roddenberry's Earth: Final Conflict*, the remake of *The Outer Limits*, *Smallville*, *The X-Files*, and many more. And nothing makes a Canadian heart beat more proudly than to catch sight of a red street-corner mailbox that accidentally makes it into one of these shows, because it proves it was filmed in Canada.

But the creative decisions are mostly made in Los Angeles, by Americans—which is why the streets of Vancouver are trying to pass for those of American cities.

Are our SF&F books doing any better than just passing themselves off as American products? Sure, some of us set our books in Canada, but are they *really* Canadian in content and sensibility? Can they be, when the editors and publishers they have to be accepted by are Americans? In the end, are the bits of Canadiana that appear as background details in our books as irrelevant as those red mailboxes?

I don't know. But it's interesting to see which houses do the most Canadian SF. It has been said that the United States will never annex Canada, because that would mean importing thirty million Democrats— the Canadian center is well to the left of the American one. I can't think of a single Canadian whose frontlist is currently published by Baen, the U.S. publishing house most associated with the American right (although it has reprinted some of Spider Robinson's old titles). But there's a huge Canuck contingent at Tor, many of whose editors are vocally left-wing, and DAW's editors have often espoused very liberal values, too.

The Canadian SF&F reading public prefers Canadian authors, which makes it all the more puzzling that Canada's major publishers have shied away from those genres (British publishers do very well with them, after all, so why shouldn't Canadian ones?).

American and Canadian authors usually sell equally well in the United States. But whereas most American genre writers are lucky to sell one copy north of the border for every ten south of it (as one might predict, given the population ratio), many Canadians manage to sell four or five copies domestically for every ten sold in the States, proving that even when it is filtered through an American editorial lens, Canadians would much rather read work by their compatriots. (Nor is this filtering anything new: The anthology that kick-started the modern Canadian SF movement, 1985's *Tesseracts*, was edited by an American expatriate, the famed Judith Merril.)

And yet, as I said, the big Canadian publishers still routinely refuse to do science fiction and fantasy. But, in 2005, a baby step was taken in the right direction. I mentioned the Canadian small press earlier; it's something I've been proud to be part of, editing a line called (cough, cough) Robert J. Sawyer Books for Calgary's Red Deer Press since 2003. Red Deer is tiny; just four full-time employees. But in 2005, Fitzhenry and Whiteside, a much bigger company (with thirty-four full-time employees) bought up Red Deer. I thought my SF line was going to fall by the wayside in this purchase, but it turned out, to my astonishment, to be one of the main reasons Fitzhenry wanted Red Deer.

Fitzhenry also recently bought up another tiny press, even smaller than Red Deer, an outfit called Trifolium that had been doing SF anthologies edited by DAW mainstay Julie E. Czerneda. And it acquired distribution rights to the list produced by Calgary's Edge Science Fiction and Fantasy, a small press that, in addition to doing the *Tesseracts* anthologies, has been publishing first-rate genre novels.

Together, Julie and I are now building the fantasy and SF lists of the first decent-sized Canadian publisher since the days of Laser Books to have its own science fiction and fantasy imprints. We're providing a domestic home for authors such as Terence M. Green (two-time World Fantasy Award finalist), Matthew Hughes (a staple of *The Magazine of Fantasy & Science Fiction*), hard-SF superstar Karl Schroeder, and Andrew Weiner (a contributor to *Asimov's Science Fiction*).

What the future holds, only time will tell. But it's encouraging to note that the tide is turning a bit in Canadian genre television, too. As

I write this, a TV series based on Tanya Huff's fantasy novels about private investigator Vicki Nelson and her vampire companion is in production. As usual, the show is being made in Vancouver—and while it's pretending yet again to be a different city, this time the city it's standing in for is Toronto. Will wonders never cease?

I'm partial to this story, since I commissioned it for an anthology of hard-boiled private-eye stories set in the future. Robert J. Sawyer, who has won both the Hugo and Nebula for different novels (and who has practically retired the Japanese Hugo, the Seiun), came up with a title that would have been meaningless twenty years ago but resonates with just about everyone today—and a story worthy of that title.

IDENTITY THEFT

ROBERT J. SAWYER

The door to my office slid open. "Hello," I said, rising from my chair. "You must be my nine o'clock." I said it as if I had a ten o'clock and an eleven o'clock, but I didn't. The whole Martian economy was in a slump, and, even though I was the only private detective on Mars, this was the first new case I'd had in weeks.

"Yes," said a high, feminine voice. "I'm Cassandra Wilkins."

I let my eyes rove up and down her body. It was very good work; I wondered if she'd had quite so perfect a figure before transferring. People usually ordered replacement bodies that, at least in broad strokes, resembled their originals, but few could resist improving them. Men got buffer, women got curvier, and everyone modified their faces, removing asymmetries, wrinkles, and imperfections. If and when I transferred myself, I'd eliminate the gray in my blond hair and get a new nose that would look like my current one had before it'd been broken a couple of times.

"A pleasure to meet you, Ms. Wilkins," I said. "I'm Alexander Lomax. Please have a seat."

She was a little thing, no more than a hundred and fifty centimeters, and she was wearing a stylish silver-gray blouse and skirt, but no makeup or jewelry. I'd expected her to sit down with a catlike, fluid movement, given her delicate features, but she just sort of plunked herself into the chair. "Thanks," she said. "I do hope you can help me, Mr. Lomax. I really do."

Rather than immediately sitting down myself, I went to the coffeemaker. I filled my own mug, then opened my mouth to offer Cassandra a cup, but closed it before doing so; transfers, of course, didn't drink. "What seems to be the problem?" I said, returning to my chair.

It's hard reading a transfer's expression: the facial sculpting was usually very good, but the movements were somewhat restrained. "My husband—oh, my goodness, Mr. Lomax, I hate to even say this!" She looked down at her hands. "My husband . . . he's disappeared."

I raised my eyebrows; it was pretty damned difficult for someone to disappear here. New Klondike was only three kilometers in diameter, all of it locked under the dome. "When did you last see him?"

"Three days ago."

My office was small, but it did have a window. Through it, I could see one of the supporting arches that helped to hold up the transparent dome over New Klondike. Outside the dome, a sandstorm was raging, orange clouds obscuring the sun. Auxiliary lights on the arch compensated for that, but Martian daylight was never very bright. That's a reason why even those who had a choice were reluctant to return to Earth: after years of only dim illumination, apparently the sun as seen from there was excruciating. "Is your husband, um, like you?" I asked.

She nodded. "Oh, yes. We both came here looking to make our fortune, just like everyone else."

I shook my head. "I mean is he also a transfer?"

"Oh, sorry. Yes, he is. In fact, we both just transferred."

"It's an expensive procedure," I said. "Could he have been skipping out on paying for it?"

Cassandra shook her head. "No, no. Joshua found one or two nice specimens early on. He used the money from selling those pieces to buy the New You franchise here. That's where we met—after I threw in the towel on sifting dirt, I got a job in sales there. Anyway, of course, we both got to transfer at cost." She was actually wringing her synthetic hands. "Oh, Mr. Lomax, please help me! I don't know what I'm going to do without my Joshua!"

"You must love him a lot," I said, watching her pretty face for more than just the pleasure of looking at it; I wanted to gauge her sincerity as she replied. After all, people often disappeared because things were bad at home, but spouses are rarely forthcoming about that.

"Oh, I do!" said Cassandra. "I love him more than I can say. Joshua is a wonderful, wonderful man." She looked at me with pleading eyes. "You have to help me get him back. You just have to!"

I looked down at my coffee mug; steam was rising from it. "Have you tried the police?"

Cassandra made a sound that I guessed was supposed to be a snort: it had the right roughness, but was dry as Martian sand. "Yes. They—oh, I hate to speak ill of anyone, Mr. Lomax! Believe me, it's not my way, but—well, there's no ducking it, is there? They were useless. Just totally useless."

I nodded slightly; it's a story I heard often enough—I owed most of what little livelihood I had to the local cops' incompetence and indifference. "Who did you speak to?"

"A—a detective, I guess he was; he didn't wear a uniform. I've forgotten his name."

"What did he look like?"

"Red hair, and—"

"That's Mac," I said. She looked puzzled, so I said his full name. "Dougal McCrae."

"McCrae, yes," said Cassandra. She shuddered a bit, and she must have noticed my surprised reaction to that. "Sorry," she said. "I just didn't like the way he looked at me."

I resisted running my eyes over her body just then; I'd already done so, and I could remember what I'd seen. I guess her original figure hadn't been like this one; if it had, she'd certainly be used to admiring looks from men by now.

"I'll have a word with McCrae," I said. "See what's already been done. Then I'll pick up where the cops left off."

"Would you?" Her green eyes seemed to dance. "Oh, thank you, Mr. Lomax! You're a good man—I can tell!"

I shrugged a little. "I can show you two ex-wives and a half-dozen bankers who'd disagree."

"Oh, no," she said. "Don't say things like that! You *are* a good man, I'm sure of it. Believe me, I have a sense about these things. You're a good man, and I know you won't let me down."

Naïve woman; she'd probably thought the same thing about her husband—until he'd run off. "Now, what can you tell me about your husband? Joshua, is it?"

"Yes, that's right. His full name is Joshua Connor Wilkins—and it's Joshua, never just Josh, thank you very much." I nodded. Guys who were anal about being called by their full first names never bought a round, in my experience. Maybe it was a good thing that this clown was gone.

"Yes," I said. "Go on." I didn't have to take notes, of course. My office computer was recording everything, and would extract whatever was useful into a summary file for me.

Cassandra ran her synthetic lower lip back and forth beneath her artificial upper teeth, thinking for a moment. Then: "Well, he was born in Calgary, Alberta, and he's thirty-eight years old. He moved to Mars seven mears ago." Mears were Mars-years; about double the length of those on Earth.

"Do you have a picture?"

"I can access one," she said. She pointed at my desk terminal. "May I?"

I nodded, and Cassandra reached over to grab the keyboard. In doing so, she managed to knock over my coffee mug, spilling hot joe all over her dainty hand. She let out a small yelp of pain. I got up, grabbed a towel, and began wiping up the mess. "I'm surprised that hurt," I said. "I mean, I *do* like my coffee hot, but . . ."

"Transfers feel pain, Mr. Lomax," she said, "for the same reason that biologicals do. When you're flesh-and-blood, you need a signaling system to warn you when your parts are being damaged; same is true for those of us who have transferred. Admittedly, artificial bodies are much more durable, of course."

"Ah," I said.

"Sorry," she replied. "I've explained this so many times now—you know, at work. Anyway, please forgive me about your desk."

I made a dismissive gesture. "Thank God for the paperless office, eh? Don't worry about it." I gestured at the keyboard; fortunately, none of the coffee had gone down between the keys. "You were going to show me a picture?"

"Oh, right." She spoke some commands, and the terminal responded—making me wonder what she'd wanted the keyboard for. But then she used it to type in a long passphrase; presumably she didn't want to say hers aloud in front of me. She frowned as she was typing it in, and backspaced to make a correction; multiword passphrases were easy to say, but hard to type if you weren't adept with a keyboard—and the more security conscious you were, the longer the passphrase you used.

Anyway, she accessed some repository of her personal files, and brought up a photo of Joshua-never-Josh Wilkins. Given how attractive Mrs. Wilkins was, he wasn't what I expected. He had cold, gray eyes, hair buzzed so short as to be nonexistent, and a thin, almost lipless mouth; the overall effect was reptilian. "That's before," I said. "What about after? What's he look like now that he's transferred?"

"Umm, pretty much the same," she said.

"Really?" If I'd had that kisser, I'd have modified it for sure. "Do you have pictures taken since he moved his mind?"

"No actual pictures," said Cassandra. "After all, he and I only just transferred. But I can go into the NewYou database, and show you the plans from which his new face was manufactured." She spoke to the terminal some more, and then typed in another lengthy passphrase. Soon enough, she had a computer-graphics rendition of Joshua's head on my screen.

"You're right," I said, surprised. "He didn't change a thing. Can I get copies of all this?"

She nodded, and spoke some more commands, transferring various documents into local storage.

"All right," I said. "My fee is two hundred solars an hour."

"That's fine, that's fine, of course! I don't care about the money, Mr. Lomax—not at all. I just want Joshua back. Please tell me you'll find him."

"I will," I said, smiling my most reassuring smile. "Don't you worry about that. He can't have gone far."

Actually, of course, Joshua Wilkins *could* perhaps have gone quite far—so my first order of business was to eliminate that possibility.

No spaceships had left Mars in the last ten days, so he couldn't be off-planet. There was a giant airlock in the south through which large spaceships could be brought inside for dry-dock work, but it hadn't been cracked open in weeks. And, although a transfer could exist freely on the Martian surface, there were only four personnel air locks leading out of the dome, and they all had security guards. I visited each of those air locks and checked, just to be sure, but the only people who had gone out in the last three days were the usual crowds of hapless fossil hunters, and every one of them had returned when the dust storm began.

I remember when this town had started up: "The Great Fossil Rush," they called it. Weingarten and O'Reilly, two early private explorers who had come here at their own expense, had found the first fossils on Mars, and had made a fortune selling them back on Earth. More valuable than any precious metal; rarer than anything else in the solar system—actual evidence of extraterrestrial life! Good fist-sized specimens went for millions in online auctions; excellent football-sized ones for billions. There was no greater status symbol than to own the petrified remains of a Martian pentaped or rhizomorph.

Of course, Weingarten and O'Reilly wouldn't say precisely where they'd found their specimens, but it had been easy enough to prove that their spaceship had landed here, in the Isidis Planitia basin. Other treasure hunters started coming, and New Klondike—the one and only town on Mars—was born.

Native life was never widely dispersed on Mars; the single ecosystem that had ever existed here seemed to have been confined to an area not much bigger than Rhode Island. Some of the prospectors—excuse me, fossil hunters—who came shortly after W&O's first expedition found a few nice specimens, although most had been badly blasted by blowing sand.

Somewhere, though, was the mother lode: a bed that produced fossils more finely preserved than even those from Earth's famed Burgess Shale. Weingarten and O'Reilly had known where it was—they'd stumbled on it by pure dumb luck, apparently. But they'd both been killed when their heat shield separated from their lander when reentering Earth's atmosphere after their third expedition here—and, in the twenty mears since, no one had yet rediscovered it.

People were still looking, of course. There'd always been a market for transferring consciousness; the potentially infinite lifespan was hugely appealing. But here on Mars, the demand was particularly brisk, since artificial bodies could spend days or even weeks on the surface, searching for paleontological gold, without worrying about running out of air. Of course, a serious sandstorm could blast the synthetic flesh from metal bones, and scour those bones until they were whittled to nothing; that's why no one was outside right now.

Anyway, Joshua-never-Josh Wilkins was clearly not outside the dome, and he hadn't taken off in a spaceship. Wherever he was hiding, it was somewhere in New Klondike. I can't say he was breathing the same air I was, because he wasn't breathing at all. But he was *here*, somewhere. All I had to do was find him.

I didn't want to duplicate the efforts of the police, although "efforts" was usually too generous a term to apply to the work of the local constabulary; "cursory attempts" probably was closer to the truth, if I knew Mac.

New Klondike had twelve radial roadways, cutting across the nine concentric rings of buildings under the dome. My office was at dome's edge; I could have taken a hovertram into the center, but I preferred to walk. A good detective knew what was happening on the streets, and the hovertrams, dilapidated though they were, sped by too fast for that.

I didn't make any bones about staring at the transfers I saw along the way. They ranged in style from really sophisticated models, like Cassandra

Wilkins, to things only a step up from the tin woodman of Oz. Of course, those who'd contented themselves with second-rate synthetic forms doubtless believed they'd trade up when they eventually happened upon some decent specimens. Poor saps; no one had found truly spectacular remains for mears, and lots of people were giving up and going back to Earth, if they could afford the passage, or were settling in to lives of, as Thoreau would have it, quiet desperation, their dreams as dead as the fossils they'd never found.

I continued walking easily along; Mars gravity is about a third of Earth's. Some people were stuck here because they'd let their muscles atrophy; they'd never be able to hack a full gee again. Me, I was stuck here for other reasons, but I worked out more than most—Gully's Gym, over by the shipyards—and so still had reasonably strong legs; I could walk comfortably all day if I had to.

The cop shop was a five-story building—it could be that tall, this near the center of the dome—with walls that had once been white, but were now a grimy grayish pink. The front doors were clear alloquartz, same as the overhead dome, and they slid aside as I walked up to them. At the side of the lobby was a long red desk—as if we don't see enough red on Mars—with a map showing the Isidis Planitia basin; New Klondike was a big circle off to one side.

The desk sergeant was a flabby lowbrow named Huxley, whose uniform always seemed a size too small for him. "Hey, Hux," I said, walking over. "Is Mac in?"

Huxley consulted a monitor, then nodded. "Yeah, he's in, but he don't see just anyone."

"I'm not just anyone, Hux. I'm the guy who picks up the pieces after you clowns bungle things."

Huxley frowned, trying to think of a rejoinder. "Yeah, well . . ." he said, at last.

"Oooh," I said. "Good one, Hux! Way to put me in my place."

He narrowed his eyes. "You ain't as funny as you think you are, Lomax," he said.

"Of course I'm not," I said. "Nobody could be *that* funny." I nodded at the secured inner door. "Going to buzz me through?"

"Only to be rid of you," said Huxley. So pleased was he with the wit of this remark that he repeated it: "Only to be rid of you."

Huxley reached below the counter, and the inner door—an unmarked black panel—slid aside. I pantomimed tipping a nonexistent hat at Hux, and headed into the station proper. I then walked down the corridor to McCrae's office; the door was open, so I rapped my knuckles against the plastic jamb.

"Lomax!" he said, looking up. "Decided to turn yourself in?"

"Very funny, Mac," I said. "You and Hux should go on the road together."

He snorted. "What can I do for you, Alex?"

Mac was a skinny biological, with shaggy orange eyebrows shielding his blue eyes. "I'm looking for a guy named Joshua Wilkins."

Mac had a strong Scottish brogue—so strong, I figured it must be an affectation. "Ah, yes," he said. "Who's your client? The wife?"

I nodded.

"A bonnie lass," he said.

"That she is," I said. "Anyway, you tried to find her husband, this Wilkins . . ."

"We looked around, yeah," said Mac. "He's a transfer, you knew that?"

I nodded.

"Well," Mac said, "she gave us the plans for his new face—precise measurements, and all that. We've been feeding all the video made by public security cameras through facial-recognition software. So far, no luck."

I smiled. That's about as far as Mac's detective work normally went: things he could do without hauling his bony ass out from behind his desk. "How much of New Klondike do they cover now?" I asked.

"It's down to sixty percent of the public areas," said Mac. People kept smashing the cameras, and the city didn't have the time or money to replace them.

"You'll let me know if you find anything?"

Mac drew his shaggy eyebrows together. "You know the privacy laws, Alex. I can't divulge what the security cameras see."

I reached into my pocket, pulled out a fifty-solar coin, and flipped it. It went up rapidly, but came down in what still seemed like slow motion to me, even after all these years on Mars; Mac didn't require any special reflexes to catch it in midair. "Of course," he said, "I suppose we could make an exception . . ."

"Thanks. You're a credit to law-enforcement officials everywhere."

He snorted again, then: "Say, what kind of heat you packing these days? You still carrying that old Smith & Wesson?"

"I've got a license," I said, narrowing my eyes.

"Oh, I know, I know. But be careful, eh? The times, they are a-changin'. Bullets aren't much use against a transfer, and getting to be more of those each day."

I nodded. "So I've heard. How do you guys handle them?"

"Until recently, as little as possible," said Mac. "Turning a blind eye, and all that."

"Saves getting up," I said.

Mac didn't take offense. "Exactly. But let me show you something." We left his office, went further down the corridor and entered another room. He pointed to a device on the table. "Just arrived from Earth," he said. "The latest thing."

It was a wide, flat disk, maybe half a meter in diameter, and five centimeters thick. There were a pair of U-shaped handgrips attached to the edge, opposite each other. "What is it?" I asked.

"A broadband disrupter," he said. He picked it up and held it in front of himself, like a gladiator's shield. "It discharges an oscillating multifrequency electromagnetic pulse. From a distance of four meters or less, it will completely fry the artificial brain of a transfer—killing it as effectively as a bullet kills a human."

"I don't plan on killing anyone," I said.

"That's what you said the last time."

Ouch. Still, maybe he had a point. "I don't suppose you have a spare one I can borrow?"

Mac laughed. "Are you kidding? This is the only one we've got so far."

"Well, then," I said, heading for the door, "I guess I'd better be careful."

My next stop was the NewYou building. I took Third Avenue, one of the radial streets of the city, out the five blocks to it. The building was two stories tall and was made, like most structures here, of red laser-fused Martian sand bricks. Flanking the main doors were a pair of wide alloquartz display windows, showing dusty artificial bodies dressed in fashions from about two mears ago; it was high time somebody updated things.

Inside, the store was part showroom and part workshop, with spare parts scattered about: here, a white-skinned artificial hand; there, a black lower leg; on shelves, synthetic eyes and spools of colored monofilament that I guessed were used to simulate hair. There were also all sorts of internal parts on worktables: motors and hydraulic pumps and joint hinges. A half-dozen technicians were milling around, assembling new bodies or repairing old ones.

Across the room, I spotted Cassandra Wilkins, wearing a beige suit today. She was talking with a man and a woman, who were biological; potential customers, presumably. "Hello, Cassandra," I said, after I'd closed the distance between us.

"Mr. Lomax!" she said, excusing herself from the couple. "I'm so glad you're here—so very glad! What news do you have?"

"Not much," I said. "I've been to visit the cops, and I thought I should start my investigation here. After all, your husband owned this franchise, right?"

Cassandra nodded enthusiastically. "I knew I was doing the right thing hiring you," she said. "I just knew it! Why, do you know that lazy detective McCrae never stopped by here—not even once!"

I smiled. "Mac's not the outdoorsy type," I said. "And, well, you get what you pay for."

"Isn't that the truth?" said Cassandra. "Isn't that just the God's honest truth!"

"You said your husband moved his mind recently?"

She nodded her head. "Yes. All of that goes on upstairs, though. This is just sales and service down here."

"Can you show me?" I asked.

She nodded again. "Of course—anything you want to see, Mr. Lomax!" What I wanted to see was under that beige suit—nothing beat the perfection of a transfer's body—but I kept that thought to myself. Cassandra looked around the room, then motioned for another staff member—also female, also a transfer, also gorgeous, and this one did wear tasteful makeup and jewelry—to come over. "I'm sorry," Cassandra said to the two customers she'd abandoned a few moments ago. "Miss Takahashi here will look after you." She then turned to me. "This way."

We went through a curtained doorway and up a set of stairs. "Here's our scanning room," said Cassandra, indicating the left-hand one of a pair of doors; both doors had little windows in them. She stood on tiptoe to look in the scanning-room window, and nodded, apparently satisfied by what she saw, then opened the door. Two people were inside: a balding man of about forty, who was seated, and a standing woman who looked twenty-five; the woman was a transfer herself, though, so there was no way of knowing her real age. "So sorry to interrupt," Cassandra said. She looked at the man in the chair, while gesturing at me. "This is Alexander Lomax. He's providing some, ah, consulting services for us."

The man looked at me, surprised, then said, "Klaus Hansen," by way of introduction.

"Would you mind ever so much if Mr. Lomax watched while the scan was being done?" asked Cassandra.

Hansen considered this for a moment, frowning his long, thin face. But then he nodded. "Sure. Why not?"

"Thanks," I said. "I'll just stand over here." I moved to the far wall and leaned back against it.

The chair Hansen was sitting in looked a lot like a barber's chair. The female transfer who wasn't Cassandra reached up above the chair and pulled down a translucent hemisphere that was attached by an articulated arm to the ceiling. She kept lowering it until all of Hansen's head was covered, and then she turned to a control console.

The hemisphere shimmered slightly, as though a film of oil was washing over its surface; the scanning field, I supposed.

Cassandra was standing next to me, arms crossed in front of her chest. It was an unnatural-looking pose, given her large bosom. "How long does the scanning take?" I asked.

"It's a quantum-mechanical process," she replied. "So the scanning is rapid. But it'll take about ten minutes to move the data into the artificial brain. And then . . ."

"And then?" I said.

She lifted her shoulders, as if the rest didn't need to be spelled out. "Why, and then Mr. Hansen will be able to live forever."

"Ah," I said.

"Come along," said Cassandra. "Let's go see the other side." We left that room, closing its door behind us, and entered the one next door. This room was a mirror image of the previous one, which I guess was appropriate. Standing erect in the middle of the room, supported by a metal armature, was Hansen's new body, dressed in a fashionable blue suit; its eyes were closed. Also in the room was a male NewYou technician, who was biological.

I walked around, looking at the artificial body from all angles. The replacement Hansen still had a bald spot, although its diameter had been reduced by half. And, interestingly, Hansen had opted for a sort of permanent designer-stubble look; the biological him was clean-shaven at the moment.

Suddenly the simulacrum's eyes opened. "Wow," said a voice that was the same as the one I'd heard from the man next door. "That's incredible."

"How do you feel, Mr. Hansen?" asked the male technician.

"Fine," he said. "Just fine."

"Good," the technician said. "There'll be some settling-in adjustments, of course. Let's just check to make sure all your parts are working . . ."

"And there it is," said Cassandra, to me. "Simple as that." She led me out of the room, back into the corridor.

"Fascinating," I said. I pointed at the left-hand door. "When do you take care of the original?"

"That's already been done. We do it in the chair."

I stared at the closed door, and I like to think I suppressed my shudder enough so that Cassandra was unaware of it. "All right," I said. "I guess I've seen enough."

Cassandra looked disappointed. "Are you sure you don't want to look around some more?"

"Why?" I said. "Is there anything else worth seeing?"

"Oh, I don't know," said Cassandra. "It's a big place. Everything on this floor, everything downstairs . . . everything in the basement."

I blinked. "You've got a basement?" Almost no Martian buildings had basements; the permafrost layer was very hard to dig through.

"Yes," she said. "Oh, yes." She paused, then looked away. "Of course, no one ever goes down there; it's just storage."

"I'll have a look," I said.

And that's where I found him.

He was lying behind some large storage crates, face down, a sticky pool of machine oil surrounding his head. Next to him was a fusion-powered jackhammer, the kind many of the fossil hunters had for removing surface rocks. And next to the jackhammer was a piece of good old-fashioned paper. On it, in block letters, was written, "I'm so sorry, Cassie. It's just not the same."

It's hard to commit suicide, I guess, when you're a transfer. Slitting your wrists does nothing significant. Poison doesn't work, and neither does drowning.

But Joshua-never-anything-else-at-all-anymore Wilkins had apparently found a way. From the looks of it, he'd leaned back against the rough cement wall, and, with his strong artificial arms, had held up the jackhammer, placing its bit against the center of his forehead. And then he'd held down on the jackhammer's twin triggers, letting the unit run until it had managed to pierce through his titanium skull and scramble the soft material of his artificial brain. When his brain died, his thumbs let up on the triggers, and he dropped the jackhammer, then tumbled over himself. His head had twisted sideways when it hit the concrete floor. Everything below his eyebrows was intact; it was clearly the same face Cassandra Wilkins had shown me.

I headed up the stairs and found Cassandra, who was chatting in her animated style with another customer.

"Cassandra," I said, pulling her aside. "Cassandra, I'm very sorry, but . . ."

She looked at me, her green eyes wide. "What?"

"I've found your husband. And he's dead."

She opened her pretty mouth, closed it, then opened it again. She looked like she might fall over, even with gyroscopes stabilizing her. I put an arm around her shoulders, but she didn't seem comfortable with it, so I let her go. "My . . . God," she said at last. "Are you . . . are you positive?"

"Sure looks like him," I said.

"My God," she said again. "What . . . what happened?"

No nice way to say it. "Looks like he killed himself."

A couple of Cassandra's coworkers had come over, wondering what all the commotion was about. "What's wrong?" asked one of them— the same Miss Takahashi I'd seen earlier.

"Oh, Reiko," said Cassandra. "Joshua is dead!"

Customers were noticing what was going on, too. A burly flesh-and-blood man, with arms as thick around as most men's legs, came across the room; he seemed to be the boss here. Reiko Takahashi had already drawn Cassandra into her arms—or vice-versa; I'd been looking away when it had happened—and was stroking Cassandra's artificial hair. I let the boss do what he could to calm the crowd, while I used my comm-link to call Mac and inform him of Joshua Wilkins's suicide.

Detective Dougal McCrae of New Klondike's finest arrived about twenty minutes later, accompanied by two uniforms. "How's it look, Alex?" Mac asked.

"Not as messy as some of the biological suicides I've seen," I said. "But it's still not a pretty sight."

"Show me."

I led Mac downstairs. He read the note without picking it up.

The burly man soon came down, too, followed by Cassandra Wilkins, who was holding her artificial hand to her artificial mouth.

"Hello, again, Mrs. Wilkins," said Mac, moving to interpose his body between her and the prone form on the floor. "I'm terribly sorry, but I'll need you to make an official identification."

I lifted my eyebrows at the irony of requiring the next of kin to actually look at the body to be sure of who it was, but that's what we'd gone back to with transfers. Privacy laws prevented any sort of ID chip or tracking device being put into artificial bodies. In fact, that was one of the many incentives to transfer; you no longer left fingerprints or a trail of identifying DNA everywhere you went.

Cassandra nodded bravely; she was willing to accede to Mac's request. He stepped aside, a living curtain, revealing the artificial body with the gaping head wound. She looked down at it. I'd expected her to quickly avert her eyes, but she didn't; she just kept staring.

Finally, Mac said, very gently, "Is that your husband, Mrs. Wilkins?"

She nodded slowly. Her voice was soft. "Yes. Oh, my poor, poor Joshua . . ."

Mac stepped over to talk to the two uniforms, and I joined them. "What do you do with a dead transfer?" I asked. "Seems pointless to call in the medical examiner."

By way of answer, Mac motioned to the burly man. The man touched his own chest and raised his eyebrows in the classic, "Who, me?" expression. Mac nodded again. The man looked left and right, like he was crossing some imaginary road, and then came over. "Yeah?"

"You seem to be the senior employee here," said Mac. "Am I right?"

The man nodded. "Horatio Fernandez. Joshua was the boss, but, yeah, I guess I'm in charge until head office sends somebody new out from Earth."

"Well," said Mac, "you're probably better equipped than we are to figure out the exact cause of death."

Fernandez gestured theatrically at the synthetic corpse, as if it were—well not *bleedingly* obvious, but certainly apparent.

Mac nodded. "It's just a bit too pat," he said, his voice lowered conspiratorially. "Implement at hand, suicide note." He lifted his shaggy orange eyebrows. "I just want to be sure."

Cassandra had drifted over without Mac noticing, although of course I had. She was listening in.

"Yeah," said Fernandez. "Sure. We can disassemble him, check for anything else that might be amiss."

"No," said Cassandra. "You can't."

"I'm afraid it's necessary," said Mac, looking at her. His Scottish brogue always put an edge on his words, but I knew he was trying to sound gentle.

"No," said Cassandra, her voice quavering. "I forbid it."

Mac's voice got a little firmer. "You can't. I'm legally required to order an autopsy in every suspicious case."

Cassandra wheeled on Fernandez. "Horatio, I order you not to do this."

Fernandez blinked a few times. "Order?"

Cassandra opened her mouth to say something more, then apparently thought better of it. Horatio moved closer to her, and put a hulking arm around her small shoulders. "Don't worry," he said. "We'll be gentle." And then his face brightened a bit. "In fact, we'll see what parts we can salvage—give them to somebody else; somebody who couldn't afford such good stuff if it was new." He smiled beatifically. "It's what Joshua would have wanted."

The next day, I was siting in my office, looking out the small window. The dust storm had ended. Out on the surface, rocks were strewn everywhere, like toys on a kid's bedroom floor. My wrist commlink buzzed, and I looked at it in anticipation, hoping for a new case; I could use the solars. But the ID line said NKPD. I told the device to accept the call, and a little picture of Mac's red-headed face appeared on my wrist. "Hey, Lomax," he said. "Come on by the station, would you?"

"What's up?"

The micro-Mac frowned. "Nothing I want to say over open airwaves."

I nodded. Now that the Wilkins case was over, I didn't have anything better to do anyway. I'd only managed about seven billable hours, damnitall, and even that had taken some padding.

I walked into the center along Ninth Avenue, entered the lobby of the police station, traded quips with the ineluctable Huxley, and was admitted to the back.

"Hey, Mac," I said. "What's up?"

" 'Morning, Alex," Mac said, rolling the R in "Morning." "Come in; sit down." He spoke to his desk terminal, and turned its monitor around so I could see it. "Have a look at this."

I glanced at the screen. "The report on Joshua Wilkins?" I said.

Mac nodded. "Look at the section on the artificial brain."

I skimmed the text, until I found that part. "Yeah?" I said, still not getting it.

"Do you know what 'baseline synaptic web' means?" Mac asked.

"No, I don't. And you didn't either, smart-ass, until someone told you."

Mac smiled a bit, conceding that. "Well, there were lots of bits of the artificial brain left behind. And that big guy at NewYou—Fernandez, remember?—he really got into this forensic stuff, and decided to run it through some kind of instrument they've got there. And you know what he found?"

"What?"

"The brain stuff—the raw material inside the artificial skull—was pristine. It had never been imprinted."

"You mean no scanned mind had ever been transferred into that brain?"

Mac folded his arms across his chest and leaned back in his chair. "Bingo."

I frowned. "But that's not possible. I mean, if there was no mind in that head, who wrote the suicide note?"

Mac lifted those shaggy eyebrows of his. "Who indeed?" he said. "And what happened to Joshua Wilkins's scanned consciousness?"

"Does anyone at NewYou but Fernandez know about this?" I asked.

Mac shook his head. "No, and he's agreed to keep his mouth shut while we continue to investigate. But I thought I'd clue you in, since apparently the case you were on isn't really closed—and, after all, if you don't make money now and again, you can't afford to bribe me for favors."

I nodded. "That's what I like about you, Mac. Always looking out for my best interests."

Perhaps I should have gone straight to see Cassandra Wilkins, and made sure that we both agreed that I was back on the clock, but I had some questions I wanted answered first. And I knew just who to turn to. Raoul Santos was the city's top computer expert. I'd met him during a previous case, and we'd recently struck up a small-f friendship—we both shared the same taste in bootleg Earth booze, and he wasn't above joining me at some of New Klondike's sleazier saloons to get it. I used my commlink to call him, and we arranged to meet at the Bent Chisel.

The Bent Chisel was a little hellhole off of Fourth Avenue, in the sixth concentric ring of buildings. I made sure I had my revolver, and that it was loaded, before I entered. The bartender was a surly man named Buttrick, a biological who had more than his fair share of flesh, and blood as cold as ice. He wore a sleeveless black shirt, and had a three-day growth of salt-and-pepper beard. "Lomax," he said, acknowledging my entrance. "No broken furniture this time, right?"

I held up three fingers. "Scout's honor."

Buttrick held up one finger.

"Hey," I said. "Is that any way to treat one of your best customers?"

"My best customers," said Buttrick, polishing a glass with a ratty towel, "pay their tabs."

"Yeah," I said, stealing a page from Sgt. Huxley's *Guide to Witty Repartee.* "Well." I headed on in, making my way to the back of the bar, where my favorite booth was located. The waitresses here were topless, and soon enough one came over to see me. I couldn't remember her name offhand, although we'd slept together a couple of times. I ordered a scotch on the rocks; they normally did that with carbon-dioxide ice here, which was much cheaper than water ice on Mars. A few minutes later, Raoul Santos arrived. "Hey," he said, taking a seat opposite me. "How's tricks?"

"Fine," I said. "She sends her love."

Raoul made a puzzled face, then smiled. "Ah, right. Cute. Listen, don't quit your day job."

"Hey," I said, placing a hand over my heart, "you wound me. Down deep, I'm a stand-up comic."

"Well," said Raoul, "I always say people should be true to their innermost selves, but . . ."

"Yeah?" I said. "What's your innermost self?"

"Me?" Raoul raised his eyebrows. "I'm pure genius, right to the very core."

I snorted, and the waitress reappeared. She gave me my glass. It was just a little less full than it should have been: either Buttrick was trying to curb his losses on me, or the waitress was miffed that I hadn't acknowledged our former intimacy. Raoul placed his order, talking directly into the woman's breasts. Boobs did well in Mars gravity; hers were still perky even though she had to be almost forty.

"So," said Raoul, looking over steepled fingers at me. "What's up?" His face consisted of a wide forehead, long nose, and receding chin; it made him look like he was leaning forward even when he wasn't.

I took a swig of my drink. "Tell me about this transferring game."

"Ah, yes," said Raoul. "Fascinating stuff. Thinking of doing it?"

"Maybe someday," I said.

"You know, it's supposed to pay for itself within three mears," he said, " 'cause you no longer have to pay life-support tax after you've transferred."

I was in arrears on that, and didn't like to think about what would happen if I fell much further behind. "That'd be a plus," I said. "What about you? You going to do it?"

"Sure. I want to live forever; who doesn't? 'Course, my dad won't like it."

"Your dad? What's he got against it?"

Raoul snorted. "He's a minister."

"In whose government?" I asked.

"No, no. A *minister*. Clergy."

"I didn't know there were any of those left, even on Earth," I said.

"He *is* on Earth, but, yeah, you're right. Poor old guy still believes in souls."

I raised my eyebrows. "Really?"

"Yup. And because he believes in souls, he has a hard time with this idea of transferring consciousness. He would say the new version isn't the same person."

I thought about what the supposed suicide note said. "Well, is it?"

Raoul rolled his eyes. "You, too? Of course it is! The mind is just software—and since the dawn of computing, software has been moved from one computing platform to another by copying it over, then erasing the original."

I frowned, but decided to let that go for the moment. "So, if you do transfer, what would you have fixed in your new body?"

Raoul spread his arms. "Hey, man, you don't tamper with perfection."

"Yeah," I said. "Sure. Still, how much could you change things? I mean, say you're a midget; could you choose to have a normal-sized body?"

"Sure, of course."

I frowned. "But wouldn't the copied mind have trouble with your new size?"

"Nah," said Raoul. The waitress returned. She bent over far enough while placing Raoul's drink on the table that her breast touched his bare forearm; she gave me a look that said, "See what you're missing, tiger?" When she was gone, Raoul continued. "See, when we first started copying consciousness, we let the old software from the old mind actually try to directly control the new body. It took months to learn how to walk again, and so on."

"Yeah, I read something about that, years ago," I said.

Raoul nodded. "Right. But now we don't let the copied mind do anything but give orders. The thoughts are intercepted by the new body's main computer. *That* unit runs the body. All the transferred mind has to do is *think* that it wants to pick up this glass, say." He acted out his example, and took a sip, then winced in response to the booze's kick. "The computer takes care of working out which pulleys to contract, how far to reach, and so on."

"So you could indeed order up a body radically different from your original?" I said.

"Absolutely," said Raoul. He looked at me through hooded eyes. "Which, in your case, is probably the route to go."

"Damn," I said.

"Hey, don't take it seriously," he said, taking another sip, and allowing himself another pleased wince. "Just a joke."

"I know," I said. "It's just that I was hoping it wasn't that way. See, this case I'm on: the guy I'm supposed to find owns the NewYou franchise here."

"Yeah?" said Raoul.

"Yeah, and I think he deliberately transferred his scanned mind into some body other than the one that he'd ordered up for himself."

"Why would he do that?"

"He faked the death of the body that looked like him—and, I think he'd planned to do that all along, because he never bothered to order up any improvements to his face. I think he wanted to get away, but make it look like he was dead, so no one would be looking for him anymore."

"And why would he do that?"

I frowned, then drank some more. "I'm not sure."

"Maybe he wanted to escape his spouse."

"Maybe—but she's a hot little number."

"Hmm," said Raoul. "Whose body do you think he took?"

"I don't know that, either. I was hoping the new body would have to be at least roughly similar to his old one; that would cut down on the possible suspects. But I guess that's not the case."

"It isn't, no."

I nodded, and looked down at my drink. The dry-ice cubes were sublimating into white vapor that filled the top part of the glass.

"Something else is bothering you," said Raoul. I lifted my head, and saw him taking a swig of his drink. A little bit of amber liquid spilled out of his mouth and formed a shiny bead on his recessed chin. "What is it?"

I shifted a bit. "I visited NewYou yesterday. You know what happens to your original body after they move your mind?"

"Sure," said Raoul. "Like I said, there's no such thing as moving software. You copy it, then delete the original. They euthanize the biological version, once the transfer is made, by frying the original brain."

I nodded. "And if the guy I'm looking for put his mind into the body intended for somebody else's mind, and that person's mind wasn't copied anywhere, then . . ." I took another swig of my drink. "Then it's murder, isn't it? Souls or no souls—it doesn't matter. If you shut down the one and only copy of someone's mind, you've murdered that person, right?"

"Oh, yes," said Raoul. "Deader than Mars itself is now."

I glanced down at the swirling fog in my glass. "So I'm not just looking for a husband who's skipped out on his wife," I said. "I'm looking for a cold-blooded killer."

I went by NewYou again. Cassandra wasn't in—but that didn't surprise me; she was a grieving widow now. But Horatio Fernandez—he of the massive arms—was on duty.

"I'd like a list of all the people who were transferred the same day as Joshua Wilkins," I said.

He frowned. "That's confidential information."

There were several potential customers milling about. I raised my voice so they could hear. "Interesting suicide note, wasn't it?"

Fernandez grabbed my arm and led me quickly to the side of the room. "What the hell are you doing?" he whispered angrily.

"Just sharing the news," I said, still speaking loudly, although not quite loud enough now, I thought, for the customers to hear. "People thinking of uploading should know that it's not the same—at least, that's what Joshua Wilkins said in that note."

Fernandez knew when he was beaten. The claim in the putative suicide note was exactly the opposite of NewYou's corporate position:

transferring was supposed to be flawless, conferring nothing but benefits. "All right, all right," he hissed. "I'll pull the list for you."

"Now that's service," I said. "They should name you employee of
the month."

He led me into the back room and spoke to a computer terminal. I
happened to overhear the passphrase for accessing the customer database; it was just six words—hardly any security at all.

Eleven people had moved their consciousnesses into artificial bodies
that day. I had him transfer the files on each of the eleven into my wrist
commlink. "Thanks," I said, doing that tip-of-the-nonexistent-hat
thing I do. Even when you've forced a man to do something, there's no
harm in being polite.

If I was right that Joshua Wilkins had appropriated the body of somebody else who had been scheduled to transfer the same day, it shouldn't
be too hard to figure out whose body he'd taken; all I had to do, I figured, was interview each of the eleven.

My first stop, purely because it happened to be the nearest, was the
home of a guy named Stuart Berling, a full-time fossil hunter. He must
have had some recent success, if he could afford to transfer.

Berling's home was part of a row of townhouses off Fifth Avenue, in
the fifth ring. I pushed his door buzzer, and waited impatiently for a response. At last he appeared. If I wasn't so famous for my poker face, I'd
have done a double take. The man who greeted me was a dead ringer
for Krikor Ajemian, the holovid star—the same gaunt features and intense eyes, the same mane of dark hair, the same tightly trimmed beard
and mustache. I guess not everyone wanted to keep even a semblance of
their original appearance.

"Hello," I said. "My name is Alexander Lomax. Are you Stuart
Berling?"

The artificial face in front of me surely was capable of smiling, but
choose not to. "Yes. What do you want?"

"I understand you only recently transferred your consciousness into
this body."

A nod. "So?"

"So, I work for the NewYou—the head office on Earth. I'm here to
check up on the quality of the work done by our franchise here on
Mars." Normally, this was a good technique. If Berling was who he said

he was, the question wouldn't faze him. But if he was really Joshua Wilkins, he'd know I was lying, and his expression might betray this. But transfers didn't have faces that were as malleable; if this person was startled or suspicious, nothing in his plastic features indicated it.

"So?" Berling said again.

"So I'm wondering if you were satisfied by the work done for you?"

"It cost a lot," said Berling.

I smiled. "Yes, it does. May I come in?"

He considered this for a few moments, then shrugged. "Sure, why not?" He stepped aside.

His living room was full of work tables, covered with reddish rocks from outside the dome. A giant lens on an articulated arm was attached to one of the work tables, and various geologist's tools were scattered about.

"Finding anything interesting?" I asked, gesturing at the rocks.

"If I was, I certainly wouldn't tell you," said Berling, looking at me sideways in the typical paranoid-prospector's way.

"Right," I said. "Of course. So, *are* you satisfied with the NewYou process?"

"Sure, yeah. It's everything they said it would be. All the parts work."

"Thanks for your help," I said, pulling out my PDA to make a few notes, and then frowning at its blank screen. "Oh, damn," I said. "The silly thing has a loose fusion pack. I've got to open it up and reseat it." I showed him the back of the unit's case. "Do you have a little screwdriver that will fit that?"

Everybody owned some screwdrivers, even though most people rarely needed them, and they were the sort of thing that had no standard storage location. Some people kept them in kitchen drawers, others kept them in tool chests, still others kept them under the bathroom sink. Only a person who had lived in this home for a while would know where they were.

Berling peered at the little slot-headed screw, then nodded. "Sure," he said. "Hang on."

He made an unerring beeline for the far side of the living room, going to a cabinet that had glass doors on its top half, but solid metal ones on its bottom. He bent over, opened one of the metal doors, reached in, rummaged for a bit, and emerged with the appropriate screwdriver.

"Thanks," I said, opening the case in such a way that he couldn't see inside. I then surreptitiously removed the little bit of plastic I'd used to insulate the fusion battery from the contact it was supposed to touch. Meanwhile, without looking up, I said, "Are you married, Mr. Berling?" Of course, I already knew the answer was yes; that fact was in his NewYou file.

He nodded.

"Is your wife home?"

His artificial eyelids closed a bit. "Why?"

I told him the honest truth, since it fit well with my cover story: "I'd like to ask her whether she can perceive any differences between the new you and the old."

Again, I watched his expression, but it didn't change. "Sure, I guess that'd be okay." He turned and called over his shoulder, "Lacie!"

A few moments later, a homely flesh-and-blood woman of about fifty appeared. "This person is from the head office of NewYou," said Berling, indicating me with a pointed finger. "He'd like to speak to you."

"About what?" asked Lacie. She had a deep, not-unpleasant voice.

"Might we speak in private?" I said.

Berling's gaze shifted from Lacie to me, then back to Lacie. "Hrmpph," he said, but then, a moment later, added, "I guess that'd be all right." He turned around and walked away.

I looked at Lacie. "I'm just doing a routine follow-up," I said. "Making sure people are happy with the work we do. Have you noticed any changes in your husband since he transferred?"

"Not really."

"Oh?" I said. "If there's anything at all . . ." I smiled reassuringly. "We want to make the process as perfect as possible. Has he said anything that's surprised you, say?"

Lacie crinkled her face. "How do you mean?"

"I mean, has he used any expressions or turns of phrase you're not used to hearing from him?"

A shake of the head. "No."

"Sometimes the process plays tricks with memory. Has he failed to know something he should know?"

"Not that I noticed," said Lacie.

"What about the reverse? Has he known anything that you wouldn't expect him to know?"

She lifted her eyebrows. "No. He's just Stuart."

I frowned. "No changes at all?"

"No, none . . . well, almost none."

I waited for her to go on, but she didn't, so I prodded her. "What is it? We really would like to know about any difference, any flaw in our transference process."

"Oh, it's not a flaw," said Lacie, not meeting my eyes.

"No? Then what?"

"It's just that . . ."

"Yes?"

"Well, just that he's a demon in the sack now. He stays hard forever."

I frowned, disappointed not to have found what I was looking for on the first try. But I decided to end the masquerade on a positive note. "We aim to please, ma'am. We aim to please."

I spent the next several hours interviewing four other people; none of them seemed to be anyone other than who they claimed to be.

Next on my list was Dr. Rory Pickover, whose home was an apartment in the innermost circle of buildings, beneath the highest point of the dome. He lived alone, so there was no spouse or child to question about any changes in him. That made me suspicious right off the bat: if one were going to choose an identity to appropriate, it ideally would be someone without close companions. He also refused to meet me at his home, meaning I couldn't try the screwdriver trick on him.

I thought we might meet at a coffee shop or a restaurant—there were lots in New Klondike, although none were doing good business these days. But he insisted we go outside the dome—out onto the Martian surface. That was easy for him; he was a transfer now. But it was a pain in the ass for me; I had to rent a surface suit.

We met at the south air lock just as the sun was going down. I suited up—surface suits came in three stretchy sizes; I took the largest. The fish-bowl helmet I rented was somewhat frosted on one side; sandstorm-scouring, no doubt. The air tanks, slung on my back, were good for about four hours. I felt heavy in the suit, even though in it I still weighed only about half of what I had back on Earth.

Rory Pickover was a paleontologist—an actual scientist, not a treasure-seeking fossil hunter. His pre-transfer appearance had been almost stereotypically academic: a round, soft face, with a fringe of graying hair. His new body was lean and muscular, and he had a full head of dark brown hair, but the face was still recognizably his. He was carrying a geologist's hammer, with a wide, flat blade; I rather suspected it would nicely smash my helmet. I had surreptitiously transferred the Smith & Wesson from the holster I wore under my jacket to an exterior pocket on the rented surface suit, just in case I needed it while we were outside.

We signed the security logs, and then let the technician cycle us through the air lock.

Off in the distance, I could see the highland plateau, dark streaks marking its side. Nearby, there were two large craters and a cluster of smaller ones. There were few footprints in the rusty sand; the recent storm had obliterated the thousands that had doubtless been there earlier. We walked out about five hundred meters. I turned around briefly to look back at the transparent dome and the buildings within.

"Sorry for dragging you out here," said Pickover. He had a cultured British accent. "I don't want any witnesses." Even the cheapest artificial body had built-in radio equipment, and I had a transceiver inside my helmet.

"Ah," I said, by way of reply. I slipped my gloved hand into the pocket containing the Smith & Wesson, and wrapped my fingers around its reassuring solidity.

"I know you aren't just in from Earth," said Pickover, continuing to walk. "And I know you don't work for NewYou."

We were casting long shadows; the sun, so much tinier than it appeared from Earth, was sitting on the horizon; the sky was already purpling, and Earth itself was visible, a bright blue-white evening star.

"Who do you think I am?" I asked.

His answer surprised me, although I didn't let it show. "You're Alexander Lomax, the private detective."

Well, it didn't seem to make any sense to deny it. "Yeah. How'd you know?"

"I've been checking you out over the last few days," said Pickover. "I'd been thinking of, ah, engaging your services."

We continued to walk along, little clouds of dust rising each time our feet touched the ground. "What for?" I said.

"You first, if you don't mind," said Pickover. "Why did you come to see me?"

He already knew who I was, and I had a very good idea who he was, so I decided to put my cards on the table. "I'm working for your wife."

Pickover's artificial face looked perplexed. "My . . . wife?"

"That's right."

"I don't have a wife."

"Sure you do. You're Joshua Wilkins, and your wife's name is Cassandra."

"What? No, I'm Rory Pickover. You know that. You called me."

"Come off it, Wilkins. The jig is up. You transferred your consciousness into the body intended for the real Rory Pickover, and then you took off."

"I—oh. Oh, Christ."

"So, you see, I know. Too bad, Wilkins. You'll hang—or whatever the hell they do with transfers—for murdering Pickover."

"No." He said it softly.

"Yes," I replied, and now I pulled out my revolver. It really wouldn't be much use against an artificial body, but until quite recently Wilkins had been biological; hopefully, he was still intimidated by guns. "Let's go."

"Where?"

"Back under the dome, to the police station. I'll have Cassandra meet us there, just to confirm your identity."

The sun had slipped below the horizon now. He spread his arms, a supplicant against the backdrop of the gathering night. "Okay, sure, if you like. Call up this Cassandra, by all means. Let her talk to me. She'll tell you after questioning me for two seconds that I'm not her husband. But—Christ, damn, Christ."

"What?"

"I want to find him, too."

"Who? Joshua Wilkins?"

He nodded, then, perhaps thinking I couldn't see his nod in the growing darkness, said, "Yes."

"Why?"

He tipped his head up, as if thinking. I followed his gaze. Phobos was visible, a dark form overhead. At last, he spoke again. "Because *I'm* the reason he's disappeared."

"What?" I said. "Why?"

"That's why I was thinking of hiring you myself. I didn't know where else to turn."

"Turn for what?"

Pickover looked at me. "I did go to NewYou, Mr. Lomax. I knew I was going to have an enormous amount of work to do out here on the surface now, and I wanted to be able to spend days—weeks!—in the field, without worrying about running out of air, or water, or food."

I frowned. "But you've been here on Mars for six mears; I read that in your file. What's changed?"

"*Everything,* Mr. Lomax." He looked off in the distance. "Everything!" But he didn't elaborate on that. Instead, he said. "I certainly know this Wilkins chap you're looking for; I went to his store, and had him transfer my consciousness from my old biological body into this one. But he also kept a copy of my mind—I'm sure of that."

I raised my eyebrows. "How do you know?"

"Because my computer accounts have been compromised. There's no way anyone but me can get in; I'm the only one who knows the passphrase. But someone *has* been inside, looking around; I use quantum encryption, so you can tell whenever someone has even *looked* at a file." He shook his head. "I don't know how he did it—there must be some technique I'm unaware of—but somehow Wilkins has been extracting information from the copy of my mind. That's the only way I can think of that anyone might have learned my passphrase."

"You think Wilkins did all this to access your bank accounts? Is there really enough money in them to make it worth starting a new life in somebody else's body? It's too dark to see your clothes right now, but, if I recall correctly, they looked a bit . . . shabby."

"You're right. I'm just a poor scientist. But there's something I know that could make the wrong people rich beyond their wildest dreams."

"And what's that?" I said.

He continued to walk along, trying to decide, I suppose, whether to trust me. I let him think about that, and at last, Dr. Rory Pickover, who was now just a starless silhouette against a starry sky, said, in a soft, quiet voice, "I know where it is."

"Where what is?"

"The alpha deposit."

"The what?"

"Sorry," he said. "Paleontologist's jargon. What I mean is, I've found it: I've found the mother lode. I've found the place where Weingarten and O'Reilly had been excavating. I've found the source of the best preserved, most-complete Martian fossils."

"My God," I said. "You'll be *rolling* in it."

Perhaps he shook his head; it was now too dark to tell. "No, sir," he said, in that cultured English voice. "No, I won't. I don't want to *sell* these fossils. I want to preserve them; I want to protect them from these plunderers, these . . . these *thieves*. I want to make sure they're collected properly, scientifically. I want to make sure they end up in the best museums, where they can be studied. There's so much to be learned, so much to discover!"

"Does Wilkins know now where this . . . what did you call it? This alpha deposit is?"

"No—at least, not from accessing my computer files. I didn't record the location anywhere but up here." Presumably he was tapping the side of his head.

"But you think Wilkins extracted the passphrase from a copy of your mind?"

"He must have."

"And now he's presumably trying to extract the location of the alpha deposit from that copy of your mind."

"Yes, yes! And if he succeeds, all will be lost! The best specimens will be sold off into private collections—trophies for some trillionaire's estate, hidden forever from science."

I shook my head. "But this doesn't make any sense. I mean, how would Wilkins even know that you had discovered the alpha deposit?"

Suddenly Pickover's voice was very small. "I'd gone in to NewYou—you have to go in weeks in advance of transferring, of course, so you can tell them what you want in a new body; it takes time to custom-build one to your specifications."

"Yes. So?"

"So, I wanted a body ideally suited to paleontological work on the surface of Mars; I wanted some special modifications—the kinds of things only the most successful prospectors could afford. Reinforced knees; extra arm strength for moving rocks; extended spectral response in the eyes, so that fossils will stand out better; night vision so that I could continue digging after dark; but . . ."

I nodded. "But you didn't have enough money."

"That's right. I could barely afford to transfer at all, even into the cheapest off-the-shelf body, and so . . ."

He trailed off, too angry at himself, I guess, to give voice to what was in his mind. "And so you hinted that you were about to come into some wealth," I said, "and suggested that maybe he could give you what you needed now, and you'd make it up to him later."

Pickover sounded sad. "That's the trouble with being a scientist; sharing information is our natural mode."

"Did you tell him precisely what you'd found?" I asked.

"No. No, but he must have guessed. I'm a paleontologist, I've been studying Weingarten and O'Reilly for years—all of that is a matter of public record. He must have figured out that I knew where their fossil beds are. After all, where else would a guy like me get money?" He sighed. "I'm an idiot, aren't I?"

"Well, Mensa isn't going to be calling you any time soon."

"Please don't rub it in, Mr. Lomax. I feel bad enough as it is, and—" His voice cracked; I'd never heard a transfer's do that before. "And now I've put all those lovely, lovely fossils in jeopardy! Will you help me, Mr. Lomax? Please say you'll help me!"

I nodded. "All right. I'm on the case."

We went back into the dome, and I called Raoul Santos on my comm-link, getting him to meet me at Rory Pickover's little apartment at the center of town. It was four floors up, and consisted of three small rooms—an interior unit, with no windows.

When Raoul arrived, I made introductions. "Raoul Santos, this is Rory Pickover. Raoul here is the best computer expert we've got in New Klondike. And Dr. Pickover is a paleontologist."

Raoul tipped his broad forehead at Pickover. "Good to meet you."

"Thank you," said Pickover. "Forgive the mess, Mr. Santos. I live alone. A lifelong bachelor gets into bad habits, I'm afraid." He'd already cleared debris off of one chair for me; he now busied himself doing the same with another chair, this one right in front of his home computer.

"What's up, Alex?" asked Raoul, indicating Pickover with a movement of his head. "New client?"

"Yeah," I said. "Dr. Pickover's computer files have been looked at by some unauthorized individual. We're wondering if you could tell us from where the access attempt was made."

"You'll owe me a nice round of drinks at the Bent Chisel," said Raoul.

"No problem," I said. "I'll put it on my tab."

Raoul smiled, and stretched his arms out, fingers interlocked, until his knuckles cracked. Then he took the now-clean seat in front of Pickover's computer and began to type. "How do you lock your files?" he asked, without taking his eyes off the monitor.

"A verbal passphrase," said Pickover.

"Anybody besides you know it?"

Pickover shook his artificial head. "No."

"And it's not written down anywhere?"

"No, well . . . not as such."

Raoul turned his head, looking up at Pickover. "What do you mean?"

"It's a line from a book. If I ever forgot the exact wording, I could always look it up."

Raoul shook his head in disgust. "You should always use random passphrases." He typed keys.

"Oh, I'm sure it's totally secure," said Pickover. "No one would guess—"

Raoul interrupted. "Your passphrase being, 'Those privileged to be present . . .'"

I saw Pickover's jaw drop. "My God. How did you know that?"

Raoul pointed to some data on the screen. "It's the first thing that was inputted by the only outside access your system has had in weeks."

"I thought passphrases were hidden from view when entered," said Pickover.

"Sure they are," said Raoul. "But the comm program has a buffer; it's in there. Look."

Raoul shifted in the chair so that Pickover could see the screen clearly over his shoulder. "That's . . . well, that's very strange," said Pickover.

"What?"

"Well, sure that's my passphrase, but it's not quite right."

I loomed in to have a peek at the screen, too. "How do you mean?" I said.

"Well," said Pickover, "see, my passphrase is 'Those privileged to be present at a family festival of the Forsytes'—it's from the opening of *The Man of Property*, the first book of *The Forsyte Saga* by John Galsworthy. I love that phrase because of the alliteration—'privilege to be present,' 'family festival of the Forsytes.' Makes it easy to remember."

Raoul shook his head in you-can't-teach-people-anything disgust. Pickover went on. "But, see, whoever it was typed in even more."

I looked at the glowing string of letters. In full it said: *Those privileged to be present at a family festival of the Forsytes have seen them dine at half past eight, enjoying seven courses.*

"It's too much?" I said.

"That's right," said Pickover, nodding. "My passphrase ends with the word 'Forsytes.'"

Raoul was stroking his receding chin. "Doesn't matter," he said.

"The files would unlock the moment the phrase was complete; the rest would just be discarded—systems that principally work with spoken commands don't require you to press the enter key."

"Yes, yes, yes," said Pickover. "But the rest of it isn't what Galsworthy wrote. It's not even close. *The Man of Property* is my favorite book; I know it well. The full opening line is 'Those privileged to be present at a family festival of the Forsytes have seen that charming and instructive sight—an upper middle-class family in full plumage.'" Nothing about the time they ate, or how many courses they had."

Raoul pointed at the text on screen, as if it had to be the correct version. "Are you sure?" he said.

"Of course!" said Pickover. "Galsworthy's public domain; you can do a search online and see for yourself."

I frowned. "No one but you knows your passphrase, right?"

Pickover nodded vigorously. "I live alone, and I don't have many friends; I'm a quiet sort. There's no one I've ever told, and no one who could have ever overheard me saying it, or seen me typing it in."

"Somebody found it out," said Raoul.

Pickover looked at me, then down at Raoul. "I think . . ." he said, beginning slowly, giving me a chance to stop him, I guess, before he said too much. But I let him go on. "I think that the information was extracted from a scan of my mind made by NewYou."

Raoul crossed his arms in front of his chest. "Impossible."

"What?" said Pickover, and "Why?" said I.

"Can't be done," said Raoul. "We know how to copy the vast array of interconnections that make up a human mind, and we know how to reinstantiate those connections in an artificial substrate. But we don't know how to decode them; nobody does. There's simply no way to sift through a digital copy of a mind and extract specific data."

Damn! If Raoul was right—and he always was in computing matters—then all this business with Pickover was a red herring. There probably was no bootleg scan of his mind; despite his protestations of being careful, someone likely had just overheard his passphrase, and decided to go spelunking through his files. While I was wasting time on this, Joshua Wilkins was doubtless slipping further out of my grasp.

Still, it was worth continuing this line of investigation for a few minutes more. "Any sign of where the access attempt was made?" I asked Raoul.

He shook his head. "No. Whoever did it knew what they were doing; they covered their tracks well. The attempt came over an outside line—that's all I can tell for sure."

I nodded. "Okay. Thanks, Raoul. Appreciate your help."

Raoul got up. "My pleasure. Now, how 'bout that drink."

I opened my mouth to say yes, but then it hit me—what Wilkins must be doing. "Umm, later, okay? I've—I've got some more things to take care of here."

Raoul frowned; he'd clearly hoped to collect his booze immediately. But I started maneuvering him toward the door. "Thanks for your help, Raoul. I really appreciate it."

"Um, sure, Alex," he said. He was obviously aware he was being given the bum's rush, but he wasn't fighting it too much. "Anytime."

"Yes, thank you awfully, Mr. Santos," said Pickover.

"No problem. If—"

"See you later, Raoul," I said, opening the door for him. "Thanks so much." I tipped my nonexistent hat at him.

Raoul shrugged, clearly aware that something was up, but not motivated sufficiently to find out what. He went through the door, and I hit the button that caused it to slide shut behind him. As soon as it was closed, I put an arm around Pickover's shoulders, and propelled him back to the computer. I pointed at the line Raoul had highlighted on the screen, and read the ending of it aloud: " '. . . dine at half past eight, enjoying seven courses.' "

Pickover nodded. "Yes. So?"

"Numbers are often coded info," I said. " 'Half past eight; seven courses.' What's that mean to you?"

"To me?" said Pickover. "Nothing. I like to eat much earlier than that, and I never have more than one course."

"But it could be a message," I said.

"From who?"

There was no easy way to tell him this. "From you to you."

He drew his artificial eyebrows together in puzzlement. "What?"

"Look," I said, motioning for him to sit down in front of the computer, "Raoul is doubtless right. You can't sift a digital scan of a human mind for information."

"But that must be what Wilkins is doing."

I shook my head. "No," I said. "The only way to find out what's in a mind is to ask it interactively."

"But . . . but no one's asked me my passphrase."

"No one has asked *this* you. But Joshua Wilkins must have transferred the extra copy of your mind into a body, so that he could deal with it directly. And that extra copy must be the one that's revealed your codes to him."

"You mean . . . you mean there's another me? Another *conscious* me?"

"Looks that way."

"But . . . no, no. That's . . . why, that's *illegal*. Bootleg copies of human beings—my God, Lomax, it's obscene!"

"I'm going to go see if I can find him," I said.

"It," said Pickover, forcefully.

"What?"

"It. Not him. I'm the only 'him'—the only real Rory Pickover."

"So what do you want me to do when I find it?"

"Erase it, of course. Shut it down." He shuddered. "My God, Lomax, I feel so . . . so violated! A stolen copy of my mind! It's the ultimate invasion of privacy . . ."

"That may be," I said. "But the bootleg is trying to tell you something. He—it—gave Wilkins the passphrase, and then tacked some extra words onto it, in order to get a message to you."

"But I don't recognize those extra words," said Pickover, sounding exasperated.

"Do they *mean* anything to you? Do they suggest anything?"

Pickover reread what was on the screen. "I can't imagine what," he said, "unless . . . no, no, I'd never think up a code like that."

"You obviously just *did* think of it. What's the code?"

Pickover was quiet for a moment, as if deciding if the thought was worth giving voice. Then: "Well, New Klondike is circular in layout, right? And it consists of concentric rings of buildings. Half past eight—that would be between Eighth and Ninth Avenue, no? And seven courses—in the seventh circle out from the center? Maybe the damned bootleg is trying to draw our attention to a location, a specific place here in town."

"Between Eighth and Ninth, eh? That's a rough area. I go to a gym near there."

"The old shipyards," said Pickover. "Aren't they there?"

"Yeah." I started walking toward the door. "I'm going to investigate."

"I'll go with you," said Pickover.

I looked at him and shook my head. He would doubtless be more of a hindrance than a help. "It's too dangerous," I said. "I should go alone."

Pickover looked for a few moments like he was going to protest, but then he nodded. "All right. I hope you find Wilkins. But if you find another me . . ."

"Yes?" I said. "What would you like me to do?"

Pickover gazed at me with pleading eyes. "Erase it. Destroy it." He shuddered again. "I never want to see the damned thing."

I had to get some sleep—damn, but sometimes I do wish I were a transfer. I took the hovertram out to my apartment, and let myself have five hours—Mars hours, admittedly, which were slightly longer than Earth ones—and then headed out to the old shipyards. The sun was just coming up as I arrived there. The sky through the dome was pink in the east and purple in the west.

Some active maintenance and repair work was done on spaceships here, but most of these ships were no longer spaceworthy and had been abandoned. Any one of them would make a good hideout, I thought; spaceships were shielded against radiation, making it hard to scan through their hulls to see what was going on inside.

The shipyards were large fields holding vessels of various sizes and shapes. Most were streamlined—even Mars's tenuous atmosphere required that. Some were squatting on tail fins; some were lying on their bellies; some were supported by articulated legs. I tried every hatch I could see on these craft, but, so far, they all had their air locks sealed tightly shut.

Finally, I came to a monstrous abandoned spaceliner—a great hull, some three hundred meters long, fifty meters wide, and a dozen meters high. The name *Mayflower II* was still visible in chipped paint near the bow—which is the part I came across first—and the slogan "Mars or Bust!" was also visible.

I walked a little farther alongside the hull, looking for a hatch, until—

Yes! I finally understood what a fossil hunter felt like when he at last turned up a perfectly preserved rhizomorph. There was an outer airlock door here, and it was open. The other door, inside, was open, too. I stepped through the chamber, entering the ship proper. There were stands for holding space suits, but the suits themselves were long gone.

I walked over to the far end of the room, and found another door—one of those submarine-style ones with a locking wheel in the center. This one was closed, and I figured it would probably have been sealed shut at some point, but I tried to turn the wheel anyway, just to be sure, and damned if it didn't spin freely, disengaging the locking bolts. I pulled the door open, and stepped through it, into a corridor. The door was on spring-loaded hinges; as soon as I let go of it, it closed behind me, plunging me into darkness.

Of course, I'd brought a flashlight. I pulled it off my belt and thumbed it on.

The air was dry and had a faint odor of decay to it. I headed down the corridor, the pool of illumination from my flashlight going in front of me, and—

A squealing noise. I swung around, and the beam from my flashlight caught the source before it scurried away: a large brown rat, its eyes two tiny red coals in the light. People had been trying to get rid of the rats—and cockroaches and silverfish and other vermin that had somehow made it here from Earth—for mears.

I turned back around and headed deeper into the ship. The floor wasn't quite level: it dipped a bit to—to starboard, they'd call it, and I also felt that I was gaining elevation as I walked along. The ship's floor had no carpeting; it was just bare, smooth metal. Oily water pooled along the starboard side; a pipe must have ruptured at some point. Another rat scurried by up ahead; I wondered what they ate here, aboard the dead hulk of the ship.

I thought I should check in with Pickover—let him know where I was. I activated my commlink, but the display said it was unable to connect. Of course: the radiation shielding in the spaceship's hull kept signals from getting out.

It was getting awfully cold. I held my flashlight straight up in front of my face, and saw that my breath was now coming out in visible clouds. I paused and listened. There was a steady dripping sound: condensation, or another leak. I continued along, sweeping the flashlight beam left and right in good detective fashion as I did so.

There were doors at intervals along the corridor—the automatic sliding kind you usually find aboard spaceships. Most of these panels had been pried open, and I shone my flashlight into each of the revealed rooms. Some were tiny passenger quarters, some were storage, one was a medical facility—all the equipment had been removed, but the examining beds betrayed the room's function.

I checked yet another set of quarters, then came to a closed door, the first one I'd seen along this hallway.

I pushed the open button, but nothing happened; the ship's electrical system was dead. Of course, there was an emergency handle, recessed into the door's thickness. I could have used three hands just then: one to hold my flashlight, one to hold my revolver, and one to pull on the handle. I tucked the flashlight into my right armpit, held my gun with my right hand, and yanked on the recessed handle with my left.

The door hardly budged. I tried again, pulling harder—and almost popped my arm out of its socket. Could the door's tension control have been adjusted to require a transfer's strength to open it? Perhaps.

I tried another pull, and to my astonishment, light began to spill out from the room. I'd hoped to just yank the door open, taking advantage of the element of surprise, but the damned thing was only moving a small increment with each pull of the handle. If there was someone on the other side, and he or she had a gun, it was no doubt now leveled directly at the door.

I stopped for a second, shoved the flashlight into my pocket, and— damn, I hated having to do this—holstered my revolver so that I could free up my other hand to help me pull the door open. With both hands now gripping the recessed handle, I pulled with all my strength, letting out an audible grunt as I did so.

The light from within stung my eyes; they'd grown accustomed to the soft beam from the flashlight. Another pull, and the door panel had now slid far enough into the wall for me to slip into the room by turning sideways. I took out my gun, and let myself in.

A voice, harsh and mechanical, but no less pitiful for that: "*Please . . .*"

My eyes swung to the source of the sound. There was a worktable, with a black top, attached to the far wall. And strapped to that table—

Strapped to that table was a transfer's synthetic body. But this wasn't like the fancy, almost-perfect simulacrum that my client Cassandra inhabited. This was a crude, simple humanoid form, with a boxy torso and limbs made up of cylindrical metal segments. And the face—

The face was devoid of any sort of artificial skin. The eyes, blue in color and looking startlingly human, were wide, and the teeth looked like dentures loose in the head. The rest of the face was a mess of pulleys and fiber optics, of metal and plastic.

"*Please . . .*" said the voice again. I looked around the rest of the room. There was a fusion battery, about the size of a softball, with several cables snaking out of it, including some that led to portable lights. There was also a closet, with a simple door. I pulled it open—this one slid easily—to make sure no one else had hidden in there while I was coming in. An emaciated rat that had been trapped there at some point scooted out of the closet, and through the still partially open corridor door.

I turned my attention to the transfer. The body was clothed in simple denim pants and a T-shirt.

"Are you okay?" I said, looking at the skinless face.

The metal skull moved slightly left and right. The plastic lids for the glass eyeballs retracted, making the non-face into a caricature of imploring. "*Please . . .*," he said for a third time.

I looked at the metal restraints holding the artificial body in place: thin nylon bands, pulled taut, that were attached to the tabletop. I couldn't see any release mechanism. "Who are you?" I said.

I was half-prepared for the answer, of course. "Rory Pickover." But it didn't sound anything like the Rory Pickover I'd met: the cultured British accent was absent, and this synthesized voice was much higher pitched.

Still, I shouldn't take this sad thing's statement at face value—especially since it had hardly any face. "Prove it," I said. "Prove you're Rory Pickover."

The glass eyes looked away. Perhaps the transfer was thinking of how to satisfy my demand—or perhaps he was just avoiding my eyes. "My citizenship number is 48394432."

I shook my head. "No good," I said. "It's got to be something *only* Rory Pickover would know."

The eyes looked back at me, the plastic lids lowered, perhaps in suspicion. "It doesn't matter who I am," he said. "Just get me out of here."

That sounded reasonable on the surface of it, but if this *was* another Rory Pickover . . .

"Not until you prove your identity to me," I said. "Tell me where the alpha deposit is."

"Damn you," said the transfer. "The other way didn't work, so now you're trying this." The mechanical head looked away. "But this won't work, either."

"Tell me where the alpha deposit is," I said, "and I'll free you."

"I'd rather die," he said. And then, a moment later, he added wistfully, "Except . . ."

I finished the thought for him. "Except you can't."

He looked away again. It was hard to feel for something that looked so robotic; that's my excuse, and I'm sticking to it. "Tell me where O'Reilly and Weingarten were digging. Your secret is safe with me."

He said nothing. The gun in my hand was now aimed at the robotic head. "Tell me!" I said. "Tell me before——"

Off in the distance, out in the corridor: the squeal of a rat, and—

Footfalls.

The transfer heard them, too. Its eyes darted left and right in what looked like panic.

"Please," he said, lowering his volume. As soon as he started speaking, I put a vertical index finger to my lips, indicating that he should be quiet, but he continued: "Please, for the love of God, get me out of here. I can't take any more."

I made a beeline for the closet, stepping quickly in and pulling that door most of the way shut behind me. I positioned myself so that I could see—and, if necessary, shoot—through the gap. The footfalls were growing louder. The closet smelled of rat. I waited.

I heard a voice, richer, more human, than the supposed Pickover's. "What the—?"

And I saw a person—a transfer—slipping sideways into the room, just as I had earlier. I couldn't yet see the face from this angle, but it wasn't Joshua. The body was female, and I could see that she was a brunette. I took in air, held it, and—

And she turned, showing her face now. My heart pounded. The delicate features. The wide-spaced green eyes.

Cassandra Wilkins.

My client.

She'd been carrying a flashlight, which she set now on another, smaller table. "Who's been here, Rory?" Her voice was cold.

"No one," he said.

"The door was open."

"You left it that way. I was surprised, but . . ." He stopped, perhaps realizing to say any more would be a giveaway that he was lying.

She tilted her head slightly. Even with a transfer's strength, that door must be hard to close. Hopefully she'd find it plausible that she'd given the handle a final tug, and had only assumed that the door had closed completely when she'd last left. Of course, I immediately saw the flaw with that story: you might miss the door not clicking into place, but you wouldn't fail to notice that light was still spilling out into the corridor. But most people don't consider things in such detail; I'd hoped she'd buy Pickover's suggestion.

And, after a moment more's reflection, she seemed to do just that, nodding her head, apparently to herself, then moving closer to the table onto which the synthetic body was strapped. "We don't have to do this again," said Cassandra. "If you just tell me . . ."

She let the words hang in the air for a moment, but Pickover made no response. Her shoulders moved up and down a bit in a philosophical shrug. "It's your choice," she said. And then, to my astonishment, she hauled back her right arm and slapped Pickover hard across the robotic face, and—

And Pickover screamed.

It was a long, low, warbling sound, like sheet-metal being warped, a haunted sound, an inhuman sound.

"*Please* . . ." he hissed again, the same plaintive word he'd said to me, the word I, too, had ignored.

Cassandra slapped him again, and again he screamed. Now, I've been slapped by lots of women over the years: it stings, but I've never screamed. And surely an artificial body was made of sterner stuff than me.

Cassandra went for a third slap. Pickover's screams echoed in the dead hulk of the ship.

"Tell me," she said.

I couldn't see his face; her body was obscuring it. Maybe he shook his head. Maybe he just glared defiantly. But he said nothing.

She shrugged again; they'd obviously been down this road before. She moved to one side of the bed and stood by his right arm, which was pinned to his body by the nylon strap. "You really don't want me to do this," she said. "And I don't have to, if . . ." She let the uncompleted offer hang there for a few seconds, then: "Ah, well." She reached down with her beige, realistic-looking hand, and wrapped three of her fingers around his right index finger. And then she started bending it backward.

I could see Pickover's face now. Pulleys along his jawline were working; he was struggling to keep his mouth shut. His glass eyes were rolling up, back into his head, and his left leg was shaking in spasms. It was a bizarre display, and I alternated moment by moment between feeling sympathy for the being lying there, and feeling cool detachment because of the clearly artificial nature of the body.

Cassandra let go of Pickover's index finger, and, for a second, I thought she was showing some mercy. But then she grabbed it as well as the adjacent finger, and began bending them both back. This time, despite his best efforts, guttural, robotic sounds did escape from Pickover.

"Talk!" Cassandra said. *"Talk!"*

I'd recently learned—from Cassandra herself—that artificial bodies had to have pain sensors; otherwise, a robotic hand might end up resting on a heating element, or too much pressure might be put on a joint. But I hadn't expected such sensors to be so sensitive, and—

And then it hit me, just as another of Pickover's warbling screams was torn from him. Cassandra knew all about artificial bodies; she sold them, after all. If she wanted to adjust the mind-body interface of one so that pain would register particularly acutely, doubtless she could. I'd seen a lot of evil things in my time, but this was perhaps the worst. Scan a mind, put it in a body wired for hypersensitivity to pain, and torture it until it gave up its secrets. Then, of course, you just wipe the mind, and—

"You *will* crack eventually, you know," she said, almost conversationally, as she looked at Pickover's fleshless face. "Given that it's inevitable, you might as well just tell me what I want to know."

The elastic bands that served as some of Pickover's facial muscles contracted, his teeth parted, and his head moved forward slightly but rapidly. I thought for half a second that he was incongruously blowing her a kiss, but then I realized what he was really trying to do: spit at her. Of course, his dry mouth and plastic throat were incapable of generating moisture, but his mind—a human mind, a mind accustomed to a biological body—had summoned and focused all its hate into that most primal of gestures.

"Very well," said Cassandra. She gave his fingers one more nasty yank backwards, holding them at an excruciating angle. Pickover alternated screams and whimpers. Finally, she let his fingers go. "Let's try something different," she said. She leaned over him. With her left hand, she pried his right eyelid open, and then she jabbed her right thumb into that eye. The glass sphere depressed into the metal skull, and Pickover screamed again. The artificial eye was presumably much tougher than a natural one, but, then again, the thumb pressing into it was also tougher. I felt my own eyes watering in a sympathetic response.

Pickover's artificial spine arched up slightly, as he convulsed against the two restraining bands. From time to time, I got clear glimpses of Cassandra's face, and the perfectly symmetrical artificial smile of glee on it was almost sickening.

At last, she stopped grinding her thumb into his eye. "Had enough?" she said. "Because if you haven't . . ."

Pickover was indeed still wearing clothing; it was equally gauche to walk the streets nude whether you were biological or artificial. But now, Cassandra's hands moved to his waist. I watched as she undid his belt, unsnapped and unzipped his jeans, and then pulled the pants as far down his metallic thighs as they would go before she reached the restraining strap that held his legs to the table. Transfers had no need for underwear, and Pickover wasn't wearing any. His artificial penis and testicles now lay exposed. I felt my own scrotum tightening in dread.

And then Cassandra did the most astonishing thing. She'd had no compunctions about bending back his fingers with her bare hands. And she hadn't hesitated when it came to plunging her naked thumb into his eye. But now that she was going to hurt him down there, she seemed to want no direct contact. She started looking around the room; for a second, she was looking directly at the closet door. I scrunched back against the far wall, hoping she wouldn't see me. My heart was pounding.

Finally, she found what she was looking for: a wrench, sitting on the floor. She picked it up, raised the wrench above her head, and looked directly into Pickover's one good eye—the other had closed as soon as she'd removed her thumb, and had never reopened as far as I could tell. "I'm going to smash your ball bearings into iron filings, unless . . ."

He closed his other eye now, the plastic lid scrunching.

"Count of three," she said. "One."

"I can't," he said in that low volume that served as his whisper. "You'd ruin them, sell them off—"

"Two."

"Please! They belong to science! To all humanity!"

"Three!"

Her arm slammed down, a great arc slicing through the air, the silver wrench smashing into the plastic pouch that was Pickover's scrotum. He let out a scream greater than any I'd yet heard, so loud, indeed, that it hurt my ears despite the muffling of the partially closed closet door.

She hauled her arm up again, but waited for the scream to devolve into a series of whimpers. "One more chance," she said. "Count of three." His whole body was shaking. I felt nauseous.

"One."

He turned his head to the side, as if by looking away he could make the torture stop.

"Two."

A whimper escaped his artificial throat.

"Three!"

I found myself looking away, too, unable to watch as—

"All right!"

It was Pickover's voice, shrill and mechanical, shouting.

"All right!" he shouted again. I turned back to face the tableau: the human-looking woman with a wrench held up above her head, and the terrified mechanical-looking man strapped to the table. "All right," he repeated once more, softly now. "I'll tell you what you want to know."

"You'll tell me where the alpha deposit is?" asked Cassandra, lowering her arm.

"Yes," he said. "Yes."

"Where?

Pickover was quiet.

"Where?"

"God forgive me . . ." he said softly.

She began to raise her arm again. *"Where?"*

"Sixteen-point-four kilometers south-southwest of Nili Patera," he said. "The precise coordinates are . . ." and he spoke a string of numbers.

"You better be telling the truth," Cassandra said.

"I am." His voice was tiny. "To my infinite shame, I am."

Cassandra nodded. "Maybe. But I'll leave you tied up here until I'm sure."

"But I told you the truth! I told you everything you need to know."

"Sure you did," said Cassandra. "But I'll just confirm that."

I stepped out of the closet, my gun aimed directly at Cassandra's back. "Freeze," I said.

Cassandra spun around. "Lomax!"

"Mrs. Wilkins," I said, nodding. "I guess you don't need me to find your husband for you anymore, eh? Now that you've got the information he stole."

"What? No, no. I still want you to find Joshua. Of course I do!"

"So you can share the wealth with him?"

"Wealth?" She looked over at the hapless Pickover. "Oh. Well, yes, there's a lot of money at stake." She smiled. "So much so that I'd be happy to cut you in, Mr. Lomax—oh, you're a good man. I know you wouldn't hurt me!"

I shook my head. "You'd betray me the first chance you got."

"No, I wouldn't. I'll need protection; I understand that—what with all the money the fossils will bring. Having someone like you on my side only makes sense."

I looked over at Pickover and shook my head. "You tortured that man."

"That 'man,' as you call him, wouldn't have existed at all without me. And the real Pickover isn't inconvenienced in the slightest."

"But . . . *torture*," I said. "It's inhuman."

She jerked a contemptuous thumb at Pickover. "He's not human. Just some software running on some hardware."

"That's what you are, too."

"That's *part* of what I am," Cassandra said. "But I'm also *authorized*. He's bootleg—and bootlegs have no rights."

"I'm not going to argue philosophy with you."

"Fine. But remember who works for whom, Mr. Lomax. I'm the client—and I'm going to be on my way now."

I held my gun rock-steady. "No, you're not."

She looked at me. "An interesting situation," she said, her tone even. "I'm unarmed, and you've got a gun. Normally, that would put you in charge, wouldn't it? But your gun probably won't stop me. Shoot me in the head, and the bullet will just bounce off my metal skull. Shoot me in the chest, and at worst you might damage some components that I'll eventually have to get replaced—which I can, and at a discount, to boot.

"Meanwhile," she continued, "I have the strength of ten men; I could literally pull your limbs from their sockets, or crush your head between my hands, squeezing it until it pops like a melon and your brains, such as they are, squirt out. So, what's it going to be, Mr. Lomax? Are you going to let me walk out that door and be about my business? Or are you going to pull that trigger, and start something that's going to end with you dead?"

I was used to a gun in my hand giving me a sense of power, of security. But just then, the Smith & Wesson felt like a lead weight. She was right: shooting her with it was likely to be no more useful than just throwing it at her. Of course, there were crucial components in an artificial body's makeup; I just didn't happen to know what they were, and, anyway, they probably varied from model to model. If I could be sure to drop her with one shot, I'd do it. I'd killed before in self-defense, but . . .

But this wasn't self-defense. Not really. If I didn't start something, she was just going to walk out. Could I kill in cold . . . well, not cold *blood.* But she *was* right: she was a person, even if Pickover wasn't. She was the one and only legal instantiation of Cassandra Wilkins. The cops might be corrupt here, and they might be lazy. But even they wouldn't turn a blind eye on attempted murder. If I shot her, and somehow got away, they'd hunt me down. And if I didn't get away, she *would* be attacking me in self-defense.

"So," she said, at last. "What's it going to be?"

"You make a persuasive argument, Mrs. Wilkins," I said in the most reasonable tone I could muster under the circumstances.

And then, without changing my facial expression in the slightest, I pulled the trigger.

I wondered if a transfer's time sense ever slows down, or if it is always perfectly quartz-crystal timed. Certainly, time seemed to attenuate for me then. I swear I could actually see the bullet as it followed its trajectory from my gun, covering the three meters between the barrel and—

And not, of course, Cassandra's torso.

Nor her head.

She was right; I probably couldn't harm her that way.

No, instead, I'd aimed past her, at the table on which the *faux* Pickover was lying on his back. Specifically, I'd aimed at the place where the thick nylon band that crossed over his torso, pinning his arms, was anchored on the right-hand side—the point where it made a taut diagonal line between where it was attached to the side of the table and the top of Pickover's arm.

The bullet sliced through the band, cutting it in two. The long portion, freed of tension, flew up and over his torso like a snake that had just had forty thousand volts pumped through it.

Cassandra's eyes went wide in astonishment that I'd missed her, and her head swung around. The report of the bullet was still ringing in my ears, of course, but I swear I could also hear the *zzzzinnnng!* of the restraining band snapping free. To be hypersensitive to pain, I figured you'd have to have decent reaction times, and I hoped that Pickover had been smart enough to note in advance my slight deviation of aim before I fired it.

And, indeed, no sooner were his arms free than he sat bolt upright—his legs were still restrained—and grabbed one of Cassandra's arms, pulling her toward him. I leapt in the meager Martian gravity. Most of Cassandra's body was made of lightweight composites and synthetic materials, but I was still good old flesh and blood: I outmassed her by at least fifty kilos. My impact propelled her backwards, and she slammed against the table's side. Pickover shot out his other arm, grabbing Cassandra's second arm, pinning her backside against the edge of the table. I struggled to regain a sure footing, then brought my gun up to her right temple.

"All right, sweetheart," I said. "Do you really want to test how strong your artificial skull is?"

Cassandra's mouth was open; had she still been biological, she'd probably have been gasping for breath. But her heartless chest was perfectly still. "You can't just shoot me," she said.

"Why not? Pickover here will doubtless back me up when I say it was self-defense, won't you, Pickover?"

He nodded. "Absolutely."

"In fact," I said, "you, me, this Pickover, and the other Pickover are the only ones who know where the alpha deposit is. I think the three of us would be better off without you on the scene anymore."

"You won't get away with it," said Cassandra. "You can't."

"I've gotten away with plenty over the years," I said. "I don't see an end to that in sight." I cocked the hammer, just for fun.

"Look," she said, "there's no need for this. We can all share in the wealth. There's plenty to go around."

"Except you don't have any rightful claim to it," said Pickover. "You stole a copy of my mind, and tortured me. And you want to be rewarded for that?"

"Pickover's right," I said. "It's his treasure, not yours."

"It's *humanity's* treasure," corrected Pickover. "It belongs to all mankind."

"But I'm your client," Cassandra said to me.

"So's he. At least, the legal version of him is."

Cassandra sounded desperate. "But—but that's a conflict of interest!"

"So sue me," I said.

She shook her head in disgust. "You're just in this for yourself!"

I shrugged amiably, and then pressed the barrel even tighter against her artificial head. "Aren't we all?"

"Shoot her," said Pickover. I looked at him. He was still holding her upper arms, pressing them in close to her torso. If he'd been biological, the twisting of his torso to accommodate doing that probably would have been quite uncomfortable. Actually, now that I thought of it, given his heightened sensitivity to pain, even this artificial version was probably hurting from twisting that way. But apparently this was a pain he was happy to endure.

"Do you really want me to do that?" I said. "I mean, I can understand, after what she did to you, but . . ." I didn't finish the thought; I just left it in the air for him to take or leave.

"She *tortured* me," he said. "She deserves to die."

I frowned, unable to dispute his logic—but, at the same time, wondering if Pickover knew that he was as much on trial here as she was.

"Can't say I blame you," I said again, and then added another "but," and once more left the thought incomplete.

At last, Pickover nodded. "But maybe you're right. I can't offer her any compassion, but I don't need to see her dead."

A look of plastic relief rippled over Cassandra's face. I nodded. "Good man," I said. I'd killed before, but I never enjoyed it.

"But, still," said Pickover, "I would like *some* revenge."

Cassandra's upper arms were still pinned by Pickover, but her lower arms were free. To my astonishment, they both moved. The movement startled me, and I looked down, just in time to see them jerking toward her groin, almost as if to protect . . .

I found myself staggering backward; it took a second for me to regain my balance. "*Oh, my God . . .*"

Cassandra had quickly moved her arms back to a neutral, hanging-down position—but it was too late. The damage had been done.

"You . . ." I said. I normally was never at a loss for words, but I was just then. "You're . . ."

Pickover had seen it, too; his torso had been twisted just enough to allow him to do so.

"No woman . . ." he began slowly.

Cassandra hadn't wanted to touch Pickover's groin—even though it was artificial—with her bare hands. And when Pickover had suggested exacting revenge for what had been done to him, Cassandra's hands had moved instinctively to protect—

Jesus, why hadn't I seen it before? The way she plunked herself down in a chair, the fact that she couldn't bring herself to wear makeup or jewelry on her new body; her discomfort at intimately touching or being intimately touched by men: it was obvious in retrospect.

Cassandra's hands had moved instinctively to protect *her own testicles.*

"You're not Cassandra Wilkins," I said.

"Of course I am," said the female voice.

"Not on the inside, you're not," I said. "You're a man. Whatever mind has been transferred into that body is male."

Cassandra twisted violently. Goddamned Pickover, perhaps stunned by the revelation, had obviously loosened his grip, because she got free. I fired my gun again and the bullet went straight into her chest; a streamer of machine oil, like from a punctured can, shot out, but there was no sign that the bullet had slowed her down.

"Don't let her get away!" shouted Pickover, in his rough mechanical voice. I swung my gun on him, and for a second I could see terror in his eyes, as if he thought I meant to off him for letting her twist away. But I aimed at the nylon strap restraining his legs and fired. This time, the bullet only partially severed the strap. I reached down and yanked at the remaining filaments, and so did Pickover. They finally broke and this strap, like the first, snapped free. Pickover swung his legs off the table, and immediately stood up. An artificial body had many advantages, among them not being woozy or dizzy after lying down for God-only-knew how many days.

In the handful of seconds it had taken to free Pickover, Cassandra had made it out the door that I'd pried partway open, and was now running down the corridor in the darkness. I could hear splashing sounds, meaning she'd veered far enough off the corridor's centerline to end up in the water pooling along the starboard side, and I heard her actually bump into the wall at one point, although she immediately continued on. She didn't have her flashlight, and the only illumination in the corridor would have been what was spilling out of the room I was now in—a fading glow to her rear as she ran along, whatever shadow she herself was casting adding to the difficulty of seeing ahead.

I squeezed out into the corridor. I still had my flashlight in my pocket; I fished it out and aimed it just in front of me; Cassandra wouldn't benefit much from the light it was giving off. Pickover, who, I noted, had now done his pants back up, had made his way through the half-open door and was now standing beside me. I started running, and he fell in next to me.

Our footfalls now drowned out the sound of Cassandra's; I guessed she must be some thirty or forty meters ahead. Although it was almost pitch black, she presumably had the advantage of having come down this corridor several times before; neither Pickover nor I had ever gone in this direction.

A rat scampered out of our way, squealing as it did so. My breathing was already ragged, but I managed to say, "How well can you guys see in the dark?"

Pickover's voice, of course, showed no signs of exertion. "Only slightly better than biologicals can."

I nodded, although he'd have to have had better vision than he'd just laid claim to in order to see it. My legs were a lot longer than Cassandra's, but I suspected she could pump them more rapidly. I swung the flashlight beam up, letting it lance out ahead of us for a moment. There she was, off in the distance. I dropped the beam back to the floor in front of me.

More splashing from up ahead; she'd veered off once more. I thought about firing a shot—more for the drama of it, than any serious hope of bringing her down—when I suddenly became aware that Pickover was passing me. His robotic legs were as long as my natural ones, and he could piston them up and down at least as quickly as Cassandra could.

I tried to match his speed, but wasn't able to. Even in Martian gravity, running fast is hard work. I swung my flashlight up again, but Pickover's body, now in front of me, was obscuring everything further down the corridor; I had no idea how far ahead Cassandra was now—and the intervening form of Pickover prevented me from acting out my idle fantasy of squeezing off a shot.

Pickover continued to pull ahead. I was passing open door after open door, black mouths gaping at me in the darkness. I heard more rats, and Pickover's footfalls, and—

Suddenly, something jumped on my back from behind me. A hard arm was around my neck, pressing sharply down on my Adam's apple. I tried to call out to Pickover, but couldn't get enough breath out . . . or in. I craned my neck as much as I could, and shone the flashlight beam up on the ceiling, so that some light reflected down onto my back from above.

It was Cassandra! She'd ducked into one of the other rooms, and lain in wait for me. Pickover was no detective; he had completely missed the signs of his quarry no longer being in front of him—and I'd had Pickover's body blocking my vision, plus the echoing bangs of his footfalls to obscure my hearing. I could see my own chilled breath, but, of course, not hers.

I tried again to call out to Pickover, but all I managed was a hoarse croak, doubtless lost on him amongst the noise of his own running. I was already oxygen-deprived from exertion, and the constricting of my throat was making things worse; despite the darkness I was now seeing white flashes in front of my eyes, a sure sign of asphyxiation. I only had a few seconds to act—

And act I did. I crouched down as low as I could, Cassandra still on my back, her head sticking up above mine, and I leapt with all the strength I could muster. Even weakened, I managed a powerful kick, and in this low Martian gravity, I shot up like a bullet. Cassandra's metal skull smashed into the roof of the corridor. There happened to be a lighting fixture directly above me, and I heard the sounds of shattering glass and plastic.

I was descending now in maddeningly slow motion, but as soon as I was down, Cassandra still clinging hard to me, I surged forward a couple of paces then leapt up again. This time, there was nothing but unrelenting bulkhead overhead, and Cassandra's metal skull slammed hard into it.

Again the slow-motion fall. I felt something thick and wet oozing through my shirt. For a second, I'd thought Cassandra had stabbed me— but no, it was probably the machine oil leaking from the bullet hole I'd put in her earlier. By the time we had touched down again, Cassandra had loosened her grip on my neck as she tried to scramble off me. I spun around and fell forward, pushing her backward onto the corridor floor, me tumbling on top of her. Despite my best efforts, the flashlight was knocked from my grip by the impact, and it spun around, doing a few complete circles before it ended up with its beam facing away from us.

I still had my revolver in my other hand, though. I brought it up, and, by touch, found Cassandra's face, probing the barrel roughly over it. Once, in my early days, I'd rammed a gun barrel into a thug's mouth; this time, I had other ideas. I got the barrel positioned directly over her left eye, and pressed down hard with it—a little poetic justice.

I said, "I bet if I shoot through your glass eye, aiming up a bit, I'll tear your artificial brain apart. You want to find out?"

She said nothing. I called back over my shoulder, "*Pickover!*" The name echoed down the corridor, but I had no idea whether he heard me. I turned my attention back to Cassandra—or whoever the hell this really was. I cocked the trigger. "As far as I'm concerned, Cassandra Wilkins is my client—but you're not her. Who are you?"

"I *am* Cassandra Wilkins," said the voice.

"No, you're not," I said. "You're a man—or, at least, you've got a man's mind."

"I can *prove* I'm Cassandra Wilkins," said the supine form. "My name is Cassandra Pauline Wilkins; my birth name is Collier. I was born in Sioux City, Iowa, on 30 October 2079. I immigrated to New Klondike in July 2102. My citizenship number is—"

"Facts. Figures." I shook my head. "Anyone could find those things out."

"But I know stuff no one else could possibly know. I know the name of my childhood pets; I know what I did to get thrown out of school when I was fifteen; I know precisely where the original me had a tattoo; I . . ."

She went on, but I stopped listening.

Jesus Christ, it was almost the perfect crime. No one could really get away with stealing somebody else's identity—not for long. The lack of intimate knowledge of how the original spoke, of private things the original knew, would soon enough give you away, unless—

Unless you were the *spouse* of the person whose identity you'd appropriated.

"You're not Cassandra Wilkins," I said. "You're Joshua Wilkins. You took her body; you transferred into it, and she transferred—" I felt my stomach tighten; it really was a nearly perfect crime. "And she transferred *nowhere*; when the original was euthanized, she died. And that makes you guilty of murder."

"You can't prove that," said the female voice. "No biometrics, no DNA, no fingerprints. I'm whoever I say I am."

"You and Cassandra hatched this scheme together," I said. "You both figured Pickover had to know where the alpha deposit was. But then you decided that you didn't want to share the wealth with anyone—not even your wife. And so you got rid of her, and made good your escape at the same time."

"That's crazy," the female voice said. "I *hired* you. Why on—on *Mars*—would I do that, then?"

"You expected the police to come out to investigate your missing-person report; they were supposed to find the body in the basement of NewYou. But they didn't, and you knew suspicion would fall on you—the supposed spouse!—if you were the one who found it. So you hired me—the dutiful wife, worried about her poor, missing hubby! All you wanted was for me to find the body."

"Words," said Joshua. "Just words."

"Maybe so," I said. "I don't have to satisfy anyone else. Just me. I will give you one chance, though. See, I want to get out of here alive—and I don't see any way to do that if I leave you alive, too. Do you? If you've got an answer, tell me—otherwise, I've got no choice but to pull this trigger."

"I promise I'll let you go," said Joshua.

I laughed, and the sound echoed in the corridor. "You promise? Well, I'm sure I can take that to the bank."

"No, seriously," said Joshua. "I won't tell anyone. I—"

"Are you Joshua Wilkins?" I asked.

Silence.

"Are you?"

I felt the face moving up and down a bit, the barrel of my gun shifting slightly in the eye socket as it did so. "Yes."

"Well, rest in peace," I said, and then, with relish, added, *"Josh."*

I pulled the trigger.

The flash from the gun barrel briefly lit up the female, freckled face, which was showing almost human horror. The revolver snapped back in my hand, then everything was dark again. I had no idea how much damage the bullet would do to the brain. Of course, the artificial chest wasn't rising and falling, but it never had been. And there was nowhere to check for a pulse. I decided I'd better try another shot, just to be sure. I shifted slightly, thinking I'd put this one through the other eye, and—

And Joshua's arms burst up, pushing me off him. I felt myself go airborne, and was aware of Joshua scrambling to his feet. He scooped up the flashlight, and as he swung it and himself around, it briefly illuminated his face. There was a deep pit where one eye used to be.

I started to bring the gun up and—

And Joshua thumbed off the flashlight. The only illumination was a tiny bit of light, far, far down the corridor, spilling out from the torture room; it wasn't enough to let me see Joshua clearly. But I squeezed the trigger, and heard a bullet ricochet—either off some part of Joshua's metal internal skeleton, or off the corridor wall.

I was the kind of guy who always knew *exactly* how many bullets he had left: two. I wasn't sure I wanted to fire them both off blindly, but—

I could hear Joshua moving closer. I fired again. This time, the feminine voice box made a sound between an *oomph* and the word "ouch," so I knew I'd hit him.

One bullet to go.

I started walking backward—which was no worse than walking forward; I was just as likely to trip either way in this near-total darkness. The body in the shape of Cassandra Wilkins was much smaller than mine—but also, although it shamed the macho me to admit it, much stronger. It could probably grab me by the shoulders and pound my head up into the ceiling, just as I'd pounded hers—and I rather suspect mine wouldn't survive. And if I let it get hold of my arm, it could probably wrench the gun from me; five bullets hadn't been enough to stop the artificial body, but one was all it would take to ice me for good.

And so I decided it was better to have an empty gun than a gun that could potentially be turned on me. I held the weapon out in front, took my best guess, and squeezed the trigger one last time.

The revolver barked, and the flare from the muzzle lit the scene, stinging my eyes. The artificial form cried out—I'd hit a spot its sensors felt was worth protecting with a major pain response, I guess. But the being kept moving forward. Part of me thought about turning tail and running—I still had the longer legs, even if I couldn't move them as fast—but another part of me couldn't bring myself to do that. The gun was of no more use, so I threw it aside. It hit the corridor wall, making a banging sound, then fell to the deck plates, producing more clanging as it bounced against them.

Of course, as soon as I'd thrown the gun away, I realized I'd made a mistake. *I* knew how many bullets I'd shot, and how many the gun held, but Joshua probably didn't; even an empty gun could be a deterrent if the other person thought it was loaded.

We were facing each other—but that was all that was certain. Precisely how much distance there was between us I couldn't say. Although running produced loud, echoing footfalls, either of us could have moved a step or two forward or back—or left or right—without the other being aware of it. I was trying not to make any noise, and a transfer could stand perfectly still, and be absolutely quiet, for hours on end.

I had no idea how badly I'd hurt him. In fact, given that he'd played possum once before, it was possible the sounds of pain were faked, just to make me think he was damaged. My great grandfather said clocks used to make a ticking sound with the passing of each second; I'd never heard such a thing, but I was certainly conscious of time passing in increments as we stood there, each waiting for the other to make a move.

Suddenly, light exploded in my face. He'd thumbed the flashlight back on, aiming it at what turned out to be a very good guess as to where my eyes were. I was temporarily blinded, but his one remaining mechanical eye responded more efficiently, I guess, because now that he knew exactly where I was, he leapt, propelling himself through the air and knocking me down.

This time, both hands closed around my neck. I still outmassed

Joshua and managed to roll us over, so he was on his back and I was on top. I arched my back and slammed my knee into his balls, hoping he'd release me . . .

. . . except, of course, he didn't have any balls; he only thought he did. *Damn!*

The hands were still closing around my gullet; despite the chill air, I felt myself sweating. But with his hands occupied, mine were free: I pushed my right hand onto his chest—startled by the feeling of artificial breasts there—and probed around until I found the slick, wet hole my first bullet had made. I hooked my right thumb into that hole, pulled sideways, and brought in my left thumb, as well, squeezing it down into the opening, ripping it wider and wider. I thought if I could get at the internal components, I might be able to rip out something crucial. The artificial flesh was soft, and there was a layer of what felt like foam rubber beneath it—and beneath that, I could feel hard metal parts. I tried to get my whole hand in, tried to yank out whatever I could, but I was fading fast. My pulse was thundering so loudly in my ears I couldn't hear anything else, just a *thump-thump-thumping,* over and over again, the *thump-thump-thumping* of . . .

Of footfalls! Someone was running this way, and—

And the scene lit up as flashlights came to bear on us.

"There they are!" said a harsh, mechanical voice that I recognized as belonging to Pickover. "There they are!"

"NKPD!" shouted another voice I also recognized—a deep, Scottish brogue. "Let Lomax go!"

Joshua looked up. "Back off!" he shouted—in that female voice. "If you don't, I'll finish him."

Through blurring vision, I thought I could see Mac hesitating. But then he spoke again. "If you kill him, you'll go down for murder. You don't want that."

Joshua relaxed his grip a bit—not enough to let me escape, but enough to keep me alive as a hostage, at least a little while longer. I sucked in cold air, but my lungs still felt like they were on fire. In the illumination from the flashlights I could see the improved copy of Cassandra Wilkins's face craning now to look at McCrae. Transfers didn't show as much emotion as biologicals did, but it was clear that Joshua was panicking.

I was still on top. I thought if I waited until Joshua was distracted, I could yank free of his grip without him snapping my neck. "Let go of him," Mac said firmly. It was hard to see him; he was the one holding the light source, after all, but I suddenly became aware that he was also holding a large disk. "Release his neck, or I'll deactivate you for sure."

Joshua practically had to roll his green eyes up into his head to see Mac, standing behind him. "You ever use one of those before?" he said, presumably referring to the disrupter disk. "No, I know you haven't— no transfer has been killed on Mars in weeks, and that technology only just came out. Well, I work in the transference business. I know the disruption isn't instantaneous. Yes, you can kill me—but not before I kill Lomax."

"You're lying," said McCrae. He handed his flashlight to Pickover, and brought the disk up in front of him, holding it vertically by its two U-shaped handles. "I've read the specs."

"Are you willing to take that chance?" asked Joshua.

I could only arch my neck a bit; it was very hard for me to look up and see Mac, but he seemed to be frowning, and, after a second, he turned partially away. Pickover was standing behind him, and—

And suddenly an electric whine split the air, and Joshua was convulsing beneath me, and his hands were squeezing my throat even more tightly than before. The whine—a high keening sound—must have been coming from the disrupter. I still had my hands inside Joshua's chest and could feel his whole interior vibrating as his body racked. I yanked my hands out and grabbed onto his arms, pulling with all my might. His hands popped free from my throat, and his whole luscious female form was shaking rapidly. I rolled off him; the artificial body kept convulsing as the keening continued. I gasped for breath and all I could think about for several moments was getting air into me.

After my head cleared a bit, I looked again at Joshua, who was still convulsing, and then I looked up at Mac, who was banging on the side of the disrupter disk. I realized that, now that he'd activated it, he had no idea how to deactivate it. As I watched, he started to turn it over, presumably hoping there was some control he'd missed on the side he couldn't see—and I realized that if he completed his move, the disk would be aimed backward, in the direction of Pickover. Pickover clearly saw this, too: he was throwing his robot-like arms up, as if to shield his face—not that that could possibly do any good.

I tried to shout "No!" but my voice was too raw, and all that came out was a hoarse exhalation of breath, the sound of which was lost beneath the keening. In my peripheral vision, I could see Joshua lying face down. His vicious spasms stopped as the beam from the disrupter was no longer aimed at him.

But even though I didn't have any voice left, Pickover did, and his shout of *"Don't!"* was loud enough to be heard over the electric whine of the disrupter. Mac continued to rotate the disk a few more degrees before he realized what Pickover was referring to. He flipped the disk back around, then continued turning it until the emitter surface was facing straight down. And then he dropped it, and it fell in Martian slo-mo, at last clanking against the deck plates, a counterpoint to the now-muffled electric whine. I hauled myself to my feet and moved over to check on Joshua, while Pickover and Mac hovered over the disk, presumably looking for the off switch.

There were probably more scientific ways to see if the transferred Joshua was dead, but this one felt right just then: I balanced on one foot, hauled back the other leg, and kicked the son of a bitch in the side of that gorgeous head. The impact was strong enough to spin the whole body through a quarter-turn, but there was no reaction at all from Joshua.

Suddenly, the keening died, and I heard a self-satisfied *"There!"* from Mac. I looked over at him, and he looked back at me, caught in the beam from the flashlight Pickover was holding. Mac's bushy orange eyebrows were raised and there was a sheepish grin on his face. "Who'd have thought the off switch had to be pulled out instead of pushed in?"

I tried to speak, and found that I did have a little voice now. "Thanks for coming by, Mac. I know how you hate to leave the station."

Mac nodded in Pickover's direction. "Yeah, well, you can thank this guy for putting in the call," he said. He turned, and faced Pickover full-on. "Just who the hell are you, anyway?"

I saw Pickover's mouth begin to open in his mechanical head, and a thought rushed through my mind. This Pickover was bootleg. Both the other Pickover and Joshua Wilkins had been correct: such a being shouldn't exist, and had no rights. Indeed, the legal Pickover would doubtless continue to demand that this version be destroyed; no one wanted an unauthorized copy of himself wandering around.

Mac was looking away from me, and toward the duplicate of Pickover. And so I made a wide sweeping of my head, left to right, then back again. Pickover apparently saw it, because he closed his mouth before sounds came out, and I spoke, as loudly and clearly as I could in my current condition. "Let me do the introductions," I said, and I waited for Mac to turn back toward me.

When he had, I pointed at Mac. "Detective Dougal McCrae," I said, then I took a deep breath, let it out slowly, and pointed at Pickover. "I'd like you to meet Joshua Wilkins."

Mac nodded, accepting this. "So you found your man? Congratulations, Alex." He then looked down at the motionless female body. "Too bad about your wife, Mr. Wilkins."

Pickover turned to face me, clearly seeking guidance. "It's so sad," I said quickly. "She was insane, Mac—had been threatening to kill her poor husband Joshua here for weeks. He decided to fake his own death to escape her, but she got wise to it somehow, and hunted him down. I had no choice but to try to stop her."

As if on cue, Pickover walked over to the dead artificial body, and crouched beside it. "My poor dear wife," he said, somehow managing to make his mechanical voice sound tender. He lifted his skinless face toward Mac. "This planet does that to people, you know. Makes them go crazy." He shook his head. "So many dreams dashed."

Mac looked at me, then at Pickover, then at the artificial body lying on the deck plating, then back at me. "All right, Alex," he said, nodding slowly. "Good work."

I tipped my nonexistent hat at him. "Glad to be of help."

I walked into the dark interior of the Bent Chisel, whistling.

Buttrick was behind the bar, as usual. "You again, Lomax?"

"The one and only," I replied cheerfully. That topless waitress I'd slept with a couple of times was standing next to the bar, loading up her tray. I looked at her, and suddenly her name came to me. "Hey, Diana!" I said. "When you get off tonight, how 'bout you and me go out and paint the town . . ." I trailed off: the town was *already* red; the whole damned planet was.

Diana's face lit up, but Buttrick raised a beefy hand. "Not so fast, lover boy. If you've got the money to take her out, you've got the money to settle your tab."

I slapped two golden hundred-solar coins on the countertop. "That should cover it." Buttrick's eyes went as round as the coins, and he scooped them up immediately, as if he was afraid they'd disappear—which, in this joint, they probably would.

"I'll be in the booth in the back," I said to Diana. "I'm expecting Mr. Santos; when he arrives, could you bring him over?"

Diana smiled. "Sure thing, Alex. Meanwhile, what can I get you? Your usual poison?"

I shook my head. "Nah, none of that rotgut. Bring me the best scotch you've got—and pour it over *water* ice."

Buttrick narrowed his eyes. "That'll cost extra."

"No problem," I said. "Start up a new tab for me."

A few minutes later, Diana came by the booth with my drink, accompanied by Raoul Santos. He took the seat opposite me. "This better be on you, Alex," said Raoul. "You still owe me for the help I gave you at Dr. Pickover's place."

"Indeed it is, old boy. Have whatever you please."

Raoul rested his receding chin on his open palm. "You seem in a good mood."

"Oh, I am," I said. "I got paid this week."

The man the world now accepted as Joshua Wilkins had returned to NewYou, where he'd gotten his face finished and his artificial body upgraded. After that, he told people it was too painful to continue to work there, given what had happened with his wife. So he sold the NewYou franchise to his associate, Horatio Fernandez. The money from the sale gave him plenty to live on, especially now that he didn't need food and didn't have to pay the life-support tax anymore. He gave me all the fees his dear departed wife should have—plus a very healthy bonus.

I'd asked him what he was going to do now. "Well," he said, "even if you're the only one who knows it, I'm still a paleontologist—and now I can spend days on end out on the surface. I'm going to look for new fossil beds."

And what about the other Pickover—the official one? It took some doing, but I managed to convince him that it had actually been the late Cassandra, not Joshua, who had stolen a copy of his mind, and that she was the one who had installed it in an artificial body. I told Dr. Pickover that when Joshua discovered what his wife had done, he destroyed the bootleg and dumped the ruined body that had housed it in the basement of the NewYou building.

Not too shabby, eh? Still, I wanted more. I rented a surface suit and a Mars buggy and headed out to 16.4 kilometers south-southwest of Nili Patera. I figured I'd pick myself up a lovely rhizomorph or a nifty pentaped, and never have to work again.

Well, I looked and looked and looked, but I guess the duplicate Pickover had lied about where the alpha deposit was; even under torture, he hadn't betrayed his beloved fossils. I'm sure Weingarten and O'Reilly's source is out there somewhere, though, and the legal Pickover is doubtless hard at work thinking of ways to protect it from looters.

I hope he succeeds. I really do.

But for now, I'm content just to enjoy this lovely scotch.

"How about a toast?" suggested Raoul, once Diana had brought him his booze.

"I'm game," I said. "To what?"

Raoul frowned, considering. Then his eyebrows climbed his broad forehead, and he said, "To being true to your innermost self."

We clinked glasses. "I'll drink to that."

Nancy Kress, the author of twenty-three books, is no stranger to Nebula volumes. She's won three Nebulas, and she edited the 2001 edition of this book. She also writes a regular column for *Writer's Digest* and is a fine workshop teacher; as an editor I've never had a contribution from one of Nancy's students who hadn't mastered all the basics. There is no such thing as a typical Nancy Kress story, but if there were, "My Mother, Dancing" might come close to it.

MY MOTHER, DANCING

NANCY KRESS

Fermi's Paradox, California, 1950: Since planet formation ap-
pears to be common, and since the processes that lead to the
development of life are a continuation of those that develop
planets, and since the development of life leads to intelligence and
intelligence to technology—then why hasn't a single alien civilization contacted Earth?

Where is everybody?

They had agreed, laughing, on a form of the millennium contact, what
Micah called "human standard," although Kabil had insisted on keeping
hirs konfol and Deb had not dissolved hirs crest, which waved three
inches above hirs and hummed. But, then, Deb! Ling had designed floating baktor for the entire ship, red and yellow mostly, that combined and
recombined in kaleidoscopic loveliness that only Ling could have programmed. The viewport was set to magnify, the air mixture just slightly
intoxicating, the tinglies carefully balanced by Cal, that master. Ling had
wanted "natural" sleep cycles, but Cal's arguments had been more persuasive, and the tinglies massaged the limbic so pleasantly. Even the child
had some. It was a party.

The ship slipped into orbit around the planet, a massive subJovian far
from its sun, streaked with muted color. "Lovely," breathed Deb, who
lived for beauty.

Cal, the biologist, was more practical: "I ran the equations; by now
there should be around two hundred thousand of them in the rift, if the
replication rate stayed constant."

"Why wouldn't it?" said Ling, the challenger, and the others
laughed. The tinglies really were a good idea.

The child, Harrah, pressed hirs face to the window. "When can we land?"

The adults smiled at each other. They were so proud of Harrah, and so careful. Hirs was the first gene-donate for all of them except Micah, and probably the only one for the rest of them except Cal, who was a certified intellect donor. Kabil knelt beside Harrah, bringing hirs face close to the child's height.

"Little love, we can't land. Not here. We must see the creations in holo."

"Oh," Harrah said, with the universal acceptance of childhood. It had not changed in five thousand years, Ling was fond of remarking, that child idea that whatever it lived was the norm. But, then . . . *Ling.*

"Access the data," Cal said, and Harrah obeyed, reciting it aloud as hirs parents had all taught hirs. Ling smiled to see that Harrah still closed hirs eyes to access, but opened them to recite.

"The creations were dropped on this planet 273 E-years ago. They were the one-hundred-fortieth drop in the Great Holy Mission that gives us our life. The creations were left in a closed-system rift . . . what does that mean?"

"The air in the creations' valley doesn't get out to the rest of the planet, because the valley is so deep and the gravity so great. They have their own air."

"Oh. The creations are cyborged replicators, programmed for self-awareness. They are also programmed to expect human contact at the millennium. They . . ."

"Enough," said Kabil, still kneeling beside Harrah. Hirs stroked hirs hair, black today. "The important thing, Harrah, is that you remember that these creations are beings, different from us but with the same life force, the only life force. They must be respected, just as people are, even if they look odd to you."

"Or if they don't know as much as you," said Cal. "They won't, you know."

"I know," Harrah said. They had made hirs an accommodator, with strong genes for bonding. They already had Ling for challenge. Harrah added, "Praise Fermi and Kwang and Arlbeni for the emptiness of the universe."

Ling frowned. Hirs had opposed teaching Harrah the simpler, older folklore of the Great Mission. Ling would have preferred the child receive only truth, not religion. But Deb had insisted. *Feed the imagination first,* hirs had said, *and later Harrah can separate science from prophecy.* But the tinglies felt sweet, and the air mixture was set for a party, and hirs own baktors floated in such a graceful pattern that Ling, even Ling, could not quarrel.

"I wonder," Deb said dreamily, "what they have learned in 273 years."

"When will they holo?" Harrah said. "Are we there yet?"

Our mother is coming.

Two hours more and they will come, from beyond the top of the world. When they come, there will be much dancing. Much rejoicing. All of us will dance and rejoice, even those who have detached and let the air carry them away. Those ones will receive our transmissions and dance with us.

Or maybe our mother will also transmit to where those of us now sit. Maybe they will transmit to all, even those colonies out of our transmission range. Why not? Our mother, who made us, can do whatever is necessary.

First, the dancing. Then, the most necessary thing of all. Our mother will solve the program flaw. Completely, so that none of us will die. Our mother doesn't die. We are not supposed to die, either. Our mother will transmit the program to correct this.

Then the dancing there will be!

> Kwang's Resolution, Bohr Station, 2552: Since the development of the Quantum Transport, humanity has visited nearly a thousand planets in our galaxy and surveyed many more. Not one of them has developed any life of any kind, no matter how simple. Not one.
>
> No aliens have contacted Earth because there is nobody else out there.

Harrah laughed in delight. Hirs long black hair swung through a drift of yellow baktors. "The creations look like oysters!"

The holocube showed uneven rocky ground through thick, murky air. A short distance away rose the abrupt steep walls of the rift, thousands of feet high. Attached to the ground by thin, flexible, mineral-conducting tubes were hundreds of uniform, metal-alloy double shells. The shells held self-replicating nanomachinery, including the rudimentary AI, and living eukaryotes sealed into selectively permeable membranes. The machinery ran on the feeble sunlight and on energy produced by anaerobic bacteria, carefully engineered for the thick atmospheric stew of methane, hydrogen, helium, ammonia, and carbon dioxide.

The child knew none of this. Hirs saw the "oysters" jumping up in time on their filaments, jumping and falling, flapping their shells open and closed, twisting and flapping and bobbing. Dancing.

Kabil laughed, too. "Nowhere in the original programming! They learned it!"

"But what could the stimulus have been?" Ling said. "How lovely to find out!"

"Sssshhh, we're going to transmit," Micah said. Hirs eyes glowed. Micah was the oldest of them all; hirs had been on the original drop. "Seeding 140, are you there?"

"We are here! We are Seeding 140! Welcome, our mother!"

Harrah jabbed hirs finger at the holocube. "We're not your mother!"

Instantly, Deb closed the transmission. Micah said harshly, "Harrah! Your manners!"

The child looked scared. Deb said, "Harrah, we talked about this. The creations are not like us, but their ideas are as true as ours, on their own world. Don't laugh at them."

From Kabil, "Don't you remember, Harrah? Access the learning session!"

"I . . . remember," Harrah faltered.

"Then show some respect!" Micah said. "This is the Great Mission!"

Harrah's eyes teared. Kabil, the tender-hearted, put hirs hand on Harrah's shoulder. "Small heart, the Great Mission gives meaning to our lives."

"I . . . know. . . ."

Micah said, "You don't want to be like those people who just use up all their centuries in mere pleasure, with no structure to their wanderings around the galaxy, no purpose beyond seeing what the nanos can produce that they haven't produced before, no difference between today and tomorrow, no—"

"That's sufficient," Ling said. "Harrah understands, and regrets. Don't give an Arlbeni Day speech, Micah."

Micah said stiffly, "It matters, Ling."

"Of course it matters. But so do the creations, and they're waiting. Deb, open the transmission again. . . . Seeding 140, thank you for your welcome! We return!"

Arlbeni's Vision, Planet Cadrys, 2678: We have been fools.

Humanity is in despair. Nano has given us everything, and nothing. Endless pleasures empty of effort, endless tomorrows empty of purpose, endless experiences empty of meaning. From evolution to sentience, sentience to nano, nano to the decay of sentience.

But the fault is ours. We have overlooked the greatest gift ever given humanity: the illogical emptiness of the universe. It is against evolution, it is against known physical processes. Therefore, how can it exist? And why?

It can exist only by the intent of something greater than the physical processes of the universe. A conscious Intent.

The reason can only be to give humanity, the universe's sole inheritor, knowledge of this Intent. The emptiness of the universe—anomalous, unexplainable, impossible—has been left for us to discover, as the only convincing proof of God.

Our mother has come! We dance on the seabed. We transmit the news to the ones who have detached and floated away. We rejoice together, and consult the original program.

"You are above the planetary atmosphere," we say, new words until just this moment, but now understood. All will be understood now, all corrected. "You are in a ship, as we are in our shells."

"Yes," says our mother. "You know we cannot land."

"Yes," we say, and there is momentary dysfunction. How can they help us if they cannot land? But only momentary. This is our mother. And they landed us here once, didn't they? They can do whatever is necessary.

Our mother says, "How many are you now, Seeding 140?"

"We are 79,432," we say. Sadness comes. We endure it, as we must.

Our mother's voice changes in wavelength, in frequency. "Seventy-nine thousand? Are you . . . we had calculated more. Is this replication data correct?"

A packet of data arrives. We scan it quickly; it matches our programming.

"The data is correct, but . . ." We stop. It feels like another dying ceremony, suddenly, and it is not yet time for a dying ceremony. We will wait another few minutes. We will tell our mother in another few minutes. Instead, we ask, "What is your state of replication, our mother?"

Another change in wavelength and frequency. We scan and match data, and it is in our databanks: laughter, a form of rejoicing. Our mother rejoices.

"You aren't equipped for visuals, or I would show you our replicant," our mother says. "But the rate is much, much lower than yours. We have one new replicant with us on the ship."

"Welcome new replicant!" we say, and there is more rejoicing. There, and here.

"I've restricted transmission . . . there's the t-field's visual," Micah said.

A hazy cloud appeared to one side of the holocube, large enough to hold two people comfortably, three close together. Only words spoken inside the field would now transmit. Baktors scuttled clear of the ionized haze. Deb stepped inside the field, with Harrah; Cal moved out of it. Hirs frowned at Micah.

"They can't be only seventy-nine thousand-plus if the rate of replication held steady. Check the resource data, Micah."

"Scanning. . . . no change in available raw materials. . . . no change in sunlight per square unit."

"Scan their counting program."

"I already did. Fully functional."

"Then run an historical scan of replicants created."

"That will take time . . . there, it's started. What about attrition?"

Cal said, "Of course. I should have thought of that. Do a seismic survey and match it with the original data. A huge quake could easily have destroyed two-thirds of them, poor seedings. . . ."

Ling said, "You could ask them."

Kabil said, "If it's not a cultural taboo. Remember, they have had time to evolve a culture, we left them that ability."

"Only in response to environmental stimuli. Would a quake or a mudslide create enough stimulus pressure to evolve death taboos?"

They looked at each other. Something new in the universe, something humanity had not created . . . this was why they were here! Their eyes shone, their breaths came faster. Yet they were uncomfortable, too, at the mention of death. How long since any of them . . . oh, yes. Ling's clone in that computer malfunction, but so many decades ago. . . . Discomfort, excitement, compassion for Seeding 140, yes compassion most of all, how terrible if the poor creations had actually lost so many in a quake. . . . All of them felt it, and meant it, the emotion was genuine. And in their minds the finger of God touched them for a moment, with the holiness of the tiny human struggle against the emptiness of the universe.

"Praise Fermi and Kwang and Arlbeni . . ." one of them murmured, and no one was sure who, in the general embarrassment that took them a moment later. They were not children.

Micah said, "Match the seismic survey with the original data," and moved off to savor alone the residue of natural transcendence, rarest and strangest of the few things nano could not provide.

Inside the hazy field Harrah said, "Seeding! I am dancing just like you!" and moved hirs small body back and forth, up and down on the ship's deck.

Arlbeni's Vision, Planet Cadrys, 2678: In the proof of God lies its corollary. The Great Intent has left the universe empty, but for us. It is our mission to fill it.

Look around you, look at what we've become. At the pointless destruction, the aimless boredom, the spiritual despair. The human race cannot exist without purpose, without vision, without faith. Filling the emptiness of the universe will rescue us from our own.

Our mother says, "Do you play games?"

We examine the data carefully. There is no match.

Our mother speaks again. "That was our new replicant speaking, Seeding 140. Hirs is only half-created as yet, and hirs program language is not fully functional. Hirs means, of the new programs you have created for yourselves since the original seeding, which ones in response to the environment are expressions of rejoicing? Like dancing?"

"Yes!" we say. "We dance in rejoicing. And we also throw pebbles in rejoicing and catch pebbles in rejoicing. But not for many years since."

"Do it now!" our mother says.

This is our mother. We are not rejoicing. But this is our mother. We pick up some pebbles.

"No," our mother says quickly, "you don't need to throw pebbles. That was the new replicant again. Hirs does not yet understand that seedings do what, and only what, they wish. Your . . . your mother does *not* command you. Anything you do, anything you have learned, is as necessary as what we do."

"I'm sorry again," our mother says, and there is physical movement registered in the field of transmission.

We do not understand. But our mother has spoken of new programs, of programs created since the seeding, in response to the environment. This we understand, and now it is time to tell our mother of our need. Our mother has asked. Sorrow floods us, rejoicing disappears, but now is the time to tell what is necessary.

Our mother will make all functional once more.

"Don't scold hirs like that, hirs is just a child," Kabil said. "Harrah, stop crying, we know you didn't mean to impute to them any inferiority."

Micah, hirs back turned to the tiny parental drama, said to Cal, "Seismic survey complete. No quakes, only the most minor geologic disturbances . . . really, the local history shows remarkable stability."

"Then what accounts for the difference between their count of themselves and the replication rate?"

"It can't be a real difference."

"But . . . oh! Listen. Did they just say—"

Hirs turned slowly toward the holocube.

Harrah said at the same moment, through hirs tears, "They stopped dancing."

Cal said, "Repeat that," remembered hirself, and moved into the transmission field, replacing Harrah. "Repeat that, please, Seeding 140. Repeat your last transmission."

The motionless metal oysters said, "We have created a new program in response to the Others in this environment. The Others who destroy us."

Cal said, very pleasantly, " 'Others'? What Others?"

"The new ones. The mindless ones. The destroyers."

"There are no others in your environment," Micah said. "What are you trying to say?"

Ling, across the deck in a cloud of pink bakterons, said, "Oh, oh . . . no . . . they must have divided into factions. Invented warfare amongst themselves! Oh. . . ."

Harrah stopped sobbing and stood, wide-eyed, on hirs sturdy short legs.

Cal said, still very pleasant, "Seeding 140, show us these Others. Transmit visuals."

"But if we get close enough to the Others to do that, we will be destroyed!"

Ling said sadly, "It *is* warfare."

Deb compressed hirs beautiful lips. Kabil turned away, to gaze out at the stars. Micah said, "Seeding . . . do you have any historical transmissions of the Others, in your databanks? Send those."

"Scanning . . . sending."

Ling said softly, "We always knew warfare was a possibility for any creations. After all, they have our unrefined DNA, and for millennia . . ." Hirs fell silent.

"The data is only partial," Seeding 140 said. "We were nearly destroyed when it was sent to us. But there is one data packet until the last few minutes of life."

The cheerful, dancing oysters had vanished from the holocube. In their place were the fronds of a tall, thin plant, waving slightly in the thick air. It was stark, unadorned, elemental. A multicellular organism rooted in the rocky ground, doing nothing.

No one on the ship spoke.

The holocube changed perspective, to a wide scan. Now there were whole stands of fronds, acres of them, filling huge sections of the rift. Plant after plant, drab olive green, blowing in the unseen wind.

After the long silence, Seeding 140 said, "Our mother? The Others were not there for ninety-two years. Then they came. They replicate much faster than we do, and we die. Our mother, can you do what is necessary?"

Still no one spoke, until Harrah, frightened, said, "What is it?"

Micah answered, hirs voice clipped and precise. "According to the data packet, it is an aerobic organism, using a process analogous to photosynthesis to create energy, giving off oxygen as a byproduct. The data includes a specimen analysis, broken off very abruptly as if the AI failed. The specimen is non-carbon-based, non-DNA. The energy sources sealed in Seeding 140 are anaerobic."

Ling said sharply, "Present oxygen content of the rift atmosphere?"

Cal said, "Seven point six two percent." Hirs paused. "The oxygen created by these . . . these 'Others' is poisoning the seeding."

"But," Deb said, bewildered, "why did the original drop include such a thing?"

"It didn't," Micah said. "There is no match for this structure in the gene banks. It is not from Earth."

"Our mother?" Seeding 140 said, over the motionless fronds in the holocube. "Are you still there?"

Disciple Arlbeni, Grid 743.9, 2999: As we approach this millennium marker, rejoice that humanity has passed both beyond superstition and spiritual denial. We have a faith built on physical truth, on living genetics, on human need. We have, at long last, given our souls not to a formless Deity, but to the science of life itself. We are safe, and we are blessed.

Micah said suddenly, "It's a trick."

The other adults stared at hirs. Harrah had been hastily reconfigured for sleep. Someone—Ling, most likely—had dissolved the floating bak-tons and blanked the wall displays, and only the empty transmission field added color to the room. That, and the cold stars beyond.

"Yes," Micah continued, "a trick. Not malicious, of course. But we programmed them to learn, and they did. They had some seismic event, or some interwarfare, and it made them wary of anything unusual. They learned that the unusual can be deadly. And the most unusual thing they know of is us, set to return at 3000. So they created a transmission pro-gram designed to repel us. Xenophobia, in a stimulus-response learning environment. You said it yourself, Ling, the learning components are built on human genes. And we have xenophobia as an evolved survival response!"

Cal jack-knifed across the room. Tension turned hirs ungraceful. "No. That sounds appealing, but nothing we gave Seeding 140 would let them evolve defenses that sophisticated. And there was no seismic event for the internal stimulus."

Micah said eagerly, "We're the stimulus! Our anticipated return! Don't you see . . . we're the 'Others'!"

Kabil said, "But they call us 'mother'. . . . They were thrilled to see us. They're not xenophobic to us."

Deb spoke so softly the others could barely hear. "Then it's a com-puter malfunction. Cosmic bombardment of their sensory equipment. Or at least, of the unit that was 'dying.' Malfunctioning before the end. All that sensory data about oxygen poisoning is compromised."

"Of course!" Ling said. But hirs was always honest. "At least . . . no, compromised data isn't that coherent, the pieces don't fit together so well biochemically. . . ."

"And non-terrestrially," Cal said, and at the jagged edge in his voice, Micah exploded.

"California, these are not native life! There is no native life in the galaxy except on Earth!"

"I know that, Micah," Cal said, with dignity. "But I also know this data does not match anything in the d-bees."

"Then the d-bees are incomplete!"

"Possibly."

Ling put hirs hands together. They were long, slender hands with very long nails, created just yesterday. *I want to grab the new millennium with both hands,* Ling had laughed before the party, *and hold it firm.* "Spores. Panspermia."

MY MOTHER, DANCING 193

"I won't listen to this!" Micah said.

"An old theory," Ling went on, gasping a little. "Seeding 140 said the Others weren't there for their first hundred years. But if the spores blew in from space on the solar wind and the environment was right for them to germinate—"

Deb said quickly, "Spores aren't really life. Wherever they came from, they're not alive."

"Yes, they are," said Kabil. "Don't quibble. They're alive."

Micah said loudly, "I've given my entire life to the Great Mission. I was on the original drop for this very planet."

"They're alive," Ling said, "and they're not ours."

"My entire life!" Micah said. Hirs looked at each of them in turn, hirs face stony, and something terrible glinted behind the beautiful deep-green eyes.

Our mother does not answer. Has our mother gone away?

Our mother would not go away without helping us. It must be that they are still dancing.

We can wait.

"The main thing is Harrah, after all," Kabil said. Hirs sat slumped on the floor. They had been talking so long.

"A child needs secure knowledge. Purpose. Faith," Cal said.

Ling said wearily, "A child needs truth."

"Harrah," Deb crooned softly. "Harrah, made of all of us, future of our genes, small heart Harrah. . . ."

"Stop it, Debaron," Cal said. "Please."

Micah said, "Those things down there are not real. They are not. Test it, Cal. I've said so already. Test it. Send down a probe, try to bring back samples. There's nothing there."

"You don't know that, Micah."

"I know!" Micah said, and was subtly revitalized. Hirs sprang up. "Test it!"

Ling said, "A probe isn't necessary. We have the transmitted data and—"

"Not reliable!" Micah said.

"—and the rising oxygen content. Data from our own sensors."

"Outgassing!"

"Micah, that's ridiculous. And a probe—"

"A probe might come back contaminated," Cal said.

"Don't risk contamination," Kabil said suddenly. "Not with Harrah here."

"Harrah, made of us all. . . ." Deb had turned hirs back on the rest now, and lay almost curled into a ball, lost in hirs powerful imagination. Deb!

Kabil said, almost pleadingly, to Ling, "Harrah's safety should come first."

"Harrah's safety lies in facing the truth," Ling said. But hirs was not strong enough to sustain it alone. They were all so close, so knotted together, a family. Knotted by Harrah and by the Great Mission, to which Ling, no less than all the others, had given hirs life.

"Harrah, small heart," sang Deb.

Kabil said, "It isn't as if we have proof about these 'Others.' Not real proof. We don't actually *know*."

"*I* know," Micah said.

Cal looked bleakly at Kabil. "No. And it is wrong to sacrifice a child to a supposition, to a packet of compromised data, to a . . . a superstition of creations so much less than we are. You know that's true, even though we none of us ever admit it. But I'm a biologist. The creations are limited DNA, with no ability to self-modify. Also strictly regulated nano, and AI only within careful parameters. Yes, of course they're life forms deserving respect on their own terms, of course of course I would never deny that—"

"None of us would," Kabil said.

"—but they're not *us*. Not ever us."

A long silence, broken only by Deb's singing.

"Leave orbit, Micah," Cal finally said, "before Harrah wakes up."

> Disciple Arlbeni, Grid 743.9, 2999: We are not gods, never gods, no matter what the powers evolution and technology have given us, and we do not delude ourselves that we are gods, as other cultures have done at other millennia. We are human. Our salvation is that we know it, and do not pretend otherwise.

Our mother? Are you there? We need you to save us from the Others, to do what is necessary. Are you there?

Are you still dancing?

TO BOLDLY GO: A STRANGE, BEAUTIFUL FUTURE FOR GENRE COVER ART

JOHN PICACIO

One of the things we all know but then don't spend much time dis-cussing is the fact that cover art is vitally important to the sales of a book, and the sales of a book are vitally important to the writer and the publisher. So I thought it was time to get some input on the state of science fiction art, and to do so, I asked John Picacio—Hugo nom-inee, World Fantasy Award winner, and Chesley winner.

"It is in vain to hope to please all alike. Let a man stand with his face in what direction he will, he must necessarily turn his back on one half of the world."
　　—GEORGE DENNISON PRENTICE

"Science fiction is the genre that looks at the implications of technology on society, which, in this age of exponential techno-logical growth, makes it the most relevant branch of literature going."
　　—LOU ANDERS

Earlier this year, a publisher hired me to create a cover for a science fiction novel. At the outset of the assignment I was told, "We don't want this to look like science fiction, so try to avoid any-thing too science fiction on the cover." It was an interesting comment, and it wasn't the first time I had heard a publisher say this. I'm a fan of science fiction, but not a fan of science fiction cliché, so I can respect and understand a publisher's desire to avoid cliché. As a cover artist, I try to avoid these anyway, but I never avoid the actual grammar of the field itself. In fact, I'd like to think that good cover illustration evokes, rather than represents, and celebrates a book's intentions, rather than hides them. In the case of this particular assignment, I managed to create an abstract cover illustration that directly served the integrity of the novel, made a provocative visual, and met the client's wishes. Mission accomplished. Everyone went home happy. However, months later, that comment still disturbs me. "We don't want this to look like science fiction. . . ."

What exactly does that mean? And why would a publisher say that? My initial guess was that perhaps the publisher decided that any visual association with science fiction limited the potential audience for a given book, and by avoiding that association, the book would be more marketable to a nongenre audience, and, presumably, make more money. If genre visuals are so unpalatable to the nongenre masses, then why do the *Star Wars* and *Lord of the Rings* films dominate the list of the top-twenty highest-grossing films ever? If science fiction visual concepts are so unwieldy for the masses, or so embarrassing to be associated with, then why was the first *Matrix* film one of the most influential and far-ranging cultural phenomena of the last decade? There seems to be a disconnection here.

Quality publishers are not the culprits. They're not the bogeypeople. They want to publish great, lasting works of integrity more than anyone, and they want to make money. The most important word in the previous sentence is not *integrity* or *money*, but, in fact, the word *and*. Take a step back for a moment: In the 1950s, science fiction covers were dominated by pulp-inspired visions. Publisher Ian Ballantine believed that SF was more than a phenomenon for juvenile male readers, and when he encountered the work of Richard Powers, he gave Powers the freedom to create modern, surreal illustrations for novels like Arthur C. Clarke's *Childhood's End*—covers that didn't hide the genre elements of the work, but instead presented them in a way that enticed genre *and* nongenre audiences to read the book.

Ballantine wanted two things: He wanted to evolve the genre, and he wanted to make money. He demanded both, and he believed that progressive cover illustration could help him achieve both. Powers's illustrations not only unabashedly embraced the dreamscape of science fiction, but they were unprecedented in the genre in their unconventional forms and personal vision. And guess what? They sold *lots* of books. They impressed upon the audience the notion that science fiction was very relevant to the times, and, in fact, that science fiction was as contemporary and adult as any art form. Those covers helped build a reputation of integrity that made Ballantine Books what it is today.

So what about today? Why is this important to our times? I think it's more important than ever because it's a powerful example of what science fiction can be when it's not afraid to be itself, and it's not afraid to ask questions, rather than provide answers. It doesn't have to be a choice between art *or* profit. It can be both. The best science fiction cover art can help achieve both, and I think the field's tendency to visually avoid itself (in a sense) is not only the wrong move, but counterproductive to both missions. It seems that many publishers today feel the increasing urge to neuter genre ideas from their covers, rather than embrace them in fresh and thoughtful ways. In some cases, publishers feel that illustration itself is the enemy and choose to inflict homogenous cover design approaches on the world. In contrast, Ballantine gave Powers the freedom to be liberal (or liberating, if you like), to be forward-thinking, to be personal, to be challenging, and to be otherworldly. His images were not comforting and they didn't seek to please everyone, and they were decidedly utopian and dystopian, sometimes in the same picture space. As John Clute once said, Powers's covers "tell the dream of SF, in their own terms, indelibly."

So can today's genre industry do the same thing with its cover art—be provocative and be profitable? I believe the answer is yes, and the freedom to say yes to both criteria is the path to the next strange and wonderful horizon. For example, look at the overall work of Tor Books in a given year and you'll see the vision of their art director, Irene Gallo. She's not only one of the bright lights of the SF/fantasy field, but of the entire illustration field. She gives scores of illustrators the opportunity every year to take chances and experiment in ways that serve both the given manuscript and advancement of the field, and make money for Tor year after year. John Jude Palencar, Gregory Manchess, Rick Berry, John Harris, Leo and Diane Dillon, Dave McKean, and Rafal Olbinski are amongst the many illustrators who have done provocative and thoughtful covers under her watch. It's not a coincidence that she, and the best art directors, get optimal results by choosing the right creative talent and then letting the artists create art. It sounds so simple, but in today's corporate environment, it's an increasingly valuable commodity.

The tools of art have never been more volatile and exciting. The glut of mainstream designers trying to be the next Chip Kidd has homogenized the bookstore shelves in such a way that the *illustrated* covers of science fiction have more visual presence than ever. The cultural aptitude to absorb visual information has never been higher than it is now, and the culture's appetite for visual satisfaction has never been more voracious. These are challenging political and social times, when the pressure for a publisher to financially perform is great, and the pressure to conform is even greater. It's during times of this kind of adversity when art leaps forward and carries society with it, even if it goes kicking and screaming. Will science fiction and speculative fiction publishing accept the challenge and let its cover illustrations open new doors for perception and audience, like Richard Powers and Ian Ballantine did? I think the climate is ripe. The audience is ready. Now more than ever, the future of cover art in science fiction, and all speculative fiction, resides in its ability to not be afraid of itself, to not be afraid of questions, and—dare I say it?—to boldly go.

A Look at the Accomplishments and Contributions of the Independent Press

LOU ANDERS

When I started selling science fiction there weren't as many titles being published, but a lot more publishing houses had science fiction lines. One by one, many of these lines—the good, the bad, and the ugly—have vanished, and now, as you survey the stands, it seems as if the field is at the mercy of just eight or nine editors.

Actually, nothing could be farther from the truth, and I asked Lou Anders, the editor of the much-praised new science fiction line Pyr, to do a survey and tell us what's out there.

Locus Online names seventy-seven companies in its list of science fiction, fantasy, and horror specialty publishers, from Aardwolf Press to Yard Dog Press. They range in size from single-man operations with barely a handful of titles to their credit to outfits with hundreds of books in their backlist. They include new companies that have sprung up in the advent of POD technologies and established houses utilizing more traditional printing methods. They include venerable names like Arkham House, debuting in 1939 with the aim of keeping H. P. Lovecraft in print after his death in 1937, and newcomers like MonkeyBrain Books, who appeared on the scene in 2003 as a publisher devoted to nonfiction genre studies and has since branched out into encyclopedias, art books, and fiction.

Like the aforementioned Arkham House, specialty presses exist for the express purpose of filling a specific niche—in many cases, that of preserving the illustrious and ongoing history of the genre. NESFA Press is the publishing pseudopod of the New England Science Fiction Association, whose first hardcover title was L. Sprague de Camp's *Scribblings,* published at their annual convention Boskone in 1972. NESFA press czar Anthony Lewis explains, "We started by creating and printing indexes to the SF magazines, but that is better done online these days. We primarily produce three types of books: books honoring the guest(s) of honor at our annual convention, Boskone, and at some Worldcons and other conventions; books in the NESFA's Choice series, which bring back into print the works of deserving classic SF writers such as James Schmitz, Cordwainer Smith, C. M. Kornbluth, Anthony Boucher, Robert Sheckley, and Zenna Henderson. This arose from a series of discussion groups at Boskones about these out-of-print stories and laments from fans who could not find copies of the original publications. Reference books of science fiction and science fiction fandom."

Somewhat younger than NESFA, but clearly operating in a similar space, is ISFiC, the publishing arm of Illinois Science Fiction in Chicago. Steven H. Silver explains, "ISFiC Press was begun in 2004 using surplus funds from Chicon 2000. The intention was for ISFiC Press to begin by publishing guest of honor books in conjunction with WindyCon, one of the two annual conventions ISFiC sponsors. Our first book, *Relativity*, by Robert J. Sawyer, was published in November 2004 with a cover by Jael. A collection of Sawyer's short stories, essays, and speeches, it also included an introduction by Mike Resnick and an afterword by academic Valerie Broege, who also supplied a crossword puzzle based on Sawyer's writing. In 2005, *Relativity* received an Aurora Award from the Canadian fans. ISFiC Press published its first two novels, Harry Turtledove's *Every Inch a King* and Jeff Duntemann's debut novel, *The Cunning Blood,* in November 2005 to coincide with WindyCon 32. Something ISFiC Press wanted to do from the beginning was publish nonfiction of interest to the science fiction world, and in August 2006 we published our first nonfiction book, released at the Worldcon, *Worldcon Guest of Honor Speeches*, edited by Mike Resnick and Joe Siclari. This book collected more than thirty speeches, from Frank R. Paul's 1939 speech at the first Worldcon through Christopher Priest's 2005 speech. Many of the speeches were published in the book for the first time. In 2006, the Windycon book was a collection of stories by Jack McDevitt, entitled *Outbound*."

Small press MonkeyBrain Books, run by the two-person team of Chris Roberson and Allison Baker, began life in 2003 as a publisher devoted to nonfiction genre studies. As Roberson explains, "MonkeyBrain Books exists to publish books I'd buy if I saw them on the shelf. If someone else was publishing them, I wouldn't have to do so. The thing of which I'm proudest is having the opportunity to prove to the world that Jess Nevins is the superstar I always knew he was."

Roberson refers to *Heroes & Monsters* and *A Blazing World*, annotations of Alan Moore's *The League of Extraordinary Gentlemen* graphic novels written by genre fiction scholar Jess Nevins, to date Monkey-Brain's most successful releases. Though ostensibly "unofficial" guides, Nevins's two *League* books feature interviews with and input from writer Alan Moore and artist Kevin O'Neil and are regarded by both creators as an essential companion to their work, influencing both the shape and scope of future issues of their ongoing series. (The phrase "This is for Jess Nevins" is worked backward into one panel, viewable if the page is held to a mirror.)

Spurred by their success, MonkeyBrain has recently branched out into fiction, with works available and forthcoming from Kim Newman, Rudy Rucker, and others, as well as a new anthology series of pulp-style action stories, *Adventure Vol 1.*

Another house with a special niche (and perhaps an opposite trajectory to MonkeyBrain) is BenBella Books. Publisher Glenn Yeffeth explains, "I think of us as a science fiction house, but one step removed. We publish a variety of categories, but the majority of our books are related to science fiction one way or another, even if, technically, they aren't science fiction, or even fiction. But they live in the science fiction universe. We've got a very exciting title called *Star Wars on Trial*, which is all about having the science fiction community hash out the impact, good and bad, that *Star Wars* has had on us and the world's perception of science fiction. It's organized as an actual trial, with David Brin and Matthew Woodring Stover serving as prosecution and defense, and, as you know well, the debate gets heated, and it's funny as hell at points. That's exactly the kind of book I love publishing. We have an anthology on *Lost*—which is indisputably the most commercially successful genre show on television in a long time—edited by Orson Scott Card, coming out this summer.

"We started by publishing a lot of science fiction and fantasy, mostly reprints, but we're very, very careful about that now. It's just too hard to make much (or any) money with them. We're fairly big by the standards of a small press, and with five full-time employees, all of whom expect to get paid each week, so we have to choose our quixotic moments carefully. We've had some great fiction titles that have done nicely for us, such as *The Man Who Folded Himself* by David Gerrold, *The Sheep Look Up* by John Brunner, and *Shadows Fall* by Simon Green. But all of the fiction enters an intensely competitive environment in which it's really hard to stand out. In nonfiction, it's easier to be the only or at least one of a handful of books on any particular topic. But in science fiction, existing fans of the author aside, you're essentially competing with every other SF novel. So it's tough, and we only publish fiction where we feel we're bringing something reasonably unique to the table. A good example is a book coming out this fall entitled *History Revisited*, edited by Mike Resnick, which is a collection of some of the best alternate-history stories ever published, with a commentary on each one by a historian that specializes in that area of history. No one's ever done that before, and we'll be making this into an ongoing series."

Says Michael Walsh of Old Earth Books: "Old Earth publishes what interests me, from the grand pulp action of E. E. Smith to the magical realism/slipstream of Edward Whittemore; from the short story collections of Avram Davidson to the forthcoming Howard Waldrop retrospective. I also hope the books do more than just break even."

As corporate pressure from above forces many major houses to drop stable, midlist authors with proven track records, many small and midsize houses are stepping in to pick up the pieces. One such publisher, Solaris, a newly formed imprint of role-playing game-and-media-tie-in house BL Publishing, will launch in 2007 with the specific aim of publishing original science fiction and fantasy drawn from the ranks of American and British midlist writers. Vincent Rospond, BL's sales and marketing manager, explains BL's strategy on the blog GalleyCat: "We can make a smaller print run make more money for us than Simon & Schuster or Random House can. You have authors who may be at the low end at some of those publishers who would be a priority for us. It's just a matter of economics."[1]

Tachyon publisher Jacob Weisman agrees. "In today's business climate, there are fewer large publishers than thirty years ago, and they compete for a relatively narrow range of books. This creates an increased opportunity for independent presses to publish major books by important authors, and confers on these presses an increased obligation to make sure that the general reading public knows about those books and has access to them."

Weisman sees a sea change in recent science fiction, as old tropes blend with new ideas and techniques to recreate a recent renaissance of speculative fiction. "Some of the most exciting, innovative SF/F fiction is coming from outside of the traditional New York publishing houses.

[1]"Outtakes from This Week's *PW* Cover Story," April 3, 2006, by Ron Hogan, www.mediabistro.com/galleycat/publishing/outtakes_from_this_weeks_pw_cover_story_34710.asp

Through great risk and even greater rewards, independent presses, far-flung and hungry, have become the new trendsetters. Night Shade Books (Portland, Oregon), Golden Gryphon (Urbana, Illinois), Wheatland Press (Wilsonville, Oregon), Small Beer (Northampton, Massachusetts), BenBella Books (Dallas, Texas), and Tachyon Publications (San Francisco, California) are leading the way, publishing important work by unique voices and finding a loyal, growing audience in doing so.

"These maverick presses started, out of economic necessity, by publishing short story collections that were being overlooked by the industry at large. These collections have kept the SF/F short story market vibrant, launching the careers of exciting newcomers like Kelly Link (*Magic for Beginners*) and Charles Stross (*The Atrocity Archives*), and giving a home to established icons like Peter S. Beagle (*The Rhinoceros Who Quoted Nietzsche*) and Iain M. Banks (*The Algebraist*). Buoyed by critical and commercial successes, the indie SF/F presses have, while still maintaining their commitment to the short story form, expanded into publishing novels and nonfiction."

Many of the independent presses also specialize in producing masterfully produced, archival-quality hardcovers and beautifully produced trade paperbacks attractive to the book lovers and collectors of genre fandom. Weisman continues, "At Tachyon, we are committed to mastering the marketing and distribution of books as well as their design and production. Our mission at Tachyon is to publish entertaining books that have significant literary value. Our goal is to be a publisher of significant, well-designed, lasting books that are loved by readers and writers alike, and to be recognized as such by booksellers, reviewers, writers, and the reading public."

Particularly renowned for the look of their books is Golden Gryphon Press. Editor and publisher Gary Turner explains: "Golden Gryphon Press seeks to preserve short fiction in durable, well-crafted hardcovers, typically as single-author collections. A hallmark of the books is jacket art by top artists. One of our success stories is *The Atrocity Archives* by Charles Stross, which includes the short novel 'The Atrocity Archives,' which had only been serialized in a UK publication, and the short story 'The Concrete Jungle,' which won a Hugo."

One publisher in particular, Robert J. Sawyer Books (Red Deer Press, a Fitzhenry & Whiteside Company), sees itself as deliberately picking up the discarded material viewed as too difficult or challenging for a mainstream press to handle. "In April 2003, Red Deer Press, one of Canada's leading publishers, launched the first book under its Robert J.

Sawyer Books imprint: the novel *Letters from the Flesh* by Marcos Donnelly. Robert J. Sawyer personally selects all the books under his imprint, which now does three titles a year, and the Donnelly perfectly typified what he was looking for: science fiction (not fantasy or horror), thematically and philosophically rich, stand-alone (not part of a series) books, under a hundred thousand words long. More than that, though, RJS Books is trying to do things that are problematic for big New York publishers. The Donnelly was a second novel; his first had been a critical success but commercial failure for Baen (and, frankly, as a science-versus-religion novel, that first book was quite an aberration on the Baen list).

"The second, Andrew Weiner's *Getting Near the End*, was likewise a second novel by a problematic author. Weiner's first had been fourteen years previously under the short-lived *Isaac Asimov Presents* line; while Weiner—for many years a mainstay of *F&SF* and *Asimov's*—was clearly a first-rate writer, his slow pace at producing novels made him unwelcome at the New York houses, but we were able to position him very nicely, and get him reviewed in the *Globe and Mail*, Canada's national newspaper.

"Our third title was again problematic: Tor has been building Karl Schroeder, a new star of hard SF, very nicely—but to follow up one of his novels with a short story collection from them would have shown a precipitous sales drop, since collections don't do nearly as well as novels. By letting us have his collection, it was sufficiently distanced from his Tor titles so as not to create a problem.

"The fourth and fifth books were first novels by writers who'd both gotten rejections from New York houses that had said they'd have bought the books in better economic times; as a small press, RJS Books can make a success of titles that simply aren't viable for big publishers. And our sixth book, coming in the fall of 2006, is actually a reissue of a title that came out in 1992 and was totally botched by its original publisher, a mainstream Canadian house that had no idea what to do with an SF novel—a book by two-time World Fantasy Award novelist Terence M. Green. We're going to relaunch it, and have the first edition of it ever in the United States.

"So, in addition to publishing damn fine books by damn fine writers, I've made a specialty of positioning and placing difficult books—the kind of wonderful titles that don't fit neatly into big publishers' current bottom line–driven thinking."

But as well as providing a home for writers who have been displaced from their major houses, the independent press can also work in synergy with the major houses, especially for those writers who are prolific enough to produce more than one book a year. Author John Scalzi, whose novel *Old Man's War* (Tor, January 2005) is one of the most successful debuts in recent years, has also released a novel and a chapbook through independent publisher Subterranean Press, and has a forthcoming nonfiction work as well. "My experience with them has been excellent," he says. "One of the things I like is that Subterranean Press publisher Bill Schafer sees my publishing relationship with him as complementary to my relationships with larger publishers like Tor, rather than in competition with them. This is good for me because, in fact, I have just one writing career. His seeing my SP work as part of a larger publishing portfolio—and working for my overall benefit as well as his company's own—gives me a feeling of partnership with him. Because he wants to help me succeed on my terms, I want to help him and SP succeed on theirs."

Seconding this opinion is Peter Crowther of PS Publishing, a small house that began life servicing the neglected niche of novella-length works (twenty thousand to forty thousand words) and has since grown to publish collections, full-length novels, and nonfiction. "Small and large publishers are equally important in maximizing the development and ongoing commercial potential of new writers and, of course, in cultivating and maintaining the continued interest of readers. Without either the big guns or the small imprints, the field would be much the poorer, and I think—or hope—that, in its first seven years, PS has established itself at the very forefront of genre publishing. We've moved from four books in 1999 to twenty-two titles in 2005, marrying the breaking of new talents—Adam Nevill (*Banquet for the Damned*), Tracy Knight (*The Astonished Eye*), and, most recently, Joe Hill, with the phenomenal *20th Century Ghosts*—with the celebration of household names through making newly available many hard-to-find works in expanded editions: Such projects include Ray Bradbury's *R Is for Rocket* and *S Is for Space* (plus four more upcoming Bradbury titles), Arthur C. Clarke's *Tales from the White Hart*, Michael G. Coney's *Hello Summer, Goodbye* and *I Remember Pallahaxi*, and Lawrence Block's *Random Walk*."

The independent presses can also shepherd an individual work to the attention of a larger audience. The trade paperback of the aforementioned *The Atrocity Archives* by Charles Stross was later released by Ace, an example of how independent press success primed the way for a large house. Bantam has also picked up paperback rights to several such works, including *The Thackery T. Lambshead Pocket Guide to Eccentric and Discredited Diseases,* and *City of Saints and Madmen* from Jeff Vandermeer, originally published by Night Shade Books and Prime Books, respectively.

Meanwhile, with the democratization of the landscape afforded by the Internet, and new means of advertising and distribution, small and independent publishers are emerging who can claim successes to rival even those of the major houses. One such press is Night Shade Books, whose edition of Iain M. Banks's *The Algebraist* was recently chosen by Amazon as the number one science fiction title of 2005. Night Shade publisher Jason Williams says, "A major high point for me—M. John Harrison's collection *Things That Never Happen* on the *New York Times* summer recommended reading list; our success with Harrison, who was considered unsalable before this, allowed him to get picked up by Bantam and have a career in the United States again. That's one of the main reasons Banks gave us *The Algebraist,* by the way."

Another such example is Small Beer, which burst on the scene with cofounder Kelly Link's short story collection, *Stranger Things Happen,* a title that not only captured the undivided attention of the entire SF&F field, but which catapulted Link out to wider mainstream awareness. Small Beer's Gavin Grant says, "We're interested in bringing readers to works that might have escaped their notice. Maureen F. McHugh's collection, *Mothers and Other Monsters,* is a good example. She has long been a fantasy and science fiction favorite, but less so outside of the genre. We, as many of her editors have felt, thought that given the right notice she could attract a general readership. So we put out a book that we hoped would appeal to readers new and old, and eventually the book began to reach those readers when super librarian Nancy Pearl, one of the Story Prize judges, reviewed it on NPR's *Morning Edition.* We hope the paperback, which has an interview with Maureen as well as an essay and a series of talking points, will be picked up by book clubs."

Whether they are working under the radar, picking up deserving works that have fallen off the tables of the big houses, or working in loose cooperation with these houses or even in competition with them, aided by the democratization of the Internet, the small and independent houses have been a vital part of the science fiction, fantasy, and horror genres since their inception, preserving those genres' histories and contributing to the richness of the ongoing future of the field. The reality is this: Big or small, the focus should not be on competition for eyeballs between houses; the competition is not with one another, but with other media. In a world that offers increasingly more varieties of diversions and distractions from reading in the way of television, movies, DVDs, video games, and Internet sites, every single good book published enriches the genre overall and contains within its pages the potential to grow the readership. There will always be more deserving works than there are available publishing slots in a given year. Every single work of quality that is produced benefits us all. As this brief sampling of houses and opinions demonstrates, the independent presses are doing their part to ensure that the twenty-first century truly is the science fiction and fantasy age, and that the future still lies ahead of us, as gleaming as it ever was.

A List of Independent Publisher Web Sites

www.arkhamhouse.com
www.benbellabooks.com
www.goldengryphon.com
www.isfic.org
www.lcrw.net
www.monkeybrainbooks.com
www.nesfa.org
www.nightshadebooks.com
www.oldearthbooks.com
robertjsawyerbooks.com
www.solarisbooks.com
www.tachyonpublications.com

Joe Haldeman would probably deny it, but somewhere between his first published story and the appearance of *Camouflage,* his third novel to win the Nebula, he became one of the giants of the field. A multiple Hugo and Nebula winner, a WorldCon Guest of Honor, a past president of SFWA, a screenwriter, a workshop teacher, and still a fan, there's no aspect of science fiction that he hasn't mastered. (He's also won three Rhysling Awards for his science fiction poetry.) We can't, of course, run the entire text of *Camouflage* here, but I asked Joe to excerpt about fifteen thousand words, to give you a fair taste of the state of novel writing in science fiction today.

JOE HALDEMAN

The monster came from a swarm of stars that humans call Messier 22, a globular cluster ten thousand light-years distant. A million stars with ten million planets—all but one of them devoid of significant life.

It's not a part of space where life could flourish. All of those planets are in unstable orbits, the stars swinging so close to one another that they steal planets, or pass them around, or eat them.

This makes for ferocious geological and climatic changes; most of the planets are sterile billiard balls or massive Jovian gasbags. But on the one world where life has managed a toehold, that life is *tough*.

And adaptable. What kind of organisms can live on a world as hot as Mercury, which then is suddenly as distant from its sun as Pluto within the course of a few years?

Most of that life survives by simplicity—lying dormant until the proper conditions return. The dominant form of life, though, thrives on change. It's a creature that can force its own evolution—not by natural selection, but by unnatural mutation, changing itself as conditions vary. It becomes whatever it needs to be—and after millions of swifter and swifter changes, it becomes something that can never die.

The price of eternal life had been a life with no meaning beyond simple existence. With its planet swinging wildly through the cluster, the creatures' days were spent crawling through deserts gnawing on rocks, scrabbling across ice, or diving into muck—in search of any food that couldn't get away.

The world spun this way and that, until random forces finally tossed it to the edge of the cluster, away from the constant glare of a million suns—into a stable orbit: a world that was only half day and half night;

a world where clement seas welcomed diversity. Dozens of species became millions, and animals crawled up from the warm sea onto land grown green, buzzing with life.

The immortal creatures relaxed, life suddenly easy. They looked up at night, and saw stars.

They developed curiosity, then philosophy, and then science. During the day, they would squint into a sky with a thousand sparks of sun. In the night's dark, across an ocean of space, the cool billowing oval of our Milky Way Galaxy beckoned.

Some of them built vessels, and hurled themselves into the night. It would be a voyage of a million years, but they'd lived longer than that, and had patience.

A million years before the monster's man is born and its story begins, one such vessel splashes into the Pacific Ocean. It goes deep, following an instinct to hide. The creature that it carried to Earth emerges, assesses the situation, and becomes something appropriate for survival.

For a long time it lives on the dark bottom, under miles of water, large and invincible, studying its situation. Eventually, it abandons its anaerobic hugeness and takes the form of a great white shark, the top of the food chain, and goes exploring, while most of its essence stays safe inside the vessel.

For a long time, it remembers where the vessel is, and remembers where it came from, and why. As centuries go by, though, it remembers less. After dozens of millennia, it simply lives, and observes, and changes.

It encounters humanity and notes their acquired superiority—their placement, however temporary, at the top of every food chain. It becomes a killer whale, and then a porpoise, and then a swimmer, and wades ashore naked and ignorant.

But eager to learn.

ONE

Baja California, 2019

Russell Sutton had done his stint with the U.S. government around the turn of the century, a frustrating middle-management job in two Mars exploration programs. When the second one crashed, he had said good-bye to Uncle Sam and space in general, returning to his first love, marine biology.

He was still a manager and still an engineer, heading up the small firm Poseidon Projects. He had twelve employees, half of them PhDs. They only worked on two or three projects at a time, esoteric engineering problems in marine resource management and exploration. They had a reputation for being wizards, and for keeping both promises and secrets. They could turn down most contracts—anything not sufficiently interesting; anything from the government.

So Russ was not excited when the door to his office eased open and the man who rapped his knuckles on the jamb was wearing an admiral's uniform. His first thought was that they really could afford a receptionist; his second was how to frame a refusal so that the guy would just leave, and not take up any more of his morning.

"Dr. Sutton, I'm Jack Halliburton."

That was interesting. "I read your book in graduate school. Didn't know you were in the military." The man's face was vaguely familiar from his memory of the picture on the back of *Bathyspheric Measurements and Computation;* no beard now, and a little less hair. He still looked like Don Quixote on a diet.

"Have a seat." Russ waved at the only chair not supporting stacks of paper and books. "But let me tell you right off that we don't do government work."

"I know that." He eased himself into the chair and set his hat on the floor. "That's one reason I'm here." He unzipped a blue portfolio and took out a sealed plastic folder. He turned it sideways and pressed his thumb to the corner; it read his print and popped open. He tossed it onto Russell's desk.

The first page had no title but TOP SECRET—FOR YOUR EYES ONLY, in red block letters.

"I can't open this. And as I said—"

"It's not really classified, not yet. No one in the government, outside of my small research group, even knows it exists."

"But you're here as a representative of the government, no? I assume you do own some clothes without stars on the shoulders."

"Protective coloration. I'll explain. Just look at it."

Russ hesitated, then opened the folder. The first page was a picture of a vague cigar shape looming out of a rectangle of gray smears.

"That's the discovery picture. We were doing a positron radar map of the Tonga-Kermadec Trench—"

"Why on earth?"

"That part *is* classified. And irrelevant."

Russ had the feeling that his life was on a cusp, and he didn't like it. He spun around slowly in his chair, taking in the comfortable clutter, the pictures and the charts on the wall. The picture window looking down on the Sea of Cortez, currently calm.

With his back to Halliburton, he said, "I don't suppose this is something we could do from here."

"No. We've chosen a place in Samoa."

"Now, that's attractive. Heat and humidity and lousy food."

"I tend to think pretty girls and no winter." He pushed his glasses back on his nose. "Food's not bad if you don't mind American."

Russ turned back around and studied the picture. "You have to tell me something about why you were there. Did the Navy lose something?"

"Yes."

"Did it have people in it?"

"I can't answer that."

"You just did." He turned to the second page. It was a sharper view of the object. "This isn't from positrons."

"Well, it is. But it's a composite from various angles, noise removed."

Good job, he thought. "How far down is this thing?"

"The trench is seven miles deep there. The artifact is under another forty feet of sand."

"Earthquake?"

He nodded. "A quarter of a million years ago."

Russ stared at him for a long moment. "Didn't I read about this in an old Stephen King novel?"

"Look at the next page."

It was a regular color photograph. The object lay at the bottom of a deep hole. Russ thought about the size of that digging job; the expense of it. "The Navy doesn't know about this?"

"No. We did use their equipment, of course."

"You found the thing they lost?"

"We will next week." He stared out the window. "I'll have to trust you."

"I won't turn you in to the Navy."

He nodded slowly and chose his words. "The submarine that was lost is in the trench, too. Not thirty miles from this . . . object."

"You didn't report it. Because?"

"I've been in the Navy for almost twenty years. Twenty years next month. I was going to retire anyhow."

"Disillusioned?"

"I never was 'illusioned.' Twenty years ago, I wanted to leave academia, and the Navy made me an interesting offer. It has been a fascinating second career. But it hasn't led me to trust the military, or the government.

"Over the past decade I've assembled a crew of like-minded men and women. I was going to take some of them with me when I retired—to set up an outfit like yours, frankly."

Russ went to the coffee machine and refreshed his cup. He offered one to Halliburton, who declined.

"I think I see what you're getting at."

"Tell me."

"You want to retire with your group and set up shop. But if you suddenly 'discover' this thing, the government might notice the coincidence."

"That's a good approximation. Take a look at the next page."

It was a close-up of the thing. Its curved surface mirrored perfectly the probe that was taking its picture.

"We tried to get a sample of the metal for analysis. It broke every drill bit we tried on it."

"Diamond?"

"It's harder than diamond. And massive. We can't estimate its density, because we haven't been able to budge it, let alone lift it."

"Good God."

"If it were an atomic submarine, we could have hauled it up. It's not even a tenth that size.

"If it were made of lead, we could have raised it. If it were solid uranium. It's denser than that."

"I see," Russ said. "Because we raised the *Titanic*. . . ."

"May I be blunt?"

"Always."

"We could bring it up with some version of your flotation techniques. And keep all the profit, which may be considerable. But there would be hell to pay when the Navy connection was made."

"So what's your plan?"

"Simple." He took a chart out of his portfolio and rolled it out on Russ's desk. It snapped flat. "You're going to be doing a job in Samoa. . . ."

TWO

San Guillermo, California, 1931

Before it came out of the water, it formed clothes on the outside of its body. It had observed more sailors than fishermen, so that was what it chose. It waded out of the surf wearing white utilities, not dripping wet because they were not cloth. They had a sheen like the skin of a porpoise. Its internal organs were more porpoise than human.

It was sundown, almost dark. The beach was deserted except for one man, who came running up to the changeling.

"Holy cow, man. Where'd you swim from?"

The changeling looked at him. The man was almost two heads taller than it, with prominent musculature, wearing a black bathing suit.

"Cat got your tongue, little guy?"

Mammals can be killed easily with a blow to the brain. The changeling grabbed his wrist and pulled him down and smashed his skull with one blow.

When the body stopped twitching, the changeling pinched open the thorax and studied the disposition of organs and muscles. It reconfigured itself to match, a slow and painful process. It needed to gain about 30 percent body mass, so it removed both arms, after studying them, and held them to its body until they were absorbed. It added a few handfuls of cooling entrails.

It pulled down the bathing suit and duplicated the reproductive structure that it concealed, and then stepped into the suit. Then it carried the gutted body out to deep water and abandoned it to the fishes.

It walked down the beach toward the lights of San Guillermo, a strapping handsome young man, duplicated down to the fingerprints, a process that had taken no thought, but an hour and a half of agony.

But it couldn't speak any human language and its bathing suit was on backward. It walked with a rolling sailor's gait; except for the one it had just killed, every man it had seen for the past century had been walking on board a ship or boat.

It walked toward light. Before it reached the small resort town, the sky was completely dark, moonless, and spangled with stars. Something made it stop and look at them for a long time.

The town was festive with Christmas decorations. It noticed that other people were almost completely covered in clothing. It could form more clothing on its skin, or kill another one, if it could find one the right size alone. But it didn't get the chance.

Five teenagers came out of a burger joint with a bag of hamburgers. They were laughing, but suddenly stopped dead.

"Jimmy?" a pretty girl said. "What are you doing?"

"Ain't it a little cool for that?" a boy said. "Jim?"

They began to approach it. It stayed calm, knowing it could easily kill all of them. But there was no need. They kept making noises.

"Something's wrong," an older one said. "Did you have an accident, Jim?"

"He drove out with his surfing board after lunch," the pretty girl said, and looked down the road. "I don't see his car."

It didn't remember what language was, but it knew how whales communicated. It tried to repeat the sound they had been making. "Zhim."

"Oh my God," the girl said. "Maybe he hit his head." She approached it and reached toward its face. It swatted her arms away.

"Ow! My God, Jim." She felt her forearm where it had almost fractured it.

"Mike odd," it said, trying to duplicate her facial expression.

One of the boys pulled the girl back. "Somethin' crazy's goin' on. Watch out for him."

"Officer!" the older girl shouted. "Officer Sherman!"

A big man in a blue uniform hustled across the street. "Jim Berry? What the hell?"

"He hit me," the pretty one said. "He's acting crazy."

"My God, Jim," it said, duplicating her intonation.

"Where're your clothes, buddy?" Sherman said, unbuttoning his holster.

It realized that it was in a complex and dangerous situation. It knew these were social creatures, and they were obviously communicating. Best try to learn how.

"Where're your clothes, buddy," it said in a deep bass growl.

"He might have hit his head surfing," the girl who was cradling her arm said. "You know he's not a mean guy."

"I don't know whether to take him home or to the hospital," the officer said.

"The hospital," it said.

"Probably a good idea," he said.

"Good idea," it said. When the officer touched its elbow it didn't kill him.

THREE

Mid-Pacific, 2019

It worked like this: Poseidon Projects landed a contract from a Sea World affiliate—actually a dummy corporation that Jack Halliburton had built out of money and imagination—to raise up a Spanish-American War–era relic, a sunken destroyer, from Samoa. But no sooner had they their equipment in place than they got an urgent summons from the U.S. Navy—there was a nuclear submarine down in the Tonga Trench, and the Navy couldn't lift it as fast as Poseidon could. There might be men still alive in it. They covered the five hundred miles as fast as they could.

Of course Jack Halliburton knew that the sub had ruptured and there was no chance of survivors. But it made it possible for Russell Sutton to ply down the length of the Tonga and Kermadec Trenches. He made routine soundings as he went, and discovered a mysterious wreck not far from the sub.

There was plenty of respectful news coverage of the two crews' efforts—Sutton's working out of professional courtesy and patriotism. Raising the *Titanic* had given them visibility and credibility. With all the derring-do and pathos and technological fascination of the submarine story, it was barely a footnote that Russ's team had seen something interesting on the way, and had claimed salvage rights.

It was an impressive sight when the sub came surging out of the depths, buoyed up by the house-sized orange balloons that Russ had brought to the task. The cameras shut down for the grisly business of removing and identifying the sailors' remains. They all came on again for the 121 flag-draped caskets on the deck of the carrier that wallowed in the sea next to the floating hulk of the sub.

Then the newspeople went home, and the actual story began.

FOUR

San Guillermo, California, 1931

They put a white hospital robe on it and sat it down in an examination room. It continued the safe course of imitative behavior with the doctors and nurses and with the man and woman who were the real Jimmy's father and mother, even duplicating the mother's tears.

The father and mother followed the family doctor to a room out of earshot.

"I don't know what to tell you," Dr. Farben said. "There's no evidence of any injury. He looks to be in excellent health."

"A stroke or a seizure?" the father asked.

"Maybe. Most likely. We'll keep him under observation for a few days. It might clear up. If not, you'll have to make some decisions."

"I don't want to send him to an institution," the mother said. "We can take care of this."

"Let's wait until we know more," the doctor said, patting her hand but looking at the father. "A specialist will look at him tomorrow."

They put it in a ward, where it was observant of the other patients' behavior, even to the extent of using a urinal correctly. The chemistry of the fluid it produced might have puzzled a scientist. The nurse remarked on the fishy odor, not knowing that some of it was left over from a porpoise's bladder.

It spent the night in some pain as its internal organs sorted themselves out. It kept the same external appearance. It reviewed in its mind everything it had observed about human behavior, knowing that it would be some time before it could convincingly interact.

It also reflected back about itself. It was no more a human than it had been a porpoise, a killer whale, or a great white shark. Although its memory faded over millennia, past vagueness into darkness, it had a feeling that most of it was waiting, back there in the sea. Maybe it could go back, as a human, and find the rest of itself.

A couple enjoying the salt air at dawn found a body the tide had left in a rocky pool. It had been clothed only in feasting crabs. There was nothing left of the face or any soft parts, but by its stature, the coroner could tell it had been male. A shark or something had taken both its arms, and all its viscera had been eaten away.

No locals or tourists were missing. A reporter suggested a mob murder, the arms chopped off to get rid of fingerprints. The coroner led him back to show him the remains, to explain why he thought the arms had been pulled off—twisted away—rather than chopped or sawed, but the reporter bolted halfway through the demonstration.

The coroner's report noted that from the state of decomposition of the remaining flesh, he felt the body had been immersed for no more than twelve hours. Sacramento said there were no appropriate missing persons reports. Just another out-of-work drifter. The countryside was full of them, these days, and sometimes they went for a swim with no intention of returning to shore.

Over the next two days, three brain specialists examined Jimmy, and they were perplexed and frustrated. His symptoms resembled a stroke in some ways; in others, profound amnesia from head trauma, for which there was no physical evidence. There might be a tumor involved, but the parents wouldn't give permission for X rays. This was fortunate for the changeling, because the thing in its skull was as much a porpoise brain as it was a human's, and various parts of it were nonhuman crystal and metal.

A psychiatrist spent a couple of hours with Jimmy, and got very little that was useful. His response to the word association test was interesting: he parroted back each word, mocking the doctor's German accent. In later years the doctor might classify the behavior as passive-aggressive, but what he told the parents was that at some level the boy probably had all or most of his faculties, but he had regressed to an infantile state. He suggested that the boy be sent to an asylum, where modern treatment would be available.

The mother insisted on taking him home, but first allowed the doctor to try fever therapy, injecting Jimmy with blood from a tertian malaria patient. Jimmy sat smiling for several days, his temperature unchanging—the body of the changeling consuming the malarial parasites along with other hospital food—and he was finally released to them after a week of fruitless observation.

They had retained both a male and a female nurse; their home overlooking the sea had plenty of room for both employees to stay in residence.

Both of them had worked with retarded children and adults, but within a few days they could see that Jimmy was something totally unrelated to that frustrating experience. He was completely passive but never acted bored. In fact, he seemed to be studying them with intensity.

(The female, Deborah, was used to being studied with intensity: she was pretty and voluptuous. Jimmy's intensity puzzled her because it didn't seem to be at all sexual, and a boy his age and condition ought to be brimming with sexual energy and curiosity. But her "accidental" exposures and touches provoked no response at all. He never had an erection, never tried to look down her blouse, never left any evidence of having masturbated. At this stage in its development, the changeling could only mimic behavior it had seen.)

It was learning how to read. Deborah spent an hour after dinner reading to Jimmy from children's books, tracing the words with her finger. Then she would give Jimmy the book, and he would repeat it, word for word—but in *her* voice.

She had the male nurse, Lowell, read to him, and then of course he would mimic Lowell. That made the feat less impressive, as reading. But his memory was astonishing. If Deborah held up any book he had read and pointed to it, he could recite the whole thing.

Jimmy's mother was encouraged by his progress, but his father wasn't sure, and when Jimmy's psychiatrist, Dr. Grossbaum, made his weekly visit, he sided with the father. Jimmy parroted the list of facial nerves that every medical student memorizes, and then a poem by Schiller, in faultless German.

"Unless he's secretly studied German and medicine," Grossbaum said, "he's not remembering anything from before." He told them about idiots savants, who had astonishing mental powers in some narrow specialty, but otherwise couldn't function normally. But he'd never heard of anyone changing from a normal person into an idiot savant; he promised to look into it.

Jimmy's progress in less intellectual realms was fast. He no longer was clumsy walking around the house and grounds—at first he hadn't seemed to know what doors and windows were. Lowell and Deborah taught him badminton, and after initial confusion he had a natural talent for it—not surprising, since he'd been the best tennis player in his class. They were amazed at what he could do in the swimming pool—when he first jumped in, he did two rapid lengths underwater, using a stroke neither of them could identify. When they demonstrated the Australian crawl, breast stroke, and backstroke, he "remembered" them immediately.

By the second week, he was taking his meals with the family, not only manipulating the complex dinner service flawlessly, but also communicating his desires clearly to the servants, even though he couldn't carry on a simple conversation.

His mother invited Dr. Grossbaum to dinner, so he could see how well Jimmy was getting along with the help. The psychiatrist was impressed, but not because he saw it as evidence of growth. It was like the facial nerves and German poetry; like badminton and swimming. The boy could imitate anybody perfectly. When he was thirsty, he pointed at his glass, and it was filled. That was what his mother did, too.

His parents had evidently not noticed that every time a servant made a noise at Jimmy, he nodded and smiled. When the servant's action was completed, he nodded and smiled again. That did get him a lot of food, but he was a growing boy.

Interesting that the nurses' records showed no change in weight. Exercise?

It was unscientific, but Grossbaum admitted to himself that he didn't like this boy, and for some reason was afraid of him. Maybe it was his psychiatric residency in the penal system—maybe he was projecting from that unsettling time. But he always felt that Jimmy was studying him intently, the way the intelligent prisoners had: *what can I get out of this man?*

A better psychiatrist might have noticed that the changeling treated everyone that way.

RHYSLING AWARD WINNERS

The Rhysling, named for Robert A. Heinlein's Rhysling, "the blind poet of the spaceways," is not a Nebula or an SFWA award, but we're happy to provide a few pages of the Nebula volumes to show you what our poets are doing.

Right now the Rhysling is divided into two categories: short (less than fifty lines) and long (more than fifty lines). I understand that a third category is soon to be added, but that's for future editors to contend with. For now, I'm happy to present the current Rhysling winners for long poem ("Soul Searching," by Tim Pratt) and short poem ("No Ruined Lunar City," by Greg Beatty).

TIM PRATT

On weekends I help my old neighbor look
for his soul. He says he used to be a wizard, or a giant
(the story varies from telling to telling), and, as was
the custom for his kind, he put his soul into an egg
(or perhaps a stone) for safe-keeping. He hid the egg
(or stone) inside a duck (or in the belly
of a sheep, or in a tree stump), and so long
as his soul was safe, his body could not be killed
or wounded. "Oh," he says. "I was the greatest
terror of the hills. I ate the hearts of knights,"
or sometimes, "I lived in my high
tower and none dared oppose me, and with the wave
of my hand I could turn stone to mud
and water to boiling blood."

Or sometimes, "The earth trembled
with my every step." He says this
almost wistfully.

My neighbor is seventy at least, I think,
or older (unless he is hundreds of years old
as he claims). His skin is covered in dark freckles,
liver spots, and moles, and he says that each
blemish marks a year he's lived beyond
his rightful span. All he wants is to find the egg
(or stone) that houses his soul, so that he
may break the egg (or crush the stone) and die.

I asked him once, while we looked for his soul
in the garbage cans at the park, "How
could you misplace your soul?"

"I hid it so well, I forgot
where it was hidden," he said.

"Seems like a hell of a thing
to forget," I said.

"When you don't have a soul,"
he said,
"It's harder to know which things
are important
to remember."

We go out every weekend. He's old.
I live alone. We are companions
for one another. He tells marvelous
stories. I think he must have once
taught mythology, though he tells
the tales of gods and heroes
as if he saw it all firsthand.

Once he found a robin's egg
on the ground. It must have fallen
from a nest. He held the egg
in trembling hands, cracked it,
and yolk spilled out. No soul.

He shook the egg
off his hands. Bits of shell
fell to the ground. He wiped
his hands on his pants
and went on looking, picking
up rocks, dropping them
in disgust and frustration.

We go out every weekend,
we walk the length of the town
and back, but somehow
the earth never trembles.

GREG BEATTY

There is no ruined lunar city,
no airless Macchu Picchu
on the moon.
No spires rise in leaping
Seussian whimsy,
enabled by the one-sixth gee.
There are no domes cracked
by random meteorites,
leaving homes below exposed—
dead and full of surprised dead.
There are no teddy bears
worn threadbare by loonie hands,
eyes cracked by extreme days and nights.
There are no pools of orange
Tang swirled with moondust,
homage spiraling with artistry.
There are no empty spacesuits,
their linings dry and cracked
from decades without air.
No, there are no lost
cities on the moon,
with squares that recall Topeka,
Vladivostok, Quito, or Rome
and streets that run
from crater to mare
only to stand empty
because men have moved on.
But there will be.

THINK OUTSIDE THE PAGE

KEVIN J. ANDERSON

The world is changing—including the world of science fiction publishing. I don't think anyone is more fully aware of this—and of the opportunities it presents—than Kevin J. Anderson, who spends a lot of his time these days living on the bestseller list. I asked him to tell us just how the field is evolving and—just as important—how writers must adjust and adapt to it, and not to pull his punches (not that he ever does). Basically, says Kevin, the future is here, and it would be a shame if the men and women who make a living writing about it were left behind. I think it may be the most important article to appear in a Nebula anthology.

In 1940, A. E. van Vogt published his first novel, *Slan*, in *Astounding Stories*, at the very cusp of the golden age of SF. Not only was van Vogt named Grand Master by SFWA in 1996, he was also a mentor to this year's Grand Master, Harlan Ellison. Before his death, van Vogt began work on a sequel to *Slan* (which I just completed, at the request of his widow). In 2007 that novel will be published, nearly seven decades after the first appearance of the original.

The changes that have occurred in the science fiction genre between the publication of *Slan* and its sequel are so dramatic they would have strained the capabilities of even van Vogt's most fantastical mutation machines. For many years, science fiction consisted primarily of short stories in the pulp magazines, then paperbacks and snickered-at films. SF was seen as the domain of socially inept geeks. Despite aspirations toward literary respectability, the genre was still ridiculed by many and read by few (often in secret); A-list films such as *2001* or *Soylent Green* were anomalies.

Then came a pair of bona fide breakthroughs that changed the genre as significantly as Elvis changed rock-and-roll: *Star Trek* and *Star Wars* (which, ironically, the "elite" of science fiction criticized as being derivative and uninspired). While they offered few surprises to the well-read SF fan, the two franchises achieved something remarkable among the rest of the world—*by effectively making SF accessible to everyone.* The effect on our genre was the equivalent of translating the Bible into the vernacular.

Even though *Star Wars* was following on the heels of George Lucas's very successful *American Graffiti,* he spent years trying to get a major studio to fund the $11 million to make *Star Wars.* Time and again he was turned down because "science fiction is not profitable" and "there's no audience for it." *Star Wars* changed all that. In the meantime, after being canceled from its original run, *Star Trek* was resurrected and became the longest-running franchise in science fiction history. The eleventh motion picture is scheduled to debut in 2008, forty-two years after the first episode was broadcast.

The readership of science fiction was ripe for this popular explosion. The year before the release of *Star Wars,* in 1976, Frank Herbert's *Children of Dune* became the first SF novel ever to hit *The New York Times* best-seller list. Anne McCaffrey's *The White Dragon* followed in 1978. Today SF and fantasy novels regularly appear on all major best-seller lists.

While some purists complained that the very popularity of movies and television shows cheapened the genre, the relationship between books and other entertainment media grew stronger and stronger. A spate of quick knockoffs and novelizations—often poorly written, as admitted by many of the authors who wrote them—did not make the publishing world do handstands. The *Star Trek* book line, however, thrived, and the novelizations of the *Star Wars* films sold extremely well.

Fans of the shows or movies (who were not necessarily readers) wanted to know more about their favorite characters, so they picked up the books. And when that wasn't enough, they followed the media authors to their original novels. It was a new way to create and expand a readership, a marketing tool that science fiction had not effectively used before. (I could see the data with my own eyes when I watched the sales of my original novels jump as soon as I began publishing *Star Wars* novels.)

"Serious" writers began to treat tie-in novels as real books and put in their best work. Eight years after the release of *Return of the Jedi,* and with no prospect of any further *Star Wars* films on the horizon, the first of the new *Star Wars* novels (written by Hugo winner Timothy Zahn) hit number one on *The New York Times* list. Award-winning and well-respected authors as diverse as Greg Bear, Orson Scott Card, Joe Halde-man, Mike Resnick, Elizabeth Hand, Terry Bisson, Pat Cadigan, Barbara Hambly, Vonda McIntyre, Walter Jon Williams, Gregory Benford, David Brin, and many others have written books set in preexisting universes. Successful book lines were also spun off from *X-Files*, *Stargate SG-1*, *Buffy the Vampire Slayer*, *Angel*, *Babylon 5*, *Andromeda*, *Farscape*, *Independence Day*, *Battlestar Galactica* (both versions), *Xena: Warrior Princess*, *High-lander*, and just about any other hit genre show.

In the face of this burgeoning success, a new battle cry rose from hard-core fans and authors that "Media tie-ins will kill SF publishing!" The mistaken belief was that when a media book is published, a "real" novel loses a slot, as if it's a zero-sum game. What in fact happened was that the whole field expanded dramatically. Currently, genre book pub-lishing is at record levels. In 1980, before the media tie-in boom, only about 1,000 total SF/F titles were published annually; in 2005 there were 2,516.

According to this year's *Locus* summary, 198 of those titles were "media related" (in contrast to 212 horror novels, 258 SF novels, and 414 fantasy novels). Even if we remove all of the media books from the list, the total number of SF/F titles published is still 230 percent higher than in 1980. Far from "killing the genre," media books forced stores to expand their SF/F sections from small corners to large chunks of real estate.

Major movies have also proved to be powerful engines that drive the sales of original novels. With the 1984 release of David Lynch's *Dune* film (considered a flop at the time), Frank Herbert's original twenty-year-old novel hit number one on *The New York Times* list and sold an extra million copies. The 1997 film version of Heinlein's *Starship Troop-ers* (which was not highly regarded by the fans) made the original book a *New York Times* best seller nearly four decades after its first appearance. According to *Publishers Weekly*, more copies of Tolkien's *Lord of the Rings* books were sold *in one year* during the release of Peter Jackson's film of *Fellowship of the Ring* than in all the years combined since its original publication in 1954. Since an author's primary purpose is, presumably, to get readers, movies are an extremely effective way to increase the au-dience for a book.

For those who prefer their prose fiction in some medium other than printed words on a page, the audiobook market has skyrocketed. In 2005, Audible, Inc., reported an 83 percent jump in sales from the previ-ous year and a 67 percent increase in individual customers. Currently, audiobooks comprise about 10 percent of the publishing industry, and sales projections show that the market will triple in the next few years. No longer just on cassette tapes or CDs, spoken books are available in many different formats, including downloadable MP3 files so "readers" can listen to them on their iPods.

Unfortunately, every segment of the genre doesn't have such a rosy outlook. On the downside, many of the old magazines have vanished entirely, and the circulation figures of the remaining ones are at record lows, barely a third of their numbers from 1980. Traditional short story markets are drying up. In November 2005 the largest electronic market, scifiction at scifi.com, closed its doors. (On the other hand, a major new electronic publication, Jim Baen's Universe, will debut in 2006.) More than one pundit has pointed to this trend as an indication of the death of science fiction. Without question the genre landscape is changing.

Whereas the heart and soul of SF once resided in magazine short fiction, now the brightest spotlight shines on other aspects of the genre. That doesn't mean great short fiction isn't still being written. You, the readers of this anthology, have a book full of the very best short fiction of the year, as selected by the members of the Science Fiction and Fantasy Writers of America. Short fiction will always be a vital part of SF, but it is no longer the primary source. The creative universe is in a constant state of flux.

Consider: At one time, a strong market for writers was to provide scripts for science fiction, mystery, and thriller radio shows. Those shows eventually went off the air, and the audience went elsewhere. But the demise of radio fiction programs has not meant the demise of fiction, any more than the shrinking circulations of print SF magazines will mean the end of science fiction.

As a genre, science fiction and fantasy is reaching and entertaining more people than ever before and shows no sign of slowing down. An ever-growing audience wants SF. Though they may choose not to get their fix by reading stories in magazines, they will get their SF in other ways. In a genre that prides itself on infinite possibilities and forward thinking, we must imagine—and accept—many new and diverse "delivery systems" for the entertainment that springs from our imaginations. It's time to think outside the page.

The World Science Fiction Convention, tailored primarily to readers, had about four thousand attendees in 2005. At the same time, Dragon★Con in Atlanta—which embraces not only books, but comics, film, TV, anime, and games—drew fifty thousand, while the San Diego Comic-Con handily brought in a hundred thousand.

Instead of a niche catering only to a small group of hard-core readers, science fiction has become a business—big business. In the three decades since George Lucas was told there was no audience and no profit in science fiction, the financial landscape has changed. The biggest moneymaking movies every year are genre films. Twenty-six of the thirty top-grossing films of all time are science fiction or fantasy. In the 1970s Lucas had to beg for $11 million; now the budgets for big genre movies regularly top $200 million.

Box office numbers boggle the mind, and then DVD numbers boggle the mind all over again. *The Lord of the Rings* film trilogy grossed nearly $3 billion worldwide in theaters, not counting DVD sales. The biggest international box office hit of 2005, *Harry Potter and the Goblet of Fire*, brought in $900 million worldwide. Meanwhile, the original *Star Wars* DVD pulled in $115 million on its initial day of release.

An even larger portion of the entertainment pie goes to computer/video games, most of which are science fiction or fantasy-related. In 2004, the SF video game release *Halo 2* earned $125 million in *twenty-four hours.* And the *Halo* universe is not limited to the game itself, but has spawned a series of original novels, a host of guidebooks, an art book, calendars, and two music sound tracks.

SF is dying? Yeah, right.

A critically acclaimed film was based on Andrew Lloyd Webber's *The Phantom of the Opera*, one of the most successful Broadway musicals ever, which itself was based on Gaston Leroux's classic genre novel. *Jeff Wayne's Musical Version of War of the Worlds* was one of the best-selling albums of the decade it was released. The entire Progressive Rock movement of the 1970s and 1980s was based predominantly on SF themes.

Action figures have been made out of characters I created, and the toys were packaged in a box that resembled the cover of my book, complete with my name as author. One of the negotiating points in a recent book contract I signed was for "theme park rights" to the novel.

The science fiction and fantasy genre has matured into a full-fledged player in the entertainment industry, but it consists of more than just books and magazines. Today, SF is plastered on movie marquees and the television show lineup. Games are made of novels. Original novels are based on games. Comic books are spun off of novels, and novels are written about comic book characters. Well-known authors are writing episodes of TV shows, and filmmakers are trying to get into writing books. Movies are regularly made from novels and short stories in our genre, as well as from SF video games, graphic novels, and TV shows. Science fiction has proudly marched far from the boundaries of the printed page.

Are all these major changes and distribution shifts good for short stories and the magazine market? Unfortunately, probably not.

Are the changes good for SF/F books in general? Apparently. More titles are published in almost every category than there were ten or twenty years ago. And that doesn't count audiobooks and e-books. More genre books are hitting the best-seller lists, and major mainstream authors are mining science-fictional tropes for their novels.

Is the changing landscape of genre entertainment good for writers? Of course, although authors may have to make a paradigm shift. Is that so much to ask of futurists and visionaries, creators who thrive on stretching their imaginations? It shouldn't be.

Scriptwriters are *writers*, too. So are game writers, as well as the writers who create all those spinoff projects—from films to comics to tie-in novels to original audio adventures. The end of on-air radio dramas may have put some radio writers out of business, but others changed their way of thinking, turned to new markets, and learned new skills.

Are the changes good for the genre as a whole? Absolutely. People who cling to the idea that "science fiction is only books and stories" are fandom's equivalent of the Amish, restricting themselves to a certain mind-set of a time that was "right," while the rest of the world has advanced far beyond them. The universe changes; readers with a science fiction mind-set should know and accept that better than anyone else.

SF is no longer just words printed on paper. It has branched out in a thousand different directions through numerous multimedia dimensions. Even the most creative among us can't imagine all the ways science fiction writers will be able to deliver their ideas, stories, and characters to a future audience.

Think outside the page, and enjoy your science fiction in whatever manner you choose to consume it.

And here she is again—Kelly Link, of course—this time with the Nebula-winning novelette "The Faery Handbag," which also won the Hugo. Kelly has a pair of collections out and coedits *The Year's Best Fantasy and Horror* and *Lady Churchill's Rosebud Wristlet*. (Lest you think that Kelly has settled for winning the Hugo and Nebula, I suppose I should point out that she's also won the World Fantasy Award, the James Tiptree Jr. Award, and—as an editor—the Bram Stoker Award.)

Before the raiding party arrived, the village packed up all of their belongings and moved into the handbag.

THE FAERY HANDBAG

KELLY LINK

I used to go to thrift stores with my friends. We'd take the train into Boston, and go to the Garment District, which is this huge vintage clothing warehouse. Everything is arranged by color, and somehow that makes all of the clothes beautiful. It's kind of like if you went through the wardrobe in the Narnia books, only instead of finding Aslan and the White Witch and horrible Eustace, you found this magic clothing world—instead of talking animals, there were feather boas and wedding dresses and bowling shoes, and paisley shirts and Doc Martens and everything hung up on racks so that first you have black dresses, all together, like the world's largest indoor funeral, and then blue dresses—all the blues you can imagine—and then red dresses and so on. Pink reds and orangey reds and purple reds and exit-light reds and candy reds. Sometimes I would close my eyes and Natasha and Natalie and Jake would drag me over to a rack, and rub a dress against my hand. "Guess what color this is."

We had this theory that you could learn how to tell, just by feeling, what color something was. For example, if you're sitting on a lawn, you can tell what color green the grass is, with your eyes closed, depending on how silky-rubbery it feels. With clothing, stretchy velvet stuff always feels red when your eyes are closed, even if it's not red. Natasha was always best at guessing colors, but Natasha is also best at cheating at games and not getting caught.

One time we were looking through kids' T-shirts and we found a Muppets T-shirt that had belonged to Natalie in third grade. We knew it belonged to her, because it still had her name inside, where her mother had written it in permanent marker when Natalie went to summer camp. Jake bought it back for her, because he was the only one who had money that weekend. He was the only one who had a job.

Maybe you're wondering what a guy like Jake is doing in The Garment District with a bunch of girls. The thing about Jake is that he always has a good time, no matter what he's doing. He likes everything, and he likes everyone, but he likes me best of all. Wherever he is now, I bet he's having a great time and wondering when I'm going to show up. I'm always running late. But he knows that.

We had this theory that things have life cycles, the way that people do. The life cycle of wedding dresses and feather boas and T-shirts and shoes and handbags involves The Garment District. If clothes are good, or even if they're bad in an interesting way, The Garment District is where they go when they die. You can tell that they're dead, because of the way that they smell. When you buy them, and wash them, and start wearing them again, and they start to smell like you, that's when they reincarnate. But the point is, if you're looking for a particular thing, you just have to keep looking for it. You have to look hard.

Down in the basement at The Garment District they sell clothing and beat-up suitcases and teacups by the pound. You can get eight pounds' worth of prom dresses—a slinky black dress, a poufy lavender dress, a swirly pink dress, a silvery, starry lamé dress so fine you could pass it through a key ring—for eight dollars. I go there every week, hunting for Grandmother Zofia's faery handbag.

The faery handbag: It's huge and black and kind of hairy. Even when your eyes are closed, it feels black. As black as black ever gets, like if you touch it, your hand might get stuck in it, like tar or black quicksand or when you stretch out your hand at night, to turn on a light, but all you feel is darkness.

Fairies live inside it. I know what that sounds like, but it's true.

Grandmother Zofia said it was a family heirloom. She said that it was over two hundred years old. She said that when she died, I had to look after it. Be its guardian. She said that it would be my responsibility.

I said that it didn't look that old, and that they didn't have handbags two hundred years ago, but that just made her cross. She said, "So then tell me, Genevieve, darling, where do you think old ladies used to put their reading glasses and their heart medicine and their knitting needles?"

———

I know that no one is going to believe any of this. That's okay. If I thought you would, then I couldn't tell you. Promise me that you won't believe a word. That's what Zofia used to say to me when she told me stories. At the funeral, my mother said, half-laughing and half-crying, that her mother was the world's best liar. I think she thought maybe Zofia wasn't really dead. But I went up to Zofia's coffin, and I looked her right in the eyes. They were closed. The funeral parlor had made her up with blue eyeshadow, and blue eyeliner. She looked like she was going to be a news anchor on Fox television, instead of dead. It was creepy and it made me even sadder than I already was. But I didn't let that distract me.

"Okay, Zofia," I whispered. "I know you're dead, but this is important. You know exactly how important this is. Where's the handbag? What did you do with it? How do I find it? What am I supposed to do now?"

Of course, she didn't say a word. She just lay there, this little smile on her face, as if she thought the whole thing—death, blue eyeshadow, Jake, the handbag, faeries, Scrabble, Baldeziwurlekistan, all of it—was a joke. She always did have a weird sense of humor. That's why she and Jake got along so well.

I grew up in a house next door to the house where my mother lived when she was a little girl. Her mother, Zofia Swink, my grandmother, babysat me while my mother and father were at work.

Zofia never looked like a grandmother. She had long black hair, which she plaited up in spiky towers. She had large blue eyes. She was taller than my father. She looked like a spy or ballerina or a lady pirate or a rock star. She acted like one too. For example, she never drove anywhere. She rode a bike. It drove my mother crazy. "Why can't you act your age?" she'd say, and Zofia would just laugh.

Zofia and I played Scrabble all the time. Zofia always won, even though her English wasn't all that great, because we'd decided that she was allowed to use Baldeziwurleki vocabulary. Baldeziwurlekistan is where Zofia was born, over two hundred years ago. That's what Zofia said. (My grandmother claimed to be over two hundred years old. Or maybe even older. Sometimes she claimed that she'd even met Genghis Khan. He was much shorter than her. I probably don't have time to tell that story.) Baldeziwurlekistan is also an incredibly valuable word in Scrabble points, even though it doesn't exactly fit on the board. Zofia put it down the first time we played. I was feeling pretty good because I'd gotten forty-one points for *zippery* on my turn.

Zofia kept rearranging her letters on her tray. Then she looked over at me, as if daring me to stop her, and put down *eziwurlekistan*, after *bald*. She used *delicious, zippery, wishes, kismet,* and *needle,* and made *to* into *toe*. *Baldeziwurlekistan* went all the way across the board and then trailed off down the righthand side.

I started laughing.

"I used up all my letters," Zofia said. She licked her pencil and started adding up points.

"That's not a word," I said. "*Baldeziwurlekistan* is not a word. Besides, you can't do that. You can't put an eighteen-letter word on a board that's fifteen squares across."

"Why not? It's a country," Zofia said. "It's where I was born, little darling."

"Challenge," I said. I went and got the dictionary and looked it up. "There's no such place."

"Of course there isn't nowadays," Zofia said. "It wasn't a very big place, even when it was a place. But you've heard of Samarkand, and Uzbekistan and the Silk Road and Genghis Khan. Haven't I told you about meeting Genghis Khan?"

I looked up Samarkand. "Okay," I said. "Samarkand is a real place. A real word. But Baldeziwurlekistan isn't."

"They call it something else now," Zofia said. "But I think it's important to remember where we come from. I think it's only fair that I get to use Baldeziwurleki words. Your English is so much better than me. Promise me something, mouthful of dumpling, a small, small thing. You'll remember its real name. Baldeziwurlekistan. Now when I add it up, I get three hundred and sixty-eight points. Could that be right?"

If you called the faery handbag by its right name, it would be something like *orzipanikanikcz*, which means the "bag of skin where the world lives," only Zofia never spelled that word the same way twice. She said you had to spell it a little differently each time. You never wanted to spell it exactly the right way, because that would be dangerous.

I called it the faery handbag because I put *faery* down on the Scrabble board once. Zofia said that you spelled it with an *i*, not an *e*. She looked it up in the dictionary, and lost a turn.

Zofia said that in Baldeziwurlekistan they used a board and tiles for divination, prognostication, and sometimes even just for fun. She said it was a little like playing Scrabble. That's probably why she turned out to be so good at Scrabble. The Baldeziwurlekistanians used their tiles and board to communicate with the people who lived under the hill. The people who lived under the hill knew the future. The Baldeziwurlekistanians gave them fermented milk and honey, and the young women of the village used to go and lie out on the hill and sleep under the stars. Apparently the people under the hill were pretty cute. The important thing was that you never went down into the hill and spent the night there, no matter how cute the guy from under the hill was. If you did, even if you spent only a single night under the hill, when you came out again, a hundred years might have passed. "Remember that," Zofia said to me. "It doesn't matter how cute a guy is. If he wants you to come back to his place, it isn't a good idea. It's okay to fool around, but don't spend the night."

Every once in a while, a woman from under the hill would marry a man from the village, even though it never ended well. The problem was that the women under the hill were terrible cooks. They couldn't get used to the way time worked in the village, which meant that supper always got burnt, or else it wasn't cooked long enough. But they couldn't stand to be criticized. It hurt their feelings. If their village husband complained, or even if he looked like he wanted to complain, that was it. The woman from under the hill went back to her home, and even if her husband went and begged and pleaded and apologized, it might be three years or thirty years or a few generations before she came back out.

Even the best, happiest marriages between the Baldeziwurlekistanians and the people under the hill fell apart when the children got old enough to complain about dinner. But everyone in the village had some hill blood in them.

"It's in you," Zofia said, and kissed me on the nose. "Passed down from my grandmother and her mother. It's why we're so beautiful."

When Zofia was nineteen, the shaman-priestess in her village threw the tiles and discovered that something bad was going to happen. A raiding party was coming. There was no point in fighting them. They would burn down everyone's houses and take the young men and women for slaves. And it was even worse than that. There was going to be an earthquake as well, which was bad news because usually, when raiders showed up, the village went down under the hill for a night and when they came out again, the raiders would have been gone for months or decades or even a hundred years. But this earthquake was going to split the hill right open.

The people under the hill were in trouble. Their home would be destroyed, and they would be doomed to roam the face of the earth, weeping and lamenting their fate until the sun blew out and the sky cracked and the seas boiled and the people dried up and turned to dust and blew away. So the shaman-priestess went and divined some more, and the people under the hill told her to kill a black dog and skin it and use the skin to make a purse big enough to hold a chicken, an egg, and a cooking pot. So she did, and then the people under the hill made the inside of the purse big enough to hold all of the village and all of the people under the hill and mountains and forests and seas and rivers and lakes and orchards and a sky and stars and spirits and fabulous monsters and sirens and dragons and dryads and mermaids and beasties and all the little gods that the Baldeziwurlekistanians and the people under the hill worshipped.

"Your purse is made out of dog skin?" I said. "That's disgusting!"

"Little dear pet," Zofia said, looking wistful, "dog is delicious. To Baldeziwurlekistanians, dog is a delicacy."

Before the raiding party arrived, the village packed up all of their belongings and moved into the handbag. The clasp was made out of bone. If you opened it one way, then it was just a purse big enough to hold a chicken and an egg and a clay cooking pot, or else a pair of reading glasses and a library book and a pillbox. If you opened the clasp another way, then you found yourself in a little boat floating at the mouth of a river. On either side of you was forest, where the Baldeziwurlekistanian villagers and the people under the hill made their new settlement.

If you opened the handbag the wrong way, though, you found yourself in a dark land that smelled like blood. That's where the guardian of the purse (the dog whose skin had been sewn into a purse) lived. The guardian had no skin. Its howl made blood come out of your ears and nose. It tore apart anyone who turned the clasp in the opposite direction and opened the purse in the wrong way.

"Here is the wrong way to open the handbag," Zofia said. She twisted the clasp, showing me how she did it. She opened the mouth of the purse, but not very wide, and held it up to me. "Go ahead, darling, and listen for a second."

I put my head near the handbag, but not too near. I didn't hear anything. "I don't hear anything," I said.

"The poor dog is probably asleep," Zofia said. "Even nightmares have to sleep now and then."

After he got expelled, everybody at school called Jake Houdini instead of Jake. Everybody except for me. I'll explain why, but you have to be patient. It's hard work telling everything in the right order.

Jake is smarter and also taller than most of our teachers. Not quite as tall as me. We've known each other since third grade. Jake has always been in love with me. He says he was in love with me even before third grade, even before we ever met. It took me a while to fall in love with Jake.

In third grade, Jake knew everything already, except how to make friends. He used to follow me around all day long. It made me so mad that I kicked him in the knee. When that didn't work, I threw his backpack out the window of the school bus. That didn't work either, but the next year Jake took some tests and the school decided that he could skip fourth and fifth grade. Even I felt sorry for Jake then. Sixth grade didn't work out. When the sixth graders wouldn't stop flushing his head down the toilet, he went out and caught a skunk and set it loose in the boys' locker room.

The school was going to suspend him for the rest of the year, but instead Jake took two years off while his mother homeschooled him. He learned Latin and Hebrew and Greek, how to write sestinas, how to make sushi, how to play bridge, and even how to knit. He learned fencing and ballroom dancing. He worked in a soup kitchen and made a Super 8 movie about Civil War reenactors who play extreme croquet in full costume instead of firing off cannons. He started learning how to play guitar. He even wrote a novel. I've never read it—he says it was awful.

When he came back two years later, because his mother had cancer for the first time, the school put him back with our year, in seventh grade. He was still way too smart, but he was finally smart enough to figure out how to fit in. Plus he was good at soccer and he was yummy. Did I mention that he played guitar? Every girl in school had a crush on Jake, but he used to come home after school with me and play Scrabble with Zofia and ask her about Baldeziwurlekistan.

Jake's mom was named Cynthia. She collected ceramic frogs and knock-knock jokes. When we were in ninth grade, she had cancer again. When she died, Jake smashed all of her frogs. That was the first funeral I ever went to. A few months later, Jake's father asked Jake's fencing teacher out on a date. They got married right after the school expelled Jake for his AP project on Houdini. That was the first wedding I ever went to. Jake and I stole a bottle of wine and drank it, and I threw up in the swimming pool at the country club. Jake threw up all over my shoes.

So, anyway, the village and the people under the hill lived happily ever after for a few weeks in the handbag, which they had tied around a rock in a dry well that the people under the hill had determined would survive the earthquake. But some of the Baldeziwurlekistanians wanted to come out again and see what was going on in the world. Zofia was one of them. It had been summer when they went into the bag, but when they came out again, and climbed out of the well, snow was falling and their village was ruins and crumbly old rubble. They walked through the snow, Zofia carrying the handbag, until they came to another village, one that they'd never seen before. Everyone in that village was packing up their belongings and leaving, which gave Zofia and her friends a bad feeling. It seemed to be just the same as when they went into the handbag.

They followed the refugees, who seemed to know where they were going, and finally everyone came to a city. Zofia had never seen such a place. There were trains and electric lights and movie theaters, and there were people shooting each other. Bombs were falling. A war going on. Most of the villagers decided to climb right back inside the handbag, but Zofia volunteered to stay in the world and look after the handbag. She had fallen in love with movies and silk stockings and with a young man, a Russian deserter.

Zofia and the Russian deserter married and had many adventures and finally came to America, where my mother was born. Now and then Zofia would consult the tiles and talk to the people who lived in the handbag and they would tell her how best to avoid trouble and how she and her husband could make some money. Every now and then one of the Baldeziwurlekistanians or one of the people from under the hill came out of the handbag and wanted to go grocery shopping, or to a movie or an amusement park to ride on roller coasters, or to the library.

The more advice Zofia gave her husband, the more money they made. Her husband became curious about Zofia's handbag, because he could see that there was something odd about it, but Zofia told him to mind his own business. He began to spy on Zofia, and saw that strange men and women were coming in and out of the house. He became convinced that either Zofia was a spy for the Communists, or maybe that she was having affairs. They fought and he drank more and more, and finally he threw away her divination tiles. "Russians make bad husbands," Zofia told me. Finally, one night while Zofia was sleeping, her husband opened the bone clasp and climbed inside the handbag.

"I thought he'd left me," Zofia said. "For almost twenty years I thought he'd left me and your mother and taken off for California. Not that I minded. I was tired of being married and cooking dinners and cleaning house for someone else. It's better to cook what I want to eat, and clean up when I decide to clean up. It was harder on your mother, not having a father. That was the part that I minded most.

"Then it turned out that he hadn't run away after all. He spent one night in the handbag and came out again twenty years later, exactly as handsome as I remembered, and enough time had passed that I had forgiven him all the quarrels. We made up and it was all very romantic and then when we had another fight the next morning, he went and kissed your mother, who had slept right through his visit, on the cheek, and then he climbed right back inside the handbag. I didn't see him again for another twenty years. The last time he showed up, we went to see *Star Wars* and he liked it so much that he went back inside the handbag to tell everyone else about it. In a couple of years they'll all show up and want to see it on video and all of the sequels too."

"Tell them not to bother with the prequels," I said.

The thing about Zofia and libraries is that she's always losing library books. She says that she hasn't lost them, and in fact that they aren't even overdue, really. It's just that even one week inside the faery handbag is a lot longer in library-world time. So what is she supposed to do about it? The librarians all hate Zofia. She's banned from using any of the branches in our area. When I was eight, she got me to go to the library for her and check out biographies and science books and Georgette Heyer romance novels. My mother was livid when she found out, but it was too late. Zofia had already misplaced most of them.

It's really hard to write about somebody as if they're really dead. I still think Zofia must be sitting in her living room, in her house, watching some old horror movie, dropping popcorn into her handbag. She's waiting for me to come over and play Scrabble.

Nobody is ever going to return those library books now.

My mother used to come home from work and roll her eyes. "Have you been telling them your fairy stories?" she'd say. "Genevieve, your grandmother is a horrible liar."

Zofia would fold up the Scrabble board and shrug at me and Jake. "I'm a wonderful liar," she'd say. "I'm the best liar in the world. Promise me you won't believe a single word."

But she wouldn't tell the story of the faery handbag to Jake. Only the old Baldeziwurlekistanian folktales and fairy tales about the people under the hill. She told him about how she and her husband made it all the way across Europe, hiding in haystacks and in barns. What she told me was how once, when her husband went off to find food, a farmer found her hiding in his chicken coop and tried to rape her. But she opened up the faery handbag in the way she showed me, and the dog came out and ate the farmer and all his chickens too.

She was teaching Jake and me how to curse in Baldeziwurleki. I also know how to say *I love you,* but I'm not going to ever say it to anyone again, except to Jake, when I find him.

When I was eight, I believed everything Zofia told me. By the time I was thirteen, I didn't believe a single word. When I was fifteen, I saw a man come out of her house and get on Zofia's three-speed bicycle and ride down the street. He wore funny clothes. He was a lot younger than my mother and father, and even though I'd never seen him before, he was familiar. I followed him on my bike, all the way to the grocery store. I waited just past the checkout lanes while he bought peanut butter, Jack Daniel's, half a dozen instant cameras, and at least sixty packs of Reese's peanut butter cups, three bags of Hershey's Kisses, a handful of Milky Way bars and other stuff from the rack of checkout candy. While the checkout clerk was helping him bag up all of that chocolate, he looked up and saw me. "Genevieve?" he said. "That's your name, right?"

I turned and ran out of the store. He grabbed up the bags and ran after me. I don't even think he got his change back. I was still running away, and then one of the straps on my flip-flops popped out of the sole, the way they do, and that made me really angry so I just stopped. I turned around.

"Who are you?" I said.

But I already knew. He looked like he could have been my mom's younger brother. He was really cute. I could see why Zofia had fallen in love with him.

His name was Rustan. Zofia told my parents that he was an expert in Baldeziwurlekistanian folklore who would be staying with her for a few days. She brought him over for dinner. Jake was there too, and I could tell that Jake knew something was up. Everybody except my dad knew something was going on.

"You mean Baldeziwurlekistan is a real place?" my mother asked Rustan. "My mother is telling the truth?"

I could see that Rustan was having a hard time with that one. He obviously wanted to say that his wife was a horrible liar, but then where would he be? Then he couldn't be the person that he was supposed to be.

There were probably a lot of things that he wanted to say. What he said was, "This is really good pizza."

Rustan took a lot of pictures at dinner. The next day I went with him to get the pictures developed. He'd brought back some film with him, with pictures he'd taken inside the faery handbag, but those didn't come out well. Maybe the film was too old. We got doubles of the pictures from dinner so that I could have some too. There's a great picture of Jake, sitting outside on the porch. He's laughing, and he has his hand up to his mouth, like he's going to catch the laugh. I have that picture up on my computer, and also up on my wall over my bed.

I bought a Cadbury Creme Egg for Rustan. Then we shook hands and he kissed me once on each cheek. "Give one of those kisses to your mother," he said, and I thought about how the next time I saw him, I might be Zofia's age, and he would be only a few days older. The next time I saw him, Zofia would be dead. Jake and I might have kids. That was too weird.

I know Rustan tried to get Zofia to go back with him, to live in the handbag, but she wouldn't.

"It makes me dizzy in there," she used to tell me. "And they don't have movie theaters. And I have to look after your mother and you. Maybe when you're old enough to look after the handbag, I'll poke my head inside, just long enough for a little visit."

I didn't fall in love with Jake because he was smart. I'm pretty smart myself. I know that smart doesn't mean nice, or even mean that you have a lot of common sense. Look at all the trouble smart people get themselves into.

I didn't fall in love with Jake because he could make maki rolls and had a black belt in fencing, or whatever it is that you get if you're good in fencing. I didn't fall in love with Jake because he plays guitar. He's a better soccer player than he is a guitar player.

Those were the reasons why I went out on a date with Jake. That, and because he asked me. He asked if I wanted to go see a movie, and I asked if I could bring my grandmother and Natalie and Natasha. He said sure and so all five of us sat and watched *Bring It On* and every once in a while Zofia dropped a couple of Milk Duds or some popcorn into her purse. I don't know if she was feeding the dog, or if she'd opened the purse the right way, and was throwing food at her husband.

I fell in love with Jake because he told stupid knock-knock jokes to Natalie, and told Natasha that he liked her jeans. I fell in love with Jake when he took me and Zofia home. He walked her up to her front door and then he walked me up to mine. I fell in love with Jake when he didn't try to kiss me. The thing is, I was nervous about the whole kissing thing. Most guys think that they're better at it than they really are. Not that I think I'm a real genius at kissing either, but I don't think kissing should be a competitive sport. It isn't tennis.

Natalie and Natasha and I used to practice kissing with each other. Just for practice. We got pretty good at it. We could see why kissing was supposed to be fun.

But Jake didn't try to kiss me. Instead he just gave me this really big hug. He put his face in my hair and he sighed. We stood there like that, and then finally I said, "What are you doing?"

"I just wanted to smell your hair," he said.

"Oh," I said. That made me feel weird, but in a good way. I stuck my nose in his hair, which is brown and curly. I smelled it. We stood there and smelled each other's hair, and I felt so good. I felt so happy.

Jake said into my hair, "Do you know that actor John Cusack?"

I said, "Yeah. One of Zofia's favorite movies is *Better Off Dead*. We watch it all the time."

"So he likes to go up to women and smell their armpits."

"Gross!" I said. "That's such a lie! What are you doing now? That tickles."

"I'm smelling your ear," Jake said.

Jake's hair smelled like iced tea with honey in it, after all the ice has melted.

———

Kissing Jake is like kissing Natalie or Natasha, except that it isn't just for fun. It feels like something there isn't a word for in Scrabble.

The deal with Houdini is that Jake got interested in him during Advanced Placement American History. He and I were both put in tenth-grade history. We were doing biography projects. I was studying Joseph McCarthy. My grandmother had all sorts of stories about McCarthy. She hated him for what he did to Hollywood.

Jake didn't turn in his project—instead he told everyone in our AP class except for Mr. Streep (we call him Meryl) to meet him at the gym on Saturday. When we showed up, Jake reenacted one of Houdini's escapes with a laundry bag, handcuffs, a gym locker, bicycle chains, and the school's swimming pool. It took him three and a half minutes to get free, and this guy named Roger took a bunch of photos and then put the photos online. One of the photos ended up in the *Boston Globe,* and Jake got expelled. The really ironic thing was that while his mom was in the hospital, Jake had applied to M.I.T. He did it for his mom. He thought that way she'd have to stay alive. She was so excited about M.I.T. A couple of days after he'd been expelled, right after the wedding, while his dad and the fencing instructor were in Bermuda, he got an acceptance letter in the mail and a phone call from this guy in the admissions office who explained why they had to withdraw the acceptance.

My mother wanted to know why I let Jake wrap himself up in bicycle chains and then watched while Peter and Michael pushed him into the deep end of the school pool. I said that Jake had a backup plan. Ten more seconds and we were all going to jump into the pool and open the locker and get him out of there. I was crying when I said that. Even before he got in the locker, I knew how stupid Jake was being. Afterwards, he promised me that he'd never do anything like that again.

That was when I told him about Zofia's husband, Rustan, and about Zofia's handbag. How stupid am I?

So I guess you can figure out what happened next. The problem is that Jake believed me about the handbag. We spent a lot of time over at Zofia's, playing Scrabble. Zofia never let the faery handbag out of her sight. She even took it with her when she went to the bathroom. I think she even slept with it under her pillow.

I didn't tell her that I'd said anything to Jake. I wouldn't ever have told anybody else about it. Not Natasha. Not even Natalie, who is the most responsible person in all of the world. Now, of course, if the handbag turns up and Jake still hasn't come back, I'll have to tell Natalie. Somebody has to keep an eye on the stupid thing while I go find Jake.

What worries me is that maybe one of the Baldeziwurlekistanians or one of the people under the hill or maybe even Rustan popped out of the handbag to run an errand and got worried when Zofia wasn't there. Maybe they'll come looking for her and bring it back. Maybe they know I'm supposed to look after it now. Or maybe they took it and hid it somewhere. Maybe someone turned it in at the lost-and-found at the library and that stupid librarian called the FBI. Maybe scientists at the Pentagon are examining the handbag right now. Testing it. If Jake comes out, they'll think he's a spy or a superweapon or an alien or something. They're not going to just let him go.

Everyone thinks Jake ran away, except for my mother, who is convinced that he was trying out another Houdini escape and is probably lying at the bottom of a lake somewhere. She hasn't said that to me, but I can see her thinking it. She keeps making cookies for me.

What happened is that Jake said, "Can I see that for just a second?"

He said it so casually that I think he caught Zofia off guard. She was reaching into the purse for her wallet. We were standing in the lobby of the movie theater on a Monday morning. Jake was behind the snack counter. He'd gotten a job there. He was wearing this stupid red paper hat and some kind of apron bib thing. He was supposed to ask us if we wanted to supersize our drinks.

He reached over the counter and took Zofia's handbag right out of her hand. He closed it and then he opened it again. I think he opened it the right way. I don't think he ended up in the dark place. He said to me and Zofia, "I'll be right back." And then he wasn't there anymore. It was just me and Zofia and the handbag, lying there on the counter where he'd dropped it.

If I'd been fast enough, I think I could have followed him. But Zofia had been guardian of the faery handbag for a lot longer. She snatched the bag back and glared at me. "He's a very bad boy," she said. She was absolutely furious. "You're better off without him, Genevieve, I think."

"Give me the handbag," I said. "I have to go get him."

"It isn't a toy, Genevieve," she said. "It isn't a game. This isn't Scrabble. He comes back when he comes back. If he comes back."

"Give me the handbag," I said. "Or I'll take it from you."

She held the handbag up high over her head, so that I couldn't reach it. I hate people who are taller than me. "What are you going to do now?" Zofia said. "Are you going to knock me down? Are you going to steal the handbag? Are you going to go away and leave me here to explain to your parents where you've gone? Are you going to say good-bye to your friends? When you come out again, they will have gone to college. They'll have jobs and babies and houses and they won't even recognize you. Your mother will be an old woman and I will be dead."

"I don't care," I said. I sat down on the sticky red carpet in the lobby and started to cry. Someone wearing a little metal name tag came over and asked if we were okay. His name was MISSY. Or maybe he was wearing someone else's tag.

"We're fine," Zofia said. "My granddaughter has the flu."

She took my hand and pulled me up. She put her arm around me and we walked out of the theater. We never even got to see the stupid movie. We never even got to see another movie together. I don't ever want to go see another movie. The problem is, I don't want to see unhappy endings. And I don't know if I believe in the happy ones.

"I have a plan," Zofia said. "I will go find Jake. You will stay here and look after the handbag."

"You won't come back either," I said. I cried even harder. "Or if you do, I'll be like a hundred years old and Jake will still be sixteen."

"Everything will be okay," Zofia said. I wish I could tell you how beautiful she looked right then. It didn't matter if she was lying or if she actually knew that everything was going to be okay. The important thing was how she looked when she said it. She said, with absolute certainty, or maybe with all the skill of a very skillful liar, "My plan will work. First we go to the library, though. One of the people under the hill just brought back an Agatha Christie mystery, and I need to return it."

"We're going to the library?" I said. "Why don't we just go home and play Scrabble for a while." You probably think I was just being sarcastic here, and I was being sarcastic. But Zofia gave me a sharp look. She knew that if I was being sarcastic that my brain was working again. She knew that I knew she was stalling for time. She knew that I was coming up with my own plan, which was a lot like Zofia's plan, except that I was the one who went into the handbag. *How* was the part I was working on.

"We could do that," she said. "Remember, when you don't know what to do, it never hurts to play Scrabble. It's like reading the I Ching or tea leaves."

"Can we please just hurry?" I said.

Zofia just looked at me. "Genevieve, we have plenty of time. If you're going to look after the handbag, you have to remember that. You have to be patient. Can you be patient?"

"I can try," I told her. I'm trying, Zofia. I'm trying really hard. But it isn't fair. Jake is off having adventures and talking to talking animals, and who knows, learning how to fly and some beautiful three-thousand-year-old girl from under the hill is teaching him how to speak fluent Baldeziwurleki. I bet she lives in a house that runs around on chicken legs, and she tells Jake that she'd love to hear him play something on the guitar. Maybe you'll kiss her, Jake, because she's put a spell on you. But whatever you do, don't go up into her house. Don't fall asleep in her bed. Come back soon, Jake, and bring the handbag with you.

I hate those movies, those books, where some guy gets to go off and have adventures and meanwhile the girl has to stay home and wait. I'm a feminist. I subscribe to *Bust* magazine, and I watch *Buffy* reruns. I don't believe in that kind of shit.

We hadn't been in the library for five minutes before Zofia picked up a biography of Carl Sagan and dropped it in her purse. She was definitely stalling for time. She was trying to come up with a plan that would counteract the plan that she knew I was planning. I wondered what she thought I was planning. It was probably much better than anything I'd come up with.

"Don't do that!" I said.

"Don't worry," Zofia said. "Nobody was watching."

"I don't care if nobody saw! What if Jake's sitting there in the boat, or what if he was coming back and you just dropped it on his head!"

"It doesn't work that way," Zofia said. Then she said, "It would serve him right, anyway."

That was when the librarian came up to us. She had a name tag on as well. I was so sick of people and their stupid name tags. I'm not even going to tell you what her name was. "I saw that," the librarian said.

"Saw what?" Zofia said. She smiled down at the librarian, like she was Queen of the Library, and the librarian was a petitioner.

The librarian stared hard at her. "I know you," she said, almost sounding awed, like she was a weekend bird-watcher who had just seen Bigfoot. "We have your picture on the office wall. You're Ms. Swink. You aren't allowed to check out books here."

"That's ridiculous," Zofia said. She was at least two feet taller than the librarian. I felt a bit sorry for the librarian. After all, Zofia had just stolen a seven-day book. She probably wouldn't return it for a hundred years. My mother has always made it clear that it's my job to protect other people from Zofia. I guess I was Zofia's guardian before I became the guardian of the handbag.

The librarian reached up and grabbed Zofia's handbag. She was small but she was strong. She jerked the handbag and Zofia stumbled and fell back against a work desk. I couldn't believe it. Everyone except for me was getting a look at Zofia's handbag. What kind of guardian was I going to be?

"Genevieve," Zofia said. She held my hand very tightly, and I looked at her. She looked wobbly and pale. She said, "I feel very bad about all of this. Tell your mother I said so."

Then she said one last thing, but I think it was in Baldeziwurleki.

The librarian said, "I saw you put a book in here. Right here." She opened the handbag and peered inside. Out of the handbag came a long, lonely, ferocious, utterly hopeless scream of rage. I don't ever want to hear that noise again. Everyone in the library looked up. The librarian made a choking noise and threw Zofia's handbag away from her. A little trickle of blood came out of her nose and a drop fell on the floor. What I thought at first was that it was just plain luck that the handbag was closed when it landed. Later on I was trying to figure out what Zofia said. My Baldeziwurleki isn't very good, but I think she was saying something like "Figures. Stupid librarian. I have to go take care of that damn dog." So maybe that's what happened. Maybe Zofia sent part of herself in there with the skinless dog. Maybe she fought it and won and closed the handbag. Maybe she made friends with it. I mean, she used to feed it popcorn at the movies. Maybe she's still in there.

What happened in the library was Zofia sighed a little and closed her eyes. I helped her sit down in a chair, but I don't think she was really there anymore. I rode with her in the ambulance, when the ambulance finally showed up, and I swear I didn't even think about the handbag until my mother showed up. I didn't say a word. I just left her there in the hospital with Zofia, who was on a respirator, and I ran all the way back to the library. But it was closed. So I ran all the way back again, to the hospital, but you already know what happened, right? Zofia died. I hate writing that. My tall, funny, beautiful, book-stealing, Scrabble-playing, storytelling grandmother died.

But you never met her. You're probably wondering about the hand-bag. What happened to it. I put up signs all over town, like Zofia's hand-bag was some kind of lost dog, but nobody ever called.

So that's the story so far. Not that I expect you to believe any of it. Last night Natalie and Natasha came over and we played Scrabble. They don't really like Scrabble, but they feel like it's their job to cheer me up. I won. After they went home, I flipped all the tiles upside-down and then I started picking them up in groups of seven. I tried to ask a ques-tion, but it was hard to pick just one. The words I got weren't so great either, so I decided that they weren't English words. They were Baldezi-wurleki words.

Once I decided that, everything became perfectly clear. First I put down *kirif*, which means "happy news," and then I got a *b*, an *o*, an *l*, an *e*, a *f*, another *i*, an *s*, and a *z*. So then I could make *kirif* into *bolekirifisz*, which could mean "the happy result of a combination of diligent effort and patience."

I would find the faery handbag. The tiles said so. I would work the clasp and go into the handbag and have my own adventures and would rescue Jake. Hardly any time would have gone by before we came back out of the handbag. Maybe I'd even make friends with that poor dog and get to say good-bye, for real, to Zofia. Rustan would show up again and be really sorry that he'd missed Zofia's funeral and this time he would be brave enough to tell my mother the whole story. He would tell her that he was her father. Not that she would believe him. Not that you should believe this story. Promise me that you won't believe a word.

JAMES PATRICK KELLY

James Patrick Kelly, a two-time Hugo winner and frequent Nebula nominee, has quite a few arrows in his literary quiver: novels, short fiction, anthologies, collections, plays, poems, essays, even planetarium shows. In 2004 the governor of New Hampshire appointed him chair of the State Council on the Arts. Jim is also on the faculty of the Stonecoast creative writing MFA program at the University of Southern Maine. "Men Are Trouble" shows his versatility, successfully bringing the outlook and language of Raymond Chandler to science fiction.

MEN ARE TROUBLE

JAMES PATRICK KELLY

ONE

I stared at my sidekick, willing it to chirp. I'd already tried watching the door, but no one had even breathed on it. I could've been writing up the Rashmi Jones case, but then I could've been dusting the office. It needed dusting. Or having a consult with Johnnie Walker, who had just that morning opened an office in the bottom drawer of my desk. Instead, I decided to open the window. Maybe a new case would arrive by carrier pigeon. Or wrapped around a brick.

Three stories below me, Market Street was as empty as the rest of the city. Just a couple of plain janes in walking shoes and a granny in a blanket and sandals. She was sitting on the curb in front of a dead Starbucks, strumming street guitar for pocket change, hoping to find a philanthropist in hell. Her singing was faint but sweet as peach ice cream. *My guy, talking 'bout my guy.* Poor old bitch, I thought. There are no guys—not yours, not anyone's. She stopped singing as a devil flapped over us, swooping for a landing on the next block. It had been a beautiful June morning until then, the moist promise of spring not yet broken by summer in our withered city. The granny struggled up, leaning on her guitar. She wrapped the blanket tight around her and trudged downtown.

My sidekick did chirp then, but it was Sharifa, my about-to-be ex-lover. She must have been calling from the hospital; she was wearing her light blue scrubs. Even on the little screen, I could see that she had been crying. "Hi, Fay."

I bit my lip.

"Come home tonight," she said. "Please."

"I don't know where home is."

"I'm sorry about what I said." She folded her arms tight across her chest. "It's your body. Your life."

I loved her. I was sick about being seeded, the abortion, everything that had happened between us in the last week. I said nothing.

Her voice was sandpaper on glass. "Have you had it done yet?" That made me angry all over again. She was wound so tight she couldn't even say the word.

"Let me guess, Doctor," I said. "Are we talking about me getting scrubbed?"

Her face twisted. "Don't."

"If you want the dirt," I said, "you could always hire me to shadow myself. I need the work."

"Make it a joke, why don't you?"

"Okey-doke, Doc," I said and clicked off. So my life was cocked—not exactly main menu news. Still, even with the window open, Sharifa's call had sucked all the air out of my office. I told myself that all I needed was coffee, although what I really wanted was a rich aunt, a vacation in Fiji, and a new girlfriend. I locked the door behind me, slogged down the hall and was about to press the down button when the elevator chimed. The doors slid open to reveal George, the bot in charge of our building, and a devil—no doubt the same one that had just flown by. I told myself this had nothing to do with me. The devil was probably seeing crazy Martha down the hall about a tax rebate or taking piano lessons from Abby upstairs. Sure, and drunks go to bars for the peanuts.

"Hello, Fay," said George. "This one had true hopes of finding you in your office."

I goggled, slack-jawed and stupefied, at the devil. Of course, I'd seen them on vids and in the sky and once I watched one waddle into City Hall but I'd never been close enough to slap one before. I hated the devils. The elevator doors shivered and began to close. George stuck an arm out to stop them.

"May this one borrow some of your time?" George said.

The devil was just over a meter tall. Its face was the color of an old bloodstain and its maw seemed to kiss the air as it breathed with a wet, sucking sound. The wings were wrapped tight around it; the membranes had a rusty translucence that only hinted at the sleek bullet of a body beneath. I could see my reflection in its flat compound eyes. I looked like I had just been hit in the head with a lighthouse.

"Something is regrettable, Fay?" said George.

That was my cue for a wisecrack to show them that no invincible mass-murdering alien was going to intimidate Fay Hardaway.

"No," I said. "This way."

If they could've sat in chairs, there would've been plenty of room for us in my office. But George announced that the devil needed to make itself comfortable before we began. I nodded as I settled behind my desk, grateful to have something between the two of them and me. George dragged both chairs out into the little reception room. The devil spread its wings and swooped up onto my file cabinet, ruffling the hardcopy on my desk. It filled the back wall of my office as it perched there, a span of almost twenty feet. George wedged himself into a corner and absorbed his legs and arms until he was just a head and a slab of gleaming blue bot stuff. The devil gazed at me as if it were wondering what kind of rug I would make. I brought up three new icons on my desktop. *New Case. Searchlet. Panic button.*

"Indulge this one to speak for Seeren?" said George. "Seeren has a bright desire to task you to an investigation."

The devils never spoke to us, never explained what they were doing. No one knew exactly how they communicated with the army of bots they had built to prop us up.

I opened the *New Case* folder and the green light blinked. "I'm recording this. If I decide to accept your case, I will record my entire investigation."

"A thoughtful gesture, Fay. This one needs to remark on your client Rashmi Jones."

"She's not my client." It took everything I had not to fall off my chair. "What about her?"

"Seeren conveys vast regret. All deaths diminish all."

I didn't like it that this devil knew anything at all about Rashmi, but especially that she was dead. I'd found the body in Room 103 of the Comfort Inn just twelve hours ago. "The cops already have the case." I didn't mind that there was a snarl in my voice. "Or what's left of it. There's nothing I can do for you."

"A permission, Fay?"

The icon was already flashing on my desktop. I opened it and saw a pix of Rashmi in the sleeveless taupe dress that she had died in. She had the blue ribbon in her hair. She was smiling, as carefree as a kid on the last day of school. The last thing she was thinking about was sucking on an inhaler filled with hydrogen cyanide. Holding her hand was some brunette dressed in a mannish chalk-stripe suit and a matching pillbox hat with a veil as fine as smoke. The couple preened under a garden arch that dripped with pink roses. They faced right, in the direction of the hand of some third party standing just off camera. It was an elegant hand, a hand that had never been in dishwater or changed a diaper. There was a wide silver ring on the fourth finger, engraved with a pattern or maybe some kind of fancy writing. I zoomed in on the ring and briefly tormented pixels but couldn't get the pattern resolved.

I looked up at the devil and then at George. "So?"

"This one notices especially the digimark," said George. "Date-stamped June 12, 2:52."

"You're saying it was taken yesterday afternoon?"

That didn't fit—except that it did. I had Rashmi downtown shopping for shoes late yesterday morning. At 11:46 she bought a $13 pair of this season's Donya Durands and, now missing. At 1:23 she charged 89¢ for a Waldorf salad and an iced tea at Maison Diana. She checked into the Comfort Inn at 6:40. She didn't have a reservation, so maybe this was a spur of the moment decision. The desk clerk remembered her as distraught. That was the word she used. A precise word, although a bit highbrow for the Comfort Inn. Who buys expensive shoes the day she intends to kill herself? Somebody who is distraught. I glanced again at my desktop. Distraught was precisely what Rashmi Jones was not in this pix. Then I noticed the shoes: ice and taupe Donya Durands.

"Where did you get this?" I said to the devil.

It stared through me like I was a dirty window.

I tried the bot. I wouldn't say that I liked George exactly, but he'd always been straight with me. "What's this about, George? Finding the tommy?"

"The tommy?"

"The woman holding Rashmi's hand."

"Seeren has made this one well aware of Kate Vermeil," said George. "Such Kate Vermeil takes work at 44 East Washington Avenue and takes home at 465 12th Avenue, Second Floor Left."

I liked that, I liked it a lot. Rashmi's mom had told me that her daughter had a Christer friend called Kate, but I didn't even have a last name, much less an address. I turned to the devil again. "You know this how?"

All that got me was another empty stare.

"Seeren," I said, pushing back out of my chair, "I'm afraid George has led you astray. I'm the private investigator." I stood to show them out. "The mind reader's office is across the street."

This time George didn't ask permission. My desktop chirped. I waved open a new icon. A certified bank transfer in the amount of a thousand dollars dragged me back onto my chair.

"A cordial inducement," said George. "With a like amount offered after the success of your investigation."

I thought of a thousand dinners in restaurants with linen tablecloths. "Tell me already." A thousand bottles of smoky scotch.

"This one draws attention to the hand of the unseen person," said the bot. "Seeren has the brightest desire to meeting such person for fruitful business discussions."

The job smelled like the dumpster at Fran's Fish Fry. Precious little money changed hands in the pretend economy. The bots kept everything running, but they did nothing to create wealth. That was supposed to be up to us, I guess, only we'd been sort of discouraged. In some parts of town, that kind of change could hire a Felony 1, with a handful of Misdemeanors thrown in for good luck.

"That's more than I'm worth," I said. "A hundred times more. If Seeren expects me to break the arm attached to that hand, it's talking to the wrong jane."

"Violence is to be deplored," said George. "However, Seeren tasks Fay to discretion throughout. Never police, never news, never even rumor if possible."

"Oh, discretion." I accepted the transfer. "For two large, I can be as discreet as the Queen's butler."

TWO

I could've taken a cab, but they're almost all driven by bots now, and bots keep nobody's secrets. Besides, even though I had a thousand dollars in the bank, I thought I'd let it settle in for a while. Make itself at home. So I bicycled over to 12th Avenue. I started having doubts as I hit the 400 block. This part of the city had been kicked in the head and left bleeding on the sidewalk. Dark bars leaned against pawnshops. Board-ups turned their blank plywood faces to the street. There would be more bots than women in this neighborhood and more rats than bots.

The Adagio Spa squatted at 465 12th Avenue. It was a brick building with a reinforced luxar display window that was so scratched it looked like a thin slice of rainstorm. There were dusty plants behind it. The second floor windows were bricked over. I chained my bike to a dead car, set my sidekick to record and went in.

The rear wall of the little reception area was bright with pix of some Mediterranean seaside town. A clump of bad pixels made the empty beach flicker. A bot stepped through the door that led to the spa and took up a position at the front desk. "Good afternoon, Madam," he said. "It's most gratifying to welcome you. This one is called . . ."

"I'm looking for Kate Vermeil." I don't waste time on chitchat with bots. "Is she in?"

"It's regrettable that she no longer takes work here."

"She worked here?" I said. "I was told she lived here."

"You was told wrong." A granny filled the door, and then hobbled through, leaning on a metal cane. She was wearing a yellow flowered dress that was not quite as big as a circus tent and over it a blue smock with *Noreen* embroidered over the left breast. Her face was wide and pale as a hardboiled egg, her hair a ferment of tight gray curls. She had the biggest hands I had ever seen. "I'll take care of this, Barry. Go see to Helen Ritzi. She gets another needle at twelve, then turn down the heat to 101."

The bot bowed politely and left us.

"What's this about then?" The cane wobbled and she put a hand on the desk to steady herself.

I dug the sidekick out of my slacks, opened the PI license folder and showed it to her. She read it slowly, sniffed and handed it back. "Young fluffs working at play jobs. Do something useful, why don't you?"

"Like what?" I said. "Giving perms? Face peels?"

She was the woman of steel; sarcasm bounced off her. "If nobody does a real job, pretty soon the damn bots will replace us all."

"Might be an improvement." It was something to say, but as soon as I said it I wished I hadn't. My generation was doing better than the grannies ever had. Maybe someday our kids wouldn't need bots to survive.

Our kids. I swallowed a mouthful of ashes and called the pix Seeren had given me onto the sidekick's screen. "I'm looking for Kate Vermeil." I aimed it at her.

She peered at the pix and then at me. "You need a manicure."

"The hell I do."

"I work for a living, fluff. And my hip hurts if I stand up too long." She pointed her cane at the doorway behind the desk. "What did you say your name was?"

The battered manicure table was in an alcove decorated with fake grapevines that didn't quite hide the water stains in the drop ceiling. Dust covered the leaves, turning the plastic fruit from purple to gray.

Noreen rubbed a thumb over the tips of my fingers. "You bite your nails, or do you just cut them with a chainsaw?"

She wanted a laugh so I gave her one.

"So, nails square, round, or oval?" Her skin was dry and mottled with liver spots.

"Haven't a clue." I shrugged. "This was your idea."

Noreen perched on an adjustable stool that was cranked low so that her face was only a foot above my hands. There were a stack of stainless steel bowls, a jar of Vaseline, a round box of salt, a bowl filled with packets of sugar stolen from McDonald's, and a liquid soap dispenser on the table beside her. She started filing each nail from the corner to the center, going from left to right and then back. At first she worked in silence. I decided not to push her.

"Kate was my masseuse up until last week," she said finally. "Gave her notice all of a sudden and left me in the lurch. I've had to pick up all her appointments and me with the bum hip. Some days I can't hardly get out of bed. Something happen to her?"

"Not as far as I know."

"But she's missing."

I shook my head. "I don't know where she is, but that doesn't mean she's missing."

Noreen poured hot water from an electric kettle into one of the stainless steel bowls, added cool water from a pitcher, squirted soap and swirled the mixture around. "You soak for five minutes." She gestured for me to dip my hands into the bowl. "I'll be back. I got to make sure that Barry doesn't burn Helen Ritzi's face off." She stood with a grunt.

"Wait," I said. "Did she say why she was quitting?"

Noreen reached for her cane. "Couldn't stop talking about it. You'd think she was the first ever."

"The first to what?"

The granny laughed. "You're one hell of a detective, fluff. She was supposed to get married yesterday. Tell me that pix you're flashing ain't her doing the deed."

She shuffled off, her white nursemate shoes scuffing against dirty linoleum. From deeper in the spa, I heard her kettle drum voice and then the bot's snare. I was itching to take my sidekick out of my pocket, but I kept my hands in the soak. Besides, I'd looked at the pix enough times to know that she was right. A wedding. The hand with the ring would probably belong to a Christer priest. There would have been a witness and then the photographer, although maybe the photographer was the witness. Of course, I had tumbled to none of this in the two days I'd worked Rashmi Jones's disappearance. I was one hell of a detective, all right. And Rashmi's mom must not have known either. It didn't make sense that she would hire me to find her daughter and hold something like that back.

"I swear," said Noreen, leaning heavily on the cane as she creaked back to me, "that bot is scary. I sent down to City Hall for it just last week and already it knows my business left, right, up, and down. The thing is, if they're so smart, how come they talk funny?"

"The devils designed them to drive us crazy."

"They didn't need no bots to do that, fluff."

She settled back onto her stool, tore open five sugar packets and emptied their contents onto her palm. Then she reached for the salt box and poured salt onto the sugar. She squirted soap onto the pile and then rubbed her hands together. "I could buy some fancy exfoliating cream but this works just as good." She pointed with her chin at my hands. "Give them a shake and bring them here."

I wanted to ask her about Kate's marriage plans, but when she took my hands in hers, I forgot the question. I'd never felt anything quite like it; the irritating scratch of the grit was offset by the sensual slide of our soapy fingers. Pleasure with just the right touch of pain—something I'd certainly be telling Sharifa about, if Sharifa and I were talking. My hands tingled for almost an hour afterward.

Noreen poured another bowl of water and I rinsed. "Why would getting married make Kate want to quit?" I asked.

"I don't know. Something to do with her church?" Noreen patted me dry with a threadbare towel. "She went over to the Christers last year. Maybe Jesus don't like married women giving backrubs. Or maybe she got seeded." She gave a bitter laugh. "Everybody does eventually."

I let that pass. "Tell me about Kate. What was she like to work with?"

"Average for the kind of help you get these sorry days." Noreen pushed at my cuticles with an orangewood stick. "Showed up on time mostly; I could only afford to bring her in two days a week. No go-getter, but she could follow directions. Problem was she never really got close to the customers, always acting like this was just a pitstop. Kept to herself mostly, which was how I could tell she was excited about getting married. It wasn't like her to babble."

"And the bride?"

"Some Indian fluff—Rashy or something."

"Rashmi Jones."

She nodded. "Her I never met."

"Did she go to school?"

"Must have done high school, but damned if I know where. Didn't make much of an impression, I'd say. College, no way." She opened a drawer where a flock of colored vials was nesting. "You want polish or clear coat on the nails?"

"No color. It's bad for business."

She leered at me. "Business is good?"

"You say she did massage for you?" I said. "Where did she pick that up?"

"Hold still now." Noreen uncapped the vial; the milky liquid that clung to the brush smelled like super glue's evil twin. "This is fast dry." She painted the stuff onto my nails with short, confident strokes. "Kate claimed her mom taught her. Said she used to work at the health club at the Radisson before it closed down."

"Did the mom have a name?"

"Yeah." Noreen chewed her lower lip as she worked. "Mom. Give the other hand."

I extended my arm. "So if Kate didn't live here, where did she live?"

"Someplace. Was on her application." She kept her head down until she'd finished. "You're done. Wave them around a little—that's it."

After a moment, I let my arms drop to my side. We stared at each other. Then Noreen heaved herself off the stool and led me back out to the reception room.

"That'll be eighty cents for the manicure, fluff." She waved her desktop on. "You planning on leaving a tip?"

I pulled out the sidekick and beamed two dollars at the desk. Noreen opened the payment icon, grunted her approval and then opened another folder. "Says here she lives at 44 East Washington Avenue."

I groaned.

"Something wrong?"

"I already have that address."

"Got her call too? Kate@Washington.03284."

"No, that's good. Thanks." I went to the door and paused. I don't know why I needed to say anything else to her, but I did. "I help people, Noreen. Or at least I try. It's a real job, something bots can't do."

She just stood there, kneading the bad hip with a big, dry hand.

I unchained my bike, pedaled around the block and then pulled over. I read Kate Vermeil's call into my sidekick. Her sidekick picked up on the sixth chirp. There was no pix.

"You haven't reached Kate yet, but your luck might change if you leave a message at the beep." She put on the kind of low, smoky voice that doesn't come out to play until dark. It was a nice act.

"Hi Kate," I said. "My name is Fay Hardaway and I'm a friend of Rashmi Jones. She asked me to give you a message about yesterday so please give me a call at Fay@Market.03284." I wasn't really expecting her to respond, but it didn't hurt to try.

I was on my way to 44 East Washington Avenue when my sidekick chirped in the pocket of my slacks. I picked up. Rashmi Jones's mom, Najma, stared at me from the screen with eyes as deep as wells.

"The police came," she said. "They said you were supposed to notify them first. They want to speak to you again."

They would. So I'd called the law after I called the mom—they'd get over it. You don't tell a mother that her daughter is dead and then ask her to act surprised when the cops come knocking. "I was working for you, not them."

"I want to see you."

"I understand."

"I hired you to find my daughter."

"I did," I said. "Twice." I was sorry as soon as I said it.

She glanced away; I could hear squeaky voices in the background. "I want to know everything," she said. "I want to know how close you came."

"I've started a report. Let me finish it and I'll bring it by later. . . ."

"Now," she said. "I'm at school. My lunch starts at eleven-fifty and I have recess duty at twelve-fifteen." She clicked off.

I had nothing to feel guilty about, so why was I tempted to wriggle down a storm drain and find the deepest sewer in town? Because a mom believed that I hadn't worked fast enough or smart enough to save her daughter? Someone needed to remind these people that I didn't fix lost things, I just found them. But that someone wouldn't be me. My play now was simply to stroll into her school and let her beat me about the head with her grief. I could take it. I ate old Bogart movies for breakfast and spit out bullets. And at the end of this cocked day, I could just forget about Najma Jones, because there would be no Sharifa reminding me how much it cost me to do my job. I took out my sidekick, linked to my desktop and downloaded everything I had in the Jones file. Then I swung back onto my bike.

The mom had left a message three days ago, asking that I come out to her place on Ashbury. She and her daughter rattled around in an old

Victorian with gingerbread gables and a front porch the size of Cuba. The place had been in the family for four generations. Theirs had been a big family—once. The mom said that Rashmi hadn't come home the previous night. She hadn't called and didn't answer messages. The mom had contacted the cops, but they weren't all that interested. Not enough time would have passed for them. Too much time had passed for the mom.

The mom taught fifth grade at Reagan Elementary. Rashmi was a twenty-six-year-old grad student, six credits away from an MFA in Creative Writing. The mom trusted her to draw money from the family account, so at first I thought I might be able to find her by chasing debits. But there was no activity in the account we could attribute to the missing girl. When I suggested that she might be hiding out with friends, the mom went prickly on me. Turned out that Rashmi's choice of friends was a cause of contention between them. Rashmi had dropped her old pals in the last few months and taken up with a new, religious crowd. Alix, Gratiana, Elaine, and Kate—the mom didn't know their last names—were members of the Church of Christ the Man. I'd had trouble with Christers before and wasn't all that eager to go up against them again, so instead I biked over to campus to see Rashmi's advisor. Zelda Manotti was a dithering old granny who would have loved to help except she had all the focus of paint spatter. She did let me copy Rashmi's novel-in-progress. And she did let me tag along to her advanced writing seminar, in case Rashmi showed up for it. She didn't. I talked to the three other students after class, but they either didn't know where she was or wouldn't say. None of them was Gratiana, Alix, or Elaine.

That night I skimmed *The Lost Heart,* Rashmi's novel. It was a nostalgic and sentimental weeper set back before the devils disappeared all the men. Young Brigit Bird was searching for her father, a famous architect who had been kidnapped by Colombian drug lords. If I was just a fluff doing a fantasy job in the pretend economy, then old Noreen would have crowned Rashmi Jones queen of fluffs.

I'd started day two back at the Joneses' home. The mom watched as I went through Rashmi's room. I think she was as worried about what I might find as she was that I would find nothing. Rashmi listened to the Creeps, had three different pairs of Kat sandals, owned everything Denise Pepper had ever written, preferred underwire bras and subscribed to *News for the Confused.* She had kicked about a week's worth of dirty clothes under her bed. Her wallpaper mix cycled through koalas, the World's Greatest Beaches, ruined castles, and *Playgirl* Center-folds 2000–2010. She'd kept a handwritten diary starting in the sixth grade and ending in the eighth in which she often complained that her mother was strict and that school was boring. The only thing I found that rattled the mom was a Christer Bible tucked into the back of the bottom drawer of the nightstand. When I pulled it out, she flushed and stalked out of the room.

I found my lead on the Joneses' home network. Rashmi was not par-ticularly diligent about backing up her sidekick files, and the last one I found was almost six months old, which was just about when she'd got-ten religion. She'd used simple encryption, which wouldn't withstand a serious hack, but which would discourage the mom from snooping. I doglegged a key and opened the file. She had multiple calls. Her mother had been trying her at Rashmi@Ashbury.03284. But she also had an al-ternate: Brigitbird@Vincent.03284. I did a reverse lookup and that turned an address: The Church of Christ the Man, 348 Vincent Avenue. I wasn't keen for a personal visit to the church, so I tried her call.

"Hello," said a voice.

"Is this Rashmi Jones?"

The voice hesitated. "My name is Brigit. Leave me alone."

"Your mother is worried about you, Rashmi. She hired me to find you."

"I don't want to be found."

"I'm reading your novel, Rashmi." It was just something to say; I wanted to keep her on the line. "I was wondering, does she find her fa-ther at the end?"

"No." I could hear her breath caressing the microphone. "The dev-ils come. That's the whole point."

Someone said something to her and she muted the speaker. But I knew she could still hear me. "That's sad, Rashmi. But I guess that's the way it had to be."

Then she hung up.

The mom was relieved that Rashmi was all right, furious that she was with Christers. So what? I'd found the girl: case closed. Only Najma Jones begged me to help her connect with her daughter. She was already into me for twenty bucks plus expenses, but for another five I said I'd try to get her away from the church long enough for them to talk. I was on my way over when the searchlet I'd attached to the Jones account turned up the hit at Grayle's Shoes. I was grateful for the reprieve, even more pleased when the salesbot identified Rashmi from her pix. As did the waitress at Maison Diana.

And the clerk at the Comfort Inn.

THREE

Ronald Reagan Elementary had been recently renovated, no doubt by a squad of janitor bots. The brick façade had been cleaned and repointed; the long row of windows gleamed like teeth. The asphalt playground had been ripped up and resurfaced with safe-t-mat, the metal swingsets swapped for gaudy towers and crawl tubes and slides and balance beams and decks. The chain link fences had been replaced by redwood lattice through which twined honeysuckle and clematis. There was a boxwood maze next to the swimming pool that shimmered, blue as a dream. Nothing was too good for the little girls—our hope for the future.

There was no room in the rack jammed with bikes and scooters and goboards, so I leaned my bike against a nearby cherry tree. The very youngest girls had come out for first recess. I paused behind the tree for a moment to let their whoops and shrieks and laughter bubble over me. My business didn't take me to schools very often; I couldn't remember when I had last seen so many girls in one place. They were black and white and yellow and brown, mostly dressed like janes you might see anywhere. But there were more than a few whose clothes proclaimed their mothers' lifestyles. Tommys in hunter camo and chaste Christers, twists in chains and spray-on, clumps of sisters wearing the uniforms of a group marriage, a couple of furries and one girl wearing a body suit that looked just like bot skin. As I lingered there, I felt a chill that had nothing to do with the shade of a tree. I had no idea who these tiny creatures were. They went to this well-kept school, led more or less normal lives. I grew up in the wild times, when everything was falling apart. At that moment, I realized that they were as far removed from me as I was from the grannies. I would always watch them from a distance.

Just inside the fence, two sisters in green-striped shirtwaists and green knee socks were turning a rope for a ponytailed jumper who was executing nimble criss-crosses. The turners chanted,

"Down in the valley where the green grass grows,

"There sits Stacy pretty as a rose! She sings, she sings, she sings so sweet,

"Then along comes Chantall to kiss her on the cheek!"

Another jumper joined her in the middle, matching her step for step, her dark hair flying. The chant continued,

"How many kisses does she get?

"One, two, three, four, five. . . ."

The two jumpers pecked at each other in the air to the count of ten without missing a beat. Then Ponytail skipped out and the turners began the chant over again for the dark-haired girl. Ponytail bent over for a moment to catch her breath; when she straightened, she noticed me.

"Hey you, behind the tree." She shaded her eyes with a hand. "You hiding?"

I stepped into the open. "No."

"This is our school, you know." The girl set one foot behind the other and then spun a hundred and eighty degrees to point at the door to the school. "You supposed to sign in at the office."

"I'd better take care of that then."

As I passed through the gate into the playground, a few of the girls stopped playing and stared. This was all the audience Ponytail needed. "You someone's mom?"

"No."

"Don't you have a job?" She fell into step beside me.

"I do."

"What is it?"

"I can't tell you."

She dashed ahead to block my path. "Probably because it's a pretend job."

Two of her sisters in green-striped shirtwaists scrambled to back her up.

"When we grow up," one of them announced, "we're going to have real jobs."

"Like a doctor," the other said. "Or a lion tamer."

Other girls were joining us. "I want to drive a truck," said a tommy. "Big, big truck." She specified the size of her rig with outstretched arms.

"That's not a real job. Any bot could do that."

"I want to be a teacher," said the dark-haired sister who had been jumping rope.

"Chantall loves school," said a furry. "She'd marry school if she could." Apparently this passed for brilliant wit in the third grade; some girls laughed so hard they had to cover their mouths with the backs of their hands. Me, I was flummoxed. Give me a spurned lover or a mean drunk or a hardcase cop and I could figure out some play, but just then I was trapped by this giggling mob of children.

"So why you here?" Ponytail put her fists on her hips.

A jane in khakis and a baggy plum sweater emerged from behind a blue tunnel that looked like a centipede. She pinned me with that penetrating but not unkind stare that teachers are born with, and began to trudge across the playground toward me. "I've come to see Ms. Jones," I said.

"Oh." A shadow passed over Ponytail's face and she rubbed her hands against the sides of her legs. "You better go then."

Someone called, "Are you the undertaker?"

A voice that squeaked with innocence asked, "What's an undertaker?"

I didn't hear the answer. The teacher in the plum sweater rescued me and we passed through the crowd.

I didn't understand why Najma Jones had come to school. She was either the most dedicated teacher on the planet or she was too numb to accept her daughter's death. I couldn't tell which. She had been reserved when we met the first time; now she was locked down and welded shut. She was a bird of a woman with a narrow face and thin lips. Her gray hair had a few lingering strands of black. She wore a long-sleeved white kameez tunic over shalwar trousers. I leaned against the door of her classroom and told her everything I had done the day before. She sat listening at her desk with a sandwich that she wasn't going to eat and a carton of milk that she wasn't going to drink and a napkin that she didn't need.

When I had finished, she asked me about cyanide inhalers.

"Hydrogen cyanide isn't hard to get in bulk," I said. "They use it for making plastic, engraving, tempering steel. The inhaler came from one of the underground suicide groups, probably Our Choice. The cops could tell you for sure."

She unfolded the napkin and spread it out on top of her desk. "I've heard it's a painful death."

"Not at all," I said. "They used to use hydrogen cyanide gas to execute criminals, back in the bad old days. It all depends on the first breath. Get it deep into your lungs and you're unconscious before you hit the floor. Dead in less than a minute."

"And if you don't get a large enough dose?"

"Ms. Jones . . ."

She cut me off hard. "If you don't?"

"Then it takes longer, but you still die. There are convulsions. The skin flushes and turns purple. Eyes bulge. They say it's something like having a heart attack."

"Rashmi?" She laid her daughter's name down gently, as if she were tucking it into bed. "How did she die?"

Had the cops shown her the crime scene pictures? I decided they hadn't. "I don't think she suffered," I said.

She tore a long strip off the napkin. "You don't think I'm a very good mother, do you?"

I don't know exactly what I expected her to say, but this wasn't it. "Ms. Jones, I don't know much about you and your daughter. But I do know that you cared enough about her to hire me. I'm sorry I let you down."

She shook her head wearily, as if I had just flunked the pop quiz. One third does not equal .033 and Los Angeles has never been the capital of California. "Is there anything else I should know?" she said.

"There is." I had to tell her what I'd found out that morning, but I wasn't going to tell her that I was working for a devil. "You mentioned before that Rashmi had a friend named Kate."

"The Christer?" She tore another strip off the napkin.

I nodded. "Her name is Kate Vermeil. I don't know this for sure yet, but there's reason to believe that Rashmi and Kate were married yesterday. Does that make any sense to you?"

"Maybe yesterday it might have." Her voice was flat. "It doesn't anymore."

I could hear stirring in the next classroom. Chairs scraped against linoleum. Girls were jabbering at each other.

"I know Rashmi became a Christer," she said. "It's a broken religion. But then everything is broken, isn't it? My daughter and I . . . I don't think we ever understood each other. We were strangers at the end." The napkin was in shreds. "How old were you when it happened?"

"I wasn't born yet." She didn't have to explain what *it* was. "I'm not as old as I look."

"I was nineteen. I remember men, my father, my uncles. And the boys. I actually slept with one." She gave me a bleak smile. "Does that shock you, Ms. Hardaway?"

I hated it when grannies talked about having sex, but I just shook my head.

"I didn't love Sunil, but I said I'd marry him just so I could get out of my mother's house. Maybe that was what was happening with Rashmi and this Kate person?"

"I wouldn't know."

The school bell rang.

"I'm wearing white today, Ms. Hardaway, to honor my darling daughter." She gathered up the strips of napkin and the sandwich and the carton of milk and dropped them in the trashcan. "White is the Hindu color of mourning. But it's also the color of knowledge. The goddess of learning, Saraswati, is always shown wearing a white dress, sitting on a white lotus. There is something here I must learn." She fingered the gold embroidery at the neckline of her kameez. "But it's time for recess."

We walked to the door. "What will you do now?" She opened it. The fifth grade swarmed the hall, girls rummaging through their lockers.

"Find Kate Vermeil," I said.

She nodded. "Tell her I'm sorry."

FOUR

I tried Kate's call again, but when all I got was the sidekick I biked across town to 44 East Washington Avenue. The Poison Society turned out to be a jump joint; the sign said it opened at nine PM. There was no bell on the front door, but I knocked hard enough to wake Marilyn Monroe. No answer. I went around to the back and tried again. If Kate was in there, she wasn't entertaining visitors.

A sidekick search turned up an open McDonald's on Wallingford, a ten-minute ride. The only other customers were a couple of twists with bound breasts and identical acid-green vinyl masks. One of them crouched on the floor beside the other, begging for chicken nuggets. A bot took my order for the 29¢ combo meal—it was all bots behind the counter. By law, there was supposed to be a human running the place, but if she was on the premises, she was nowhere to be seen. I thought about calling City Hall to complain, but the egg rolls arrived crispy and the McLatte was nicely scalded. Besides, I didn't need to watch the cops haul the poor jane in charge out of whatever hole she had fallen into.

A couple of hardcase tommys in army surplus fatigues had strutted in just after me. They ate with their heads bowed over their plastic trays so the fries didn't have too far to travel. Their collapsible titanium nightsticks lay on the table in plain sight. One of them was not quite as wide as a bus. The other was nothing special, except that when I glanced up from my sidekick, she was giving me a freeze-dried stare. I waggled my shiny fingernails at her and screwed my cutest smile onto my face. She scowled, said something to her partner and went back to the trough.

My sidekick chirped. It was my pal Julie Epstein, who worked Self-Endangerment/Missing Persons out of the second precinct.

"You busy, Fay?"

"Yeah, the Queen of Cleveland just lost her glass slipper and I'm on the case."

"Well, I'm about to roll through your neighborhood. Want to do lunch?"

I aimed the sidekick at the empties on my table. "Just finishing."

"Where are you?"

"McD's on Wallingford."

"Yeah? How are the ribs?"

"Couldn't say. But the egg rolls are triple dee."

"That the place where the owner is a junkliner? We've had complaints. Bots run everything?"

"No, I can see her now. She's shortchanging some beat cop."

She gave me the laugh. "Got the coroner's on the Rashmi Jones. Cyanide induced hypoxia."

"You didn't by any chance show the mom pix of the scene?"

"Hell no. Talk about cruel and unusual." She frowned. "Why?"

"I was just with her. She seemed like maybe she suspected her kid wrestled with the reaper."

"We didn't tell her. By the way, we don't really care if you call your client, but next time how about trying us first?"

"That's cop law. Me, I follow PI law."

"Where did you steal that line from, *Chinatown*?"

"It's got better dialogue than *Dragnet*." I swirled the last of my latte in the cup. "You calling a motive on the Rashmi Jones?"

"Not yet. What do you like?" She ticked off the fingers of her left hand. "Family? School? Money? Broke a fingernail? Cloudy day?"

"Pregnancy? Just a hunch."

"You think she was seeded? We'll check that. But that's no reason to kill yourself."

"They've all got reasons. Only none of them makes sense."

She frowned. "Hey, don't get all invested on me here."

"Tell me, Julie, do you think I'm doing a pretend job?"

"Whoa, Fay." Her chuckle had a sharp edge. "Maybe it's time you and Sharifa took a vacation."

"Yeah." I let that pass. "It's just that some granny called me a fluff."

"Grannies." She snorted in disgust. "Well, you're no cop, that's for sure. But we do appreciate the help. Yeah, I'd say what you do is real. As real as anything in this cocked world."

"Thanks, flatfoot. Now that you've made things all better, I'll just click off. My latte is getting cold and you're missing so damn many persons."

"Think about that vacation, shamus. Bye."

As I put my sidekick away, I realized that the tommys were waiting for me. They'd been rattling ice in their cups and folding McWrappers for the past ten minutes. I probably didn't need their brand of trouble. The smart move would be to bolt for the door and leave my bike for now; I could lose them on foot. But then I hadn't made a smart move since April. The big one was talking into her sidekick when I sauntered over to them.

"What can I do for you ladies?" I said.

The big one pocketed the sidekick. Her partner started to come out of her seat but the big one stretched an arm like a telephone pole to restrain her.

"Do we know you?" The partner had close-set eyes and a beak nose; her black hair was short and stiff as a brush. She was wearing a black tee under her fatigue jacket and black leather combat boots. Probably had steel toes. "No," she continued, "I don't think we do."

"Then let's get introductions out of the way," I said. "I'm Fay Hardaway. And you are . . . ?"

They gave me less than nothing.

I sat down. "Thanks," I said. "Don't mind if I do."

The big one leaned back in her chair and eyed me as if I was dessert. "Sure you're not making a mistake, missy?"

"Why, because you're rough, tough, and take no guff?"

"You're funny." She smirked. "I like that. People who meet us are usually so very sad. My name is Alix." She held out her hand and we shook. "Pleased to know you."

The customary way to shake hands is to hold on for four, maybe five seconds, squeeze goodbye, then loosen the grip. Maybe big Alix wasn't familiar with our customs—she wasn't letting go.

I wasn't going to let a little thing like a missing hand intimidate me.

"Oh, then I do know you," I said. We were in the McDonald's on Wallingford Street—a public place. I'd just been talking to my pal the cop. I was so damn sure that I was safe, I decided to take my shot. "That would make the girlfriend here Elaine. Or is it Gratiana?"

"Alix." The beak panicked. "Now we've got to take her."

Alix sighed, then yanked on my arm. She might have been pulling a tissue from a box for all the effort she expended. I slid halfway across the table as the beak whipped her nightstick to full extension. I lunged away from her and she caught me just a glancing blow above the ear but then Alix stuck a popper into my face and spattered me with knockout spray. I saw a billion stars and breathed the vacuum of deep space for maybe two seconds before everything went black.

Big Ben chimed between my ears. I could feel it deep in my molars, in the jelly of my eyes. It was the first thing I had felt since World War II. Wait a minute, was I alive during World War II? No, but I had seen the movie. When I wiggled my toes, Big Ben chimed again. I realized that the reason it hurt so much was that the human head didn't really contain enough space to hang a bell of that size. As I took inventory of body parts, the chiming became less intense. By the time I knew I was all there, it was just the sting of blood in my veins.

I was laid out on a surface that was hard but not cold. Wood. A bench. The place I was in was huge and dim but not dark. The high ceiling was in shadow. There was a hint of smoke in the air. Lights flickered. Candles. That was a clue, but I was still too groggy to understand what the mystery was. I knew I needed to remember something, but there was a hole where the memory was supposed to be. I reached back and touched just above my ear. The tip of my finger came away dark and sticky.

A voice solved the mystery for me. "I'm sorry that my people overreacted. If you want to press charges, I've instructed Gratiana and Alix to surrender to the police."

It came back to me then. It always does. McDonald's. Big Alix. A long handshake. That would make this a church. I sat up. When the world stopped spinning, I saw a vast marble altar awash in light with a crucifix the size of a Cessna hanging behind it.

"I hope you're not in too much pain, Miss Hardaway." The voice came from the pew behind me. A fortyish woman in a black suit and a Roman collar was on the kneeler. She was wearing a large silver ring on the fourth finger of her left hand.

"I've felt worse."

"That's too bad. Do you make a habit of getting into trouble?" She looked concerned that I might be making some bad life choices. She had soft eyes and a kindly face. Her short hair was the color of ashes. She was someone I could tell my guilty secrets to, so I could sleep at night. She would speak to Christ the Man himself on my behalf, book me into the penthouse suite in heaven.

"Am I in trouble?"

She nodded gravely. "We all are. The devils are destroying us, Miss Hardaway. They plant their seed not only in our bodies, but our minds and our souls."

"Please, call me Fay. I'm sure we're going to be just the very best of friends." I leaned toward her. "I'm sorry, I can't read your name tag."

"I'm not wearing one." She smiled. "I'm Father Elaine Horváth."

We looked at each other.

"Have you ever considered suicide, Fay?" said Father Elaine.

"Not really. It's usually a bad career move."

"Very good. But you must know that since the devils came and changed everything, almost a billion women have despaired and taken their lives."

"You know, I think I did hear something about that. Come on, lady, what's this about?"

"It is the tragedy of our times that there are any number of good reasons to kill oneself. It takes courage to go on living with the world the way it is. Rashmi Jones was a troubled young woman. She lacked that courage. That doesn't make her a bad person, just a dead one."

I patted my pocket, looking for my sidekick. Still there. I pulled it out and pressed *record*. I didn't ask for permission. "So I should mind my own business?"

"That would be a bad career move in your profession. How old are you, Fay?"

"Thirty-three."

"Then you were born of a virgin." She leaned back, slid off the kneeler and onto the pew. "Seeded by the devils. I'm old enough to have had a father, Fay. I actually remember him a little. A very little."

"Don't start." I spun out of the pew into the aisle. I hated cock nostalgia. This granny had me chewing aluminum foil; I would have spat it at Christ himself if he had dared come down off his cross. "You want to know one reason why my generation jumps out of windows and sucks on cyanide? It's because twists like you make us feel guilty about how

we came to be. You want to call me devil's spawn, go ahead. Enjoy
yourself. Live it up. Because we're just waiting for you old bitches to die
off. Someday this foolish church is going to dry up and blow away and
you know what? We'll go dancing that night, because we'll be a hell of
a lot happier without you to remind us of what you lost and who we
can never be."

She seemed perversely pleased by my show of emotion. "You're an
angry woman, Fay."

"Yeah," I said, "but I'm kind to children and small animals."

"What is that anger doing to your soul? Many young people find
solace in Christ."

"Like Alix and Gratiana?"

She folded her hands; the silver ring shone dully. "As I said, they have
offered to turn themselves . . ."

"Keep them. I'm done with them." I was cooling off fast. I paused,
considering my next move. Then I sat down on the pew next to Father
Elaine, showed her my sidekick and made sure she saw me pause the
recording. Our eyes met. We understood each other. "Did you marry
Kate Vermeil and Rashmi Jones yesterday?"

She didn't hesitate. "I performed the ceremony. I never filed the
documents."

"Do you know why Rashmi killed herself?"

"Not exactly." She held my gaze. "I understand she left a note."

"Yeah, the note. I found it on her sidekick. She wrote, 'Life is too
hard to handle and I can't handle it so I've got to go now. I love you
Mom sorry.' A little generic for a would-be writer, wouldn't you say?
And the thing is, there's nothing in the note about Kate. I didn't even
know she existed until this morning. Now I have a problem with that.
The cops would have the same problem if I gave it to them."

"But you haven't."

"Not yet."

She thought about that for a while.

"My understanding," said Father Elaine at last, "is that Kate and
Rashmi had a disagreement shortly after the ceremony." She was tiptoe-
ing around words as if one of them might wake up and start screaming.
"I don't know exactly what it was about. Rashmi left, Kate stayed here.
Someone was with her all yesterday afternoon and all last night."

"Because you thought she might need an alibi?"

She let that pass. "Kate was upset when she heard the news. She
blames herself, although I am certain she is without blame."

"She's here now?"

"No." Father Elaine shrugged. "I sent her away when I learned you were looking for her."

"And you want me to stop."

"You are being needlessly cruel, you know. The poor girl is grieving."

"Another poor girl is dead." I reached into my pocket for my penlight. "Can I see your ring?"

That puzzled her. She extended her left hand and I shone the light on it. Her skin was freckled but soft, the nails flawless. She would not be getting them done at a dump like the Adagio Spa.

"What do these letters mean?" I asked. "IHS?"

"*In hoc signo vinces.* 'In this sign you will conquer.' The emperor Constantine had a vision of a cross in the sky with those words written in fire on it. This was just before a major battle. He had his soldiers paint the cross on their shields and then he won the day against a superior force."

"Cute." I snapped the light off. "What's it mean to you?"

"The Bride of God herself gave this to me." Her face lit up, as if she were listening to an angelic chorus chant her name. "In recognition of my special vocation. You see, Fay, our Church has no intention of drying up and blowing away. Long after my generation is gone, believers will continue to gather in Christ's name. And someday they'll finish the work we have begun. Someday they will exorcise the devils."

If she knew how loopy that sounded, she didn't show it. "Okay, here's the way it is," I said. "Forget Kate Vermeil. I only wanted to find her so she could lead me to you. A devil named Seeren hired me to look for a certain party wearing a ring like yours. It wants a meeting."

"With me?" Father Elaine went pale. "What for?"

"I just find them." I enjoyed watching her squirm. "I don't ask why."

She folded her hands as if to pray, then leaned her head against them and closed her eyes. She sat like that for almost a minute. I decided to let her brood, not that I had much choice. The fiery pit of hell could've opened up and she wouldn't have noticed.

Finally, she shivered and sat up. "I have to find out how much they know." She gazed up at the enormous crucifix. "I'll see this devil, but on one condition: you guarantee my safety."

"Sure." I couldn't help myself; I laughed. The sound echoed, profaning the silence. "Just how am I supposed to do that? They disappeared half the population of Earth without breaking a sweat."

"You have their confidence," she said. "And mine."

A vast and absurd peace had settled over her; she was seeing the world through the gauze of faith. She was a fool if she thought I could go up against the devils. Maybe she believed Christ the Man would swoop down from heaven to protect her, but then he hadn't been seen around the old neighborhood much of late. Or maybe she had projected herself into the mind of the martyrs who would embrace the sword, kiss the ax that would take their heads. I reminded myself that her delusions were none of my business.

Besides, I needed the money. And suddenly I just had to get out of that big, empty church.

"My office is at 35 Market," I said. "Third floor. I'll try to set something up for six tonight." I stood. "Look, if they want to take you, you're probably gone. But I'll record everything and squawk as loud as I can."

"I believe you will," she said, her face aglow.

FIVE

I didn't go to my office after I locked my bike to the rack on Market Street. Instead I went to find George. He was stripping varnish from the beadboard wainscoting in Donna Belasco's old office on the fifth floor. Donna's office had been vacant since last fall, when she had closed her law practice and gone south to count waves at Daytona Beach. At least, that's what I hoped she was doing; the last I'd heard from her was a Christmas card. I missed Donna; she was one of the few grannies who tried to understand what it was like to grow up the way we did. And she had been generous about steering work my way.

"Hey George," I said. "You can tell your boss that I found the ring."

"This one offers the congratulations." The arm holding the brush froze over the can of stripper as he swiveled his head to face me. "You have proved true superiority, Fay." George had done a good job maintaining our building since coming to us a year ago, although he had something against wood grain. We had to stop him from painting over the mahogany paneling in the foyer.

I hated to close the door, but this conversation needed some privacy. "So I've set up a meeting." The stink of the varnish stripper was barbed wire up my nose. "Father Elaine Horváth will be here at six."

George said nothing. Trying to read a bot is like trying to read a refrigerator. I assumed that he was relaying this information to Seeren. Would the devil be displeased that I had booked its meeting into my office?

"Seeren is impressed by your speedy accomplishment," George said at last. "Credit has been allotted to this one for suggesting it task you."

"Great, take ten bucks a month off my rent. Just so you know, I promised Father Elaine she'd be safe here. Seeren is not going to make a liar out of me, is it?"

"Seeren rejects violence. It's a regrettable technique."

"Yeah, but if Seeren disappears her to wherever, does that count?"

George's head swiveled back toward the wainscoting. "Father Elaine Horváth will be invited to leave freely, if such is her intention." The brush dipped into the can. "Was Kate Vermeil also found?"

"No," I said. "I looked, but then Father Elaine found me. By the way, she didn't live at 465 12th Avenue."

"Seeren had otherwise information." The old varnish bubbled and sagged where George had applied stripper. "Such error makes a curiosity."

It was a little thing, but it pricked at me as I walked down to the third floor. Was I pleased to discover that the devils were neither omnipotent nor infallible? Not particularly. For all their crimes against humanity, the devils and their bots were pretty much running our world now. It had been a small if bitter comfort to imagine that they knew exactly what they were doing.

I passed crazy Martha's door, which was open, on the way to my office. "Yaga combany wading," she called.

I backtracked. My neighbor was at her desk, wearing her Technoprogas mask, which she claimed protected her from chlorine, hydrogen sulfide, sulfur dioxide, ammonia, bacteria, viruses, dust, pollen, cat dander, mold spores, nuclear fallout, and sexual harassment. Unfortunately, it also made her almost unintelligible.

"Try that again," I said.

"You've. Got. Company. Waiting."

"Who is it?"

She shook the mask and shrugged. The light of her desktop was reflected in the faceplate. I could see numbers swarming like black ants across the rows and columns of a spreadsheet.

"What's with the mask?"

"We. Had. A. Devil. In. The. Building."

"Really?" I said. "When?"

"Morning."

There was no reason why a devil shouldn't come into our building, no law against having one for a client. But there was an accusation in Martha's look that I couldn't deny. Had I betrayed us all by taking the case? She said, "Hate. Devils."

"Yeah," I said. "Me too."

I opened my door and saw that it was Sharifa who was waiting for me. She was trying on a smile that didn't fit. "Hi Fay," she said. She looked as elegant as always and as weary as I had ever seen her. She was wearing a peppered black linen dress and black dress sandals with thin crossover straps. Those weren't doctor shoes—they were pull down the shades and turn up the music shoes. They made me very sad.

As I turned to close the door, she must have spotted the patch of blood that had dried in my hair. "You're hurt!" I had almost forgotten about it—there was no percentage in remembering that I was in pain. She shot out of her chair. "What happened?"

"I slipped in the shower," I said.

"Let me look."

I tilted my head toward her and she probed the lump gently. "You could have a concussion."

"PI's don't get concussions. Says so right on the license."

"Sit," she said. "Let me clean this up. I'll just run to the bathroom for some water."

I sat and watched her go. I thought about locking the door behind her but I deserved whatever I had coming. I opened the bottom drawer of the desk, slipped two plastic cups off the stack and brought Johnnie Walker in for a consultation.

Sharifa bustled through the doorway with a cup of water in one hand and a fistful of paper towels in the other but caught herself when she saw the bottle. "When did this start?"

"Just now." I picked up my cup and slugged two fingers of Black Label Scotch. "Want some?"

"I don't know," she said. "Are we having fun or are we self-medicating?"

I let that pass. She dabbed at the lump with a damp paper towel. I could smell her perfume, lemon blossoms on a summer breeze and just the smallest bead of sweat. Her scent got along nicely with the liquid smoke of the scotch. She brushed against me and I could feel her body beneath her dress. At that moment I wanted her more than I wanted to breathe.

"Sit down," I said.

"I'm not done yet," she said.

I pointed at a chair. "Sit, damn it."

She dropped the paper towel in my trash as she went by.

"You asked me a question this morning," I said. "I should've given you the answer. I had the abortion last week."

She studied her hands. I don't know why; they weren't doing anything. They were just sitting in her lap, minding their own business.

"I told you when we first got together, that's what I'd do when I got seeded," I said.

"I know."

"I just didn't see any good choices," I said. "I know the world needs children, but I have a life to lead. Maybe it's a rude, pointless, dirty life but it's what I have. Being a mother . . . that's someone else's life."

"I understand," said Sharifa. Her voice was so small it could have crawled under a thimble. "It's just . . . it was all so sudden. You told me and then we were fighting and I didn't have time to think things through."

"I got tested in the morning. I told you that afternoon. I wasn't keeping anything a secret."

She folded her arms against her chest as if she were cold. "And when I get seeded, what then?"

"You'll do what's best for you."

She sighed. "Pour me some medication, would you?"

I poured scotch into both cups, came around the desk, and handed Sharifa hers. She drank, held the whiskey in her mouth for a moment and then swallowed.

"Fay, I . . ." The corners of her mouth were twitchy and she bit her lip. "Your mother told me once that when she realized she was pregnant with you, she was so happy. So happy. It was when everything was crashing around everyone. She said you were the gift she needed to . . . not to . . ."

"I got the gift lecture, Sharifa. Too many times. She made the devils sound like Santa Claus. Or the stork."

She glanced down as if surprised to discover that she was still holding the cup. She drained it at a gulp and set it on my desk. "I'm a doctor. I know they do this to us; I just wish I knew how. But it isn't a bad thing. Having you in the world can't be a bad thing."

I wasn't sure about that, but I kept my opinion to myself.

"Sometimes I feel like I'm trying to carry water in my hands but it's all leaking out and there's nothing I can do to stop it." She started rubbing her right hand up and down her left forearm. "People keep killing themselves. Maybe it's not as bad as it used to be, but still. The birth rate is barely at replacement levels. Maybe we're doomed. Did you ever think that? That we might go extinct?"

"No."

Sharifa was silent for a long time. She kept rubbing her arm. "It should've been me doing your abortion," she said at last. "Then we'd both have to live with it."

I was one tough PI. I kept a bottle of scotch in the bottom drawer and had a devil for a client. Tommys whacked me with nightsticks and pumped knockout spray into my face. But even I had a breaking point, and Dr. Sharifa Ramirez was pushing me up against it hard. I wanted to pull her into my arms and kiss her forehead, her cheeks, her graceful neck. But I couldn't give in to her that way—not now anyway. Maybe never again. I had a case, and I needed to hold the best part of myself in reserve until it was finished. "I'll be in charge of the guilt, Sharifa," I said. "You be in charge of saving lives." I came around the desk. "I've got work to do, so you go home now, sweetheart." I kissed her on the forehead. "I'll see you there."

Easier to say than to believe.

SIX

Sharifa was long gone by the time Father Elaine arrived at ten minutes to six. She brought muscle with her; Gratiana loitered in the hallway surveying my office with sullen calculation, as if estimating how long it would take to break down the door, leap over the desk, and wring somebody's neck. I shouldn't have been surprised that Father Elaine's faith in me had wavered—hell, I didn't have much faith in me either. However, I thought she showed poor judgment in bringing this particular thug along. I invited Gratiana to remove herself from my building. Perhaps she might perform an autoerotic act in front of a speeding bus? Father Elaine dismissed her, and she slunk off.

Father Elaine appeared calm, but I could tell that she was as nervous as two mice and a gerbil. I hadn't really had a good look at her in the dim church, but now I studied her in case I had to write her up for the

Missing Persons Index. She was a tallish woman with round shoulders and a bit of a stoop. Her eyes were the brown of wet sand; her cheeks were bloodless. Her smile was not quite as convincing in good light as it had been in gloom. She made some trifling small talk, which I did nothing to help with. Then she stood at the window, watching. A wingtip loafer tapped against bare floor.

It was about ten after when my desktop chirped. I waved open the icon and accepted the transfer of a thousand dollars. Seeren had a hell of a calling card. "I think they're coming," I said. I opened the door and stepped into the hall to wait for them.

"It gives Seeren the bright pleasure to meet you, Father Elaine Horváth," said George as they shuffled into the office.

She focused everything she had on the devil. "Just Father, if you don't mind." The bot was nothing but furniture to her.

"It's kind of crowded in here," I said. "If you want, I can wait outside. . . ."

Father Elaine's façade cracked for an instant, but she patched it up nicely. "I'm sure we can manage," she said.

"This one implores Fay to remain," said George.

We sorted ourselves out. Seeren assumed its perch on top of the file cabinet and George came around and compacted himself next to me. Father Elaine pushed her chair next to the door. I think she was content to be stationed nearest the exit. George looked at Father Elaine. She looked at Seeren. Seeren looked out the window. I watched them all.

"Seeren offers sorrow over the regrettable death of Rashmi Jones," said George. "Such Rashmi was of your church?"

"She was a member, yes."

"According to Fay Hardaway, a fact is that Father married Kate Vermeil and Rashmi Jones."

I didn't like that. I didn't like it at all.

Father Elaine hesitated only a beat. "Yes."

"Would Father permit Seeren to locate Kate Vermeil?"

"I know where she is, Seeren," said Father Elaine. "I don't think she needs to be brought into this."

"Indulge this one and reconsider, Father. Is such person pregnant?"

Her manner had been cool, but now it dropped forty degrees. "Why would you say that?"

"Perhaps such person is soon to become pregnant?"

"How would I know? If she is, it would be your doing, Seeren."

"Father well understands *in vitro* fertilization?"

"I've heard of it, yes." Father Elaine's shrug was far too elaborate. "I can't say I understand it."

"Father has heard then of transvaginal oocyte retrieval?"

She thrust out her chin. "No."

"Haploidisation of somatic cells?"

She froze.

"Has Father considered then growing artificial sperm from embryonic stem cells?"

"I'm a priest, Seeren." Only her lips moved. "Not a biologist."

"Does the Christer Church make further intentions to induce pregnancies in certain members? Such as Kate Vermeil?"

Father Elaine rose painfully from the chair. I thought she might try to run, but now martyr's fire burned through the shell of ice that had encased her. "We're doing Christ's work, Seeren. We reject your obscene seeding. We are saving ourselves from you and you can't stop us."

Seeren beat its wings, once, twice, and crowed. It was a dense, jarring sound, like steel scraping steel. I hadn't known that devils could make any sound at all, but hearing that hellish scream made me want to dive under my desk and curl up in a ball. I took it though, and so did Father Elaine. I gave her credit for that.

"Seeren makes no argument with the Christer Church," said George. "Seeren upholds only the brightest encouragement for such pregnancies."

Father Elaine's face twitched in disbelief and then a flicker of disappointment passed over her. Maybe she was upset to have been cheated of her glorious death. She was a granny after all, of the generation that had embraced the suicide culture. For the first time, she turned to the bot. "What?"

"Seeren tasks Father to help numerous Christers become pregnant. Christers who do such choosing will then give birth."

She sank back onto her chair.

"Too many humans now refuse the seeding," said the bot. "Not all then give birth. This was not foreseen. It is regrettable."

Without my noticing, my hands had become fists. My knuckles were white.

"Seeren will announce its true satisfaction with the accomplishment of the Christer Church. It offers a single caution. Christers must assure all to make no XY chromosome."

Father Elaine was impassive. "Will you continue to seed all nonbelievers?"

"It is prudent for the survival of humans."

She nodded and faced Seeren. "How will you know if we do try to bring men back into the world?"

The bot said nothing. The silence thickened as we waited. Maybe the devil thought it didn't need to make threats.

"Well, then." Father Elaine rose once again. Some of the stoop had gone out of her shoulders. She was trying to play it calm, but I knew she'd be skipping by the time she hit the sidewalk. Probably she thought she had won a great victory. In any event, she was done with this little party.

But it was my little party, and I wasn't about to let it break up with the devils holding hands with the Christers. "Wait," I said. "Father, you better get Gratiana up here. And if you've got any other muscle in the neighborhood, call them right now. You need backup fast."

Seeren glanced away from the window and at me.

"Why?" Father Elaine already had her sidekick out. "What is this?"

"There's a problem."

"Fay Hardaway," said George sharply. "Indulge this one and recall your task. Your employment has been accomplished."

"Then I'm on my own time now, George." I thought maybe Seeren would try to leave, but it remained on its perch. Maybe the devil didn't care what I did. Or else it found me amusing. I could be an amusing girl, in my own obtuse way.

Gratiana tore the door open. She held her nightstick high, as if expecting to dive into a bloodbath. When she saw our cool tableau, she let it drop to her side.

"Scooch over, Father," I said, "and let her in. Gratiana, you can leave the door open but keep that toothpick handy. I'm pretty sure you're going to be using it before long."

"The others are right behind me, Father," said Gratiana as she crowded into the room. "Two, maybe three minutes."

"Just enough time." I let my hand fall to the middle drawer of my desk. "I have a question for you, Father." I slid the drawer open. "How did Seeren know all that stuff about haploid this and *in vitro* that?"

"It's a devil." She watched me thoughtfully. "They come from two hundred light years away. How do they know anything?"

"Fair enough. But they also knew that you married Kate and Rashmi. George here just said that I told them, except I never did. That was a mistake. It made me wonder whether they knew who you were all along. It's funny, I used to be convinced that the devils were infallible, but now I'm thinking that they can screw up any day of the week, just like the rest of us. They're almost human that way."

"A regrettable misstatement was made." The bot's neck extended until his head was level with mine. "Indulge this one and refrain from further humiliation."

"I've refrained for too long, George. I've had a bellyful of refraining." I was pretty sure that George could see the open drawer, which meant that the devil would know what was in it as well. I wondered how far they'd let me go. "The question is, Father, if the devils already knew who you were, why would Seeren hire me to find you?"

"Go on," she said.

My chest was tight. Nobody tried to stop me, so I went ahead and stuck my head into the lion's mouth. Like that little girl at school, I'd always wanted to have a real job when I grew up. "You've got a leak, Father. Your problem isn't devil super-science. It's the good old-fashioned Judas kiss. Seeren has an inside source, a mole among your congregation. When it decided the time had come to meet with you, it wanted to be sure that none of you would suspect where its information was actually coming from. It decided that the way to give the mole cover was to hire some gullible PI to pretend to find stuff out. I may be a little slow and a lot greedy but I do have a few shreds of pride. I can't let myself be played for an idiot." I thought I heard footsteps on the stairs, but maybe it was just my own blood pounding. "You see, Father, I don't think that Seeren really trusts you. I sure didn't hear you promise just now not to be making little boys. And yes, if they find out about the boy babies, the devils could just disappear them, but you and the Bride of God and all your batty friends would find ways to make that very public, very messy. I'm guessing that's part of your plan, isn't it? To remind us who the devils are, what they did? Maybe get people into the streets again. Since the devils still need to know what you're up to, the mole had to be protected."

Father Elaine flushed with anger. "Do you know who she is?"

"No," I said. "But you could probably narrow it down to a very few. You said you married Rashmi and Kate, but that you never filed the documents. But you needed someone to witness the ceremony. Someone who was taking pix and would send one to Seeren. . . ."

Actually, my timing was a little off. Gratiana launched herself at me just as big Alix hurtled through the doorway. I had the air taser out of the drawer, but my plan had been for the Christers to clean up their own mess. I came out of my chair and raised the taser but even fifty thousand volts wasn't going to keep that snarling bitch off me.

I heard a huge wet pop, not so much an explosion as an implosion. There was a rush of air through the doorway but the room was preternaturally quiet, as if someone had just stopped screaming. We humans gaped at the void that had formerly been occupied by Gratiana. The familiar surroundings of my office seemed to warp and stretch to accommodate that vacancy. If she could vanish so completely, then maybe chairs could waltz on the ceiling and trashcans could sing *Carmen*. For the first time in my life I had a rough sense of what the grannies had felt when the devils disappeared their men. It would be one thing if Gratiana were merely dead, if there were blood, and bone and flesh left behind. A body to be buried. But this was an offense against reality itself. It undermined our common belief that the world is indeed a fact, that we exist at all. I could understand how it could unhinge a billion minds. I was standing next to Father Elaine beside the open door to my office holding the taser and I couldn't remember how I had gotten there.

Seeren hopped down off the bookcase as if nothing important had happened and wrapped its translucent wings around its body. The devil didn't seem surprised at all that a woman had just disappeared. Maybe there was no surprising a devil.

And then it occurred to me that this probably wasn't the first time since they had taken all the men that the devils had disappeared someone. Maybe they did it all the time. I thought of all the missing persons whom I had never found. I could see the files in Julie Epstein's office bulging with unsolved cases. Had Seeren done this thing to teach us the fragility of being? Or had it just been a clumsy attempt to cover up its regrettable mistakes?

As the devil waddled toward the door, Alix made a move as if to block its exit. After what had just happened, I thought that was probably the most boneheaded, brave move I had ever seen.

"Let them go." Father Elaine's voice quavered. Her eyes were like wounds.

Alix stepped aside and the devil and the bot left us. We listened to the devil scrabble down the hall. I heard the elevator doors open and then close.

Then Father Elaine staggered and put a hand on my shoulder. She looked like a granny now.

"There are no boy babies," she said. "Not yet. You have to believe me."

"You know what?" I shook free of her. "I don't care." I wanted them gone. I wanted to sit alone at my desk and watch the room fill with night.

"You don't understand."

"And I don't want to." I had to set the taser on the desk or I might have used it on her.

"Kate Vermeil is pregnant with one of our babies," said Father Elaine. "It's a little girl, I swear it."

"So you've made Seeren proud. What's the problem?"

Alix spoke for the first time. "Gratiana was in charge of Kate."

SEVEN

The Poison Society was lit brightly enough to give a camel a headache. If you forgot your sunglasses, there was a rack of freebies at the door. Set into the walls were terrariums where diamondback rattlers coiled in the sand, black neck cobras dangled from dead branches and brown scorpions basked on ceramic rocks. The hemlock was in bloom; clusters of small, white flowers opened like umbrellas. Upright stems of monkshood were interplanted with death cap mushrooms in wine casks cut in half. Curare vines climbed the pergola over the alcohol bar.

I counted maybe fifty customers in the main room, which was probably a good crowd for a Wednesday night. I had no idea yet how many might be lurking in the specialty shops that opened off this space, where a nice girl might arrange for a guaranteed-safe session of sexual asphyxia either by hanging or drowning, or else get her cerebrum toasted by various brain lightning generators. I was hoping Kate was out in the open with the relatively sane folks. I thought I owed it to Rashmi Jones.

I strolled around, pretending to look at various animals and plants, carrying a tumbler filled with a little Johnnie Walker Black Label and a lot of water. I knew Kate would be disguised but if I could narrow the field of marks down to three or four, I might actually snoop her. Of course, she might be on the other side of town, but this was my only play. My guess was that she'd switch styles, so I wasn't necessarily looking for a tommy. Her hair wouldn't be brunette, and her skin would probably be darker, and contacts could give her cat's eyes or zebra eyes or American flags, if she wanted. But even with padding and lifts she couldn't change her body type enough to fool a good scan. And I had her data from the Christer medical files loaded into my sidekick.

Father Elaine had tried Kate's call, but she wouldn't pick up. That made perfect sense since just about anyone could put their hands on software that could replicate voices. There were bots that could sing enough like Velma Stone to fool her own mother. Kate and Gratiana would have agreed on a safe word. Our problem was that Gratiana had taken it with her to hell, or wherever the devil had consigned her.

The first mark my sidekick picked out was a redhead in silk pajamas and lime green bunny slippers. A scan matched her to Kate's numbers to within 5 percent. I bumped into her just enough to plant the snoop, a sticky homing device the size of a baby tooth.

" 'Scuse me, sorry." I said. "S-so sorry." I slopped some of my drink onto the floor.

She gave me a glare that would have withered a cactus and I noodled off. As soon as I was out of her sight, I hit the button on my sidekick to which I'd assigned Kate's call. When Kate picked up, the snoop would know if the call had come from me and signal my sidekick that I had found her. The redhead wasn't Kate. Neither was the bald jane in distressed leather.

The problem with trying to locate her this way was that if I kept calling her, she'd get suspicious and lose the sidekick.

I lingered by a pufferfish aquarium. Next to it was a safe, and in front of that a tootsie fiddled with the combination lock. I scanned her and got a match to within 2 percent. She was wearing a spangle wig and a stretch lace dress with a ruffle front. When she opened the door of the safe, I saw that it was made of clear luxar. She reached in, then slammed the door and trotted off as if she were late for the last train of the night.

I peeked through the door of the safe. Inside was a stack of squat blue inhalers like the one Rashmi had used to kill herself. On the wall above the safe, the management of The Poison Society had spray-painted a mock graffiti. *21L 4R 11L*. There was no time to plant a snoop. I pressed the call button as I tailed her.

With a strangled cry, the tootsie yanked a sidekick from her clutch purse, dropped it to the floor, and stamped on it. She was wearing Donya Durand ice and taupe flat slingbacks.

As I moved toward her, Kate Vermeil saw me and ducked into one of the shops. She dodged past fifty-five-gallon drums of carbon tetrachloride and dimethyl sulfate and burst through the rear door of the shop into an alley. I saw her fumbling with the cap of the inhaler. I hurled myself at her and caught at her legs. Her right shoe came off in my hand, but I grabbed her left ankle and she went down. She still had the inhaler and was trying to bring it to her mouth. I leapt on top of her and wrenched it away.

"Do you really want to kill yourself?" I aimed the inhaler at her face and screamed at her. "Do you, Kate? Do you?" The air in the alley was thick with despair and I was choking on it. "Come on, Kate. Let's do it!"

"No." Her head thrashed back and forth. "No, please. Stop."

Her terror fed mine. "Then what the hell are you doing with this thing?" I was shaking so badly that when I tried to pitch the inhaler into the dumpster, it hit the pavement only six feet away. I had come so close to screwing up. I climbed off her and rolled on my back and soaked myself in the night sky. When I screwed up, people died. "Cyanide is awful bad for the baby," I said.

"How do you know about my baby?" Her face was rigid with fear. "Who are you?"

I could breathe again, although I wasn't sure I wanted to. "Fay Hardaway." I gasped: "I'm a PI; I left you a message this morning. Najma Jones hired me to find her daughter."

"Rashmi is dead."

"I know," I said. "So is Gratiana." I sat up and looked at her. "Father Elaine will be glad to see you."

Kate's eyes were wide, but I don't think she was seeing the alley. "Gratiana said the devils would come after me." She was still seeing the business end of the inhaler. "She said that if I didn't hear from her by tomorrow then we had lost everything and I should . . . do it. You know, to protect the church. And just now my sidekick picked up three times in ten minutes only there was nobody there and so I knew it was time."

"That was me, Kate. Sorry." I retrieved the Donya Durand slingback I'd stripped off her foot and gave it back to her. "Tell me where you got this?"

"It was Rashmi's. We bought them together at Grayles. Actually I picked them out. That was before . . . I loved her, you know, but she was crazy. I can see that now, although it's kind of too late. I mean, she was okay when she was taking her meds, but she would stop every so often. She called it taking a vacation from herself. Only it was no vacation for anyone else, especially not for me. She decided to go off on the day we got married and didn't tell me and all of a sudden after the ceremony we got into this huge fight about the baby and who loved who more and she started throwing things at me—these shoes—and then ran out of the church barefoot. I don't think she ever really understood about . . . you know, what we were trying to do. I mean, I've talked to the Bride of God herself . . . but Rashmi." Kate rubbed her eye and her hand came away wet.

I sat her up and put my arm around her. "That's all right. Not really your fault. I think poor Rashmi must have been hanging by a thread. We all are. The whole human race, or what's left of it."

We sat there for a moment.

"I saw her mom this morning," I said. "She said to tell you she was sorry."

Kate sniffed. "Sorry? What for?"

I shrugged.

"I know she didn't have much use for me," said Kate. "At least that's what Rashmi always said. But as far as I'm concerned the woman was a saint to put up with Rashmi and her mood swings and all the acting out. She was always there for her. And the thing is, Rashmi hated her for it."

I got to my knees, then to my feet. I helped Kate up. The alley was dark, but that wasn't really the problem. Even in the light of day, I hadn't seen anything.

EIGHT

I had no trouble finding space at the bike rack in front of Ronald Reagan Elementary. The building seemed to be drowsing in the heavy morning air, its brick wings enfolding the empty playground. A janitor bot was vacuuming the swimming pool, another was plucking spent blossoms from the clematis fence. The bots were headache yellow; the letters RRE in puffy orange slanted across their torsos. The gardening bot informed me that school wouldn't start for an hour. That was fine with me. This was just a courtesy call, part of the total service commitment I made to all the clients whom I had failed. I asked if I could see Najma Jones and he said he doubted that any of the teachers were in quite this early but he walked me to the office. He paged her; I signed the visitors' log. When her voice crackled over the intercom, I told the bot that I knew the way to her classroom.

I paused at the open door. Rashmi's mom had her back to me. She was wearing a sleeveless navy dress with a cream-colored dupatta scarf draped over her shoulders. She passed down a row of empty desks, perching origami animals at the center of each. There were three kinds of elephants, ducks and ducklings, a blue giraffe, a pink cat that might have been a lion.

"Please come in, Ms. Hardaway," she said without turning around. She had teacher radar; she could see behind her back and around a corner.

"I stopped by your house." I slouched into the room like a kid who had lost her civics homework. "I thought I might catch you before you left for school." I leaned against a desk in the front row and picked up the purple crocodile on it. "You fold these yourself?"

"I couldn't sleep last night," she said, "so finally I gave up and went for a walk. I ended up here. I like coming to school early, especially when no one else is around. There is so much time." She had one origami swan left over that she set on her own desk. "Staying after is different. If you're always the last one out at night, you're admitting that you haven't got anything to rush home to. It's pathetic, actually." She settled behind her desk and began opening windows on her desktop. "I've been teaching the girls to fold the ducks. They seem to like it. It's a challenging grade, the fifth. They come to me as bright and happy children and I am supposed to teach them fractions and pack them off to middle school. I shudder to think what happens to them there."

"How old are they?"

"Ten when they start. Most of them have turned eleven already. They graduate next week." She peered at the files she had opened. "Some of them."

"I take it on faith that I was eleven once," I said, "but I just don't remember."

"Your generation grew up in unhappy times." Her face glowed in the phosphors. "You haven't had a daughter yet, have you, Ms. Hardaway?"

"No."

We contemplated my childlessness for a moment.

"Did Rashmi like origami?" I didn't mean anything by it. I just didn't want to listen to the silence anymore.

"Rashmi?" She frowned, as if her daughter were a not-very-interesting kid she had taught years ago. "No. Rashmi was a difficult child."

"I found Kate Vermeil last night," I said. "I told her what you said, that you were sorry. She wanted to know what for."

"What for?"

"She said that Rashmi was crazy. And that she hated you for having her."

"She never hated me," said Najma quickly. "Yes, Rashmi was a sad girl. Anxious. What is this about, Ms. Hardaway?"

"I think you were at the Comfort Inn that night. If you want to talk about that, I would like to hear what you have to say. If not, I'll leave now."

She stared at me for a moment, her expression unreadable. "You know, I actually wanted to have many children." She got up from the desk, crossed the room and shut the door as if it were made of hand-blown glass. "When the seeding first began, I went down to City Hall and volunteered. That just wasn't done. Most women were horrified to find themselves pregnant. I talked to a bot, who took my name and address and then told me to go home and wait. If I wanted more children after my first, I was certainly encouraged to make a request. It felt like I was joining one of those mail order music clubs." She smiled and tugged at her dupatta. "But when Rashmi was born, everything changed. Sometimes she was such a needy baby, fussing to be picked up, but then she would lie in her crib for hours, listless and withdrawn. She started anti-depressants when she was five and they helped. And the Department of Youth Services issued me a full-time bot helper when I started teaching. But Rashmi was always a handful. And since I was all by myself, I didn't feel like I had enough to give to another child."

"You never married?" I asked. "Found a partner?"

"Married who?" Her voice rose sharply. "Another woman?" Her cheeks colored. "No. I wasn't interested in that."

Najma returned to her desk but did not sit down. "The girls will be coming soon." She leaned toward me, fists on the desktop. "What is it that you want to hear, Ms. Hardaway?"

"You found Rashmi before I did. How?"

"She called me. She said that she had had a fight with her girlfriend who was involved in some secret experiment that she couldn't tell me about and they were splitting up and everything was shit, the world was shit. She was off her meds, crying, not making a whole lot of sense. But that was nothing new. She always called me when she broke up with someone. I'm her mother."

"And when you got there?"

"She was sitting on the bed." Najma's eyes focused on something I couldn't see. "She put the inhaler to her mouth when I opened the door." Najma was looking into room 103 of the Comfort Inn. "And I thought to myself, what does this poor girl want? Does she want me to witness her death or stop it? I tried to talk to her, you know. She seemed to listen. But when I asked her to put the inhaler down, she wouldn't. I moved toward her, slowly. Slowly. I told her that she didn't have to do anything. That we could just go home. And then I was this close." She reached a hand across the desk. "And I couldn't help myself. I tried to swat it out of her mouth. Either she pressed the button or I set it off." She sat down abruptly and put her head in her hands. "She didn't get the full dose. It took forever before it was over. She was in agony."

"I think she'd made up her mind, Ms. Jones." I was only trying to comfort her. "She wrote the note."

"I wrote the note." She glared at me. "I did."

There was nothing I could say. All the words in all the languages that had ever been spoken wouldn't come close to expressing this mother's grief. I thought the weight of it must surely crush her.

Through the open windows, I heard the snort of the first bus pulling into the turnaround in front of the school. Najma Jones glanced out at it, gathered herself and smiled. "Do you know what Rashmi means in Sanskrit?"

"No, ma'am."

"Ray of sunlight," she said. "The girls are here, Ms. Hardaway." She picked up the origami on her desk. "We have to be ready for them." She held it out to me. "Would you like a swan?"

By the time I came through the door of the school, the turnaround was filled with busses. Girls poured off them and swirled onto the playground: giggling girls, whispering girls, skipping girls, girls holding hands. And in the warm June sun, I could almost believe they were happy girls.

They paid no attention to me.

I tried Sharifa's cell. "Hello?" Her voice was husky with sleep.

"Sorry I didn't make it home last night, sweetheart," I said. "Just wanted to let you know that I'm on my way."

HARLAN ELLISON: THE MAN IN E MINOR

BARRY N. MALZBERG

A long time coming. But here it is: manifest.

As has been observed, we can be judged as well by the enemies we have made as by our friends. I would not write that Harlan has no enemies at all—heaven forfend. Couldn't sell that one, even though he is at heart just another lovable superannuated kid from the provinces like your own faithful celebrant here. Harlan has a few. But more to the point, I suggest that Harlan has made more of the population crazy per capita than perhaps any writer of the twentieth century; Harlan has always been the guy without whom we might have slept more and cared less . . . and the people Harlan has made crazy are the right kind of people. That guy over in the corner talking to himself is the former comptroller of Stealem, Beatem, and Blind; those three furies in playsuits and straitjackets over in the other corner are Winken, Blinken, and Nod, editor in chief, publisher, and president of Crass Books, Inc. Harlan, as I wrote long ago, has never ducked a fight other than in the cause of finding an even more menacing opponent, and it has been a good fight, one that will be carried forth long after our time and in the name of higher and eventual judgment.

Grand Master. The first (1975), Heinlein; the penultimate (2005), Silverberg. Asimov somewhere near the middle. In between (scattered recall), Pohl, Williamson, Simak, Clarke, Le Guin, Bester, del Rey. Bester. (Repeat the name: surely worth a Mass.) The name Ellison fits here as comfortably as Ralph Vaughan Williams's Ninth Symphony in E Minor fits with Dvorak's Ninth in E Minor. Or Beethoven's Ninth in D Minor. Or Bruckner's Ninth in D Minor.

Slides right in there, he does. The kid in E minor.

And what also slides in deservedly and at last, this stunning, if awkwardly titled novella: a work of splendor. "The Resurgence of Miss Ankle-Strap Wedgie"—when I saw this in typescript I wanted to call it "Lone"—was written almost forty years ago, no magazine sale, saw light in the 1968 Trident collection *Love Ain't Nothing But Sex Misspelled,* and in a couple of the author's subsequent collections. Twenty-five thousand words is an awkward length. Not particularly well-known, however; perhaps Harlan's least-known story of the first rank. And not even remotely science fiction, as will shortly become evident. But it belongs here in the *Nebula Awards Showcase* as surely as Harlan Ellison belongs in the ranks of the Grand Masters. "I want to be what you are," his friend Isaac Asimov wrote Harlan decades ago. "I want to be called what you are. A writer." Ellison's public persona, one so well-known as to need no parsing here, has been powerfully effective in terms of the public life at which it is aimed, but its sheer force has obscured the still, small voice of truth: He is a driven, a central, an important writer. He has outlasted— as could be said of our greatest writers: Hemingway, Faulkner, Roth— his own impulse toward self-destruction, an impulse unfortunately almost intrinsic to writers of the first rank. Perhaps writers of the first rank—like the doomed actress of Harlan's story—yearn for nothing more than to subside to the second rank, no longer to be first in the line of fire.

Fitzgerald, in a late letter to his agent, Harold Ober, speculated that the great Hollywood novel, which had yet to be written, would be a novel dealing not with the myth, not with the glamour, not with the corruption or destruction inherent in the business, but would instead be a novel dealing with process, with the actual business of filmmaking. Such a novel, through its concentration on the actual technique of film, would be refractory, would by implication take in the entire, terrible mythic and practical range of what Otto Friedrich called "the city of nets." This novella comes closer than any I know to Fitzgerald's dictum. It is closer than any I know to this submerged and terrific cemetery of our collective dreams. It may be the best work of fiction ever to have come out of the film business, and it was written by a man, then thirty-four, who had been so involved for less than a decade. Reading this as I did in manuscript in April 1968 as the young fiction editor of *Escapade* so long ago, I thought, "This writer can do anything. He is capable of anything at all. It is impossible to conceive where he might be twenty years from now." I desperately wanted to publish this story. It was insanely out of range of length for a monthly men's magazine; it was about as sexually arousing as, say, *Day of the Locust*; it was scheduled for that Trident collection to be published in the summer of 1968, which meant that I wouldn't even have had first publication . . . and I still wanted it, and would have found a way to have taken it if the ownership of the magazine had not, instead, made a distress sale of the publication to its distributor, Kable News, and triumphantly fired us all. My largest regret—it still bothers me all these decades later—in forty years of part-time freelance and staff editing is that I was unable to take this story. Campaigning furiously and (obviously) successfully for its inclusion in this volume represents a kind of delayed and wistful balancing. I wish this had been possible forty years ago, but in a way understandable only to the old, this is better.

Other possibilities present, and Harlan, perhaps a little self-intimidated by the centrality and power of his own story and the possibility it indicated, had other places he wanted to be, other fiction to explore; some of it was science fiction and some was fantasy and some, like the long 1993 *Mefisto in Onyx*, was, like this, contemporary realism, but all of it was distinctly and irremediably Ellison, an outcome for which we were only half-prepared. Touch the whirlwind, inherit the wind, and the body of work, not really to be paraphrased in any terms other than its own, is unimpeachable.

There is that point in enconium where celebration begins to crumble into catalog, into recitation and repetition; let it not happen here. Let the work be its own statement; let this great novella be its surest testimony: He was here, this is what he gave, this is what he wrote. This is what he could do. This is in both part and full the sum of his work. We give him honor as he did all of us.

"I want to be called what you are. I want to be a writer."

May 2006, New Jersey

THE RESURGENCE OF MISS ANKLE-STRAP WEDGIE

(Dedicated to the Memory of Dorothy Parker)

HARLAN ELLISON®

Handy

In Hollywood our past is so transitory we have little hesitation about tearing down our landmarks. The Garden of Allah where Benchley and Scott Fitzgerald lived is gone; it's been replaced by a savings and loan. Most of the old, sprawling 20th lot has been converted into shopping center and beehive-faceted superhotel. Even historic relics of fairly recent vintage have gone under the cultural knife: the Ziv television studios on Santa Monica, once having been closed down, became the eerie, somehow surrealistic, weed-overgrown and bizarre jungle in which tamed cats that had roamed sound stages became cannibals, eating one another. At night, passing the studio, dark and padlocked, you could hear the poor beasts tearing each other apart. They had lived off the film industry too long and, unable to survive in the streets, lost and bewildered, they had turned into predators.

That may be an apocryphal story. It persists in my thoughts when I remember Valerie Lone.

The point is, we turn the past into the present here in Hollywood even before it's finished being the future. It's like throwing a meal into the Disposall before you eat it.

But we do have one recently erected monument here in the glamour capital of the world.

It is a twenty-three-foot-high billboard for a film called *Subterfuge*. It is a lighthearted adventure-romance in the James Bond tradition, and the billboard shows the principal leads—Robert Mitchum and Gina Lollobrigida—in high fashion postures intended to convey, well, adventure and, uh, romance.

The major credits are listed in smaller print on this billboard: produced by Arthur Crewes, directed by James Kencannon, written by John D. F. Black, music by Lalo Schifrin. The balance of the cast is there, also. At the end of the supplementary credits is a boxed line that reads:

ALSO FEATURING MISS VALERIE LONE as Angela. This line is difficult to read; it has been whited-out.

The billboard stands on a rise overlooking Sunset Boulevard on the Strip near King's Road; close by a teenie-bopper discothèque called Spectrum 2000 that once was glamorous Ciro's. But we tear down our past and convert it to the needs of the moment. The billboard will come down. When the film ends its first run at the Egyptian and opens in neighborhood theaters and drive-ins near you.

At which point even *that* monument to Valerie Lone will have been removed, and almost all of us can proceed to forget. Almost all of us, but not all. I've got to remember . . . my name is Fred Handy. I'm responsible for that billboard. Which makes me a singular man, believe me.

After all, there are so few men who have erected monuments to the objects of their homicide.

ONE

They came out of the darkness, a lightless tunnel with a highway at the bottom of it. The headlights were animal eyes miles away down the flat roadbed, and slowly slowly the sound of the engine grew across the emptiness on both sides of the concrete. California desert night, heat of the long day sunk just below the surface of the land, and a car, ponderous, plunging, straight out of nowhere along a white centerline. Gophers and rabbits bounded across the deadly open road and were gone forever.

Inside the limousine, men dozed in jump seats, and far in the rear two bull-necked cameramen discussed the day's work. Beside the driver, Fred Handy stared straight ahead at the endless stretch of State Highway 14 out of Mojave. He had been under the influence of road hypnosis for the better part of twenty minutes, and did not know it. The voice from the secondary seats behind him jarred him back to awareness. It was Kencannon.

"Jim, how long till we hit Lancaster or Palmdale?"

The driver craned his head back and slightly to the side, awkwardly, like some big bird, keeping his eyes on the road. "Maybe another twenty, twenty-five miles, Mr. K'ncannon. That was Rosamond we passed, little while ago."

"Let's stop and eat at the first clean place we see," the director said, thumbing his eyes to remove the sleep from them. "I'm starving."

There was vague movement from the third seats, where Arthur Crewes was folded sidewise, fetuslike, sleeping. A mumbled, "Where are we what time izit?"

Handy turned around. "It's about three forty-five, Arthur. Middle of the desert."

"Midway between Mojave and Lancaster, Mr. Crewes," the driver added. Crewes grunted acceptance of it.

The producer sat up in sections, swinging his legs down heavily, pulling his body erect sluggishly, cracking his shoulders back as he arched forward. With his eyes closed. "Jeezus, remind me next time to do a picture without location shooting. I'm too old for this crap." There was the murmur of trained laughter from somewhere in the limousine.

Handy thought of Mitchum, who had returned from the Mojave location earlier that day, riding back in the air-conditioned land cruiser the studio provided. But the thought only reminded him that he was not one of the Immortals, one of the golden people; that he was merely a two-fifty-a-week publicist who was having one helluva time trying to figure out a promotional angle for just another addle-witted spy-romance. Crewes had come to the genre belatedly, after the Bond flicks, after *Ipcress,* after *Arabesque* and *Masquerade* and *Kaleidoscope* and *Flint* and *Modesty Blaise* and they'd *all* come after *The 39 Steps* so what the hell did it matter; with Arthur Crewes producing, it would get serious attention and good play dates. *If.* If Fred Handy could figure out a Joe Levine William Castle Sam Katzman Alfred Hitchcock *shtick* to pull the suckers in off the streets. He longed for the days back in New York when he had had ulcers working in the agency. He still had them, but the difference was *now* he couldn't even *pretend* to be enjoying life enough to compensate for the aggravation. He longed for the days of his youth writing imbecilic poetry in Figaro's in the Village. He longed for the faintly moist body of Julie, away in the Midwest somewhere doing *Hello, Dolly!* on the strawhat circuit. He longed for a hot bath to leach all the weariness out of him. He longed for a hot bath to clean all the Mojave dust and grit out of his pores.

He longed *desperately* for something to eat.

"Hey, Jim, how about that over there . . . ?"

He tapped the driver on the forearm, and pointed down the highway to the neon flickering off and on at the roadside. The sign said SHIVEY'S TRUCK STOP and EAT. There were no trucks parked in front.

"It must be good food," Kencannon said from behind him. "I don't see any trucks there; and you know what kind of food you get at the joints truckers eat at."

Handy smiled quickly at the reversal of the old road-runner's myth. It was that roundabout sense of humor that made Kencannon's direction so individual.

"That okay by you, Mr. Crewes?" Jim asked.

"Fine, Jim," Arthur Crewes said, wearily.

The studio limousine turned in at the diner and crunched gravel. The diner was an anachronism. One of the old railroad car style, seen most frequently on the New Jersey thruways. Aluminum hide leprous with rust. Train windows fogged with dirt. Lucky Strike and El Producto decals on the door. Three steps up to the door atop a concrete stoop. Parking lot surrounding it like a gray pebble lake, cadaverously cold in the intermittent flashing of the pale yellow neon EAT off EAT off EAT . . .

The limousine doors opened, all six of them, and ten crumpled men emerged, stretched, trekked toward the diner. They fell into line almost according to the pecking order. Crewes and Kencannon; Fred Handy; the two cameramen; three grips; the effeminate makeup man, Sancher; and Jim, the driver.

They climbed the stairs, murmuring to themselves, like sluggish animals emerging from a dead sea of sleep. The day had been exhausting. Chase scenes through the rural town of Mojave. And Mitchum in his goddam land cruiser, phoning ahead to have *escargots* ready at La Rue.

The diner was bright inside, and the grips, the cameramen and Jim took booths alongside the smoked windows. Sancher went immediately to the toilet, to moisten himself with 5-Day Deodorant Pads. Crewes sat at the counter with Handy and Kencannon on either side of him. The producer looked ancient. He was a dapper man in his middle forties. He clasped his hands in front of him and Handy saw him immediately begin twisting and turning the huge diamond ring on his right hand, playing with it, taking it off and replacing it. *I wonder what that means,* Handy thought.

Handy had many thoughts about Arthur Crewes. Some of them were friendly, most were impartial. Crewes was a job for Handy. He had seen the producer step heavily when the need arose: cutting off a young writer when the script wasn't being written fast enough to make a shooting date; literally threatening an actor with bodily harm if he didn't cease the senseless wrangling on set that was costing the production money; playing agents against one another to catch a talented client unrepresented between them, available for shaved cost. But he had seen him perform unnecessary kindnesses. Unnecessary because they bought nothing, won him nothing, made him no points. Crewes had blown a tire on a freeway one day and a motorist had stopped to help. Crewes had taken his name and sent him a three thousand dollar color television-stereo. A starlet ready to put out for a part had been investigated by the detective agency Crewes kept on retainer at all times for assorted odd jobs. They had found out her child was a paraplegic. She had not been required to go the couch route; Crewes had refused her the job on grounds of talent, but had given her a check in the equivalent amount had she gotten the part.

Arthur Crewes was a very large man indeed in Hollywood. He had not always been immense, however. He had begun his career as a film editor on "B" horror flicks, worked his way up and directed several productions, then been put in charge of a series of low-budget films at the old RKO studio. He had suffered in the vineyards and somehow run the time very fast. He was still a young man, and he was ancient, sitting there turning his ring.

Sancher came out of the toilet and sat down at the far end of the counter. It seemed to jog Kencannon. "Think I'll wash off a little Mojave filth," he said, and rose. Crewes got up. "I suddenly realized I haven't been to the bathroom all day."

They walked away, leaving Handy sitting, toying with the sugar shaker.

He looked up for the first time, abruptly realizing how exhausted he was. There was a waitress shaking a wire basket of french fries, her back to him. The picture was on schedule, no problems, but no hook, no gimmick, no angle, no *shtick* to sell it; there was a big quarterly payment due on the house in Sherman Oaks; it was all Handy had, no one was going to get it; he had to keep the job. The waitress turned around for the first time and started laying out napkin, water glass, silverware, in front of him. You could work in a town for close to nine years, and still come away with nothing; not even living high, driving a '65 Impala that wasn't ostentatious; but a lousy forty-five-day marriage to a clip artist and it was all in jeopardy; he had to keep the job, just to fight her off, keep her from using California divorce logic to get that house; nine years was *not* going down the tube; God, he felt weary. The waitress was in the booth, setting up the grips and cameramen. Handy mulled the nine years, wondering what the hell he was doing out here: oh yeah, I was getting divorced, that's what I was doing. Nine years seemed so long, so ruthlessly long, and so empty suddenly, to be here with Crewes on another of the endless product that got fed into the always-yawning maw of the Great American Moviegoing Public. The waitress returned and stood before him.

"Care to order now?"

He looked up.

Fred Handy stopped breathing for a second. He looked at her, and the years peeled away. He was a teenage kid in the Utopia Theater in St. Louis, Missouri, staring up at a screen with gray shadows moving on it. A face from the past, a series of features, very familiar, were superimposing themselves.

She saw he was staring. "Order?"

He had to say it just right. "Excuse me, is, uh, is your name Lone?"

Until much later, he was not able to identify the expression that swam up in her eyes. But when he thought back on it, he knew it had been terror. Not fear, not trepidation, not uneasiness, not wariness. Terror. Complete, total, gagging terror. She said later it had been like calling the death knell for her . . . again.

She went stiff, and her hand slid off the counter edge. "Valerie Lone?" he said, softly, frightened by the look on her face. She swallowed so that the hollows in her cheeks moved liquidly. And she nodded. The briefest movement of the head.

Then he knew he had to say it just right. He was holding all that fragile crystal, and a wrong phrase would shatter it. Not: *I used to see your movies when I was a kid* or: *Whatever happened to you* or: *What are you doing here.* It had to be just right.

Handy smiled like a little boy. It somehow fit his craggy features. "You know," he said gently, "many's the afternoon I've sat in the movies and been in love with you."

There was gratitude in her smile. Relief, an ease of tensions, and the sudden rush of her own memories; the bittersweet taste of remembrance as the glories of her other life swept back to her. Then it was gone, and she was a frowzy blonde waitress on Route 14 again. "Order?"

She wasn't kidding. She turned it off like a mercury switch. One moment there was life in the faded blue eyes, the next moment it was ashes. He ordered a cheeseburger and french fries. She went back to the steam table.

Arthur Crewes came out of the men's room first. He was rubbing his hands. "Damned powdered soap, almost as bad as those stiff paper towels." He slipped onto the stool beside Handy.

And in that instant, Fred Handy saw a great white light come up. Like the buzz an acid-head gets from a fully drenched sugar cube, his mind burst free and went trembling outward in waves of color. The *shtick*, the bit, the handle, ohmigod there it is, as perfect as a blue-white diamond.

Arthur Crewes was reading the menu as Handy grabbed his wrist. "Arthur, do you know who that is?"

"Who *who* is?"

"The waitress."

"Madame Nehru."

"I'm serious, Arthur."

"All right, who?"

"Valerie Lone."

Arthur Crewes started as though he had been struck. He shot a look at the waitress, her back to them now, as she ladled up navy bean soup from the stainless steel tureen in the steam table. He stared at her, silently.

"I don't believe it," he murmured.

"It is, Arthur, I'm telling you that's just who it is."

He shook his head. "What the hell is she doing out here in the middle of nowhere. My God, it must be, what? Fifteen, twenty years?"

Handy considered a moment. "About eighteen years, if you count that thing she did for Ross at UA in forty-eight. Eighteen years and here she is, slinging hash in a diner."

Crewes mumbled something.

"What did you say?" Handy asked him.

Crewes repeated it, with an edge Handy could not place. "Lord, how the mighty have fallen."

Before Handy could tell the producer his idea, she turned, and saw Crewes staring at her. There was no recognition in her expression. But it was obvious she knew Handy had told him who she was. She turned away and carried the plates of soup to the booth.

As she came back past them, Crewes said, softly, "Hello, Miss Lone."

She paused and stared at him. She was almost somnambulistic, moving by rote. He added, "Arthur Crewes . . . remember?"

She did not answer for a long moment, then nodded as she had to Handy. "Hello. It's been a long time."

Crewes smiled a peculiar smile. Somehow victorious. "Yes, a long time. How've you been?"

She shrugged, as if to indicate the diner. "Fine, thank you."

They fell silent.

"Would you care to order now?"

When she had taken the order and moved to the grill, Handy leaned in close to the producer and began speaking intensely. "Arthur, I've got a fantastic idea."

His mind was elsewhere. "What's that, Fred?"

"Her. Valerie Lone. What a sensational idea. Put her in the picture. The comeback of . . . what was it they used to call her, that publicity thing, oh yeah . . . the comeback of 'Miss Ankle-Strap Wedgie.' It's good for space in any newspaper in the country."

Silence.

"Arthur? What do you think?"

Arthur Crewes smiled down at his hands. He was playing with the ring again. "You think I should bring her back to the industry after eighteen years."

"I think it's the most natural winning promotion idea I've ever had. And I can tell you like it."

Crewes nodded, almost absently. "Yes, I like it, Fred. You're a very bright fellow. I like it just fine."

Kencannon came back and sat down. Crewes turned to him. "Jim, can you do cover shots on the basement scenes with Bob and the stunt men for a day or two?"

Kencannon bit his lip, considering. "I suppose so. It'll mean replotting the schedule, but the board's Bernie's problem, not mine. What's up?"

Crewes twisted the ring and smiled distantly. "I'm going to call Johnny Black in and have him do a rewrite on the part of Angela. Beef it up."

"For what? We haven't even cast it yet."

"We have now." Handy grinned hugely. "Valerie Lone."

"Valerie—you're *kidding*. She hasn't even *made* a film in God knows how long. What makes you think you can get her?"

Crewes turned back to stare at the sloped shoulders of the woman at the sizzling grill. "I can get her."

HANDY

We talked to Valerie Lone, Crewes and myself. First I talked, then he talked; then when she refused to listen to him, I talked again.

She grabbed up a huge pan with the remains of macaroni and cheese burned to the bottom, and she dashed out through a screen door at the rear of the diner.

We looked at each other, and when each of us saw the look of confusion on the other's face, the looks vanished. We got up and followed her. She was leaning against the wall of the diner, scraping the crap from the pan as she cried. The night was quiet.

But she didn't melt as we came through the screen door. She got uptight. Furious. "I've been out of all that for over fifteen years, can't you leave me alone? You've got a lousy sense of humor if you think this is funny!"

Arthur Crewes stopped dead on the stairs. He didn't know what to say to her. There was something happening to Crewes; I didn't know what it was, but it was more than whatever it takes to get a gimmick for a picture.

I took over.

Handy, the salesman. Handy, the *schmacheler*, equipped with the very best butter. "It isn't fifteen years, Miss Lone. It's eighteen plus."

Something broke inside her. She turned back to the pan. Crewes didn't know whether to tell me to back off or not, so I went ahead. I pushed past Crewes, standing there with his hand on the peeling yellow paint banister, his mouth open. (The color of the paint was the color of a stray dog I had run down in Nevada one time. I hadn't seen the animal. It had dashed out of a gully by the side of the road and I'd gone right over it before I knew what had happened. But I stopped and went back. It was the same color as that banister. A faded lonely yellow, like cheap foolscap, a dollar a ream. I couldn't get the thought of that dog out of my mind.)

"You like it out here, right?"

She didn't turn around.

I walked around her. She was looking into that pan of crap. "Miss Lone?"

It was going to take more than soft-spoken words. It might even take sincerity. I wasn't sure I knew how to do *that* any more. "If I didn't know better . . . having seen all the feisty broads you played . . . I'd think you *enjoyed* feeling sorry for your—"

She looked up, whip-fast; I could hear the cartilage cracking in her neck muscles. There was a core of electrical sparks in her eyes. She was pissed-off. "Mister, I just met your face. What makes you think you can talk that way . . ." it petered out. The steam leaked off, and the sparks died, and she was back where she'd been a minute before.

I turned her around to face us. She shrugged my hand off. She wasn't a sulky child, she was a woman who didn't know how to get away from a giant fear that was getting more gigantic with every passing second. And even in fear she wasn't about to let me manhandle her.

"Miss Lone, we've got a picture working. It isn't *Gone with the Wind* and it isn't *The Birth of a Nation,* it's just a better-than-average coupla million dollar spectacular with Mitchum and Lollobrigida, and it'll make a potful for everybody concerned . . ."

Crewes was staring at me. I didn't like his expression. He was the bright young wunderkind who had made *Lonely in the Dark* and *Ruby Bernadette* and *The Fastest Man,* and he didn't like to hear me pinning his latest opus as just a nice, money-making color puffball. But Crewes wasn't a wunderkind any longer, and he wasn't making Kafka; he was making box-office bait, and he needed this woman, and so dammit did I! So screw his expression.

"Nobody's under the impression you're one of the great ladies of the theater; you never were Katherine Cornell, or Bette Davis, or even Pat Neal." She gave me that core of sparks look again. If I'd been a younger man it might have woofed me; I'm sure it had stopped legions of assistant gophers in the halcyon days. But—it suddenly scared me to realize it—I was running hungry, and mere looks didn't do it. I pushed her a little harder, my best Raymond Chandler delivery. "But you *were* a star, you were someone that people paid money to see, because whatever you had it was *yours.* And whatever that was, we want to rent it for a while, we want to bring it back."

She gave one of those little snorts that says very distinctly *You stink, Jack.* It was disdainful. She had my number. But that was cool; I'd given it to her; I wasn't about to shuck her.

"Don't think we're humanitarians. We *need* something like you on this picture. We need a handle, something that'll get us that extra two inches in the Wichita *Eagle.* That means bucks in the ticket wicket. Oh, shit, lady!"

Her lips skinned back, feral, teeth showed.

I was getting to her.

"We can help each other." She sneered and started to turn away. I reached out and slammed the pan as hard as I could. It spun out of her hands and hit the steps. She was rocked quiet for an instant, and I rapped on her as hard as I could. "Don't tell me you're in love with scraping crap out of a macaroni dish. You lived too high, too long. This is a free ride back. Take it!"

There was blood coursing through her veins now. Her cheeks had bright, flushed spots on them, high up under the eyes. "I can't do it; stop pushing at me."

Crewes moved in, then. We worked like a pair of good homicide badges. I beat her on the head, and he came running with Seidlitz powders. "Let her alone a minute, Fred. This is all at once, come on, let her think."

"What the hell's to think?"

She was being rammed from both sides, and knew it, but for the first time in years something was *happening*, and her motor was starting to run again, despite herself.

"Miss Lone," Crewes said gently, "a contract for this film, and options for three more. Guaranteed, from first day of shooting, straight through, even if you sit around after your part is shot, till last day of production."

"I haven't been anywhere near a camera—"

"That's what we have cameramen for. They turn it on you. That's what we have a director for. He'll tell you where to stand. It's like swimming or riding a bike: once you learn, you never forget . . ."

Crewes again. "Stop it, Fred. Miss Lone . . . I remember you from before. You were always good to work with. You weren't one of the cranky ones, you were a doer. You knew your lines, always."

She smiled. A wee timorous slippery smile. She remembered. And she chuckled. "Good memory, that's all."

Then Crewes and I smiled, too. She was on our side. Everything she said from here on out would be to win us the argument. She was ours.

"You know, I had the world's all-time great crush on you, Miss Lone," Arthur Crewes, a very large man in town, said. She smiled a little-girl smile of graciousness.

"I'll think about it." She stooped for the pan.

He reached it before she did. "I won't give you time to think. There'll be a car here for you tomorrow at noon."

He handed her the pan.

She took it reluctantly.

We had dug up Valerie Lone; from under uncounted strata of self-pity and anonymity; from a kind of grave she had chosen for herself for reasons I was beginning to understand. As we went back inside the diner, I had The Thought for the first time:

The Thought: *What if we ain't doing her no favors?*

And the voice of Donald Duck came back at me from the Clown Town of my thoughts: With friends like you, Handy, she may not need any enemies.

Screw you, Duck.

TWO

The screen flickered, and Valerie Lone, twenty years younger, wearing the pageboy and padded shoulders of the Forties, swept into the room. Cary Grant looked up from the microscope with his special genteel exasperation, and asked her *precisely* where she had been. Valerie Lone, the coiffed blonde hair carefully smoothed, removed her gloves and sat on the laboratory counter. She crossed her legs. She was wearing ankle-strap wedgies.

"I think the legs are still damned good, Arthur," Fred Handy said. Cigar smoke rose up in the projection room. Arthur Crewes did not answer. He was busy watching the past.

Full hips, small breasts, blonde; a loveliness that was never wispy like a Jean Arthur, never chill like a Joan Crawford, never cultured like a Greer Garson. If Valerie Lone had been identifiable with anyone else working in her era, it would have been with Ann Sheridan. And the comparison was by no means invidious. There was the same forceful *womanliness* in her manner; a wise kid who knew the score. Dynamic. Yet there was a quality of availability in the way she arched her eyebrows, the way she held her hands and neck. Sensuality mixed with reality. What had broken that spine of self-control, turned it into the fragile wariness Handy had sensed? He studied the film as the story unreeled, but there was none of that showing in the Valerie Lone of twenty years before.

As the deep, silken voice faded from the screen, Arthur Crewes reached to the console beside his contour chair, and punched a series of buttons. The projection light cut off from the booth behind them, the room lights went up, and the chair tilted forward. The producer got up and left the room, with Handy behind him, waiting for comments. They had spent close to eight hours running old prints of Valerie Lone's biggest hits.

Arthur Crewes's home centered around the projection room. As his life centered around the film industry. Through the door, and into the living room, opulent beneath fumed and waxed, shadowed oak beams far above them. The two men did not speak. The living room was immense, only slightly smaller than a basketball court. And in one corner, Crewes, now settled into a deep armchair, before a roaring walk-in fireplace. The rest of the living room was empty and quiet; one could hear the fall of dust. It had been a gay house many times in the past, and would be again, but at the moment, far down below the vaulting ceiling, their voices rising like echoes in a mountain pass, Arthur Crewes spoke to his publicist.

"Fred, I want the full treatment. I want her seen everywhere by everyone. I want her name as big as it ever was."

Handy pursed his lips, even as he nodded. "That takes money, Arthur. We're pushing the publicity budget now."

Crewes lit a cigar. "This is above-the-line expense. Keep it a separate record, and I'll take care of it out of my pocket. I want it all itemized for the IRS, but don't spare the cost."

"Do you know how much you're getting into here?"

"It doesn't matter. Whatever it is, however much you need, come and ask, and you'll get it. But I want a real job done for that money, Fred."

Handy stared at him for a long moment.

"You'll get mileage out of Valerie Lone's comeback, Arthur. No doubt about it. But I have to tell you right now it isn't going to be anything near commensurate with what you'll be spending. It isn't that kind of appeal."

Crewes drew deeply on the cigar, sent a thin streamer of blue smoke toward the darkness above them. "I'm not concerned about the value to the picture. It's going to be a good property, it can take care of itself. This is something else."

Handy looked puzzled. "Why?"

Crewes did not answer. Finally, he asked, "Is she settled in at the Beverly Hills?"

Handy rose to leave. "Best bungalow in the joint. You should have seen the reception they gave her."

"That's the kind of reception I want everywhere for her, Fred. A lot of bowing and scraping for the old queen."

Handy nodded, walked toward the foyer. Across the room, forcing him to raise his voice to reach Crewes, still lost in the dimness of the living room, the fireplace casting spastic shadows of blood and night on the walls, Fred Handy said, "Why the extra horsepower, Arthur? I get nervous when I'm told to spend freely."

Smoke rose from the chair where Arthur Crewes was hidden. "Good night, Fred."

Handy stood for a moment; then, troubled, he let himself out. The living room was silent for a long while, only the faint crackling of the logs on the fire breaking the stillness. Then Arthur Crewes reached to the sidetable and lifted the telephone receiver from its cradle. He punched out a number.

"Miss Valerie Lone's bungalow, please . . . yes, I know what time it is. This is Arthur Crewes calling . . . thank you."

There was a pause, then sound from the other end.

"Hello, Miss Lone? Arthur Crewes. Yes, thank you. Sorry if I disturbed you . . . oh, really? I rather thought you might be awake. I had the feeling you might be a little uneasy, first night back and all."

He listened to the voice at the other end. And did not smile. Then he said, "I just wanted to call and tell you not to be afraid. Everything will be fine. There's nothing to be afraid of. Nothing at all."

His eyes became light, and light fled down the wires to see her at the other end. In the elegant bungalow, still sitting in the dark. Through a window, moonlight lay like a patina of dull gold across the room, tinting even the depressions in the sofa pillows where a thousand random bottoms had rested, a vaguely yellow ocher.

Valerie Lone. Alone.

Misted by a fine down of Beverly Hills moonlight—the great gaffer in the sky working behind an amber gel keylighting her with a senior, getting fill light from four broads and four juniors, working the light outside in the great celestial cyclorama with a dozen sky-pans, and catching her just right with a pair of inky-dinks, scrims, gauzes and cutters—displaying her in a gown of powdered moth-wing dust. Valerie Lone, off-camera, trapped by the lens of God, and the electric eyes of Arthur Crewes. But still in XTREME CLOSEUP.

She thanked him, seeming bewildered by his kindness. "Is there anything you need?" he asked.

He had to ask her to repeat her answer, she had spoken so softly. But the answer was *nothing,* and he said *good night,* and was about to hang up when she called him.

To Crewes it was a sound from farther away than the Beverly Hills

Hotel. It was a sound that came by way of a Country of Mildew. From a land where oily things moved out of darkness. From a place where the only position was hunched safely into oneself with hands about knees, chin tucked down, hands wrapped tightly so that if the eyes with their just-born-bird membranes should open, through the film could be seen the relaxed fingers. It was a sound from a country where there was no hiding place.

After a moment he answered, shaken by her frightened sound. "Yes, I'm here."

Now he could not see her, even with eyes of electricity.

For Valerie Lone sat on the edge of the bed in her bungalow, not bathed in moth-wing dust, but lighted harshly by every lamp and overhead in the bungalow. She could not turn out those lights. She was petrified with fear. A nameless fear that had no origin and had no definition. It was merely *there with her*, a palpable presence.

And something else was in the room with her.

"They . . ."

She stopped. She knew Crewes was straining at the other end of the line to hear what followed.

"They sent your champagne."

Crewes smiled to himself. She was touched.

Valerie Lone did not smile, was incapable of a smile, was by no means touched. The bottle loomed huge across the room on the glass-topped table. "Thank you. It was. Very. Kind. Of. You."

Slowly, because of the way she had told him the champagne had arrived, Crewes asked, "Are you all right?"

"I'm frightened."

"There's nothing to be frightened about. We're all on your team, you know that . . ."

"I'm frightened of the champagne . . . it's been so long."

Crewes did not understand. He said so.

"I'm afraid to drink it."

Then he understood.

He didn't know what to say. For the first time in many years he felt pity for someone. He was fully conversant with affection, and hatred, and envy, and admiration and even stripped-to-the-bone lust. But pity was something he somehow hadn't had to deal with, for a long time. His ex-wife and the boy, they were the last, and that had been eight years before. He didn't know what to say.

"I'm afraid, isn't that silly? I'm afraid I'll like it too much again. I've managed to forget what it tastes like. But if I open it, and taste it, and remember . . . I'm afraid . . ."

He said, "Would you like me to drive over?"

She hesitated, pulling her wits about her. "No. No, I'll be all right. I'm just being silly. I'll talk to you tomorrow." Then, hastily: "You'll call tomorrow?"

"Yes, of course. Sure I will. I'll call first thing in the morning, and you'll come down to the Studio. I'm sure there are all sorts of people you'll want to get reacquainted with."

Silence, then, softly: "Yes. I'm just being silly. It's very lonely here."

"Well, then. I'll call in the morning."

"Lonely . . . hmmm? Oh, yes! Thank you. Good night, Mr. Crewes."

"Arthur. That's first on the list. Arthur."

"Arthur. Thank you. Good night."

"Good night, Miss Lone."

He hung up, still hearing the same voice he had heard in darkened theaters rich with the smell of popcorn (in the days before they started putting faintly rancid butter on it) and the taste of Luden's Menthol Cough Drops. The same deep, silken voice that he had just this moment past heard break, ever so slightly, with fear.

Darkness rose up around him.

Light flooded Valerie Lone. The lights she would keep burning all night, because out there was darkness and it was so lonely in here. She stared across the room at the bottle of champagne, sitting high in its silver ice bucket, chipped base of ice melting to frigid water beneath it.

Then she stood and took a drinking glass from the tray on the bureau, ignoring the champagne glasses that had come with the bottle. She walked across the room to the bathroom and went inside, without turning on the light. She filled the water glass from the tap, letting the cold faucet run for a long moment. Then she stood in the doorway of the bathroom, drinking the water, staring at the bottle of champagne, that bottle of champagne.

Then slowly, she went to it and pulled the loosened plastic cork from the mouth of the bottle. She poured half a glass.

She sipped it slowly.

Memories stirred.

And a dark shape fled off across hills in the Country of Mildew.

THREE

Handy drove up the twisting road into the Hollywood Hills. The call he had received an hour before was one he would never have expected. He had not heard from Huck Barkin in over two years. Haskell Barkin, the tall. Haskell Barkin, the tanned. Haskell Barkin, the handsome. Haskell Barkin, the amoral. The last time Fred had seen Huck, he was busily making a precarious living hustling wealthy widows with kids. His was a specialized con: he got next to the kids—Huck was one of the more accomplished surf-bums extant—even as he seduced the mother, and before the family attorney knew what was happening, the pitons and grapnels and tongs had been sunk in deep, through the mouth and out the other side, and friendly, good-looking, rangy Huck Barkin was living in the house, driving the Imperial, ordering McCormick's bourbon from the liquor store, eating like Quantrill's Raiders, and clipping bucks like the Russians were in Pomona.

There had been one who had tried to saturate herself with barbiturates when Huck had said, *"À bientot."*

There had been one who had called in her battery of attorneys in an attempt to have him make restitution, but she had been informed that Huck Barkin was one of those rare, seldom, not-often, random "judgment-proof" people.

There had been one who had gone away to New Mexico, where it was warm, and no one would see her drinking.

There had been one who had bought a tiny gun, but had never used it on him.

There had been one who had already had the gun, and she *had* used it. But not on Huck Barkin.

Fearsome, in his strangeness; without ethic. Animal.

He was one of the more unpleasant Hollywood creeps Handy had met in the nine Hollywood years. Yet there was an unctuous charm about the man; it sat well on him, if the observers weren't the most perceptive. Handy chuckled, remembering the one and only time he had seen Barkin shot down. By a woman. (And how seldom *any* woman can *really* put down a man, with such thoroughness that there is no comeback, no room to rationalize that it wasn't such a great zinger, with the full certainty that the target has been utterly destroyed, and nothing is left but to slink away. He remembered.)

It had been at a party thrown by CBS, to honor the star of their new ninety-minute Western series. Big party. Century City Hotel. All the silkies were there, all the sleek, well-fed types who went without eating a full day to make it worthwhile at the barbecue and buffet. Barkin had somehow been invited. Or crashed. No one ever questioned his appearance at these things; black mohair suit is ticket enough in a scene where recognition is predicated on the uniform of the day.

He had sidled into a conversational group composed of Handy and his own Julie, Spencer Lichtman the agent and two very expensive call girls—all pale silver hair and exquisite faces; hundred and a half per night girls; the kind a man could talk to afterward, learn something from, probably with Masters earned in photochemistry or piezoelectricity; nothing even remotely cheap or brittle about them; master craftsmen in a specialized field—and Barkin had unstrapped his Haskellesque charm. The girls had sensed at once that he was one of the leeches, hardly one of the cruisable meal tickets with wherewithal. They had been courteous, but chill. Barkin had gone from unctuous to rank in three giant steps, without saying, "May I?"

Finally, in desperation, he had leaned in close to the taller of the two silver goddesses, and murmured (loud enough for all in the group to overhear) with a Richard Widmark thinness: "How would you like me down in your panties?"

Silence for a beat, then the silver goddess turned to him with eyes of anthracite, and across the chill polar wastes came her reply. "I have one asshole down there now . . . what would I want with you?"

Handy chuckled again, smugly, remembering the look on Barkin as he had broken down into his component parts, reformed as a puddle of strawberry jam sliding down one of the walls, and oozed out of the scene, not to return that night.

Yet there was a roguish good humor about the big blond beach-bum that most people took at face value; only if Huck's back was put to the wall did the façade of affability drop away to reveal the granite foundation of amorality. The man was intent on sliding through life with as little effort as possible.

Handy had spotted him for what he was almost immediately upon meeting him, but for a few months Huck had been an amusing adjunct to Handy's new life in the film colony. They had not been in touch for three years. Yet this morning the call had come from Barkin. Using Arthur Crewes's name. He had asked Handy to come to see him, and given him an address in the Hollywood Hills.

Now, as he tooled the Impala around another snakeback curve, the top of the mountain came into view, and Handy saw the house. As it was the *only* house, dominating the flat, he assumed it was the address Barkin had given him, and he marveled. It was a gigantic circle of a structure, a flattened spool of sandblasted gray rock whose waist was composed entirely of curved panels of dark-smoked glass. Barkin could never have afforded an Orwellian feast of a home like this.

Handy drove up the flaring spiral driveway and parked beside the front door: an ebony slab with a rhodium-plated knob as big as an Impala headlight.

The grounds were incredibly well-tailored, sloping down all sides of the mountain to vanish over the next flat. Bonsai trees pruned in their abstracted Zen artfulness, bougainvillea rampant across one entire outcropping, banks of flowers, dichondra everywhere, ivy.

Then Handy realized the house was turning. To catch the sun. Through a glass roof. The front door was edging past him toward the west. He walked up to it, and looked for a doorbell. There was none.

From within the house came the staccato report of hardwood striking hardwood. It came again and again, in uneven, frantic bursts. And the sound of grunting.

He turned the knob, expecting the gigantic door to resist, but it swung open on a center-pin, counterbalanced, and he stepped through into the front hall of inlaid onyx tiles.

The sounds of wood on wood, and grunting, were easy to follow. He went down five steps into a passageway, and followed it toward the sound, emerging at the other end of the passage into a living room ocean-deep in sunshine. In the center of the room Huck Barkin and a tiny Japanese, both in loose-fitting ceremonial robes, were jousting with sawed-off quarterstaffs—*shoji* sticks.

Handy watched silently. The diminutive Japanese was electric. Barkin was no match for him, though he managed to get in a smooth rap or two from moment to moment. But the Oriental rolled and slid, barely seeming to touch the deep white carpet. His hands moved like propellers, twisting the hardwood staff to counter a swing by the taller man, jabbing sharply to embed the point of the staff in Barkin's ribs. In and out and gone. He was a blur.

As Barkin turned in almost an *entrechat,* to avoid a slantwise flailing maneuver by the Oriental, he saw Handy standing in the entranceway to the passage. Barkin stepped back from his opponent.

"That'll do it for now, Mas," he said.

They bowed to one another, the Oriental took the staffs, and left through another passageway at the far end of the room. Barkin came across the rug liquidly, all the suntanned flesh rippling with the play of solid muscle underneath. Handy found himself once again admiring the shape Barkin kept himself in. *But if you do nothing but spend time on your body, why not?* he thought ruefully. The idea of honest labor had never taken up even temporary residence in Huck's thoughts. And yet one bodybuilding session was probably equal to all the exertion a common laborer would expend in a day.

Handy thought Huck was extending his hand in greeting, but halfway across the room the robed beach-bum reached over to a Saarinen chair and snagged a huge, fluffy towel. He swabbed his face and chest with it, coming to Handy.

"Fred, baby."

"How are you, Huck?"

"Great, fellah. Just about king of the world these days. Like the place?"

"Nice. Whose is it?"

"Belongs to a chick I've been seeing. Old man's one of the big things happening in some damned banana republic or other. I don't give it too much thought; she'll be back in about a month. Till then I've got the run of the joint. Want a drink?"

"It's eleven o'clock."

"Coconut milk, friend buddy friend. Got all the amino acids you can use all day. Very important."

"I'll pass."

Barkin shrugged, walking past him to a mirrored wall that was jeweled with the reflections of pattering sunlight streaming in from above. He seemed to wipe his hand over the mirror, and the wall swung out to reveal a fully stocked bar. He took a can of coconut milk from the small freezer unit, and opened it, drinking straight from the can. "Doesn't that smart a bit?" Handy asked.

"The coconut mil—oh, you mean the *shoji* jousting. Best damned thing in the world to toughen you up. Teak. Get whacked across the belly half a dozen times with one of those and your stomach muscles turn to leather."

He flexed.

"Leather stomach muscles. Just what I've always yearned for."

Handy walked across the room and stared out through the dark glass at the incredible Southern California landscape, blighted by a murmuring, hanging pall of sickly smog over the Hollywood Freeway. With his back turned to Barkin, he said, "I tried to call Crewes after you spoke to me. He wasn't in. I came anyway. How come you used his name?" He turned around.

"He told me to."

"Where did *you* meet Arthur Crewes!" Handy snapped, sudden anger in his voice. This damned beach stiff, it had to be a shuck; he had to have used Handy's name somehow.

"At that pool party you took me to, about—what was it—about three years ago. You remember, that little auburn-haired thing, what was her name, Binnie, Bunny, something . . . ?"

"Billie. Billie Landewyck. Oh, yeah, I'd forgotten Crewes was there."

Huck smiled a confident smile. He downed the last of the coconut milk and tossed the can into a wastebasket. He came around the bar and slumped onto the sofa. "Yeah, well. Crewes remembered me. Got me through Central Casting. I keep my SAG dues up, never know when you can pick up a few bucks doing stunt or a bit. You know."

Handy did not reply. He was waiting. Huck had simply said Arthur Crewes wanted him to get together with the beach-bum, so Handy had come. But there was something stirring that Barkin didn't care to open up just yet.

"Listen, Huck, I'm getting to be an old man. I can't stand on my feet too long any more. So if you've got something shaking, let's to it, friend buddy friend."

Barkin nodded silently, as though resigned to whatever it was he had to say. "Yeah, well. Crewes wants me to meet Valerie Lone."

Handy stared.

"He remembered me."

Handy tried to speak, found he had nothing to say. It was too ridiculous. He turned to leave.

"Hold it, Fred. Don't do that, man. I'm talking to you."

"You're talking *nothing,* Barkin. You've gotta be straight out of a jug. Valerie Lone, my ass. Who do you think you're shucking? Not me, not good old friend buddy friend Handy. I know you, you deadbeat."

Barkin stood up, unfurled something over six feet of deltoid, trapezius and bicep, toned till they hummed, and planted himself in front of the passageway. "Fred, you continue to make the mistake of thinking I'm a hulk without a brain in it. You're wrong. I am a very clever lad, not merely pretty, but smart. Now if I have to drop five big ones into your pudding-trough, lover, I will do so."

Handy stopped moving toward him. Barkin was not fooling. He was angry. "What is all this, Barkin? What are you trying to climb onto? No, forget it, don't answer. What I want to know is why?"

Barkin spread hands as huge as catcher's mitts. The fingers were oddly long and graceful. And tanned. "She is a lovely woman who finds the company of handsome young men refreshing. Mr. Crewes, sir, has decided I will brighten her declining years."

"She is a scared creature who doesn't know where it's at, not right now she doesn't. And turning you loose on her would be a sudden joy like the Dutch Elm Blight."

Barkin smiled thinly. It was a mean smile. For the time it took the smile to vanish, he was not handsome. "Call Arthur Crewes. He'll verify."

"I can't get through to him, he's in a screening."

"Then go ask him. I'll be here all day."

He stepped aside. Handy waited, as though Barkin might surprise him and leap back suddenly, with a fist in the mouth. Huck stood grinning like a little boy. Ain't I cute.

"I'll do that."

Handy moved past and entered the passageway. As he walked hurriedly down the length of the corridor, he heard Barkin speak again. He turned to see the giant figure framed in the blazing sunlight rectangle at the other end of the dark tunnel. "You know, Fred chum, you need a good workout. You're gettin' flabbier than hell."

Handy fled, raising dust as he wheeled the Impala out of the driveway and down the mountainside. There was the stink of fuel oil rising up from the city. Or was it the smell of fear?

FOUR

When he burst into Arthur Crewes's office at the Studio, the reception room was filled with delight. All that young stuff. A dozen girls, legs crossed high to show off the rounded thigh, waiting to be seen. As he slammed in, Twiggyeyes blinked rapidly.

He careened through the door and brought up short, turning quickly to see an unbroken panorama of gorgeous young-twenties starlets. Roz, fifty and waspish, behind the desk, snickered at his double-take. Handy recognized the tone of the snicker. He was a man periodically motivated from somewhere low in his anatomy, and Roz never failed to hold it against him. He had never asked her out.

"Hello, Fred," one of the girls said. He had to strain to single her out. They all looked alike. Teased; long flat blonde hair; freaky Twiggy styles; backswept bouffant; short mannish cuts; all of them, no matter what mode, they all looked alike. It was Randi. She had had a thing about touching his privates. It was all he could remember about her. Not even if she'd been good. But a publicist must remember names, and with the remembrance of her touching his penis and drawing in her breath as though it had been something strange and new and wonderful like the Inca Codex or one of the Dead Sea Scrolls, the name Randi popped up like the NO SALE clack on a cash register.

"Hi, Randi. How's it going?"

He didn't even wait for an answer. He turned back to Roz. "I want to see him."

Her mouth became the nasty slit opening of a mantis. "He's got someone in with him now."

"I want to *see* him."

"I *said,* Mr. Handy, he has someone in there now. We *are* still interviewing girls, you know . . ."

"Bloody damn it, lady, I said get your ass in there and tell him Handy is coming through that door, open or not, in exactly ten seconds."

She drew herself up, no breasts at all, straight lines and Mondrian sterility, and started to huff at him. Handy said, "Fuck," and went through into Crewes's office.

He said it softly, but he made noise entering the office.

Another of the pretties was showing Arthur Crewes her 8×10 glossies, under plastic, out of an immense black leather photofolio. Starlets. Arthur was saying something about their needing a few more dark-haired girls, as Handy came through the door.

Crewes looked up, surprised at the interruption.

The starlet smiled automatically.

"Arthur, I have to talk to you."

Crewes seemed puzzled by the tone in Handy's voice. But he nodded. "In a minute, Fred. Why don't you sit down. Georgia and I were talking."

Handy realized his error. He had gone a step too far with Arthur Crewes. Throughout the industry, one thing was common knowledge about Crewes's office policy: any girl who came in for an interview was treated courteously, fairly, without even the vaguest scintilla of a hustle. Crewes had been known to can men on his productions who had used their positions to get all-too-willing actresses into bed with promises of three-line bits, or a walk-on. For Handy to interrupt while Crewes was talking to even the lowliest day-player was an affront Crewes would not allow to pass unnoticed. Handy sat down, ambivalent as hell.

Georgia was showing Crewes several shots from a Presley picture she had made the year before. Crewes was remarking that she looked good in a bikini. It was a businesslike, professional tone of voice, no leer. The girl was standing tall and straight. Handy knew that under other circumstances, in other offices where the routine was different, if Crewes had been another sort of man and had said, *why don't you take off your clothes so I can get a better idea of how you'll look in the nude shots we're shooting for the overseas market,* this girl, this Georgia, would be pulling the granny dress with its baggy mini material over her head and displaying herself in bikini briefs and maybe no brassiere to hold up all that fine young meat. But in this office she was standing tall and straight. She was being asked to be professional, to take pride in herself and whatever degree of craft she might possess. It was why there were so few lousy rumors around town about Arthur Crewes.

"I'm not certain, Georgia, but let me check with Kenny Heller in Casting, see what he's already done, and what parts are left open. I know there's a very nice five- or six-line comedy walk-on with Mitchum that we haven't found a girl for yet. Perhaps that might work. No promises, you understand, but I'll check with Kenny and get back to you later in the day."

"Thank you, Mr. Crewes. I'm very grateful."

Crewes smiled and picked up one of the 8 × 10's from a thin sheaf at the rear of the photofolio. "May we keep one of these here, for the files . . . and also to remind me to get through to Kenny?" She nodded, and smiled back at him. There was no subterfuge in the interchange, and Handy sank a trifle lower on the sofa.

"Just give it to Roz, at the desk out there, and leave your number . . . would you prefer we let you know through your agent, or directly?"

It was the sort of question, in any other office, that might mean the producer was trying to wangle the home number for his own purposes. But not here. Georgia did not hesitate as she said. "Oh, either way. It makes no difference. Herb is very good about getting me out on interviews. But if it looks possible, I'll give you my home number. There's a service on the line that'll pick up if I'm out."

"You can leave it with Roz, Georgia. And thank you for coming in." He stood and they shook hands. She was quite happy. Even if the part did not come through, she knew she had been *considered,* not merely as-sayed as a possible quickie on an office sofa. As she started for the door, Crewes added, "I'll have Roz call one way or the other, as soon as we know definitely."

She half-turned, displaying a fine length of leg, taut against the baggy dress, "Thank you. 'Bye."

"Goodbye."

She left the office, and Crewes sat down again. He pushed papers around the outer perimeter of his desk, making Handy wait. Finally, when Handy had allowed Crewes as much punishment as he felt his recent original sin deserved, he spoke.

"You've got to be out of your mind, Arthur!"

Crewes looked up then. Stopped in the midst of his preparations to remark on Handy's discourtesy in entering the office during an interview. Crewes waited, but Handy said nothing. Then Crewes thumbed the comm button on the phone. He picked up the receiver and said, "Roz, ask them if they'll be kind enough to wait about ten minutes. Fred and I have some details to work out." He listened a moment, then racked the receiver and turned to Handy.

"Okay. What?"

"Jesus Christ, Arthur. Haskell Barkin, for Christ's sake. You've got to be *kid*ding."

"I talked to Valerie Lone last night. She sounded all by herself. I thought it might be smart therapy to get her a good-looking guy, as company, a chaperone, someone who'd be nice to her. I remembered this Barkin from—"

Handy stood up, frenzy impelling his movement. Banging off walls, vibrating at supersonic speeds, turning invisible with teeth-gritting. "I *know* where you remembered this Barkin from, Arthur. From Billie Landewyck's party, three years ago; the pool party; where you met Vivvi. I know. He told me."

"You've been to see Barkin already?"

"He had me out of bed too much before I wanted to get up."

"An honest day's working time won't hurt you, Fred. I was here at seven thir—"

"Arthur, I frankly, God forgive my talking to my producer this way, frankly don't give a flying *shit* what time you were behind your desk. Barkin, Arthur! You're insane."

"He seemed like a nice chap. Always smiling."

Handy leaned over the desk, talking straight into Arthur Crewes's cerebrum, eliminating the middleman. "So does the crocodile smile, Arthur. Haskell Barkin is a crud. He is a slithering, creeping, crawling, essentially reptilian monster who slices and eats. He is Jack the Ripper, Arthur. He is a vacuum cleaner. He is a loggerhead shark. He *hates* like we *urinate*—it's a basic bodily function for him. He leaves a wet trail when he walks. Small children run shrieking from him, Arthur. He's a killer in a suntan. Women who chew nails, who destroy men for giggles, women like *that* are afraid of him, Arthur. If you were a broad and he French-kissed you, Arthur, you'd have to go get a tetanus shot. He uses human bones to bake his bread. He's declared war on every woman who ever carried a crotch. This man is death, Arthur. And *that's* what you wanted to turn loose on Valerie Lone, God save her soul. He's Paris green, he's sump water, he's axle grease, Arthur! He's—"

Arthur Crewes spoke softly, looking battered by Handy's diatribe. "You made your point, Fred. I stand corrected."

Handy slumped down into the chair beside the desk.

To himself: "Jeezus, Huck Barkin, Jeezus . . ."

And when he had run down completely, he looked up. Crewes seemed poised in time and space. His idea had not worked out. "Well, whom would *you* suggest?"

Handy spread his hands.

"I don't know. But not Barkin, or anyone like him. No Strip killers, Arthur. That would be lamb to slaughter time."

Crewes: "But she needs *some*one."

Handy: "What's your special interest, Arthur?"

Crewes: "Why say that?"

Handy: "Arthur . . . c'mon. I can tell. There's a thing you've got going where she's concerned."

Crewes turned in his chair. Staring out the window at the lot, a series of flat-trucks moving scenery back to the storage bins. "You only work for me, Fred."

Handy considered, then decided what the hell. "If I worked for Adolph Eichmann, Arthur, I'd still ask where all them Jews was going."

Crewes turned back, looked levelly at his publicist. "I keep thinking you're nothing more than a flack-man. I'm wrong, aren't I?"

Handy shrugged. "I have a thought of my own from time to time."

Crewes nodded, acquiescing. "Would you just settle for my saying she once did me a favor? Not a big favor, just a little favor, something she probably doesn't even remember, or if she does she doesn't think of it in relation to the big producer who's giving her a comeback break. Would you settle for my saying I mean her nothing but good things, Fred? Would that buy it?"

Handy nodded. "It'll do."

"So who do we get to keep her reassured that she isn't ready for the dustbin just yet?"

Again Handy spread his hands. "I don't know, it's been eighteen years since she had anything to do with—hey! Wait a bit. What's his name . . . ?"

"Who?"

"Oh, hell, *you* know . . ." Handy said, fumbling with his memory, ". . . the one who got fouled up with the draft during the war, blew his career, something, I don't remember . . . aw, c'mon Arthur, you know who I mean, used to play all the bright young attorney defending the dirty-faced delinquent parts." He snapped his fingers trying to call back a name from crumbling fan magazines, from rotogravure coming attraction placards in theater windows.

Crewes suggested, "Call Sheilah Graham."

Handy came around the desk, dialed 9 to get out, and Sheilah Graham's private number, from memory. "Sheilah? Fred Handy. Yeah, hi. Hey, who was it Valerie Lone used to go with?" He listened. "No, huh-uh, the one that was always in the columns, he was married, but they had a big thing, he does bits now, guest shots, who—"

She told him.

"Right. Right, that's who. Okay, hey thanks, Sheilah. What? No, huh-uh, huh-uh; as soon as we get something right, it's yours. Okay, luv. Thanks. 'Bye."

He hung up and turned to Crewes. "Emery Romito."

Crewes nodded. "Jeezus, is he still alive?"

"He was on *Bonanza* about three weeks ago. Guest shot. Played an alcoholic veterinarian."

Crewes lifted an eyebrow. "Type casting?"

Handy was leafing through the volume of the PLAYERS DIRECTORY that listed leading men. "I don't think so. If he'd been a stone sauce-hound he'd've been planted long before this. I think he's just getting old, that's the worst."

Crewes gave a sharp, short bitter laugh. "That's enough."

Handy slammed the PLAYERS DIRECTORY closed. "He's not in there."

"Try character males."

Handy found it, in the R's. Emery Romito. A face out of the past, still holding a distinguished mien but, even through the badly reproduced photo that had been an 8×10 glossy, showing weariness and the indefinable certainty that this man knew he had lost his chance at picking up all the marbles.

Handy showed Crewes the photo.

"Do you think this is a good idea?" The producer looked at him with trepidation.

Handy looked back at him. "It's a helluva lot better idea than *yours,* Arthur."

Crewes sucked on the edge of his lower lip between clenched teeth. "Okay. Go get him. But make him look like a knight on a white charger. I want her very happy."

"Knights on white chargers these days come barrel-assing down the streets of suburbia with their phalluses in hand, blasting women's underwear whiter-than-white. Would you settle for merely *mildly* happy?"

FIVE

Cotillions could have been held in the main drawing room of the Stratford Beach Hotel. Probably had been. In the days when Richard Dix had his way with Leatrice Joy, in the days when Zanuck had his three rejected scenarios privately published as a "book" and sent them around to the studios in hopes of building his personal stock, in the days when Virginia Rappe was being introduced to the dubious sexual joys of a fat kid named Arbuckle. In those days the Stratford Beach Hotel had been a showplace, set out on the lovely Santa Monica shore, overlooking the triumphant Pacific.

Architecturally, the hotel was a case in point for Frank Lloyd Wright's contention that the Sunshine State looked as though "someone had tipped the United States up on its east coast, and everything that was loose went tumbling into California." Great and bulky, sunk to its hips in the earth, with rococo flutings at every possible juncture, portico'd and belfry'd, the Stratford Beach had passed through fifty years of scuffling feet, spuming salt-spray, drunken orgies, changed bed-linen and insipid managers to end finally in this backwash eddy of a backwash suburb.

In the main drawing room of the Stratford Beach, standing on the top step of a wide, spiraling staircase of onyx that ran down into a room where the dust in the ancient carpets rose at each step to mingle with the downdrifting film of shattered memories, fractured yesterdays, mote-infested yearnings and the unmistakable stench of dead dreams, Fred Handy knew what had killed F. Scott Fitzgerald. This room, and the thousands of others like it, that held within their ordered interiors a kind of deadly magic of remembrance; a pull and tug of eras that refused to give up the ghost, that had not the common decency to pass away and let new times be born. The embalmed forevers that never came to be . . . they were here, lurking in the colorless patinas of dust that covered the rubber plants, that settled in the musty odor of the velvet plush furniture, that shone dully up from inlaid hardwood floors where the Charleston had been danced as a racy new thing.

This was the terrifying end-up for all the refuse of nostalgia. Hooked on this scene had been Fitzgerald, lauding and singing of something that was dead even as it was born. And so easily hooked could *anyone* get on this, who chose to live after their time was passed.

The words tarnish and mildew again formed in Handy's mind, superimposed as subtitles over a mute sequence of Valerie Lone shrieking in closeup. He shook his head, and not a moment too soon. Emery Romito came down the stairs from the second floor of the hotel, walking up behind Handy across the inlaid tiles of the front hall. He stood behind Handy, staring down into the vast living room. As Handy shook his head, fighting to come back to today.

"Elegant, isn't it?" Emery Romito said.

The voice was cultivated, the voice was deep and warm, the voice was histrionic, the voice was filled with memory, the voice was a surprise in the silence, but none of these were the things that startled Handy. The present tense, *isn't it.* Not: wasn't it, isn't it.

Oh my God, Handy thought.

Afraid to turn around, Fred Handy felt himself sucked into the past. This room, this terrible room, it was so help him God a portal to the past. The yesterdays that had never gone to rest were all here, crowding against a milky membrane separating them from the world of right here and now, like eyeless soulless wraiths, hungering after the warmth and presence of his corporeality. They wanted . . . what? They wanted his *au courant.* They wanted his today, so they could hear "Nagasaki" and "Vagabond Lover" and "Please" sung freshly again. So they could rouge their knees and straighten their headache bands over their foreheads. Fred Handy, man of today, assailed by the ghosts of yesterday, and terrified to turn around and see one of those ghosts standing behind him.

"Mr. Handy? You *are* the man who called me, aren't you?"

Handy turned and looked at Emery Romito.

"Hello," he said, through the dust of decades.

Handy

Jefferson once said people get pretty much the kind of government they deserve, which is why I refuse to listen to any bullshit carping by my fellow Californians about Reagan and his gubernatorial gang-banging—what I chose to call government by artificial insemination when I was arguing with Julie, a registered Republican, when we weren't making love—because it seems to me they got just what they were asking for. The end-product of a hundred years of statewide paranoia and rampant lunacy. That philosophy—stripped of Freudian undertones—has slopped over into most areas of my opinion. Women who constantly get stomped on by shitty guys generally have a streak of masochism in them; guys who get their hearts eaten away by rodent females are basically self-flagellants. And when you see someone who has been ravaged by life, it is a safe bet he has been a willing accomplice at his own destruction.

All of this passed through my mind as I said hello to Emery Romito. The picture in the PLAYERS DIRECTORY had softened the sadness. But in living color he was a natural for one of those billboards hustling Forest Lawn pre-need cemetery plots. *Don't get caught with your life down.*

He was one of the utterly destroyed. A man familiar to the point of incest with the forces that crush and maim, a man stunned by the hammer. And I could conceive of *no one* who would aid and abet those kind of forces in self-destruction. No. No one.

Yet no man could have done it to himself without the help of the Furies. And so, I was ambivalent. I felt both pity and cynicism for Emery Romito, and his brave foolish elegance.

Age lay like soot in the creases of what had once been a world-famous face. The kind of age that means merely growing old, without wistfulness or delight. This man had lived through all the days and nights of his life with only one thought uppermost: let me forget what has gone before.

"Would you like to sit out on the terrace?" Romito asked. "Nice breeze off the ocean today."

I smiled acquiescence, and he made a theatrical gesture in the direction of the terrace. As he preceded me down the onyx steps into the living room, I felt a clutch of nausea, and followed him. Cheyne-Stokes breathing as I walked across the threadbare carpet, among the deep rest-ful furniture that called to me, suggested I try their womb comfort, sink into them never to rise again. Or if I did, it would be as a shriveled, mummified old man. (And with the memory of a kid who grew up on movies, I saw Margo as Capra had seen her in 1937, aging horribly, shriveling, in a matter of seconds, as she was being carried out of Shangri-La. And I shuddered. A grown man, and I shuddered.)

It was like walking across the bottom of the sea; shadowed, filtered with sounds that had no names, caught by shafts of sunlight from the skylight above us that contained freshets of dust-motes rising tumbling surging upward, threading between sofas and Morris chairs like whales in shoal, finally arriving at the fogged dirty French doors that gave out onto the terrace.

Romito opened them smoothly, as if he had done it a thousand times in a thousand films—and probably had—for a thousand Anita Louises. He stepped out briskly, and drew a deep breath. In that instant I realized he was in extremely good shape for a man his age, built big across the back and shoulders, waist still trim and narrow, actually quite dapper. Then why did I think of him as a crustacean, as a pitted fossil, as a gray and wasted relic?

It was the air of fatality, of course. The superimposed chin-up-through-it-all horseshit that all Hollywood hangers-on adopted. It was an atrophied devolutionary extension of the *Show Must Go On* shuck; the myth that owns everyone in the Industry: that getting forty-eight minutes of hack cliché situation comedy filmed—only the barest minimally innervating—to capture the boggle-eyed interest of the Great Unwashed sucked down in the doldrum mire of The Great American Heartland, so they will squat there for twelve minutes of stench odor poison and artifact hardsell, is an occupation somehow inextricably involved with advancing the course of Western Civilization. A myth that has oozed over into all areas of modern thought, thus turning us into a "show biz culture" and spawning such creatures as Emery Romito. Like the cats in the empty Ziv Studios, nibbling at the leftover garbage of the film industry, but loath to leave it. (Echoes of the old saw about the carnival assistant whose job it was to shovel up elephant shit who, when asked why he didn't get a better job, replied, "What? And leave show biz?") Emery Romito was one of the clingers to the underside of the rock that was show biz, that dominated like Gibraltar the landscape of Americana.

He had forfeited his humanity in order to remain "with it." He was dead, and didn't know it. *What, and leave show biz?*

The terrace was half the size of the living room, which made it twice as large as the foyer of Grauman's Chinese. Gray stone balustrades bounded it, and earthquake tremors had performed an intricate calligraphy across the inlaid and matched flaggings. It was daylight, but that didn't stop the shadowy images of women with bobbed hairdos and men with pomaded glossiness from weaving in and around us as we stood there, staring out at the ocean. It was ghost-time again, and secret liaisons were being effected out on the terrace by dashing sheiks (whose wives [married before their men had become nickelodeon idols] were inside slugging the gin-spiked punch) and hungry little hopefuls with waxed shins and a dab of alum in their vaginas, anxious to grasp magic.

"Let's sit down," Emery Romito said. To me, not the ghosts. He indicated a conversation grouping of cheap tubular aluminum beach chairs, their once-bright webbing now hopelessly faded by sun and seamist.

I sat down and he smiled ingratiatingly.

Then he sat down, careful to pull up the pants creases in the Palm Beach suit. The suit was in good shape, but perhaps fifteen years out of date.

"Well," he said.

I smiled back. I hadn't the faintest idea what "well" was a preamble to, nor what I was required to answer. But he waited, expecting me to say something.

When I continued to smile dumbly, his expression crumpled a little, and he tried another tack. "Just what sort of part *is* it that Crewes has in mind?"

Oh my God, I thought. *He thinks it's an interview.*

"Uh, well, it isn't precisely a part in the film I'm here to talk to you about, Mr. Romito." It was much too intricate a syntax for a man whose heart might attack him at any moment.

"It isn't a part," he repeated.

"No, it was something rather personal . . ."

"It isn't a part." He whispered it, barely heard, lost instantly in the overpowering sound of the Santa Monica surf not far beyond us.

"It's about Valerie Lone," I began.

"Valerie?"

"Yes. We've signed her for *Subterfuge* and she's back in town and—"

"Subterfuge?"

"The film Mr. Crewes is producing."

"Oh. I see."

He didn't see at all. I was sure of that. I didn't know how in the world I could tell this ruined shell that his services were needed as escort, not actor. He saved me the trouble. He ran away from me, into the past.

"I remember once, in 1936 I believe . . . no, it was '37, that was the year I did *Beloved Liar* . . ."

I let the sound of the surf swell inside me. I turned down the gain on Emery Romito and turned up the gain on nature. I knew I would be able to get him to do what needed to be done—he was a lonely, helpless man for whom *any* kind of return to the world of glamor was a main chance. But it would take talking, and worse . . . listening.

". . . Thalberg called me in, and he was smiling, it was a very unusual thing, you can be sure. And he said: 'Emery, we've just signed a girl for your next picture,' and of course it was Valerie. Except that wasn't her name then, and he took me over to the Commissary to meet her. We had the special salad, it was little slivers of ham and cheese and turkey, cut so they were stacked one on top of the other, so you tasted the ham first, then the cheese, then the turkey, all in one bite, and the freshest green crisp lettuce, they called it the William Powell Salad . . . no, that isn't right . . . the William Powell was crab meat . . . I think it was the Norma Talmadge Salad . . . or was it . . ."

As I sat there talking to Emery Romito, what I did not know was that all the way across the city, at the Studio, Arthur was entering the lot with Valerie Lone, in a chauffeured Bentley. He told me about it that night, and it was horrible. But it served as the perfect counterpoint to the musty warm monologue being delivered to me that moment by the Ghost of Christmas Past.

How lovely, how enriching, to sit there in sumptuous, palatial Santa Monica, Showplace of the Western World, listening to the voice from beyond reminisce about tuna fish and avocado salads. I prayed for deafness.

SIX

Crewes had called ahead. "I want the red carpet, do I make my meaning clear?" The Studio public relations head had said yes, he understood. Crewes had emphasized the point: "I don't want any fuckups, Barry. Not even the smallest. No gate police asking for a drive-on pass, no secretary making her wait. I want every carpenter and grip and mail boy to know we're bringing Valerie Lone back today. And I want *deference,*

Barry. If there's a fuckup, even the smallest fuckup, I'll come down on you the way Samson brought down the temple."

"Christ, Arthur, you don't have to threaten me!"

"I'm not threatening, Barry, I'm making the point so you can't weasel later. This isn't some phony finger-popping rock singer, this is Valerie Lone."

"All *right,* Arthur! Stop now."

When they came through the gate, the guards removed their caps, and waved the Bentley on toward the sound stages. Valerie Lone sat in the rear, beside Arthur Crewes, and her face was dead white, even under the makeup she had applied in the latest manner: for 1945.

There was a receiving line outside Stage 16.

The Studio head, several members of the foreign press, the three top producers on the lot, and half a dozen "stars" of current tv series. They made much over her, and when they were finished, Valerie Lone had almost been convinced someone gave a damn that she was not dead.

When the flashing red gumball light on its tripod went out—signifying that the shot had been completed inside the sound stage—they entered. Valerie took three steps beyond the heavy soundproof door, and stopped. Her eyes went up and up, into the dim reaches of the huge barnlike structure, to the catwalks with their rigging, the lights anchored to their brace boards, the cool and wonderful air from the conditioners that rose to heat up there, where the gaffers worked. Then she stepped back into the shadows as Crewes came up beside her, and he knew she was crying, and he turned to ask the others if they would come in later, to follow Miss Lone on her visit. The others did not understand, but they went back outside, and the door sighed shut on its pneumatic hinges.

Crewes went to her, and she was against the wall, the tears standing in her eyes, but not running down to ruin the makeup. In that instant Crewes knew she would be all right: she was an actress, and for an actress the only reality is the fantasy of the sound stages. She would not let her eyes get red. She was tougher than he'd imagined.

She turned to him, and when she said, "Thank you, Arthur," it was so soft, and so gentle, Crewes took her in his arms and she huddled close to him, and there was no passion in it, no striving to reach bodies, only a fine and warm protectiveness. He silently said no one would hurt her, and silently she said my life is in your hands.

After a while, they walked past the coffee machine and Willie, who said hello Miss Lone it's good to have you back; and past the assistant director's lectern where the shooting schedule was tacked onto the sloping board, where Bruce del Vaille nodded to her, and looked awed; and past the extras slumped in their straight-backed chairs, reading Irving Wallace and knitting, waiting for their calls, and they had been told who it was, and they all called to her and waved and smiled; and past the high director's chair which was at that moment occupied by the script supervisor, whose name was Henry, and he murmured hello, Miss Lone, we worked together on suchandsuch, and she went to him and kissed him on the cheek, and he looked as though he wanted to cry, too. For Arthur Crewes, in the sound stage somewhere, a bird twittered gaily. He shrugged and laughed, like a child.

Someone yelled, "Okay, settle down! Settle down!"

The din fell only a decibel. James Kencannon was talking to Mitchum, to one side of the indoor set that was decorated to be an outdoor set. It was an alley in a Southwestern town, and the cyclorama in the background had been artfully rigged to simulate a carnival somewhere in the middle distance. Lights played off the canvas, and for Valerie Lone it was genuine; a real carnival erected just for her. The alley was dirty and extremely realistic. Extras lounged against the brick walls that were not brick walls, waiting for the call to roll it. The cameraman was setting the angle of the shot, the big piece of equipment on its balloon tires set on wooden tracks, ready to dolly back when the grips pulled it. The assistant cameraman with an Arriflex on his shoulder was down on one knee, gauging an up-angle for action shooting.

Del Vaille came onto the set and Kencannon nodded to him. "Okay, roll—" Kencannon stopped the preparations for the shot, and asked the first assistant director to measure off the shot once more, as Mitchum stepped into the position that had, till that moment, been held by his stand-in. The first assistant unreeled the tape measure, announced it; the cameraman gave a turn to one of the flywheels on the big camera, and nodded ready to the assistant director, who turned and bawled, "Okay! Roll it!"

A strident bell clanged in the sound stage and dead silence fell. People in mid-step stopped. No one coughed. No one spoke. Tony, the sound mixer, up on his high platform with his earphones and his console, announced, "Take thirty-three Bravo!" which resounded through the cavernous set and was picked up through the comm box by the sound truck outside the sound stage. When it was up to speed, Tony yelled, "Speed!" and the first assistant director stepped forward into the shot with his wooden clackboard bearing Kencannon's name and the shot number. He clacked the stick to establish sound synch and get the board photographed, and there was a beat as he withdrew, as Mitchum drew in a breath for the action to come, as everyone poised hanging in limbo and Kencannon—like all directors—relished the moment of absolute power waiting for his voice to announce action.

Infinite moment.

Birth of dreams.

The shadow and the reality.

"Action!"

As five men leaped out of darkness and grabbed Robert Mitchum, shoving him back up against the wall of the alley. The camera dollied in rapidly to a closeup of Mitchum's face as one of the men grabbed his jaw with brutal fingers. "Where'd you take her . . . tell us where you took her!" the assailant demanded with a faint Mexican accent. Mitchum worked his jaw muscles, tried to shove the man away. The Arriflex operator was down below them, out of the master shot, purring away his tilted angles of the scuffling men. Mitchum tried to speak, but couldn't with the man's hand on his face. "Let'm talk, Sanchez!" another of the men urged the assailant. He released Mitchum's face, and in the same instant Mitchum surged forward, throwing two of the men from him, and breaking toward the camera as it dollied rapidly back to encompass the entire shot. The Arriflex operator scuttled with him, tracking him in wobbly closeup. The five men dived for Mitchum, preparatory to beating the crap out of him as Kencannon yelled, "Cut! That's a take!" and the enemies straightened up, relaxed, and Mitchum walked swiftly to his mobile dressing room. The crew prepared to set up another shot.

The extras moved in. A group of young kids, obviously bordertown tourists from a *yanqui* college, down having a ball in the hotbed of sin and degradation.

They milled and shoved, and Arthur found himself once again captivated by the enormity of what was being done here. A writer had said: ESTABLISHING SHOT OF CROWD IN ALLEY and it was going to cost about fifteen thousand dollars to make that line become a reality. He glanced at Valerie beside him, and she was smiling, a thin and delicate smile part remembrance and part wonder. It really never wore off, this delight, this entrapment by the weaving of fantasy into reality.

"Enjoying yourself?" he asked softly.

"It's as though I'd never been away," she said.

Kencannon came to her, then. He held both her hands in his, and he looked at her: as a man and as a camera. "Oh, you'll do just fine . . . just fine." He smiled at her. She smiled back.

"I haven't read the part yet," she said.

"Johnny Black hasn't finished expanding it yet. And I don't give a damn. You'll do fine, just fine!" They stared at each other with the kind of intimacy known only to a man who sees reality as an image on celluloid, and by a woman confronting a man who can make her look seventeen or seventy. Trust and fear and compassion and a mutual cessation of hostilities between the sexes. It was always like this. As if to say: what does he see? What does she want? What will we settle for? I love you.

"Have you said hello to Bob Mitchum yet?" Kencannon asked her.

"No. I think he's resting." She was, in turn, deferential to a star, as the lessers had been deferential to her. "I can meet him later."

"Are there any questions you'd like to ask?" he said. He waved a hand at the set around him. "You'll be living here for the next few weeks, you'd better get to know it."

"Well . . . yes . . . there are a few questions," she said. And she began getting into the role of star once more. She asked questions. Questions that were twenty years out of date. Not stupid questions, just *not quite in focus.* (As if the clackboard had not been in synch with the sound wagon, and the words had emerged from the actors' mouths a micro-instant too soon.) Not embarrassing questions, merely awkward questions; the answers to which entailed Kencannon's educating her, reminding her that she was a relic, that time had not waited for her—even as she had not waited when she had been a star—but had gathered its notes in a rush and plunged panting heavily past her. Now she had to exercise muscles of thought that had atrophied, just to try and catch up with time, dashing on ahead there like an ambitious mailroom boy trying to make points with the Studio executives. Her questions became more awkward. Her words came with more difficulty. Crewes saw her getting—how did Handy put it?—uptight.

Three girls had come onto the set from a mobile dressing room back in a dark corner of the sound stage. They wore flowered wrappers. The assistant director was herding them toward the windows of a dirty little building facing out on the alley. The girls went around the back of the building—back where it was unpainted pine and brace-rods and Magic Marker annotated as SUBTER'GE 115/144 indicating in which scenes these sets would be used.

They appeared in three windows of the building. They would be spectators at the stunt-man's fight with the assailants in the alley . . . Mitchum's fight with the assailants in the alley. They were intended to represent three Mexican prostitutes, drawn to their windows by the sounds of combat. They removed their wrappers.

Their naked, fleshy breasts hung on the window ledges like Daliesque melting casabas, waiting to ripen. Valerie Lone turned and saw the array of deep-brown nipples, and made a strange sound, "Awuhhh!" as if they had been something put on sale at such a startlingly low price she was amazed, confused and repelled out of suspicion.

Kencannon hurriedly tried to explain the picture was being shot in two versions, one for domestic and eventual television release, the other for foreign marketing. He went into a detailed comparison of the two versions, and when he had finished—with the entire cast of extras listening, for the explication of hypocrisy is always fascinating—Valerie Lone said:

"Gee, I hope none of *my* scenes have to be shot without clothes . . ."

And one of the extras gave a seal-like bark of amusement. "Fat chance," he murmured, just a bit too loud.

Arthur Crewes went around in a fluid movement that was almost choreography, and hit the boy—a beach-bum with long blond hair and fine deltoids—a shot that traveled no more than sixteen inches. It was a professional fighter's punch, no windup, no bolo, just a short hard piston jab that took the boy directly under the heart. He vomited air and lost his lower legs. He sat down hard.

If Crewes had thought about it, he would not have done it. The effect on the cast. The inevitable lawsuit. The Screen Extras Guild complaint. The bad form of striking someone who worked for him. The look on Valerie Lone's face as she caught the action with peripheral vision. The sight of an actor sitting down in pain, like a small child seeking a sandpile.

But he didn't think, and he did it, and Valerie Lone turned and ran . . .

Questions that were not congruent with a film that has to take into account television rerun, accelerated shooting schedules, bankability of stars, the tenor of the kids who make up the yeoman cast of every film, the passage of time and the improvement of techniques, and the altered thinking of studio magnates; the sophisticated tastes and mores of a new filmgoing audience.

A generation of youth with no respect for roots and heritage and the past. With no understanding of what has gone before. With no veneration of age. The times had conspired against Valerie Lone. Even as the times had conspired against her twenty years before. The simple and singular truth of it was that Valerie Lone had not been condemned by a lack of talent—though a greater talent might have sustained her—nor by a weakness in character—though a more ruthless nature might have carried her through the storms—nor by fluxes and flows in the Industry, but by all of these things, and by Fate and the times. But mostly the times. She was simply, singularly, not one with her world. It was a Universe that had chosen to care about Valerie Lone. For most of the world, the Universe didn't give a damn. For rare and singular persons from time to time in all ages, the Universe felt a compassion. It felt a need to succor and warm, to aid and bolster. That disaster befell all of these "wards of the Universe" was only proof unarguable that the Universe was inept, that God was insane.

It would have been better by far had the Universe left Valerie Lone to her own destiny. But it wouldn't, it couldn't; and it combined all the chance random elements of encounter and happenstance to litter her path with roses. For Valerie Lone, in the inept and compassionate Universe, the road was broken glass and dead birds, as far down the trail as she would ever be able to see.

The Universe had created the tenor of cynicism that hummed silently through all the blond beach-bums of the Hollywood extra set . . . the Universe had dulled Valerie Lone's perceptions of the Industry as it was today . . . the Universe had speeded up the adrenaline flow in Arthur Crewes at the instant the blond beach-bum had made his obnoxious comment . . . and the Universe had, in its cockeyed, simple-ass manner, thought it was benefiting Valerie Lone.

Obviously not.

And it would be this incident, this rank little happening, that would inject the tension into her bloodstream, that would cause her nerves to fray just that infinitesimal amount necessary, that would bring about metal fatigue and erosion and rust. So that when the precise moment came when optimum efficiency was necessary . . . Valerie Lone would be hauled back to this instant, this remark, this vicious little scene; and it would provide the weakness that would doom her.

From that moment, Valerie Lone began to be consumed by her shadow. And nothing could prevent it. Not even the wonderful, wonderful Universe that had chosen to care about her.

A Universe ruled by a mad God, who was himself being consumed by his shadow.

Valerie Lone turned and ran . . .

Through the sound stage, out the door, down the studio street, through Philadelphia in 1910, past the Pleasure Dome of Kubla Khan, around a Martian sand-city, into and out of Budapest during the Uprising (where castrated Red tanks still lay drenched in the ashdrunkenness of Molotov cocktails), and through Shade's Wells onto a sun-baked plain where the idiotically gaping mouth of the No. 3 Anaconda Mine received her.

She dashed into the darkness of the Anaconda, and found herself in the midst of the Springhill Mine Disaster. Within and without, reality was self-contained.

Arthur Crewes and James Kencannon dashed after her.

At the empty opening to the cave, Crewes stopped Kencannon. "Let me, Jim."

Kencannon nodded, and walked slowly away, pulling his pipe from his belt, and beginning to ream it clean with a tool from his shirt pocket.

Arthur Crewes let the faintly musty interior of the prop cave swallow him. He stood there silently, listening for murmurings of sorrow, or madness. He heard nothing. The cave only went in for ten or fifteen feet, but it might well have been the entrance to the deepest pit in Dante's Inferno. As his eyes grew accustomed to the gloom, he saw her, slumped down against some prop boulders.

She tried to scuttle back out of sight, even as he moved toward her.

"Don't." He spoke the one word softly, and she held.

Then he came to her, and sat down on a boulder low beside her. Now she wasn't crying.

It hadn't been that kind of rotten little scene.

"He's an imbecile," Crewes said.

"He was right," she answered. There was a sealed lock-vault on pity. But self-realization could be purchased over the counter.

"He *wasn't* right. He's an ignorant young pup and I've had him canned."

"I'm sorry for that."

"Sorry doesn't get it. What he did was inexcusable." He chuckled softly, ruefully. "What *I* did was inexcusable, as well. I'll hear from SEG about it." That chuckle rose. "It was worth it."

"Arthur, let me out."

"I don't want to hear that."

"I have to say it. Please. Let me out. It won't work."

"It *will* work. It *has* to work."

She looked at him through darkness. His face was blank, without features, barely formed in any way. But she knew if she could see him clearly that there would be intensity in his expression. "Why is this so important to you?"

For many minutes he did not speak, while she waited without understanding. Then, finally, he said, "Please let me do this thing for you. I want . . . very much . . . for you to have the good things again."

"But, why?"

He tried to explain, but it was not a matter of explanations. It was a matter of pains and joys remembered. Of being lonely and finding pleasure in motion pictures. Of having no directions and finding a future in what had always been a hobby. Of having lusted for success and coming at last to it with the knowledge that movies had given him everything, and she had been part of it. There was no totally rational explanation that Arthur Crewes could codify for her. He had struggled upward and she had given him a hand. It had been a small, a tiny, a quickly forgotten little favor—if he told her now she would not remember it, nor would she think it was at all comparable to what he was trying to do for her. But as the years had hung themselves on Arthur Crewes's past, the tiny favor had grown out of all proportion in his mind, and now he was trying desperately to pay Valerie Lone back.

All this, in a moment of silence.

He had been in the arena too long. He could not speak to her of these nameless wondrous things, and hope to win her from her fears. But even in his silence there was clarity. She reached out to touch his face.

"I'll try," she said.

And when they were outside on the flat, dry plain across which Kencannon started toward them, she turned to Arthur Crewes and she said, with a rough touch of the wiseacre that had been her trademark eighteen years before, "But I still ain't playin' none of your damn scenes in the noood, buster."

It was difficult, but Crewes managed a smile.

HANDY

Meanwhile, back at my head, things were going from Erich von Stroheim to Alfred Hitchcock. No, make that from Fritz Lang to Val Lewton. Try bad to worse.

I'd come back from Never-Never Land and the song of the turtle, and had called in to Arthur's office. I simply could not face a return to the world of show biz so soon after polishing tombstones in Emery Romito's private cemetery. I needed a long pull on something called quiet, and it was not to be found at the Studio.

My apartment was hot and stuffy. I stripped and took a shower. For a moment I considered flushing my clothes down the toilet: I was sure they were impregnated with the mold of the ages, fresh from Santa Monica.

Then I chivvied and worried the thought that maybe possibly I ought just to send myself out to Filoy Cleaners, *in toto.* "Here you go, Phil," I'd say. "I'd like myself cleaned and burned." *You need sleep, Handy,* I thought. *Maybe about seven hundred years' worth.*

Rip Van Winkle, old Ripper-poo, it occurred to me, in a passing flash of genuine lunacy, knew precisely where it was at. I could see it now, a Broadway extravaganza

RIP!
starring Fred Handy

who will sleep like a mother stone log for seven hundred years right before your perspiring eyes—at $2.25 / $4.25 / and $6.25 for Center Aisle Orchestra Seats.

The shower did little to restore my sanity.

I decided to call Julie.

I checked her itinerary—which I'd blackmailed out of her agent—and found that *Hello, Dolly!* was playing Pittsburgh, Pennsylvania. I dialed the O-lady and told her all kindsa stuff. After a while she got into conversations with various kindly folks in the state of Pennsylvania, who confided in her, strictly *entre-nous,* that my Lady of the moist thighs, the fair Julie Glynn, *née* Rowena Glyckmeier, was out onna town somewheres, and O-lady 212 in Hollywood would stay right there tippy-tap up against the phone all night if need be, just to bring us two fine examples of Young American Love together, whenever.

As I racked the receiver, just as suddenly as I'd gotten *into* the mood, all good humor and fancy footwork deserted me. I realized I was sadder than I'd been in years. What the hell was happening? Why this feeling of utter depression; why this sense of impending disaster?

Then the phone rang, and it was Arthur, and he told me what had happened at the Studio. I couldn't stop shuddering.

He also told me there was an opening at the Coconut Grove that night, and he thought Valerie might like to attend. He had already called the star—it was Bobby Vinton, or Sergio Franchi, or Wayne Newton, or someone in that league—and there would be an announcement from the stage that Valerie Lone was in the audience, and a spontaneous standing ovation. I couldn't stop shuddering.

He suggested I get in touch with Romito and set up a date. Help wash away the stain of that afternoon. Then he told me the name of the extra who had insulted Valerie Lone—he must have been reading it off a piece of paper, he spoke the name with a flatness like the striking trajectory of a cobra—and suggested I compile a brief dossier on the gentleman. I had the distinct impression Arthur Crewes could be as vicious an enemy as he was cuddly a friend. The blond beach-bum would probably find it very hard getting work in films from this point on, though it was no longer the antediluvian era in which a Cohen or a Mayer or a Skouras could kill a career with a couple of phone calls. I couldn't stop shuddering.

Then I called Emery Romito and advised him he was to pick up Valerie Lone at six-thirty at the Beverly Hills. Tuxedo. He fumphuh'd and I knew he didn't have the price of a rental tux. So I called Wardrobe at the Studio and told them to send someone out to Santa Monica . . . and to dress him *au courant,* not in the wing-collar style of the Twenties, which is what I continued to shudder at in my mind.

Then I went back and took another shower. A hot shower. It was getting chilly in my body.

I heard the phone ringing through the pounding noise of the shower spray, and got to the instrument as my party was hanging up. There was a trail of monster wet footprints all across the living room behind me, vanishing into the bedroom and thence the bath, from whence I had comce.

"Yeah, who?" I yelled.

"Fred? Spencer."

A pungent footnote on being depressed. When you have just received word from the IRS that an audit of your returns will be necessary for the years 1956–66 in an attempt to pinpoint the necessity for a $13,000 per year entertainment exemption; when the ASPCA rings you up and asks you to come down and identify a body in their cold room, and they're describing your pet basset hound as he would look had he been through a McCormick reaper; when your wife, from whom you are separated, and whom you screwed last month only by chance when you took over her separation payment, calls and tells you she is with child—yours; when World War Nine breaks out and they are napalming your patio; when you've got the worst summer cold of your life, the left-hand corner of your mouth is cracked and chapped, your prostate is acting up again and oozing shiny drops of a hideous green substance; when all of this links into one gigantic chain of horror threatening to send you raving in the direction of Joe Pyne or Lawrence Welk, then, and only then, do agents named Spencer Lichtman call.

It is not a nice thing.

New horrors! I moaned silently. *New horrors!*

"Hey, you there, Fred?"

"I died."

"Listen, I want to talk to you."

"Spencer, please. I want to sleep for seven hundred years."

"It's the middle of a highly productive day."

"*I've* produced three asps, a groundhog and a vat of stale eels. Let me sleep, perchance to dream."

"I want to talk about Valerie Lone."

"Come over to the apartment." I hung up.

The wolf pack was starting to move in. I called Crewes. He was in conference. I said break in. Roz said fuckoff. I thanked her politely and retraced my monster wet footprints to the shower. Cold shower. Cold, hot, cold: if my moods continued to fluctuate, it was going to be double pneumonia time. (I might have called it my manic-depressive phase, except my moods kept going from depressive to depressiver. With not a manic in sight.)

Wearing a thick black plastic weight-reducing belt—compartments filled with sand—guaranteed to take five pounds of unsightly slob off my drooling gut—and a terry cloth wraparound, I built myself an iced tea in the kitchen. There were no ice cubes. I had a bachelor's icebox: a jar of maraschino cherries, an opened package of Philadelphia cream cheese with fungus growing on it, two tv dinners—Hawaiian shrimp and Salisbury steak—and a tin of condensed milk. If Julie didn't start marrying me or mothering me, it was certain I would be found starved dead, lying in a corner, clutching an empty carton of Ritz crackers, some fateful morning when they came to find out why I hadn't paid the rent in a month or two.

I went out onto the terrace of the lanai apartments, overlooking the hysterectomy-shaped swimming pool used for the 1928 Lilliputian Olympics. There were two slim-thighed creatures named Janice and Pegeen lounging near the edge. Pegeen had an aluminum reflector up to her chin, making sure no slightest inch of epidermis escaped UV scorching. Janice was on her stomach, oiled like the inside of a reservoirtip condom. "Hey!" I yelled. "How're you fixed for ice cubes?" Janice turned over, letting her copy of Kahlil Gibran's THE PROPHET fall flat, and shaded her eyes toward me.

"Oh, hi, Fred. Go help yourself."

I waved thanks and walked down the line to their apartment. The door was open. I went in through the debris of the previous evening's amphetamine frolic, doing a dance to avoid the hookah and the pillows on the floor. There were no ice cubes. I filled their trays, reinserted them in the freezer compartment, and went back outside. "Everything groovy?" Janice yelled up at me.

"Ginchy," I called back, and went into my apartment.

Warm iced tea is an ugly.

I heard Spencer down below, shucking the two pairs of slim thighs. I waited a full sixty-count, hoping he would pass, just once. At sixty, I went to the door and yowled, "Up here, Spencer."

"Be right there, Fred," he called over his shoulder, his moist eyeballs fastened like snails to Pegeen's bikini.

"The specialist tells me I've only got twenty minutes to live, Spencer. Get your ass up here."

He murmured something devilishly clever to the girls, who regarded his retreating back with looks that compared it unfavorably to a haunch of tainted venison. Spencer mounted the stairs two at a time, puffing hideously, trying desperately to do a Steve McQueen for the girls.

"Hey, buhbie." He extended his hand as he came through the door.

Spencer Lichtman had been selected by the monthly newsletter and puff-sheet of the Sahara Hotel & Casino in Las Vegas, Nevada, U.S.A., in their August 1966 mailing, as Mr. Charm. They noted that he was charming whether he won or lost at the tables, and they quoted him as saying, after picking up eleven hundred dollars at craps, "It's only money." The newsletter thought that was mighty white of Spencer Lichtman. The newsletter also thought it was historically clever of him to have said it, and only avoided adding their usual editorial (Ha! Ha! Isn't old Spencer a wow!) with a non-Vegas reserve totally out of character for the "editor," a former junior ad exec well into hock to the management of the hotel, working it off by editing the puff-sheet in a style charitably referred to as Hand-Me-Down Mark Hellinger.

Spencer Lichtman was, to me, one of the great losers of all time, eleven hundred Vegan jellybeans notwithstanding. That he was a brilliant agent cannot be denied. But he did it *despite* himself, dear God let me have it pegged correctly otherwise my entire world-view is ass-backwards, not *because* of himself.

He was a tall, broad-shouldered, well-fried, blue-eyed specimen, handsomely cocooned within a Harry Cherry suit. Light-blue button-down shirts (no high-rise collars for Spencer, he knew his neck was too thick for them), black knee-length socks, highly polished black loafers, diminutive cuff links, and a paisley hankie in the breast pocket. He might have sprung full-blown like Adolph Menjou from the forehead of *Gentleman's Quarterly.*

Then tell me this: if Spencer Lichtman was good-looking, mannerly, talented, in good taste, and successful, why the hell did I know as sure as Burton made little green Elizabeths, that Spencer Lichtman was a bummer?

It defied analysis.

So I shook hands with him.

"Jesus, it's hot," he wheezed, falling onto the sofa, elegantly. Even collapsing, he had panache. "Can I impose on you for something cold?"

"I'm out of ice cubes."

"Oh."

"My neighbors are out of ice cubes, too."

"Those were your neighbors—"

"Right. Out there. The girls."

"Nice neighbors."

"Yeah. But they're *still* out of ice cubes."

"So I suppose we'd better talk. Then we can go over to the Luau and get something cold."

I didn't bother telling him I'd rather undergo intensive Hong Kong acupuncture treatments with needles in my cheeks, than go to the Luau for a drink. The cream of the Hollywood and Beverly Hills show biz set always made the Luau in the afternoons, hustling secretaries from the talent agencies who were, in actuality, the daughters of Beverly Hills merchants, the daughters of Hollywood actors, the daughters of Los Angeles society, the daughters of delight. The cream. That *is* the stuff that floats to the top, isn't it? Cream?

No, Spencer, I am not going with you to the Luau so you can hustle for me, and get me bedded down with one of your puffball-haired steno-typists, thereby giving you an edge on me for future dealings. No, indeed not, Spencer, my lad. I am going to pass on all those fine trim young legs exposed beneath entirely too inflammatory minis. I am probably going to go into the bedroom after you've

gone and play with myself, but it is a far far better thing I do than to let you get
your perfectly white capped molars into me.

"You talk, Spencer. I'll listen." I sat down on the floor. "That's what
I call cooperation."

He wanted desperately to undo his tie. But that would have been
non-Agency. "I was talking to some of the people at the office . . ."

Translation: I read in the trades that Crewes has found this *altacockuh,*
this old hag Valerie Whatshername, and at the snake-pit session this
morning I suggested to Morrie and Lew and Marty that I take a crack at
maybe we should rep her, there might be a dime or a dollar or both in
it, so what are the chances?

I stared at him with an expression like Raggedy Andy.

"And, uh, we felt it would be highly prestigious for the Agency to
represent Valerie Lone . . ."

Translation: At least we can clip ten percent off of this deal with
Crewes, and she ought to be good for a second deal with him at the Studio, and if *anything* at *all* happens with her, there're two or three short
line deals we can make, maybe at American-International for one of
those *Baby Jane/Lady in a Cage* horrorifics; shit, she'd sit still for *any* kind
of star billing, even in a screamer like that. Play her right, and we can
make thirty, forty grand before she falls in her traces.

I segued smoothly from Raggedy Andy into Lenny: *Of Mice and
Men.* Except I didn't dribble.

"I think we can really move Valerie, in the field of features. And, of
course, there's a *lot* of television open to her . . ."

Translation: We'll book the old broad into a guest shot on every
nitwit series shooting now for a September air-date. Guest cameos are
perfect for a warhorse like her. It's like every asshole in America had a
private tube to the freak show. Come and see the Ice Age return! Witness the resurrection of Piltdown Woman! See the resurgence of Miss
Ankle-Strap Wedgie! Gape and drool at the unburied dead! She'll play
dance hall madams on *Cimarron Strip* and aging actresses on *Petticoat
Junction*; she'll play a frontier matriarch on *The Big Valley* and the mother
of a kidnapped child on *Felony Squad.* A grand per day, at first, till the
novelty wears off. We'll book her five or six deep till they get the word
around. Then we'll make trick deals with the network for multiples.
There's a potload in this.

Lenny slowly vanished to be replaced by Huck Finn.

"Well, *say* something, Fred! What do you think?"

Huck Finn vanished and in his stead Spencer Lichtman was staring down at Captain America, bearing his red-white-and-blue shield, decked out in his patriotic uniform with the wings on the cowl, with the steely gaze and the outthrust chin of the defender of widows and orphans.

Captain America said, softly, "You'll take five percent commission and I'll make sure she signs with you."

"Ten, Fred. You know that's standard. We can't—"

"Five." Captain America wasn't fucking around.

"Eight. *Maybe* I can swing eight. Morrie and Lew—"

Captain America shifted his star-studded shield up his arm and pulled his gauntlet tighter. "I'll be fair. Six."

Lichtman stood up, started toward the door, whirled on Captain America. "She's got to have representation, Handy. Lots of it. You know it. I know it. Name me three times you know of, when an agent took less than ten? We're working at twelve and even thirteen on some clients. This is a chancy thing. She might go, she might not. We're willing to gamble. You're making it lousy for both of us. I came to you because I know you can handle it. But we haven't even talked about *your* percentage."

Captain America's jaw muscles jumped. The inference that he could be bought was disgusting. He breathed the sweet breath of patriotic fervor and answered Spencer Lichtman—alias the Red Skull—with the tone he deserved. "No kickback for me, Spencer. Straight six."

Lichtman's expression was one of surprise. But in a moment he had it figured out, in whatever form his cynicism and familiarity with the hunting habits of the scene allowed him best and most easily to rationalize. There was an angle in it for me, he was sure of that. It was a sneaky angle, it had to be, because he couldn't find a trace of it, which meant it was subtler than most. On that level he was able to talk to me. Not to Captain America, never to old Cap; because Lichtman couldn't conceive of a purely altruistic act, old Spence couldn't. So there was a finagle here somewhere; he didn't know just where, but as thief to thief, he was delighted with the dealing.

"Seven."

"Okay."

"I should have stuck with eight."

"You wouldn't have made a deal if you had."

"You're sure she'll sign?"

"You sure you'll work your ass off for her, and keep the leeches away from her, and give her a straight accounting of earnings, and try to build the career and not just run it into the ground for a fast buck?"

"You know I—"

"You know *I*, baby! *I* have an eye on you. Arthur *Crewes* will have an eye on you. And if you fuck around with her, and louse her up, and then drop her, both Arthur and myself will do some very heavy talking with several of your clients who are currently under contract to Arthur, such as Steve and Raquel and Julie and don't you forget it."

"What's in this for you, Handy?"

"I've got the detergent concession."

"And I thought I was coming up here to hustle *you*."

"There's only one reason you're getting the contract, Spencer. She needs an agent, you're as honest as most of them—excluding Hal and Billy—and I believe *you* believe she can be moved."

"I do."

"I figured it like that."

"I'll set up a meet with Morrie and Lew and Marty. Early next week."

"Fine. Her schedule's pretty tight now. She starts rehearsals with the new scene day after tomorrow."

Spencer Lichtman adjusted his tie, smoothed his hair, and pulled down his suit jacket in the back. He extended his hand. "Pleasure doing business, Fred."

I shook once again. "Dandy, Spencer."

Then he smirked, suggesting broadly that he knew I must have a boondoggle only slightly smaller than the Teapot Dome going. And, so help me God, he winked. Conspiratorially.

Tonstant weader fwowed up.

When he left, I called Arthur, and told him what I'd done, and why. He approved, and said he had to get back to some work on his desk. I started to hang up, but heard his voice faintly, calling me back. I put the receiver up to my ear and said, "Something else, Arthur?"

There was a pause, then he said, gently, "You're a good guy, Fred." I mumbled something and racked it.

And sat there for twenty minutes, silently arguing with Raggedy Andy, Lenny, Huck and old Captain America. *They* thought I was a good guy, too. And *I* kept trying to get them to tell me where the sleazy angle might be, so I could stop feeling so disgustingly humanitarian. Have you ever tried to pull on a turtleneck over a halo?

SEVEN

Valerie Lone had only been told she would be picked up at six-thirty, for dinner and an opening at the Grove. The flowers arrived at five-fifteen. Daisies. Roses were a makeout flower, much too premeditated. Daisies. With their simplicity and their honesty and their romance. Daisies. With one rose in the center of the arrangement.

At six-thirty the doorbell to Valerie Lone's bungalow was rung, and she hurried to open the door. (She had turned down the offer of a personal maid. "The hotel is very nice to me; their regular maid is fine, Arthur, thank you.")

She opened the door, and for a moment she did not recognize him. But for her, there had only been one like him; only one man that tall, that elegant, that self-possessed. The years had not touched him. He was the same. Not a hair out of place, not a line where no line had been, and the smile—the same gentle, wide pixie smile—it was the same, unaltered. Soft, filtered lights were unnecessary. For Valerie Lone he was the same.

But in the eye of the beheld . . .

Emery Romito looked across the past and all the empty years between, and saw his woman. There had been gold, and quicksilver, and soft murmurings in the night, and crystal, and water as sweet as Chablis, and velvet and plumes of exotic birds . . . and now

there was arthritis, and difficult breathing, and a heaviness in the air, and perspiration and nervousness, and stale rum cake, and the calling of children far away across the misty landscape, and someone very dark and hungry always coming toward him.

Now there was only now. And he lamented all the days that had died without joy. Hope had sung its song within him, in reverie, on nights when the heat had been too much for him and he had gone to sit at the edge of the ocean. Far out, beyond the lights of the amusement park at Lick Pier, beyond the lights of the night, the song had been raised against dark stars and darker skies. But had never been heard. Had gone to tremolo and wavering and finally sighed into the silent vacuum of despair, where sound can only be heard by striking object against object. And in that nowhere, there was no object for Emery Romito.

"Hello, Val . . ."

Tear loneliness across its pale surface; rend it totally and find the blood of need welling up in a thick, pale torrent. Let the horns of growth blare a message in rinky-tink meter. Turn a woman carrying all her years into a sloe-eyed gamine. Peel like an artichoke the scar-tissue heart of a lost dream, and find in the center a pulsing golden light with a name. She looked across yesterday and found him standing before her, and she could do no other than cry.

He came through the door as she sagged in upon herself. Her tears were soundless, so desperate, so overwhelming, they made her helpless. He closed the door behind him and gathered her to himself. Shrunken though he was, not in her arms, not in her eyes. He was still tall, gentle Emery, whose voice was silk and softness. Collapsed within the eternity of his love, she beat back the shadows that had come to devour her, and she knew that now, *now* she would live. She spoke his name a hundred times in a second.

That night, *her* name was spoken by a hundred voices in a second; but this time, as she stood to applause for the first time in eighteen years, she did not cry. Emery Romito was with her, beside her, and she held his hand as she rose. Fred Handy was there; with the girl Randi, from the office that afternoon. Arthur Crewes was there; alone. Smiling. Jubilant. Radiating warmth for Valerie Lone and the good people who had never forgotten her. Spencer Lichtman was there; with Miss American Airlines and an orange-haired girl of pneumatic proportions starring in Joseph E. Levine's production of *Maciste and the Vestal Virgins*. ("You've got a better chance of convincing the public she's Maciste than a virgin," Handy muttered, as they passed in the lobby of the Ambassador Hotel.)

Valerie Lone! they cried. Valerie Lone!

She stood, holding Romito's hand, and the dream had come full circle.

Like the laocoönian serpent, swallowing its own tail. Ouroboros in Clown Town.

The next day John D. F. Black delivered the rewritten pages. The scenes for Valerie were exquisite. He asked if he might be introduced to Valerie Lone, and Fred took him over to the Beverly Hills, where Valerie was guardedly trying to get a suntan. It was the first time in many years that she had performed that almost religious Hollywood act: the deep-frying. She rose to meet Black, a tall and charming man with an actor's leathery good looks. In a few minutes he had charmed her completely, and told her he had been delighted to write the scenes for her, that they were just what she had always done best in her biggest films, that they gave her room to expand and color the part, that he knew she would be splendid. She asked if he would be on the set during shooting. Black looked at Handy. Handy looked away. Black shrugged and said he didn't know, he had another commitment elsewhere. But Valerie Lone knew that things had not changed all *that* much in Hollywood: the writer was still chattel. When his work on the script was done, it was no longer his own. It was given to the Producer, and the Director, and the Production Manager, and the Actors, and he was no longer welcome.

"I'd like Mr. Black to be on the set when I shoot, Mr. Handy," she said to Fred. "If Arthur doesn't mind."

Fred nodded, said he would see to it; and John D. F. Black bent, took Valerie Lone's hand in his own, and kissed it elegantly. "I love you," he said.

Late that night, Arthur and Fred took Valerie to the Channel 11 television studios on Sunset, and sat offstage as Valerie prepared for her on-camera live-action full-living-color interview with Adela Seddon, the Marquesa of Malice. A female counterpart of Joe Pyne, Adela Seddon spoke with forked tongue. She was much-watched and much-despised. Impartial voters learned their politics from her show. Wherever she was at, they were not. If she had come out in favor of Motherhood, Apple Pie and The American Way, tens of thousands of noncommitted people would instantly take up the banners of Misogyny, Macrobiotics and Master Racism. She was a badgerer, a harridan, a snarling viper with a sure mouth for the wisecrack and a ready fang for the jugular. Beneath a Tammy Grimes tousle of candy-apple red hair, her face was alternately compared with that of a tuba player confronting a small child sucking a lemon, and a prize shoat for the first time encountering the butcher's blade. She had been married six times, divorced five, was currently separated, hated being touched, and was rumored in private circles to have long-since gone mad from endless masturbation. Her nose job was not entirely successful.

Valerie was justifiably nervous.

"I've never seen her, Arthur. Working out there in the diner, nights, you know, I've never seen her."

Handy, who thought it was lunacy to bring Valerie anywhere near the Seddon woman, added, "To see is to believe."

Valerie looked at him, concern showing like a second face upon the carefully drawn mask of cosmetics the Studio makeup head had built for her. She looked good, much younger, rejuvenated by the acclaim she had received at the Ambassador's Coconut Grove. (It had been the Righteous Brothers. They had come down into the audience and belted "My Babe" in her honor, right at her.)

"You don't think much of her, do you, Mr. Handy?"

Handy expelled air wearily. "About as charming as an acrobat in a polio ward. Queen of the Yahoos. The Compleat Philistine. Death warmed over. A pain in the—"

Crewes cut him off.

"No long lists, Fred. I had one of those from you already today. Remember?"

"It's been a long day, Arthur."

"Relax, please. Adela called me this afternoon, and *asked* for Valerie. She promised to be good. Very good. She's been a fan of Valerie's for years. We talked for almost an hour. She wants to do a nice interview."

Handy grimaced. Pain. "I don't believe it. The woman would do a Bergen-Belsen on her own Granny if she thought it would jump her rating."

Crewes spoke softly, carefully, as if telling a child. "Fred, I would not for a moment jeopardize Valerie if I thought there was any danger here. Adela Seddon is not my idea of a lady, either, but her show is *watched*. It's syndicated, and it's popular. If she says she'll behave, it behooves us to take the chance."

Valerie touched Handy's sleeve. "It's all right, Fred. I trust Arthur. I'll go on."

Crewes smiled at her. "Look, it's even live, not taped earlier in the evening, the way she usually does the show. This way we know she'll behave; they tape it in case someone guests who makes her look bad, they can dump the tape. But live like this, she has to be a nanny, or she could get killed. It stands to reason."

Handy looked dubious. "There's a flaw in that somewhere, Arthur, but I haven't the strength to find it. Besides," he indicated a flashing red light on the wall above them, "Valerie is about to enter the Valley of the Shadow . . ."

The stage manager came and got Valerie, and took her out onto the set, where she was greeted with applause from the studio audience. She sat in one of the two comfortable chairs behind the low desk, and waited patiently for Adela Seddon to arrive from her offstage office.

When she made her appearance, striding purposefully to the desk and seating herself, and instantly shuffling through a sheaf of research papers (presumably on Valerie Lone), the audience once again transported itself with wild applause. Which Adela Seddon did not deign to acknowledge. The signals were given, the control booth marked, and in a moment the offstage announcer was bibble-bibbling the intro. The audience did its number, and Camera No. 2 glowed red as a ghastly closeup of Adela Seddon appeared on the studio monitors. It was like a microscopic view of a rotted watermelon rind.

"This evening," Adela Seddon began, a smile that was a rictus stretching her mouth, "we are coming to you live, not on tape. The reason for this is my very special guest, a great lady of the American cinema, who agreed to come on only if we were aired live, thus ensuring a fair and unedited interview . . ."

"I *told* you she was a shit!" Handy hissed to Crewes. Crewes shushed him with a wave of his hand.

". . . not been seen for eighteen years on the wide-screens of motion picture theaters, but she is back in a forthcoming Arthur Crewes production, *Subterfuge*. I'd like a big hand for Miss Valerie Lone!"

The audience did tribal rituals, rain dances, ju–ju incantations and a smattering of plain and fancy warwhooping. Valerie was a lady. She smiled demurely and nodded her thank-yous. Adela Seddon seemed uneasy at the depth of response, and shifted in her chair.

"She's getting out the blowdarts," Handy moaned.

"Shut up!" Crewes snarled. He was not happy.

"Miss Lone," Adela Seddon said, turning slightly more toward the nervous actress, "precisely *why* have you chosen this time to come back out of retirement? Do you think there's still an audience for your kind of acting?"

OhmiGod, thought Handy, *here it comes.*

EDITED TRANSCRIPT OF SEDDON
"LOOKING IN" / 11-23-67
(. . . *indicates deletion*)

VALERIE LONE: I don't know what you mean, "my kind of acting"?

ADELA SEDDON: Oh, come on now, Miss Lone.

VL: No, really. I don't.

AS: Well, I'll be specific then. The 1930s style: overblown and gushy.

VL: I didn't know that was my style, Miss Seddon.

AS: Well, according to your latest review, which is, incidentally, eighteen years old, in something called *Pearl of the Antilles* with Jon Hall, you are, quote, "a fading lollipop of minuscule

talent given to instant tears and grandiose arm-waving."
Should I go on?

VL: If it gives you some sort of pleasure.

AS: Pleasure isn't why I'm up here twice a week, Miss Lone. The
truth is, I sit up here with kooks and twistos and people who
denigrate our great country, and I let them have their say,
without interrupting, because I firmly believe in the First
Amendment of the Constitution of these United States of
America, that everyone has the right to speak his mind. If that
also happens to mean they have the right to make asses of
themselves before seventy million viewers, it isn't my fault.

VL: What has all that to do with me?

AS: I don't mind your *thinking* I'm stupid, Miss Lone; just kindly
don't *talk* to me as if I were stupid. The truth, Miss Lone,
that's what all this has to do with you.

VL: Are you sure you'd recognize it?
(*Audience applause*)

AS: I recognize that there are many old-time actresses who are so
venal, so egocentric, that they refuse to acknowledge their age,
who continue to embarrass audiences by trying to cling to the
illusion of sexuality.

VL: You shouldn't air your problems so openly, Miss Seddon.
(*Audience applause*)

AS: I see retirement hasn't dampened your wit.

VL: Nor made me immune to snakebites.

AS: You're getting awfully defensive, awfully early in the game.

VL: I wasn't aware this was a game. I thought it was an interview.

AS: This is *my* living room, Miss Lone. We call it a game, here, and
we play it *my* way.

VL: I understand. It's not how you play, it's who wins.

AS: Why don't we just talk about your new picture for a while?

VL: That would be a refreshing change.

     . . .

AS: Is it true Crewes found you hustling drinks in a roadhouse?

VL: Not quite. I was a waitress in a diner.

AS: I suppose you think slinging hash for the last eighteen years
puts you in tip-top trim to tackle a major part in an important
motion picture?

VL: No, but I think the fifteen years I spent in films prior to that *does*. A good actress is like a good doctor, Miss Seddon. She has the right to demand high pay not so much for the short amount of time she puts in on a picture, but for all the years before that, years in which she learned her craft properly, so she could perform in a professional manner. You don't pay a doctor merely for what he does for you *now*, but for all the years he spent learning how to do it.

AS: That's very philosophical.

VL: It's very accurate.

AS: I think it begs the question.

VL: *I* think *you'd* like to *think* it does.

. . .

AS: Wouldn't you say actresses are merely self-centered little children playing at make-believe?

VL: I would find it very difficult to say anything even remotely like that. I'm surprised you aren't embarrassed saying it.

AS: I'm hard to embarrass, Miss Lone. Why don't you answer the question?

VL: I thought I *had* answered it.

AS: Not to my satisfaction.

VL: I can see that not being satisfied has made you an unhappy woman, so I—
(*Audience applause*)
—so, so I don't want to dissatisfy you any further; I'll answer the question a little more completely. No, I think acting at its best can be something of a holy chore. If it emerges from a desire to portray life as it is, rather than just to put in a certain amount of time in front of the cameras for a certain amount of money, then it becomes as important as teaching or writing, because it crystallizes the world for an audience; it preserves the past; it lets others, living more confined lives, examine a world they may never come into contact with . . .

AS: We have to take a break now, for a commercial—

. . .

VL: I'd rather not discuss my personal life, if you don't mind.

AS: A "star" has no personal life.

VL: That may be *your* opinion, Miss Seddon, it isn't mine.

AS: Is there some special reason you won't talk about Mr. Romito?

VL: We have always been good friends—

AS: Oh, come *on*, Valerie dear, you're starting to sound like a prepared press release: "We're just friends."

VL: You find it difficult to take yes for an answer.

AS: Well, I'll tell you, Miss Lone, I had a phone call today from a
gentleman who volunteered to come into our dock tonight,
to ask you a few questions. Let's go to the dock . . . what is
your name, sir?

HASKELL BARKIN: My name is Barkin. Haskell Barkin.

AS: I understand you know Miss Lone.

HB: In a manner of speaking.

VL: I don't understand. I don't think I've ever met this gentleman.

HB: You almost did.

VL: What?

AS: Why don't you just let Mr. Barkin tell his story, Miss Lone.

She came offstage shaking violently. Romito had seen the first half
of the interview, at his hotel in Santa Monica. He had hurried to the
studio. When she stumbled away from the still-glaring lights of the set,
he was there, and she almost fell into his arms. "Oh God, Emery, I'm so
frightened . . ."

Crewes was furious. He moved into the darkness offstage, heading
for Adela Seddon's dressing room/office. Handy had another mission.

The audience was filing out of the studio. Handy dashed for the side
exit, came out in the alley next to the studio, and circled the building till
he found the parking lot. Barkin was striding toward a big yellow Con-
tinental.

"Barkin! You motherfucker!" Handy screamed at him.

The tall man turned and stopped in mid-step. His long hair had been
neatly combed for the evening television appearance, and in a suit he
looked anachronistic, like King Kong in knickers. But the brace of his
chest and shoulders was no less formidable.

He was waiting for Handy.

The little publicist came fast, across the parking lot. "How much did
they pay you, you sonofabitch? How much? *How much, motherfucker!*"

Barkin began to crouch, waiting for Handy, fists balled, knees bent,
the handsome face cold and impassive, anticipating the crunch of
knuckles against face. Handy was howling now, like a Confederate
trooper charging a Union gun emplacement. At a dead run he came
down on Barkin, standing between a Corvette and a station wagon
parked in the lot.

At the last moment, instead of breaking around the Corvette, Handy miraculously *leaped up* and came across the bonnet of the Corvette, still running, like a decathlon hurdler. Barkin had half-turned, expecting Handy's rush from the front of the sports car. But the publicist was suddenly above him, bearing down on him like a hunting falcon, before he could correct position.

Handy plunged across the Corvette, denting the red louvered bonnet, and dove full-out at Barkin. Blind with fury, he was totally unaware that he had bounded up onto the car, that he was across it in two steps, that he was flying through the air and crashing into Barkin with all the impact of a human cannonball.

He took Barkin high on the chest, one hand and wrist against the beach-bum's throat. Barkin whooshed air and sailed backward, into the station wagon. Up against the half-lowered radio antenna, which bent under his spine, then cracked and broke off in his back. Barkin screamed, a delirious, half-crazed spiral of sound as the sharp edge of the antenna cut through his suit jacket and shirt, and ripped his flesh. The pain bent him sidewise, and Handy slipped off him, catching his heel on the Corvette and tumbling into the narrow space between the cars. Barkin kicked out, his foot sinking into Handy's stomach as the publicist fell past him. Handy landed on his shoulders, the pain surging up into his chest and down into his groin. His rib cage seemed filled with nettles, and he felt for a moment he might lose control of his bladder.

Barkin tried to go for him, but the antenna was hooked through his jacket. He tried wrenching forward and there was a ripping sound, but it held. He struggled forward toward Handy awkwardly, bending from the waist, but could not get a hold on the publicist. Handy tried to rise, and Barkin stomped him, first on the hand, cracking bones and breaking skin, then on the chest, sending Handy scuttling backward on his buttocks and elbows.

Handy managed to get to his feet and pulled himself around the station wagon. Barkin was trying frantically to get himself undone, but the antenna had hooked in and out of the jacket material, and he was awkwardly twisted.

Handy climbed up onto the hood of the station wagon and on hands and knees, like a child, came across toward Barkin. The big man tried to reach him, but Handy fell across his neck and with senseless fury sank his teeth into Barkin's ear. The beach-bum shrieked again, a woman's sound, and shook his head like an animal trying to lose a flea. Handy hung on, bringing the taste of blood to his mouth. His hand came across and dug into the corner of Barkin's mouth, pulling the lip up and away. The fingers spread, he poked at Barkin's eye, and the beach-bum rattled against the car like a bird in a cage. Then all the pains merged and Barkin sagged in a semiconscious boneless mass. He hung against the weight of Handy and the hooking antenna. The strain was too great, the jacket ripped through, and Barkin fell face-forward hitting the side of the Corvette, pulling Handy over the top of the station wagon. Barkin's face hit the sports car; the nose broke. Barkin fainted with the pain, and slipped down into a Buddha-like position, Handy tumbling over him and landing on his knees between the cars.

Handy pulled himself up against the station wagon, and without realizing Barkin was unconscious, kicked out with a loose-jointed vigor, catching the beach-bum in the ribs with the toe of his shoe. Barkin fell over on his side, and lay there.

Handy, gasping, breathing raggedly, caromed off the cars, struggling to find his way to his own car. He finally made it to the Impala, got behind the wheel and through a fog of gray and red managed to get the key into the ignition. He spun out of the parking lot, scraping a Cadillac and a Mercury, his headlights once sweeping across a row of cars in which a station wagon and a Corvette were parked side by side, seeing a bleeding bag of flesh and fabric inching its way along the concrete, trying to get to its feet, touching softly at the shattered expanse of what had been a face, what had once been a good living.

Handy drove without knowing where he was going.

When he appeared at Randi's door twenty minutes later—having left her off from their date only a few hours before—she was wearing a shortie nightgown that ended at her thighs. "Jesus, Fred, what happened?" she asked, and helped him inside. He collapsed on her bed, leaving dark streaks of brown blood on the candy-striped sheets. She pulled his clothes off him, managing to touch his genitals as often as possible, and tended to his needs, all sorts of needs.

He paid no attention. He had fallen asleep.

It had been a full day for Handy.

EIGHT

The columns had picked it up. They said Valerie Lone had carried it off beautifully, coming through the barrage of viciousness and sniping with

Adela Seddon like a champ. Army Archerd called Seddon a "shrike" and suggested she try her dictionary for the difference between "argument" and "controversy," not to mention the difference between "intimidation" and "interview." Valerie was a minor folk heroine. She had gone into the lair of the dragon and had emerged dragging its fallopians behind her. Crewes and Handy were elated. There had been mutterings from Haskell Barkin's attorney, a slim and good-looking man named Taback who had seemed ashamed even to be handling Barkin's complaint. When Handy and Crewes and the Studio battery of lawyers got done explaining *precisely* what had happened, and Taback had met Handy, the attorney returned to Barkin and advised him to use Blue Cross to take care of the damage it would cover, get his current paramour to lay out for the facial rebuilding, and drop charges: no one would believe that a hulk the size of Haskell Barkin could get so thoroughly dribbled by a pigeonweight like Handy.

But that was only part of the Crewes-Handy elation. Valerie had begun to be seen everywhere with Emery Romito. The fan magazines were having a field day with it. To a generation used to reviling their elders, with no respect for age, there was a kind of sentimental Albert Payson Terhune loveliness to the reuniting of old lovers. No matter where Valerie and Emery went, people beamed on them. Talk became common that after all those years of melancholy and deprivation, at long last the lovers might be together permanently.

For Emery Romito it was the first time he had been truly alive since *they* had killed his career during the draft-dodging scandal. But that was all forgotten now; he seemed to swell with the newfound dignity he had acquired squiring the columns' hottest news item. That, combined with his rediscovery of what Valerie had always meant to him, made him something greater than the faded character actor the years had forced him to become. The fear was still there, but it could be forgotten for short times now.

Valerie had begun rehearsals with her fellow cast-members, and she was growing more confident day by day. The Seddon show had served to fill her once again with fear, but its repercussions—demonstrated in print—had effectively drained it away. These rises and fallings in temperament had an unconscious effect on her, but it was not discernible to those around her.

On the night of the second day of rehearsals, Emery came to pick her up at the Studio, in a car the Studio had rented for him. He took her to dinner at a small French restaurant near the Hollywood Ranch Market, and after the final Drambuie they drove up to Sunset, turned left, and cruised toward Beverly Hills.

It was a Friday night.

The hippies were out.

The teenie-boppers. The flower children. The new ones. The long hair, the tight boots, the paisley shirts, the mini-skirts, the loose sexuality, the hair vests, the shirts with the sleeves cut off, the noise, the jeering. The razored crevasse that existed between *their* time, when they had been golden and fans had pressed up against sawhorses at the premieres to get their autographs, and *today,* a strange and almost dreamlike time of Surrealistic youth who spoke another tongue, moved with liquid fire and laughed at things that were painful. At a stoplight near Laurel Canyon, they stopped and were suddenly surrounded by hippies hustling copies of an underground newspaper, the *L.A. Free Press.* They were repelled by the disordered, savage look of the kids, like barbarians. And though the news vendors spoke politely, though they merely pressed up against the car and shoved their papers into the windows, the terror their very presence evoked in the two older people panicked Romito and he floored the gas pedal, spurting forward down Sunset, sending one beaded and flowered news-hippie sprawling, journals flying.

Romito rolled up his window, urging Valerie to do the same. It was something Kafka-esque to them as they whirled past the discothèques and the psychedelic book shops and the outdoor restaurants where the slim, hungry children of the strobe age languished, turned on, grooving heavy behind meth or grass.

He drove fast. All the way out Sunset to the Coast Highway and out the coast to Malibu.

Finally, Valerie said softly, "Emery, do you remember The Beach House? We used to go there all the time for dinner. Remember? Let's stop there. For a drink."

Romito smiled, the lines around his eyes gathering in gentle humor. "Do I remember? I remember the night Dick Barthelmess did the tango on the bar with that swimmer, the girl from the Olympics . . . you know the one . . ."

But she didn't know the one. That particular memory had been lost. He had had the time to nurse the old memories—she had been slinging hash. No, she didn't remember the girl. But she did remember the old roadhouse that had been so popular with their set one of those years.

But when they came to the spot, they found the old roadhouse—predictably—had been razed. In its stead was a tiny beach-serving shopping center, and on the spot where Dick Barthelmess had danced the tango on the bar with that swimmer from the Olympics, there was an all-night liquor store, with a huge neon sign.

Emery Romito drove a few miles down the Coast Highway, past the liquor store, more by reflex than design. He pulled off on a side road paralleling the ocean, and there, on a ridge that sloped quickly down into darkness and surf somewhere below them, he stopped. They sat there silently together, the car turned off, their minds turned off, trapped in the darkness of loneliness, the landscape and their past.

Then, in a rush, all of it came back to Valerie Lone. The rush of thoughts waiting to be reexamined after twenty years. The reasons, the situations, the circumstances.

"Emery, why didn't we get married?"

And she answered her own question with a smile he could not see in the darkness. It was possible he had not even heard her, for he did not answer. And in her mind she ticked off the answers, all the deadly answers.

It was the dreams each of them had substituted for reality; the tenacity with which they had tried to clutch smoke and dream-mist; the stubborn refusal of each of them to acknowledge that the dream-mist and the smoke were bound to become ashes. And when each had been swallowed whole by the very careers they had thought would free them, they had become strangers. They were frightened to commit to one another, to anyone really, to anything but the world that stood and called their names a hundred times in a second, and beat hands in praise.

Then Emery spoke. As though his thoughts had been tracking similarly to her own, heading on a collision course for her mind and *her* thoughts hurtling toward him.

"You know, darling Val, you always made more money than me. Your name was always star-billing . . . at best, mine was always 'Also Featuring.' It wouldn't have worked."

She was nodding agreement, at the complete validity of it, and then, in an instant, the shock of what she was accepting without argument, believing *again* as she had the first time, the insanity of it hit her. Twenty years in the fantasy-world, yes, those *might* have been real reasons—in the loony way that blasted and twisted logic seems rational in nightmares—but she had spent almost two decades in another life, and now she *knew* they were false, as specious as the life that claimed her on the screen.

But for a moment, for a long moment she had accepted it all again. It was the town, the industry, the way the show biz life sucked one under. For those in the industry it had rapidly become that way, as they had fallen under the spell of their own weird and golden lives; it had taken over twenty years to catch on completely, to permeate the culture. But now it was possible never to come up from under the thick fog of delusion. Because it hung like a Los Angeles smog across the entire nation, perhaps the world.

But not for Valerie Lone. Never again for her.

"Emery, listen to me . . ."

He was talking softly to himself, the sound of moths in the fog. Talking about screen credits and money and days that had never really been alive, and now had to be put to death fully and finally.

"Emery! Darling! Please, listen to me!"

He turned to her. She saw him, then. Even dimly, only by moonlight, she saw him as he really was, not as she had wished him to be, standing there in the doorway of the bungalow at the Beverly Hills Hotel that first night of her new life with him. She saw what had happened to the man who had been strong enough to deny war and say he would lose everything rather than fight against his fellow man. Emery Romito had become a willing prisoner of his own show biz life. He had never escaped.

She knew she had to explain it all to him, to unlearn him, and then teach him anew. An infinite sadness filled her as she readied her arguments, her coercion, her explanations of what the other world was like . . . the world he had always thought of as dull and empty and wasted.

"Darling, I've been out in the desert, out in nowhere, for almost twenty years. You've got to believe me when I tell you, none of this matters. The billing, the money, the life at the studios, it doesn't *matter!* It's all make-believe, we always said it was that, but we let it get us, grab hold of us. We have to understand there is a whole world without any of it. What if the show *doesn't* go on? What then? Why worry? We can do other things, if we care about each other. Do you understand what I'm saying? It doesn't matter if your picture is in the PLAYERS DIRECTORY, as long as you come home at night and turn the key in the door and know there's someone on the other side who cares whether or not you were killed in the traffic on the Freeway. Emery, *talk to me!*"

Silence. Straining on her part, toward him. Silence. Then, "Val, why don't we go dancing . . . like we used to do?"

The shadow came again to devour her. It showed its teeth and it prodded her, looking for the most vulnerable places, the places still filled with the juice of life, which it would eat to the bone, and then suck the marrow from the bone, till it collapsed into despair as had the rest of her.

She fought it.

She talked to him.

Her voice was the low, insistent voice she had cultivated in the star years. Now she turned it to its full-power, and used it to win the most important part of her career.

We have a chance to make it together at last.

God has given us a second chance.

We can have what we lost twenty years ago.

Please, Emery, listen.

Emery Romito had been falling for many years. A great, shrieking fall down a long tunnel of despair. Her voice came to him down the length of that tunnel, and he clutched for it, missed, clutched again and found it. He let it hold him, swaying above the abyss, and slowly pulled himself back up that fragile thread.

Pathetically, he asked her, "Really? Do you think we can? Really?"

No one is more convincing than a woman fighting for her life. Really? She showed him, really. She told him, and she charmed him, and she gave him the strength he had lost so long ago. With her career burgeoning again, it was certain they would have all the good things they had lost on the way to this place, this night.

And finally, he leaned across, this old man, and he kissed her, this tired woman. A shy kiss, almost immature, as though his lips had never touched all the lips of starlets and chorus girls and secretaries and women so much less important than this woman beside him in a rented car on a dark oceanside road.

He was frightened, she could feel it. Almost as frightened as she was. But he was willing to try; to see if they could dredge up something of permanence from the garbage-heaps of the love they had spent twenty years wasting.

Then he started the car, backed and filled and started the return to Hollywood.

The shadow was with her, still hungry, but it was set to waiting. She was no less frightened of the long-haired children and the sharp-tongued interviewers and the merciless lights of the sound stages, but at least now there was a goal; now there was something to move toward.

A gentle breeze came up, and they opened the windows.

Handy

My first premonition of disaster to come was during the conversation Crewes had with Spencer Lichtman. It was two days before he was to shoot her initial scenes for the film. Spencer had made an appointment to discuss Valerie, and Crewes had asked me to be present.

I sat mute and alert. Spencer made his pitch; it was a good one, and a brief one. A three-picture deal with Crewes and the Studio. Sharpel, the Studio business head, was there, and he did some of the finest broken-field running I've ever seen. He suggested everyone wait to see how Valerie did in *Subterfuge*.

Spencer looked terribly disturbed at the conversation as he left. He said nothing to me. Neither did Sharpel, who seemed uneasy that I'd been in the room at all.

When they'd gone, I sat waiting for Arthur Crewes to say something. Finally, he said, "How's the publicity coming?"

"You've got the skinnys on your desk, Arthur. You know what's happening." Then I added, "I wish *I* knew what was happening."

He played dumb. "What would you like to know, Fred?"

I looked at him levelly. He knew I was on to him. There was very little point in obfuscation. "Who's dogged down the pressure on you, Arthur?" He sighed, shrugged as if to say *welllll, y'found me out,* and answered me wearily. "The Studio. They're nervous. They said Valerie is having trouble with the lines, she's awkward, the usual succotash."

"How the hell do *they* know? She hasn't even worked yet; only rehearsing. And Jimmy's kept the sessions strictly closed off."

Crewes hit the desk with the palm of his hand, then again. "They've got a spy in the crew."

"Oh, *c'mon,* you're kidding!"

"I'm *not* kidding. They've got a pile tied up in this one. That ski troops picture Jenkey made is bombing. They won't get back negative costs. They don't want to take any chances with this one. So they've got a fink in the company."

"Want me to sniff him out?"

"Why bother. They'll only plant another one. It's probably Jeanine, the assistant wardrobe mistress . . . or old Whatshisname . . . Skelly, the makeup man. No, there's no sense trying to pry out the rotten apple; it won't help her performance any."

I listened to all of it with growing concern. There was a new tone in Crewes's voice. A tentative tone, one just emerging for the first time, trying its flavor in the world. I could tell he was unhappy with the sound of it, that he was fighting it. But it was getting stronger. It was the tone of amelioration, of shading, of backing-off. It was the caterpillar tremble of fear that could metamorphose easily into the lovely butterfly of cowardice.

"You aren't planning on dumping her, are you, Arthur?"

He looked up sharply, annoyed. "Don't be stupid. I didn't go through all this just to buckle when the Studio gets nervous. Besides, I wouldn't do that to her."

"I hope not."

"I *said* not!"

"But there's always the chance they can sandbag you; after all, they *do* tend the cash register."

Crewes ran a nervous hand through his hair. "Let's see how she does. Shooting starts in two days. Kencannon says she's coming along. Let's just wait . . . and see how she does . . ."

How she did was not good.

I was on the set from the moment they started. Valerie's call was for seven o'clock in the morning. For makeup and wardrobe. The Studio limo went to get her. She was in makeup for the better part of an hour. Johnny Black showed up as she was going into Wardrobe. He kissed her on the cheek and she said, "I hope I do justice to your lines. It's a very nice part, Mr. Black." We walked over to the coffee truck and had a cup each. Neither of us spoke. Finally, Black looked down at me and asked—a bit too casually—"How's it look?"

I shrugged. No answer. I didn't have one.

Kencannon came on the set a few minutes later, and got things tight. The crew was alert, ready, they'd been put on special notice that these scenes were going to be tough enough, so let's have a whole gang of co-operation. Everyone wanted her to make it.

It was bright-eyed/bushy-tailed time.

She came out of Wardrobe and walked straight to Jim Kencannon. He took her aside and whispered to her in a dark corner for fully twenty minutes.

Then they started shooting.

She knew her lines, but her mannerisms were strictly by rote. There was an edge of fear in even the simplest of movements. Kencannon tried to put her at ease. It only made her more tense. She was locked into fear, a kind of fear no one could penetrate deeply enough to erode. She had lived with it unconsciously for too long. There was too much at stake for her here. The only defense she had was what she knew instinctively as an actress. Unfortunately, the actress who remembered all of it, and who put it to use, almost somnambulistically, was an actress of the Forties. Miss Ankle-Strap Wedgie. An actress who had not really been required to act . . . merely to look good, snap out her lines and show a lot of leg.

They ran through the first shot again and again. It was horrible to watch. Repetition after repetition, with Kencannon trying desperately to get a quality out of her that gibed with the modern tone of the film as a whole. It simply was not there.

"Scene eighty-eight, take seven, Apple!"

"Scene eighty-eight, take seven, Bravo!"

"Scene eighty-eight, take seven, China!"

"Scene eighty-eight, take fifteen, Hotel!"

"Scene ninety-one, take three, X-ray!"

Over and over and over. She blew it each time. The crew grew restless, then salty, then disgusted. The other actors began making snotty remarks off-camera. Kencannon was marvelous with her, but it was a disaster, right from speed and roll it. Finally, they got *something* shot.

Kencannon wandered off into the darkness of the sound stage. Valerie went to her dressing room. Presumably to collapse. The crew started setting up the next shot. I followed Kencannon back into the corner.

"Jim?"

He turned around, the unlit pipe hanging from the corner of his mouth. It was still before lunch, early in the day, and he looked exhausted.

"Will it be all right?" I asked him.

He started to turn away. He didn't need me bugging him. I guess the tone of concern in my voice stopped him. "Maybe I can cut it together so it'll work."

And he walked away from me.

That afternoon Kencannon got a visit from Crewes on the set, and they talked quietly for a long time, back by the prop wagon. Then they began pruning Valerie's part. A line here, a reaction shot there. Not much at first, but enough to let her know they were worried. It only served to deepen her nervousness. But they had no choice. They were backed against a wall.

But then, so was she.

The remainder of the shooting, over the next week, was agony.

There was no doubt from the outset that she couldn't make it, that the footage was dreadful. But we always harbored the secret hope that the magic of the film editor could save her.

The dailies were even more horrifying, for there, up on the projection room screen, we could see the naked failure of what we had tried to do. The day's footage went from flat and unnatural to genuinely inept. Kencannon had tried to cover as much as he could with two and three angles or reaction shots by supporting actors, by trick photography, by bizarre camerawork. None of it made it. There was still Valerie in the center of it, like the silent eye of a whirling dervish. Technique could not cover up what was lacking: a focus, a central core, a soul, a fire. Her scenes were disastrous.

When the lights came up in the projection room, and Crewes and myself were alone—we wouldn't allow anyone else to see the dailies, not then we wouldn't—we looked at each other, and Arthur breathed heavily, "Oh God, Fred! What are we going to do?"

I stared at the blank projection screen. There was such a helplessness in his voice, I didn't know what to say. "Can we keep the Studio from finding out, at least till Kencannon cuts it together?"

He shook his head. "Not a chance."

"They move along behind you?"

"Close as they can. I think they've got the labs printing up duplicate sets of dailies. They've probably already run what we just saw here."

Why? I asked myself. Why?

And the answer ran through my head the way those dailies had been run. Behold, without argument, self-explanatory. The answer was simple: Valerie Lone had never been a very good actress, not ever. The films she had made were for an audience hungry for *any* product, which was why Veda Ann Borg and Vera Hruba Ralston and Sonja Henie and Jeanne Crain and Rhonda Fleming and Ellen Drew and all the other pretty, not-particularly-talented ones had made it. It was a nation before teevee, that had theaters to fill, with "A" features starring Paul Muni and Spencer Tracy and John Garfield and Bogart and Ingrid Bergman; but those theaters also needed a lower half to the bill, the "B" pictures with Rory Calhoun and Lex Barker and Ann Blyth and Wanda Hendrix. They needed *product,* not Helen Hayes.

So all the semi-talented had made fabulous livings. *Anything* sold. But now, films for theatrical release were budgeted in the millions, for even the second-class product, and no one could risk the semi-talented.

Oh, there were still the pretty ones who got in the films without the talent to get themselves arrested, but they were in the minority, in the quickie flicks. But *Subterfuge* was no quickie. It was a heavy sugar operation into which the Studio had poured millions already, not to mention unspoken but desperate needs and expectations.

Valerie Lone was one of the last of that extinct breed of "semi-stars" who were still vaguely in the public memory—though the new generations, the kids, didn't know her from a white rabbit—but she didn't have the moxie to cut it the way Bette Davis had, or Joan Crawford, or Barbara Stanwyck. She was just plain old Valerie Lone, and that simply wasn't good enough.

She was one of the actresses who had made it then, because almost anyone who could stand up on good legs could make it . . . but not now, because now it took talent of a high order, or a special something that was called "personality." And it wasn't the same kind of "personality" Valerie had used in her day.

"What're you going to do, Arthur?"

He didn't look at me. He just stared straight ahead, at the empty screen. "I don't know. So help me God, I just don't know."

They didn't sign her for a multiple.

At the premiere, held at the Egyptian, Valerie showed with Emery Romito. She was poised, she was elegant, she signed autographs and, as Crewes remarked under his breath to me, as she came up to be interviewed by the television emcee, she was dying at the very moment of what she thought was her greatest triumph. We had not, of course, told her how much Kencannon had had to leave on the cutting-room floor. It was, literally, a walk-on.

When she emerged from the theater, after the premiere, her face was dead white. She knew what was waiting for her. And there was nothing we could say. We stood there, numbly shaking hands with all the well-wishers who told us we had a smash on our hands, as Valerie Lone walked stiffly through the crowd, practically leading the dumbfounded Romito. Their car came to the curb, and they started to get into it. Then Mitchum emerged from the lobby, and the crowd behind their ropes went mad.

There had not been a single cheer or ooh-ahhh for Valerie Lone as she had stood waiting for the limousine to pull up. She was dead, and she knew it.

I tried to call Julie that night, after the big party at the Daisy. She was out. I took a bottle of charcoal Jack Daniels and put it inside me as quickly as I could.

I fell out on the floor. But it wasn't punishment enough. I dreamed.

In the dreams I was trying to explain. My tongue was made of cloth, and it wouldn't form words. But it didn't matter, because the person I was trying to talk to couldn't hear me. It was a corpse. I could not make out the face of the corpse.

NINE

This was the anatomy of the sin against Valerie Lone:

The Agency called. Not Spencer Lichtman; he was in Florida negotiating a contract for one of their female clients with Ivan Tors for his new *Everglades* pilot. He wouldn't be back for six weeks. It was a difficult contract: the pilot, options for the series if it sold, billing, transportation, and Spencer was screwing her. So the Agency called. A voice of metallic precision that may or may not have had a name attached to it, informed her that they were reorganizing, something to do with the fiscal debenture cutback of post-merger personnel concerned with bibble-bibble-bibble. She asked the voice of the robot what that meant, and it meant she did not have a contract with the Agency, which meant she had no representation.

She called Arthur Crewes. He was out.

The Beverly Hills Hotel management called. The Studio business office had just rung them up to inform them that rent on the bungalow would cease as of the first of the month. Two weeks away.

She called Arthur Crewes. He was out.

She called long distance to Shivey's Diner. She wanted to ask him if he had gotten a replacement for her. Shivey was delighted to hear from her, hey! Everybody was just tickled pink to hear how she'd made good again, hey! Everybody was really jumping with joy at the way the papers said she was so popular again, hey! It's great she got back up on top again, and boy, nobody deserved it better than their girl Val, hey! Don't forget your old friends, don't get uppity out there just because you're a big star and famous again, doncha know!

She thanked him, told him she wouldn't forget them and hung up. Hey!

She could not go back to the desert, to the diner.

She had tasted the champagne again, and the taste of champagne lingers.

She called Arthur Crewes. He was in the cutting room and could not be disturbed.

She called Arthur Crewes. He was in New York with the promotion people, he would be back first of the week.

She called Handy. He was with Crewes.

She called Emery Romito. He was shooting a Western for CBS. His service said he would call back later. But when he did, it was late at night, and she was half-asleep. When she called him the next day, he was at the Studio still shooting. She left her name, but the call did not get returned.

The hungry shadow came at a dead run.

And there was no place to hide.

Disaster is a brush-fire. If it reaches critical proportions, nothing can stop it, nothing can put out the fire. Disaster observes a scorched earth policy.

She called Arthur Crewes. She told Roz she was coming in to see him the next morning.

There was no Studio limousine on order. She took a taxi. Arthur Crewes had spent a sleepless night, knowing she was coming, rerunning her films in his private theater. He was waiting for her.

"How is the picture doing, Arthur?"

He smiled wanly. "The opening grosses are respectable. The Studio is pleased."

"I read the review in *Time*. They were very nice to you."

"Yes. Ha-ha, very unexpected. Those smart alecks usually go for the clever phrase."

Silence.

"Arthur, the rent is up in a week. I'd like to go to work."

"Uh, I'm still working on the script for the new picture, Valerie. You know, it's been five months since we ended production. The Studio kept up the rent on the bungalow through post-production. Editing, scoring, dubbing, the works. They think they've done enough. I can't argue with them, Valerie . . . not really."

"I want to work, Arthur."

"Hasn't your agent been getting you work?"

"Two television guest appearances. Not much else. I guess the word went out about me. The picture . . ."

"You were fine, Valerie, just fine."

"Arthur, don't lie to me. I know I'm in trouble. I can't get a job. You have to do something."

There was a pathetic tone in her voice, yet she was forceful. Like someone demanding unarguable rights. Crewes was desolate. His reaction was hostility.

"*I* have to do something? Good God, Valerie, I've kept you working for over six months on three days of shooting. Isn't that enough?"

Her mouth worked silently for a moment, then very softly she said: "No, it isn't enough. I don't know what to do. I can't go back to the diner. I'm back here now. I have no one else to turn to, you're the one who brought me here. You have to do something, it's your responsibility."

Arthur Crewes began to tremble. Beneath the desk he gripped his knees with his hands. "My responsibility," he said bravely, "ended with your contract, Valerie. I've extended myself, even you have to admit that. If I had another picture even *readying* for production, I'd let you read for a part, but I'm in the midst of some very serious rewrite with the screenwriter. I have nothing. What do you want me to do?"

His assault cowed her. She didn't know what to say. He *had* been fair, had done everything he could for her, recommended her to other producers. But they both knew she had failed in the film, knew that the word had gone out. He was helpless.

She started to go, and he stopped her.

"Miss Lone." Not Val, or Valerie now. A retreating back, a pall of guilt, a formal name. "Miss Lone, can I, uh, loan you some money?"

She turned and looked at him across a distance.

"Yes, Mr. Crewes. You can."

He reached into his desk and took out a checkbook.

"I can't afford pride, Mr. Crewes. Not now. I'm too scared. So make it a big check."

He dared not look at her as she said it. Then he bent to the check and wrote it in her name. It was not nearly big enough to stop the quivering of his knees. She took it, without looking at it, and left quietly. When the intercom buzzed and Roz said there was a call, he snapped at her, "Tell 'em I'm out. And don't bother me for a while!" He clicked off and slumped back in his deep chair.

What else could I do? he thought.

If he expected an answer, it was a long time in coming.

———

After she told Emery what had happened (even though he had been with her these last five months, and knew what it was from the very tomb odor of it) she waited for him to say don't worry, I'll take care of you, now that we're together again it will be all right, I love you, you're mine. But he said nothing like that.

"They won't pick up the option, no possibility?"

"You know they dropped the option, Emery. Months ago. It was a verbal promise only. For the next film. But Arthur Crewes told me he's having trouble with the script. It could be months."

He walked around the little living room of his apartment in the Stratford Beach Hotel. A depressing little room with faded wallpaper and a rug the management would not replace, despite the holes worn in it.

"Isn't there anything else?"

"A Western. TV. Just a guest shot, sometime next month. I read for it last week, they seemed to like me."

"Well, you'll take it, of course."

"*I'll take it,* Emery, but what does it mean . . . it's only a few dollars. It isn't a living."

"We all have to make do the best we can, Val—"

"Can I stay here with you for a few weeks, till things get straightened away?"

Formed in amber, held solidified in a prison of reflections that showed his insides more clearly than his outside, Emery Romito let go the thread that had saved him, and plunged once more down the tunnel of despair. He was unable to do it. He was not calloused, merely terrified. He was merely an old man trying to relate to something that had never even been a dream—merely an illusion. And now she threatened to take even that cheap thing, simply by her existence, her presence here in this room.

"Listen, Val, I've tried to come to terms. I understand what you're going through. But it's hard, very hard. I really have to hurry myself just to make ends meet . . ."

She spoke to him then, of what they had had years ago, and what they had sensed only a few months before. But he was already retreating from her, gibbering with fear, into the shadows of his little life.

"I can't do it, Valerie. I'm not a young man any more. You remember all those days, I'd do anything; anything at all; I was wild. Well, now I'm paying for it. We all have to pay for it. We should have known, we should have put some of it aside, but who'd ever have thought it would end. No, I can't do it. I haven't got the push to do it. I get a little work, an 'also featuring' once in a while. You have to be hungry, the way all the new ones, the young ones, the way *they're* hungry. I can barely manage alone, Valerie. It wouldn't work, it just wouldn't."

She stared at him.

"I have to hang on!" he shouted at her.

She pinned him. "Hang on? To what? To guest shots, a life of walk-ons, insignificant character bits, and a Saturday night at the Friars Club? What have you got, Emery? What have you really got that's worth *anything*? Do you have me, do you have a real life, do you have anything that's really yours, that they can't take away from you?"

But she stopped. The argument was hopeless.

He sagged before her. A tired, terrified old man with his picture in the PLAYERS DIRECTORY. What backbone he might have at one time possessed had been removed from his body through the years, vertebra by vertebra. He slumped before her, weighted down by his own inability to live. Left with a hideous walking death, with elegance on the outside, soot on the inside, Valerie Lone stared at the stranger who had made love to her in her dreams for twenty years. And in that instant she knew it had never really been the myth and the horror of the town that had kept them apart. It had been their own inadequacies.

She left him, then. She could not castigate him. His was such a sordid little existence, to take that from him would be to kill him.

And she was still that much stronger than Emery Romito, her phantom lover, not to need to do it.

HANDY

I came home to find Valerie Lone sitting at the edge of the pool, talking to Pegeen. She looked up when I came through the gate, and smiled a thin smile at me.

I tried not to show how embarrassed I was.

Nor how much I'd been avoiding her.

Nor how desperately I felt like bolting and running away, all the way back to New York City.

She got up, said goodbye to Pegeen, and came toward me. I had been shopping; shirt boxes from Ron Postal and bags from de Voss had to be shifted so I could take her hand. She was wearing a summer dress, quite stylish, really. She was trying to be very light, very inoffensive; trying not to shove the guilt in my face.

"Come on upstairs, where it's cooler," I suggested.

In the apartment, she sat down and looked around.

"I see you're moving," she said.

I grinned, a little nervously, making small talk. "No, it's always this way. I've got a house in Sherman Oaks, but at the moment there's a kindofa sorta almost-ex ex-wife nesting there. It's in litigation. So I live here, ready to jump out any time."

She nodded understanding.

The intricacies of California divorce horrors were not beyond her. She had had a few of those, as I recalled.

"Mr. Handy—" she began.

I did not urge her to call me Fred.

"You were the one who talked to me first, and . . ."

And there it was. I was the one responsible. It was all on me. I'd heard what had happened with Crewes, with that rat bastard Spencer Lichtman, with Romito, and now it was my turn. She must have had nowhere else to go, no one else to impale, and so it was *mea culpa* time.

I was the one who had resurrected her from the safety and sanctity of her grave; brought her back to a world as transitory as an opening night. She looked at me and knew it wouldn't do any good, but she did it.

She laid it all on me, word by word by word.

What could I do, for Christ's sake? I had done my best. I'd even watched over her with Haskell Barkin, carried her practically on my shoulders through all the shitty scenes when she'd arrived in town. What more was there for me to do . . . ?

I'm not my brother's goddam keeper, I yelled inside my head. Let me alone, woman. Get off my back. I'm not going to die for you, or for anyone. I've got a job, and I've got to keep it. I got the publicity *Subterfuge* needed, and I thank you for helping me keep my job, but dammit I didn't inherit you. I'm not your daddy, I'm not your boy friend, I'm just a puffman in off the street, trying to keep the Dragon Lady from grabbing his house, the only roots I've ever had. So stop it, stop talking, stop trying to make me cry, because I won't.

Don't call me a graverobber, you old bitch!

"I'm a proud woman, Mr. Handy. But I'm not very smart. I let you all lie to me. Not once, but twice. The first time I was too young to know better; but this time I fell into it again knowing what you would do to me. I was one of the lucky ones, do you know that? I was lucky because I got out alive. But do you know what you've done to me? You've condemned me to the kind of life poor Emery leads, and that's no life at all."

She didn't talk any more.

She just sat there staring at me.

She didn't want excuses, or escape clauses, or anything I had to give. She knew I was helpless, that I was no better and no worse than any of them. That I had helped kill her in the name of love.

And that the worst crimes are committed in the name of love, not hate.

We both knew there would be an occasional tv bit, and enough money to keep living, but here, in this fucking ugly town, that wasn't living. It was crawling like a wounded thing through the years, till one day the end came, and that was the only release you could pray for.

I knew Julie would not be coming back to me.

Julie knew. She was on the road because she couldn't stand the Town; because she knew it would delicately slice her open, if she lay down and gave it the opportunity, and then pitch her insides out onto Wilshire Blvd. She had always said she wasn't going to go the way all the others had gone, and now I knew why I hadn't been able to reach her on the road. It was Goodbye, Dolly.

And the Dragon Lady would get the house; and I would stay in Hollywood, God help me.

Until the birds came to pick out my eyes, and I wasn't Handy the fair-haired boy any longer, or even Handy the old pro, but something they called Fred Handy? Oh, yeah, I remember him, he was good in his day. Because after all, what the hell did I have to offer but a fast mouth and a few ideas, and once the one was slowed and the other had run out like sand from an hourglass, I was no better off than Valerie Lone or her poor miserable Emery Romito.

She left me standing there, in my apartment that always looked as though I was moving. But we both knew: I wasn't going anywhere.

TEN

In a very nice little restaurant-bar on Sunset Boulevard, as evening came in to Hollywood across the rim of the bowl, Valerie Lone sat high on a barstool, eating a hot roast beef sandwich with gravy covering the very crisp french fries. She sipped slowly from a glass of dark ale. At the far end of the bar a television set was mumbling softly. It was an old movie, circa 1942.

None of the players in the movie had been Valerie Lone. The Universe loved her, but was totally devoid of a sense of irony. It was simply an old movie.

Three seats down from where Valerie Lone sat, a hippie wearing wraparound shades and seven strings of beads looked up at the bartender. "Hey, friend," he said softly.

The bartender came to him, obviously disliking the hairy trade these people represented, but unable to ignore the enormous amounts of money they somehow spent in his establishment. "Uh-huh?"

"Howzabout turning something else on . . . or maybe even better turn that damn thing off, I'll put a quarter in the jukebox." The bartender gave him a surly look, then sauntered to the set and turned it off. Valerie Lone continued to eat as the world was turned off.

The hippie put the quarter in the jukebox and pressed out three rock numbers. He returned to his barstool and the music inundated the room.

Outside, night had come, and with it, the night lights. One of the lights illuminated a twenty-three-foot-high billboard for the film *Subterfuge* starring Robert Mitchum and Gina Lollobrigida; produced by Arthur Crewes; directed by James Kencannon; written by John D. F. Black; music by Lalo Schifrin.

At the end of the supplementary credits there was a boxed line that was very difficult to read: it had been whited-out.

The line had once read:

ALSO FEATURING MISS VALERIE LONE as Angela.

Angela had become a walk-on. She no longer existed.

Valerie Lone existed only as a woman in a very nice little restaurant and bar on the Sunset Strip. She was eating. And the long shadow had also begun to feed.

ABOUT THE NEBULA AWARDS

hroughout every calendar year, the members of the Science Fiction and Fantasy Writers of America read and recommend novels
and stories for the annual Nebula Awards. The editor of the
"Nebula Awards Report" collects the recommendations and publishes
them in the SFFWA *Forum*. Near the end of the year, the NAR editor
tallies the endorsements, draws up the preliminary ballot, and sends it to
all active SFFWA members. Under the current rules, each novel and
story enjoys a one-year eligibility period from its date of publication. If
the work fails to make the preliminary ballot during that interval, it is
dropped from further Nebula consideration.

The NAR editor processes the results of the preliminary ballot and
then compiles a final ballot listing the five most popular novels, novellas,
novelettes, and short stories. For purposes of the Nebula Award, a novel
is 40,000 words or more; a novella is 17,500 to 39,999 words; a novelette is 7,500 to 17,499 words; and a short story is 7,499 words or fewer.
At the present time, SFFWA impanels both a novel jury and a short-
fiction jury to oversee the voting process and, in cases where a presumably worthy title was neglected by the membership at large, to
supplement the five nominees with a sixth choice. Thus, the appearance
of extra finalists in any category bespeaks two distinct processes: jury
discretion and ties.

Founded in 1965 by Damon Knight, the Science Fiction Writers of
America began with a charter membership of seventy-eight authors.
Today it boasts over a thousand members and an augmented name. Early
in his tenure, Lloyd Biggle, Jr., SFWA's first secretary-treasurer, proposed
that the organization periodically select and publish the year's best stories. This notion quickly evolved into the elaborate balloting process, an

annual awards banquet, and a series of Nebula anthologies. Judith Ann Lawrence designed the trophy from a sketch by Kate Wilhelm. It is a block of Lucite containing a rock crystal and a spiral nebula made of metallic glitter. The prize is handmade, and no two are exactly alike.

The Damon Knight Grand Master Nebula Award goes to a living author for a lifetime of achievement in science fiction and/or fantasy. In accordance with SFFWA's bylaws, the president nominates a candidate, normally after consulting with previous presidents and the board of directors. This nomination then goes before the officers; if a majority approves, the candidate becomes a Grand Master. Past recipients include Robert A. Heinlein (1975), Jack Williamson (1976), Clifford D. Simak (1977), L. Sprague de Camp (1979), Fritz Leiber (1981), Andre Norton (1984), Arthur C. Clarke (1986), Isaac Asimov (1987), Alfred Bester (1988), Ray Bradbury (1989), Lester del Rey (1991), Frederik Pohl (1993), Damon Knight (1995), A. E. van Vogt (1996), Jack Vance (1997), Poul Anderson (1998), Hal Clement (Harry Stubbs) (1999), Brian W. Aldiss (2000), Philip José Farmer (2001), Ursula K. Le Guin (2003), Robert Silverberg (2004), and Anne McCaffrey (2005).

1965

Best Novel: *Dune* by Frank Herbert
Best Novella (tie): "The Saliva Tree" by Brian W. Aldiss
  "He Who Shapes" by Roger Zelazny
Best Novelette: "The Doors of His Face, the Lamps of His Mouth" by Roger Zelazny
Best Short Story: " 'Repent, Harlequin!' Said the Ticktockman," by Harlan Ellison

1966

Best Novel (tie): *Flowers for Algernon* by Daniel Keyes
  Babel-17 by Samuel R. Delany
Best Novella: "The Last Castle" by Jack Vance
Best Novelette: "Call Him Lord" by Gordon R. Dickson
Best Short Story: "The Secret Place" by Richard McKenna

1967

Best Novel: *The Einstein Intersection* by Samuel R. Delany
Best Novella: "Behold the Man" by Michael Moorcock
Best Novelette: "Gonna Roll the Bones" by Fritz Leiber
Best Short Story: "Aye, and Gomorrah" by Samuel R. Delany

1968

Best Novel: *Rite of Passage* by Alexei Panshin
Best Novella: "Dragonrider" by Anne McCaffrey
Best Novelette: "Mother to the World" by Richard Wilson
Best Short Story: "The Planners" by Kate Wilhelm

1969

Best Novel: *The Left Hand of Darkness* by Ursula K. Le Guin
Best Novella: "A Boy and His Dog" by Harlan Ellison
Best Novelette: "Time Considered as a Helix of Semi-Precious
    Stones" by Samuel R. Delany
Best Short Story: "Passengers" by Robert Silverberg

1970

Best Novel: *Ringworld* by Larry Niven
Best Novella: "Ill Met in Lankhmar" by Fritz Leiber
Best Novelette: "Slow Sculpture" by Theodore Sturgeon
Best Short Story: No Award

1971

Best Novel: *A Time of Changes* by Robert Silverberg
Best Novella: "The Missing Man" by Katherine MacLean
Best Novelette: "The Queen of Air and Darkness" by Poul
    Anderson
Best Short Story: "Good News from the Vatican" by Robert
    Silverberg

1972

Best Novel: *The Gods Themselves* by Isaac Asimov
Best Novella: "A Meeting with Medusa" by Arthur C. Clarke
Best Novelette: "Goat Song" by Poul Anderson
Best Short Story: "When it Changed" by Joanna Russ

1973

Best Novel: *Rendezvous with Rama* by Arthur C. Clarke
Best Novella: "The Death of Doctor Island" by Gene Wolfe
Best Novelette: "Of Mist, and Grass, and Sand" by Vonda N.
    McIntyre
Best Short Story: "Love Is the Plan, the Plan Is Death" by James
    Tiptree, Jr.
Best Dramatic Presentation: *Soylent Green*
    Stanley R. Greenberg for Screenplay (based on the novel *Make
    Room! Make Room!*), Harry Harrison for *Make Room! Make
    Room!*

1974

Best Novel: *The Dispossessed* by Ursula K. Le Guin

Best Novella: "Born with the Dead" by Robert Silverberg

Best Novelette: "If the Stars Are Gods" by Gordon Eklund and Gregory Benford

Best Short Story: "The Day Before the Revolution" by Ursula K. Le Guin

Best Dramatic Presentation: *Sleeper* by Woody Allen

Other Awards & Honors: Grand Master: Robert A. Heinlein

1975

Best Novel: *The Forever War* by Joe Haldeman

Best Novella: "Home Is the Hangman" by Roger Zelazny

Best Novelette: "San Diego Lightfoot Sue" by Tom Reamy

Best Short Story: "Catch that Zeppelin!" by Fritz Leiber

Best Dramatic Writing: Mel Brooks and Gene Wilder for *Young Frankenstein*

Other Awards & Honors: Grand Master: Jack Williamson

1976

Best Novel: *Man Plus* by Frederik Pohl

Best Novella: "Houston, Houston, Do You Read?" by James Tiptree, Jr.

Best Novelette: "The Bicentennial Man" by Isaac Asimov

Best Short Story: "A Crowd of Shadows" by Charles L. Grant

Other Awards & Honors: Grand Master: Clifford D. Simak

1977

Best Novel: *Gateway* by Frederik Pohl

Best Novella: "Stardance" by Spider and Jeanne Robinson

Best Novelette: "The Screwfly Solution" by Raccoona Sheldon

Best Short Story: "Jeffty Is Five" by Harlan Ellison

Other Awards & Honors: Special Award: *Star Wars*

1978

Best Novel: *Dreamsnake* by Vonda N. McIntyre

Best Novella: "The Persistence of Vision" by John Varley

Best Novelette: "A Glow of Candles, a Unicorn's Eye" by Charles L. Grant

Best Short Story: "Stone" by Edward Bryant
Other Awards & Honors: Grand Master: L. Sprague de Camp

1979

Best Novel: *The Fountains of Paradise* by Arthur C. Clarke
Best Novella: "Enemy Mine" by Barry Longyear
Best Novelette: "Sandkings" by George R. R. Martin
Best Short Story: "giANTS" by Edward Bryant

1980

Best Novel: *Timescape* by Gregory Benford
Best Novella: "The Unicorn Tapestry" by Suzy McKee Charnas
Best Novelette: "The Ugly Chickens" by Howard Waldrop
Best Short Story: "Grotto of the Dancing Deer" by Clifford D. Simak
Other Awards & Honors: Grand Master: Fritz Leiber

1981

Best Novel: *The Claw of the Conciliator* by Gene Wolfe
Best Novella: "The Saturn Game" by Poul Anderson
Best Novelette: "The Quickening" by Michael Bishop
Best Short Story: "The Bone Flute" by Lisa Tuttle
(This Nebula Award was declined by the author.)

1982

Best Novel: *No Enemy but Time* by Michael Bishop
Best Novella: "Another Orphan" by John Kessel
Best Novelette: "Fire Watch" by Connie Willis
Best Short Story: "A Letter from the Clearys" by Connie Willis

1983

Best Novel: *Startide Rising* by David Brin
Best Novella: "Hardfought" by Greg Bear
Best Novelette: "Blood Music" by Greg Bear
Best Short Story: "The Peacemaker" by Gardner Dozois
Other Awards & Honors: Grand Master: Andre Norton

1984

Best Novel: *Neuromancer* by William Gibson
Best Novella: "PRESS ENTER☐;" by John Varley

Best Novelette: "Bloodchild" by Octavia E. Butler
Best Short Story: "Morning Child" by Gardner Dozois

1985

Best Novel: *Ender's Game* by Orson Scott Card
Best Novella: "Sailing to Byzantium" by Robert Silverberg
Best Novelette: "Portraits of His Children" by George R. R. Martin
Best Short Story: "Out of All Them Bright Stars" by Nancy Kress
Other Awards & Honors: Grand Master: Arthur C. Clarke

1986

Best Novel: *Speaker for the Dead* by Orson Scott Card
Best Novella: "R & R" by Lucius Shepard
Best Novelette: "The Girl Who Fell into the Sky" by Kate Wilhelm
Best Short Story: "Tangents" by Greg Bear
Other Awards & Honors: Grand Master: Isaac Asimov

1987

Best Novel: *The Falling Woman* by Pat Murphy
Best Novella: "The Blind Geometer" by Kim Stanley Robinson
Best Novelette: "Rachel in Love" by Pat Murphy
Best Short Story: "Forever Yours, Anna" by Kate Wilhelm
Other Awards & Honors: Grand Master: Alfred Bester

1988

Best Novel: *Falling Free* by Lois McMaster Bujold
Best Novella: "The Last of the Winnebagos" by Connie Willis
Best Novelette: "Schrodinger's Kitten" by George Alec Effinger
Best Short Story: "Bible Stories for Adults, No. 17: The Deluge"
   by James Morrow
Other Awards & Honors: Grand Master: Ray Bradbury

1989

Best Novel: *The Healer's War* by Elizabeth Ann Scarborough
Best Novella: "The Mountains of Mourning" by Lois McMaster
   Bujold
Best Novelette: "At the Rialto" by Connie Willis
Best Short Story: "Ripples in the Dirac Sea" by Geoffrey A. Landis

1990

Best Novel: *Tehanu: The Last Book of Earthsea* by Ursula K. Le Guin
Best Novella: "The Hemingway Hoax" by Joe Haldeman
Best Novelette: "Tower of Babylon" by Ted Chiang
Best Short Story: "Bears Discover Fire" by Terry Bisson
Other Awards & Honors: Grand Master: Lester del Rey

1991

Best Novel: *Stations of the Tide* by Michael Swanwick
Best Novella: "Beggars in Spain" by Nancy Kress
Best Novelette: "Guide Dog" by Mike Conner
Best Short Story: "Ma Qui" by Alan Brennert

1992

Best Novel: *Doomsday Book* by Connie Willis
Best Novella: "City of Truth" by James Morrow
Best Novelette: "Danny Goes to Mars" by Pamela Sargent
Best Short Story: "Even the Queen" by Connie Willis
Other Awards & Honors: Grand Master: Frederik Pohl

1993

Best Novel: *Red Mars* by Kim Stanley Robinson
Best Novella: "The Night We Buried Road Dog" by Jack Cady
Best Novelette: "Georgia on My Mind" by Charles Sheffield
Best Short Story: "Graves" by Joe Haldeman

1994

Best Novel: *Moving Mars* by Greg Bear
Best Novella: "Seven Views of Olduvai Gorge" by Mike Resnick
Best Novelette: "The Martian Child" by David Gerrold
Best Short Story: "A Defense of the Social Contracts" by Martha
    Soukup
Other Awards & Honors: Grand Master: Damon Knight
    Author Emeritus: Emil Petaja

1995

Best Novel: *The Terminal Experiment* by Robert J. Sawyer
Best Novella: "Last Summer at Mars Hill" by Elizabeth Hand
Best Novelette: "Solitude" by Ursula K. Le Guin

Best Short Story: "Death and the Librarian" by Esther Friesner
Other Awards & Honors: Grand Master: A. E. van Vogt
   Author Emeritus: Wilson "Bob" Tucker

1996

Best Novel: *Slow River* by Nicola Griffith
Best Novella: "Da Vinci Rising" by Jack Dann
Best Novelette: "Lifeboat on a Burning Sea" by Bruce Holland
   Rogers
Best Short Story: "A Birthday" by Esther M. Friesner
Other Awards & Honors: Grand Master: Jack Vance
   Author Emeritus: Judith Merril

1997

Best Novel: *The Moon and the Sun* by Vonda N. McIntyre
Best Novella: "Abandon in Place" by Jerry Oltion
Best Novelette: "The Flowers of Aulit Prison" by Nancy Kress
Best Short Story: "Sister Emily's Lightship" by Jane Yolen
Other Awards & Honors: Grand Master: Poul Anderson
   Author Emeritus: Nelson Slade Bond

1998

Best Novel: *Forever Peace* by Joe Haldeman
Best Novella: "Reading the Bones" by Sheila Finch
Best Novelette: "Lost Girls" by Jane Yolen
Best Short Story: "Thirteen Ways to Water" by Bruce Holland
   Rogers
Other Awards & Honors: Grand Master: Hal Clement (Harry Stubbs)
Bradbury Award: J. Michael Straczynski
   Author Emeritus: William Tenn (Philip Klass)

1999

Best Novel: *Parable of the Talents* by Octavia E. Butler
Best Novella: "Story of Your Life" by Ted Chiang
Best Novelette: "Mars Is No Place for Children" by Mary A. Turzillo
Best Short Story: "The Cost of Doing Business" by Leslie What
Best Script: *The Sixth Sense* by M. Night Shyamalan
Other Awards & Honors: Grand Master: Brian W. Aldiss
   Author Emeritus: Daniel Keyes

2000

Best Novel: *Darwin's Radio* by Greg Bear
Best Novella: "Goddesses" by Linda Nagata
Best Novelette: "Daddy's World" by Walter Jon Williams
Best Short Story: "macs" by Terry Bisson
Best Script: *Galaxy Quest* by Robert Gordon and David Howard
Other Awards & Honors: Grand Master: Philip José Farmer
    Bradbury Award: Yuri Rasovsky and Harlan Ellison
    Author Emeritus: Robert Sheckley

2001

Best Novel: *The Quantum Rose* by Catherine Asaro
Best Novella: "The Ultimate Earth" by Jack Williamson
Best Novelette: "Louise's Ghost" by Kelly Link
Best Short Story: "The Cure for Everything" by Severna Park
Best Script: *Crouching Tiger, Hidden Dragon* by James Schamus, Kuo
    Jung Tsai, and Hui-Ling Wang; from the book by Du Lu Wang
Other Awards & Honors: President's Award: Betty Ballantine

2002

Best Novel: *American Gods* by Neil Gaiman
Best Novella: "Bronte's Egg" by Richard Chwedyk
Best Novelette: "Hell Is the Absence of God" by Ted Chiang
Best Short Story: "Creature" by Carol Emshwiller
Best Script: *The Lord of the Rings: The Fellowship of the Ring* by
    Fran Walsh and Philippa Boyens and Peter Jackson; based on
    The Lord of the Rings by J. R. R. Tolkien
Other Awards & Honors: Grand Master: Ursula K. Le Guin
    Author Emeritus: Katherine MacLean

2003

Best Novel: *The Speed of Dark* by Elizabeth Moon
Best Novella: "Coraline" by Neil Gaiman
Best Novelette: "The Empire of Ice Cream" by Jeffrey Ford
Best Short Story: "What I Didn't See" by Karen Joy Fowler
Best Script: *The Lord of the Rings: The Two Towers* by Fran Walsh
    and Philippa Boyens and Stephen Sinclair and Peter Jackson;
    based on *The Lord of the Rings* by J. R. R. Tolkien
Other Awards & Honors: Grand Master: Robert Silverberg
    Author Emeritus: Charles L. Harness

2004

Best Novel: *Paladin of Souls* by Lois McMaster Bujold

Best Novella: "The Green Leopard Plague" by Walter Jon Williams

Best Novelette: "Basement Magic" by Ellen Klages

Best Short Story: "Coming to Terms" by Eileen Gunn

Best Script: *The Lord of the Rings: The Return of the King* by Fran Walsh and Philippa Boyens and Peter Jackson; based on *The Lord of the Rings* by J. R. R. Tolkien

Other Awards and Honors: Grand Master: Anne McCaffrey

GRAND MASTER AWARD WINNERS

1975	Robert A. Heinlein
1976	Jack Williamson
1977	Clifford D. Simak
1979	L. Sprague de Camp
1981	Fritz Leiber
1984	Andre Norton
1986	Arthur C. Clarke
1987	Isaac Asimov
1988	Alfred Bester
1989	Ray Bradbury
1991	Lester del Rey
1993	Frederik Pohl
1995	Damon Knight
1996	A. E. van Vogt
1997	Jack Vance
1998	Poul Anderson
1999	Hal Clement (Harry Stubbs)
2000	Brian W. Aldiss
2001	Philip José Farmer
2003	Ursula K. Le Guin
2004	Robert Silverberg
2005	Anne McCaffrey
2006	Harlan Ellison

Emil Petaja   [1995]

Wilson "Bob" Tucker   [1996]

Judith Merril   [1997]

Nelson Slade Bond   [1998]

William Tenn (Philip Klass)   [1999]

Daniel Keyes   [2000]

Robert Sheckley   [2001]

Katherine MacLean   [2003]

Charles L. Harness   [2004]

William F. Nolan   [2006]